HETIRIA

Shadow of Cranis

By
Shawn Ganther

CHAPTER 0 | 5836-W07

Colonel William Arfey peered down the mountain. At this distance, the silver-plated war machines looked like gems glistening in the sun. *If only they were gems*, William thought, *I'd be rich*. He gazed past the machines to the neatly aligned rows of marching men. They seemed to sway with the wind like a field viewed from a great height. William didn't need to count. He knew the entirety of the Cranis invading force lay before him: five thousand soldiers supported by two hundred state-of-the-art war machines, all preparing to ascend the mountain.

William glanced at the crest tattooed on his forearm. The symbol contained a mallet and skull with a simple phrase beneath: "For justice we remain." It had been the crest of his first unit — a reserve company composed primarily of labor workers, not hardened soldiers like he had with him today. The men and women in that old unit were rough, rowdy, and undisciplined, and William loved them for it. He carried the memory of those soldiers with him, using their shared experiences to help him train and mold his current command — the most decorated infantry unit on Planet Jaber. They had fought valiantly throughout the conflict, but as he stood there among them, only 212 remained.

Not being an irrational man, William had no illusions that they would win the day. His soldiers would fight and die for him on this mountain, but at that moment, he silently wished they didn't have to.

He heard familiar footsteps approaching from behind. They crunched on the loose stone of the mountain at a hurried pace. William didn't look back at the lieutenant colonel as he approached. He knew the sound of Cole's oversized feet.

"Colonel, Command," Cole huffed, "they're still evacuating."

William inhaled through his nose and slowly exhaled. His eyes fell to the rough landscape beneath his feet. He shook his head and smiled. *Ol' Jack told me so.*

Born and raised on Planet Jaber, William grew up the son of a scientist. He had never dreamed of being a soldier, but an unexpected series of events led him to where he was now.

Finally, he looked over his shoulder at his second-in-command. When the war began, Cole had been a captain. In less than a year, he was already a lieutenant colonel. *So many men*, William thought. And yet he remained.

"Launch the fighters," William ordered. "Have 'em hold position at the peak of da mountain."

"And the men?" Cole asked.

"I'll lead 'em."

Cole said nothing for a moment, then: "Colonel?"

William looked again at the large army assembled before him. "This'll be da last fight. I want to lead it."

A young man at barely twenty-four years old, Cole's eyes pleaded with William. "Colonel," Cole said, "permission to lead the men."

William looked away. "Denied, Lieutenant Colonel."

"But, Colonel, I-"

Cole cut his words short as William turned to face him. The lieutenant colonel stood in William's shadow as he looked down at him and said, "Take da intelligence from Command and fall back to Position Omega. Report to Command that remainin' forces were either killed or captured."

Cole stood before him, saying nothing, like a disappointed child looking up at his father.

"That's an order, Cole."

With that, William turned away and looked at the sun beyond the horizon. He could feel Cole's eyes on his back. Then, the large feet trudged away.

As a young man, William's only desire was to become an artist.

He longed to swirl paint around an empty canvas and create images of a forgotten world. Paintings barely existed anymore. They were relics of a time long past and had become frivolous in a world of science; however, art's frivolity made it all the more appealing to William. His father, of course, disapproved of this dream, and William followed it blindly until his eyes opened to a beauty beyond comprehension. Her curly, golden blond hair glowed in the bright desert sun. As she turned and her piercing blue eyes landed on him, his dreams were altered in a split second. William would soon learn that she was the daughter of a Dixothine rig worker and the school's Labor Union Charter president. She attended every Labor Party debate and joined every Union protest. He was informed of this by her gushing boyfriend, who, unfortunately, was also his best friend. Jack had been his best friend since starter school, but when she smiled and shook William's hand, he silently cursed his friend's luck. He never once mentioned his feelings for her, but he loved her from the moment she insulted his haircut.

William thought of her as he ran his hand through his dirty, tangled hair. Then he focused on the landscape, dragged his foot over the rocks, and watched them turn over and tumble down the mountain. William smiled, kneeled, picked up a rock, and tossed it. A few more stones rolled downhill. That was why he chose this location. Footing going up was treacherous. This would slow the enemy's attack. His main concern was the Cranis Air Force. The aircraft he had at his disposal were fossils by comparison. Head-to-head, it would be complete annihilation.

Burners clicked and clattered behind him as the aircraft engines ignited. Sputtering engines coughed and then roared as they lifted into the air.

He glanced back at the dilapidated aircraft and quickly turned his attention toward the approaching enemy. Cranis fighters slowed and moved to a defensive position around the soldiers. A thin, vindictive grin spread across William's face. They had taken the bait.

William blinked twice, set all his augmentations to full, and closed his system tray.

"Phoenix, this is yer colonel. How read?"

"Loud and clear," William heard on his internal comms.

"On my command, make attack run and take da party elsewhere. Copy?"

"Yes, sir. Operation Timekeeper is a go."

William watched the battalion move up the mountain. His entire plan hinged on Cranis air support not engaging the ground force.

"Phoenix, pick one and do an engine flare. Make it look good."

Within seconds, a loud pop was heard from behind William, and he turned to see a puff of smoke and a fighter descending to the ground.

A roar of enemy cheers carried up the mountain.

"Icarus, form on me."

The boots of two hundred soldiers marched toward him. Rocks shifted and tumbled past. He turned to face his army. His fiery red hair glowed in the sun as the wind pushed it from his face. He was never one for speeches but felt compelled to speak as he looked at the scared faces watching him expectantly. *Jack would know what to say.* He knelt and scooped up a handful of rocks. By the end of the day, many of them would be buried on this mountain. He picked one rock from the many in his oversized hand, turned, and hurled it down the mountain.

A murmur was heard behind him. "Artillery, prepare to fire. Range to target negative 50. Fire on my command." He turned back to his soldiers. "These blokes think they know us. They come to our home, attack our factories, kill our friends and family, and laugh because they think us weak. Today, we show them that one stone can cause an avalanche. Today, we make 'em fear us. Today, we make 'em pay for their deception. Long live da Union!" William screamed.

As the cheers arose from his soldiers, he turned back toward the conquering force of the Cranis Army. He whipped the handful of rocks down the mountain. "Phoenix, engage."

Old engines roared overhead and zipped down the mountain. The vibration caused more rocks to tumble. "Artillery, fire."

A plume of dust rose into the sky as the blast's concussion rattled the mountain. Phoenix Squadron disappeared into the dust, and lasterfire erupted. The roar of engines quickly faded into the distance, and the rumbling of falling rock muffled the cries of the Cranis Army. "Artillery, call for fire, range plus seventy-five. Fire when ready."

A barrage of projectile rounds launched into the air, and the mountainside exploded. There was a momentary silence.

"Icarus, attack!" William waved his arm and descended toward the chaos. A storm of boots joined him.

CHAPTER 1 | 5856-W17

Twenty years later.

Ade jerked awake. Drenched in sweat, he glanced around the unfamiliar room as his mind separated dream from reality. Blades of sunlight broke through the cracks in the blinds, and dust particles shimmered as they drifted from one beam of light to the next. Even with the blinds drawn, the light shone brightly enough to see the empty bed and unpacked boxes shoved against the wall on the opposite side of the stark room. Ade glanced at the clock on his nightstand. It was only 3:30 a.m. Rolling onto his side, he yanked the cot sheet over his head and closed his eyes. The dreams had become more frequent and grew like boils in his mind. Then Ade woke to a different kind of nightmare. He attempted to take a deep breath. When only a shallow breath was allowed, Ade clenched his jaw, shook his head, and kicked off the sheets. *I hate this place*, he thought.

He blinked rapidly three times, stared at the boxes for a moment, blinked again, and then took a deep breath through his nose.

This was their fifth day on planet Jaber, and Ade had yet to adapt to the constant sunshine. You'll get used to it... That's what they said in the welcoming brief. Perhaps they were right, but struggling to survive on Cranis still seemed more appealing than adapting to life on a new planet. Now, it seemed his entire existence was covered in sand.

The sound of footsteps drew Ade's attention. He heard his mother scurrying about their assigned housing unit from the other room. She was always an early riser, but this was too early even for her. On Cranis, she rose and set with the sun. Unlike his father, Ann found no comfort in the quiet of the night. Ade always thought it odd, considering both his parents were born and raised on Planet Jaber. He already missed the night. Good or bad, a sunset symbolizes the end of one day and the promise of a new day in the morning. Now, the days ran together.

Swinging his lanky legs over the side of the cot and placing his bare feet on the cold, stone floor, he ran a hand over his freshly shaved head and let his fingers slide down his forehead to a large pink scar above his right eye. Ade traced the rigid line before his hands fell back to his lap. Beyond the scar, his youthful face was devoid of any distinguishing features. He had what his mother called a baby face, and she loved to remind him of this by pinching his cheeks and cooing, "Oooh, squishy cheeks." As a nineteen-year-old, this drove him mad.

Maybe I should unpack those boxes today, he thought. He clumsily pushed himself to a standing position, which caused his weary body to sidestep and collide with the corner of the nightstand. The loud bang incited a nearly instantaneous reaction, and footsteps rushed to the closed door.

"Are you okay?" his mother called from beyond the door.

Ade frowned at the door while rubbing the sore spot on his leg. "I'm fine."

Ann had been overly attentive since they got here. Ade knew it was because she felt guilty.

"Are you naked?" Ann asked.

Ade wrinkled his nose and furrowed his brow. "What, no. No. I'm not-"

The door to the room opened, and his mother rushed in.

"What happened?"

Ade just stared at her. Mildly annoyed by the invasion of privacy, he considered being snarky but thought better of it.

"Nothing. Just these stupid leg augmentations don't work as well on this planet," Ade replied, continuing to rub his sore leg.

His mother pressed her thin lips together, attempting to suppress a smile and slight chuckle. "You should see yourself right now."

Ade knew the look. "Oh sure, find enjoyment in my misery.

Seriously though, that thing didn't even budge."

Ann was once strikingly beautiful. She was a petite woman with angled features and penetrating eyes of the sea framed by rolling, sandy-blonde hair; however, the past few years had turned her into a ghost of her former self. It was as if she had defied time, but then time vengefully enforced its will. Through it all, though, she maintained a sense of determination and strength – which Ade knew was mainly for his benefit.

"That bedstand is likely twice your age," she laughed, "if not older."

Her slender fingers brushed the hair from her face and tucked it behind her ear as she watched her son hobble on one foot while shooting eye darts at the solid piece of furniture. Ann would never admit it, but her son's clumsiness brought her great joy. It reminded her of Ade as a toddler. For some time, his head was far too big for his body. And, as he learned to walk, momentum and gravity often sent him banging into the furniture. Ann thought it was the cutest thing.

"No way! That thing looks like it was made on Earth," he fired back with a smile. *It's nice to hear her laugh*, Ade thought.

Ann had an infectious laugh. The laugh everyone in the room hears, and nobody mistakes for another person. She laughed at almost everything at one point, but her laughter had been silenced in recent months. Life had become more about survival; however, since arriving on Jaber, her laughter had returned. Ade suspected part of her was happy to be home.

"You should try to get more sleep," Ann said, "but if you're awake, I can put out some rations and goat's milk."

Ade shuddered at the thought of the pasty rations. The government issued weekly rations to people in the labor class. It was the same tasteless food they sent with soldiers into battle. They were distributed in vacuum-sealed bags and closely resembled toothpaste. "What about coffee and toast?"

Ann pursed her lips while considering his request.

"I can brew a pot, but remember, you had some yesterday, and we're only allotted enough for three pots a week. When I start my job, we can get more."

"You know, I could start working too," he replied. "They don't require you to go to school on this planet." He knew her response before the final word escaped his lips, but it was too late. Even if he was more intelligent than most kids his age, he still hadn't mastered thinking before speaking.

"Ade!" she exclaimed. "If only your father were here to hear that talk!"

Ade cringed at the mention of his father, but youth's ignorance gave him the confidence to continue his argument. "I mean, maybe they would let me go back after we're settled, and it's only one semester. Oh! Maybe I could work during the day and go to night school. It's all virtual, anyway. I think I heard someone say we could do that."

Turning to face him, the bright light from the room behind her masked the disapproving look hidden in the shadows of her face. Ade didn't need to see it to know it was there – he could feel it. Both his mother and father had always stressed the importance of education. His father swore it was the only reason he earned employment as an augmentation technician at the age of 19. His father didn't talk much about his life on Jaber. He only brought up Jaber when Ade complained about completing his homework. He would sip his coffee, peek at him over his digipaper, and say, "You're lucky. Kids your age are already working in the labor camps on Jaber." His father had never mentioned working in the labor camps, but the guilt of it always compelled Ade to finish his classwork.

Ade could sense his mother staring at his profile. "I'm sorry, Mom. I just want to help."

"You can help by finishing your coursework and getting a good score on your placement test. Your father would have wanted that."

Guilt forced him to nod. There was no arguing her point. His father, Jack, would have wanted him to finish school. "I know," he mumbled.

"Good," Ann stated. "I'll go pull some rations for when you get up." She turned to leave the room but paused. "Oh, and Ade..."

"Yes, Ma'am," he deadpanned.

"You should try to get some more sleep. You look awful."

Ade fought the urge to roll his eyes. "Thanks, Mom," he said, and she turned and closed the door behind her.

If only we could have made it another five months on Cranis, he thought. *Then we wouldn't have had to move to this dump.*

He sat back down on the cot and thought about the first day of his senior year. His father walked with him to wait for the transport shuttle. Standing there in the morning glow of the rising summer sun, his father placed a hand on his shoulder and squeezed. "This is the year," his father said. "By the end of it, you'll be a man." As he turned to walk toward their house, Ade looked back at the man who'd cast the biggest shadow he'd ever seen, and as he did, fear crept in. It was a fear of never living up to his father's expectations.

His father had graduated school a year early and was already working in augmentation development by eighteen. Before reaching nineteen, he had already been awarded a scholarship for a level five brain augmentation (commonly known as a Sata 5).

Augmentations quickly became common after Earth became uninhabitable in 2412. None of the replacement planets found within reachable distance were inhabitable without an engineered evolution of the human body. It started small with things like filters for breathing and advancements in sight technology, but it soon morphed into a complete re-engineering of the human body. A Sata upgrade became the first non-essential enhancement after a child was fully grown. A Sata allowed the installation of more advanced augmentations and added an interface for easier control of those devices. Sata upgrades also added indirect storage capacity to the brain. However, level one only added a small amount of storage — only enough for primary augmentations and a small document folder.

Ade took a few deep breaths and looked from the door to the boxes. *Not today,* he thought. Lifting his feet from the floor, he swung them back onto the cot and laid on his back. The dreams were beginning to cloud Ade's memory of his father. Instead, he thought of Jack smiling. This reminded him of the events leading up to Jack's Sata 20 ceremony. Ann insisted they wear presentation clothing for the ceremony, and, having just gone through his last mapped growth spurt, none of Ade's ceremony pants fit. She planned to take Ade after school, but Jack insisted he needed to skip work and take him. "He has a leg augmentation coming up, honey," Jack said. "If I don't take him, he may get pants that don't work after the surgery." Then Jack smiled at Ade. Everyone in the room knew Jack was bluffing, but nobody questioned it. Jack Billings never skipped work. Nor did he ever allow his children to skip school. This was special. They spent the entire day in the city — just the two of them. Two pairs of the finest ceremony pants were purchased, and since they were already in the city, they decided to visit the Earth Museum and catch a football game. Ade considered it one of the best days of his life.

A pain swelled within his chest, and his breath quickened as tears began to form. Ade swallowed. *I should have said it back.* The tears broke free and dripped from his jaw onto the pillow. He wiped his eyes on his sleeve and angrily shook his head. *Not today. Not again.*

He blinked rapidly three times to access his augmentation console, selected sleep mode, and closed the system. He took a shallow breath and looked back at the dust particles shimmering in the light. *One hour*, he thought. *Maybe...* He sniffled, rolled over, and he drifted back to sleep.

CHAPTER 2 | 5856-W18

"Many indigenous plant species found on Cranis proved toxic to humans and were therefore wiped out. Our founding members began planting scientifically altered seeds derived from plants on Earth and used solid waste from space travel to fertilize the seeds and begin growing crops. However, this process wasn't as successful as hoped, and the reserve food supplies dwindled. This caused great unrest amongst the common settlers as they received small rations after a long day of work in the fields."

Ade's eyelids drooped over his eyes until he was squinting through his eyelashes. His head nodded like a bobblehead on a loose spring, and he slowly slid down in the chair of the halostation pod.

"Mr. Billings!"

Ade's eyes opened to the teacher staring at him through the halofeed. Ade felt it coming but was unable to stop it. His mouth opened wide, and a great yawn escaped him. In the background of the feed, he could hear the other students laughing.

"Am I boring you, Mr. Billings?"

Ade wiped a small amount of drool from the corner of his mouth and tried to focus. But, in a daze, he wasn't quick enough to formulate an excuse, and instead, the truth rolled plainly from his lips.

"I'm sorry, Educator Ruth, but we learned all this in intermediate school."

There was silence as Ade sat straight and returned to a state of alertness. Then, his eyes returned to the feed to meet the bitter scowl of Educator Ruth.

"Mr. Billings, care to enlighten us dullards on Jaber about the history of Cranis?"

Ade shook his head. As rebellious as he thought himself, his parents tried to instill in him respect for those in education. However, that respect quickly dissipated due to his temper or desire to be correct.

"No Educator Ruth. I'm sorry. I haven't been sleeping well."

She continued to glare at him. Her eye twitched. "I believe the entire class would like to know more from a native Cranisian."

Ade shrugged his shoulders and sighed. "Okay, Educator Ruth." Ade paused briefly as he recalled their field trip to the Cranis History Museum. "Well, half of the settlers from the Columbus voyage died in hypersleep within the first year because of an undetected toxin in the water. Many in torpor survived initially, but a plague killed a quarter of them 700 light years from Earth. This limited breeding pairs, and they had to revive some of the remaining people in hypersleep. Oh, and two-thirds of the crops they started from seeds on Earth died on the journey, which caused a food shortage. This led to rioting on the Columbus, killing a quarter of the remaining population. This all happened before they even got to Cranis. After that-"

"That's quite enough, Mr. Billings," Ruth scoffed. She sat back from the camera and scowled at him. "We are discussing the settlement of Cranis, not the voyages here."

"I know," Ade responded, "but to explain the unrest you must know the backstory."

Ruth's scowl became a glare.

"Well, class, it seems our educational system isn't good enough for some students." And then the halofeed went black.

Only the quiet hiss of the air filtration system could be heard in the housing unit as Ade sat quietly in the pod. Then, withdrawn into his thoughts, the sound of the door opening startled him. Ade peeked out to see his mother set two sacks of groceries on the kitchen counter. Ann suddenly stopped, listened to the silence, and turned toward the pod.

He quickly turned away and looked at the blank screen.

"Why aren't you in school?" Ann said with a clear tone of disapproval.

Ade leaned back to look at her and shrugged. "The teacher ended class early."

Ann's eyes narrowed on him. "And why did the teacher end the class early?"

His mother has always possessed the unnerving ability to catch Ade in a lie. He became more adept at overcoming her natural lie detector as he grew, but he often saved it for more pivotal moments.

"I was just telling them about the Columbus Voyage. They skipped over all kinds of things in history class. I didn't think she'd get mad."

She tried to suppress a grin, but Ade knew her well enough to tell when she wasn't mad. "You need to stop correcting your teachers, Ade. I know the education system isn't as good here, but they're trying."

"Dad would have wanted me to say something," he countered.

"I know, but you've only got a couple of months left," she said, unpacking the groceries. "Learn what you can and ace your test. We don't need you getting suspended for being a troublemaker."

"What if we bought the remote pass? Then I could finish at my old school on Cranis and talk to my friends," Ade countered.

Ann placed her hands on her hips and bit her lower lip. Ade cringed. He knew this response would incite as soon as the words were spoken. "You know I can't afford a remote pass."

"Mom, I just thought maybe we had enough money now. I-"

"Don't." Tears began to form in Ann's eyes. "Ade, I can't help we're here. I wanted to keep you in school on Cranis, but we spent all our savings on your brother. This was our only option."

"Mom, I didn't mean..."

"Now, do your homework. I'll make dinner later."

Ade's lips parted to speak as she retreated to her room, but no words emerged. He knew she was having a hard time. What they endured would have broken most people, but she lived in a coat of armor. Granted, every coat of armor has a weak spot, and Ade had found hers. He slumped back into the seat of the pod.

"Fug," Ade muttered. Then, leaning forward, he pressed the connect button on the pod console and watched the ellipsis scroll across the bottom of the feed. His fists clenched, and his nostrils flared as a message popped on the feed.

A parent or guardian must contact Administrator Zeinkie before the student is allowed back to class....

Without thinking, he threw a fist into the wall of the halostation. Noise from the impact echoed through the living quarters, and Ade's eyes darted through the pod's opening toward the door of his mother's room. His face grew warm as pain radiated from his knuckles. When no response came from the room, he quickly inspected the area he'd hit. A sigh of relief escaped him when no damage was found. Then, he leaned back into the seat, and his head hung heavy on his shoulders. *She doesn't need this.* Leaning forward, he hit the disconnect button on the station.

"Thank you for choosing Halo Technology Solutions. The first choice in holographic communication," the pod stated, and the screen disappeared.

Ade scowled at the space where the screen had been. Then he looked again at the door to his mother's room and then at his red knuckles. Ade slowly pushed himself out of the seat and through the small opening. Crossing the room, he stopped at her door. He raised his hand to knock, looked at his knuckles, and raised the other fist to gently knock on his mother's door.

At first, there was no answer. It was unlike Ann to not respond. She had always been there for him. If he scraped his knee, his father would tell him to toughen up and put Regen on it. His mother, however, would dote on him and fix it for him. He knocked again. "Mom, can we talk?"

"Just a minute," she called from behind the solid door.

Ade leaned in closer to the wooden door in a feeble attempt to hear what she was doing. “Mom...”

The door swung open, causing Ade to take a quick step backward.

Her face steady and emotionless, she grinned at him. “I’ll get dinner started. I can only imagine you’re starving after a day of school. I know I’m hungry.”

She swept past him and went directly for the groceries on the counter. “They really pile the work on at the factory,” Ann said. “See, that’s the type of job you don’t want. You want a job where you use your brain.”

Watching her swiftly unpack the groceries, Ade knew his father would have been disappointed in him. He walked over to her and gently placed a hand on her shoulder. “I’ll apologize to Educator Ruth and try not to do it again,” Ade began. “I’ll even do extra work.”

He could feel the tenseness of her shoulders as they raised and lowered with each anxious breath.

“And I’m sure it’ll get better. They’re probably just making sure I know the basics.”

Ann gave him a sideways glance and continued unpacking the groceries. “If I add some spices to the rations they could be quite good – like mashed potatoes.”

“Mom, I’m sorry. I don’t blame you. I want you to know that. It’s just hard being here.”

His mother paused, and her busy hands stopped moving. She gently set down the spice and turned toward Ade. Her eyes softened as the rigid determination dissipated. “I just want the best for you, Ade. I miss Cranis too.”

Without thinking, he embraced her like a parent consoling their child. She stood awkwardly in his arms before wrapping her arms around his waist and squeezing him tight.

“You haven’t hugged me in years,” she whispered.

“You always hugged me when I needed it.”

Ann nodded and rested her head on his chest. “We’re going to be okay.”

To Ade, it sounded like she was trying to convince herself as much as him.

“We will. We can start by you teaching me how to turn that mush into mashed potatoes,” Ade said, pointing at the ration bag. “Seems impossible.”

CHAPTER 3 | 5856-W19

Running his hand over the short, prickly hair on his head, Ade glowered at the chessboard. It was the last day of his mandatory quarantine, and he felt like a caged animal. All off-world arrivals were required to undergo a three-week quarantine while acclimating to their new augmentations. The high concentration of carbon dioxide in Jaber's atmosphere meant each new arrival received an air intake regulator (AIRE 1) courtesy of the Planetary Affairs Commission. Having been born on Jaber, his mother had one since birth and, therefore, wasn't required to quarantine. Meanwhile, Ade was suspended from school and trying to recreate the last game of chess he played against his father. Chess was one of the few games in which Ade could compete with his father's intellect. They would play one game for several days, and Ade would sit and study their game while his father worked.

The last game they played was unlike any before. Jack was a highly skilled player. He played in the old style using memorized strategies. This method of play often required a precision counter. However, their last game lasted less than an hour. Jack blundered repeatedly, moving pieces into jeopardy without any apparent benefit. The lack of strategy irritated Ade, but Jack laughed as if it were of no consequence.

Why would he do that? Ade thought, motioning to the board now before him. He sighed and took a drink of goat's milk. Then he moved his queen, checkmating the opposing king and laying it onto its side. Ade glanced around the room. Housing units in the Labor District were identical to avoid jealousy among the workers. They offered few amenities and little comfort. All the walls were white, and the floor a cool gray. In the main room, a simple wooden table and four chairs sat in the middle of the room. A small kitchenette with white cabinets and appliances was just past the roof access door to the right. Moving left from the roof access door was the main entry door, a halofeed screen bolted to the wall, and Ade's halostation learning pod. On the opposing side of the room were three doorways leading to two bedrooms and a bathroom.

Ade stood, finished his milk, and turned on the halofeed. A bald man with a silver mustache rambled about President Hollar's goodwill tour. Ade scowled at the feed and walked to the open doorway of his room. Standing at the threshold, he leaned against the doorframe and counted the unpacked boxes. *Fifteen boxes. What if I just did one a day?* Then he looked at the mess on his side of the room. Piles of clothing and half-read books were scattered across the floor. *He'd be pissed if he saw that*, Ade thought. He walked into the clean side of the room and kicked a book back onto his side. Turning back toward the boxes, Ade shuffled toward them. His heart sank. He had purposefully avoided those boxes. Whenever he considered unpacking them, Ade was reminded of the countless hours spent playing Special Police with his brother, Ethan. Ade was the younger of the two, which meant he was always the criminal.

Odd how differently reality plays out, he thought.

He hoisted the top box from the pile. To his surprise, it was far heavier than anticipated. Ade groaned, leaned back to counter the weight, and took four labored steps to his right before plopping the box onto the cot. "What's he got in there?" Ade pondered aloud.

"Good thing we had movers, huh," Ann said.

Ade's heart skipped, his body stiffened, and he jolted into the air. The jolt must have scared her as much as him.

"Oh, honey! I'm sorry. Thought you heard me coming," Ann said apologetically.

"It's fine," Ade said, breathing heavily. "I just, yeah, I didn't hear you."

"What are you up to?" she asked.

"Thinking about unpacking these boxes."

Ann gave him a motherly smile and took a step closer. Then, she crossed her arms and examined the boxes. "I think it's better to wait. Then you two can unpack them together. You know how particular Ethan is about his things."

Ade hadn't heard Ethan's name said aloud in six months. The last time was in a lazite-trimmed courtroom on Cranis when the judge hammered the gavel and sentenced Ethan to three years in the labor camps on Jaber. Ade would never forget the sound of that gavel. After the shock of sentencing, the sound sent a cold shiver through his body.

"I know. I'm just going a bit crazy cooped up in here."

"You could watch JSN. Get to know Jaber a little better," Ann suggested.

Ade grimaced and shook his head. "It's the same thing over and over again."

Ann smiled. "You sound like your father."

Ade walked around her to his side of the room and kicked a book under his cot.

"You could clean your room," Ann suggested.

Ade turned and sat on his cot. "It's not that bad."

Ann glanced around the room with an amused look on her face. "I bet if I picked up that glass on your nightstand there'd be a dust ring around it."

Ade looked at the glass with dried milk in the bottom. "That was only there a day," Ade lied. He had no idea how long it had been there.

"Well, I was planning on taking you to the market tomorrow, but from the look of the floor, it looks like you have enough stuff."

Ade's ears perked, and his eyes widened. Jaber's Market District was legendary. Celebrities wrote songs about it, and influencers recorded halofeed shorts there. Many of Cranis' elite came to Jaber just to visit the market. Before the War of Worlds, Jaber controlled the production and export of all consumer goods to Cranis. Elites found it easier to travel to the source to procure sought-after items rather than wait and contend with Cranis' middle class. A vast, extravagant shopping market was constructed just beyond the Labor District to accommodate off-world shopping. The market became an instant success as a tourist destination for off-worlders. After the war, the Commerce Party eliminated the import tax on Jaber goods. Analysts predicted this move would encourage shoppers to purchase their goods locally, but the steady flow of affluent shoppers continued.

Ade's excitement dissipated as he realized it was a ploy to convince him to clean his room. "Whatever," Ade scowled. "We would need a pass, anyway."

Ann's toothy grin was suddenly beaming. "Why yes, yes, my astute son. We would."

He eyed her for a moment. She was never good at hiding her excitement. A smile grew on Ade's face. "Are you serious?"

"I picked up a pass this morning."

Ade leaped to his feet, dodged several clothing items, and embraced her. A small squeak escaped his mother as he squeezed.

"Honey, you're crushing-"

Ade quickly released her and took a step back. "Sorry. Just excited to get out of this house."

Ann's face was flushed, and her smile was blinding. He knew there was more.

"What?" Ade asked.

"Oh, nothing. You're just very excited."

"Mom, I've wanted to go since I was a kid," Ade said.

"Your father was never impressed. He said most people working in the stores couldn't afford to shop there."

"Dad said many things," Ade affirmed.

"And he was usually right," Ann retorted.

She was trying to steer the conversation away from his question. Ade knew her tricks.

"So, what aren't you telling me? I can tell, you know."

"I'm not telling. It's a surprise," Ann said, turning and abruptly leaving the room.

Ade followed her into the main room.

"Mom, I think I-"

"Shhh," Ann shushed. She stood in the middle of the room watching the halofeed. The mustache man's expression had grown grim, and a video of people with bound hands played beside him.

"Violence erupted again as native Jabroians protested Hollar's work incentive program. This is the third such event in the past two weeks. Cranis officials have confirmed a meeting with the head of the Labor Department to discuss a peaceful end to these protests."

Ann shook her head. "So much has changed since I was your age. I guess war will do that."

Ade didn't much care for politics. "So, what's the surprise?"

Ann didn't immediately look at him. Instead, she waited for the feed to switch and then turned toward him. "I guess you'll have to wait until the morning to find out. In the meantime, you can clean your room."

***

The following day, Ade skipped his tradition of hitting snooze twice before getting up. His head popped off the pillow. He blinked, adjusted his augmentation, took a deep breath, and sprang from the bed. Having only made a halfhearted attempt to clean, Ade failed to remember that he had left several books lying open on the floor. Landing on the open book, the top couple of pages ripped as the weight of his foot pushed the book and himself into a skid across the floor. His arms flailed briefly before he shifted his weight, regained his balance, and planted his back foot.

Without a second thought, he kicked the book backward toward his cot. Ade had assembled all his essential items the night before and carefully laid them atop his dresser. He quickly dressed. It had been weeks since he'd donned regular clothing, and the stiff fabric of the canvas pants felt uncomfortable on his legs. *Jaber is a vile place to live. There are bugs as big as your arm,* Ade remembered his father saying.

He sat back on his cot and tugged the blousing strap on his pants over his boot. It didn't matter what was outside the door. At this point, Ade needed to be beyond these confining white dormitory walls.

"Don't forget your sand goggles and canteen," Ann yelled from her bedroom.

Ade buttoned the top button on his overcoat and slid the goggles down onto his forehead. Canteen, Ade thought. That's a good idea. Grabbing the canteen from the hook by his doorway, he walked into the main room and stood by the exterior door while impatiently waiting for his mother. He felt like a sprinter poised to erupt from the blocks. Ade didn't think the mandatory adjustment period would affect him like it did, but he was giddy about being released.

Ann strutted out of her bedroom like a model descending a runway, and a sly smile spread across her ivory face. She wore a khaki field jacket with tapered green trousers and tall boots. However, what mesmerized Ade was the scarlet scarf wrapped around her neck. Her skin seemed to glow with life for the first time in weeks.

"You're still not going to tell me?" Ade asked.

"Nope," she replied. Her hair was drawn up into her cap, and her cheekbones seemed higher and more regal than usual. Perhaps he just hadn't noticed before. "A surprise is only a surprise if the other person doesn't know. Now check your gear before we leave."

Ade rolled his eyes before appeasing his mother with an additional check of the things he'd already checked twice. Then he lifted the scarf over his nose, adjusted his goggles, and gave his mom a thumbs up. "Can we go now?"

Ann smiled, which goaded his excitement even more. "We most certainly can," she chirped.

When they exited the housing unit, the hot air hit him like heat escaping an oven.

"My god," Ade gasped. He pulled down his mask and took a deep breath. "Was it this hot the last time we were out here?"
"No," Ann said, turning toward him.

Ade watched his reflection in Ann's mirrored goggles and looked at the haze of tan landscape behind him.

"It was night last time," Ann continued. "The slight tilt on the axis makes it cooler at night. Didn't they teach you that?"

"Yeah, but it's different in real life. This is like being in a furnace," Ade sneered.

"You'll be fine. Just drink water and keep your skin covered," Ann replied.

Labor District housing stretched as far as the eye could see. The square, single-story homes had stucco siding that looked like they were built to blend into the sandy landscape.
The Labor District resided on the part of the planet directly facing the sun. Jaber rotated on an eighty-five-degree horizontal axis, which caused the nights to be slightly cooler but only by ten degrees. The average temperature of the Labor District was 110 degrees Fahrenheit. The reason for the district's placement was simple — the desert held the largest deposits of dixothine on the planet.

Ade's back was already drenched in sweat; he followed his mother down the rock path. He took a drink of water and silently thanked his mother for reminding him. Separating the houses were pathways made of white pebbles that crunched with each step.

"Why stone?" Ade asked.

"It's cheaper than packed sand and clay."

"But why not pavement?"

Ann laughed, and Ade puzzled over what was funny. Then, he came to his own conclusion.

"It gets too hot," Ade answered.

"Yeah, they learned that lesson the hard way. It was paved when I was a kid."

Ade trudged on behind his mother. Every movement felt labored; however, his mother strolled on as if it were a leisurely summer day. After what seemed like an hour of walking, the pebbled path turned into a packed sand sidewalk, and the tiny houses gave way to large factories made of steel and concrete. The factories towered above them and blocked the sun. Ade's shoulders relaxed a bit as they walked in the shadow of the buildings. He expected more noise from the factories, but all that was heard was the swirling of fans and whistling of the wind.

"Which one do you work in?" Ade asked.

Ann pointed in front of her to the right. "Factory D5, up and to the right."

"You walk this every day," Ade marveled.

"Most days. Sometimes, I take the work shuttle."

As excited as he was, Ade was already feeling the fatigue of the walk.

"Why didn't we take the shuttle?"

Ann's pace slowed, and she looked back at him.

"Sorry," Ade said quickly. He knew why. The shuttle was an additional fee if not used for work.

They continued through the buildings in silence, and Ade studied the large, maroon letter/number combinations on the buildings.

"Why is it so quiet?" He asked. "Aren't people working?"

"Production is done at night when it's cooler. Dayshift has the lighter work of packing, shipping, and paperwork."

"You pack for shipping, right?"

"Yes, sir. Six days a week," Ann replied.

Ade paused as he considered what he was about to say. "Mom," Ade began.

"Son," his mother retorted.

"Why didn't you finish school and take the placement?"

Ann chuckled. Without looking back, she continued walking forward. "I wondered how long it would take you to ask. I figured you blamed me for not having a job and being forced to move to Jaber."

"I know you didn't qualify for work on Cranis. I guess I'm just curious. You're always talking about how important school is."

"Your father was a year ahead of me in school," Ann began. "When he graduated and got his placement, we planned to stay an extra year so I could graduate. But then I became pregnant. Things were becoming more volatile between the planets, and Jack thought we needed to move before war broke out. After that, we saw no need for me to finish school. So, I just stayed home with your brother."

"What did you want to be? If you took the placement," Ade asked.

"Politics. I wanted to go into government. You know, help make things better. My school scores were good enough."

"Couldn't you go back?"

"Maybe after you graduate. Hadn't thought about it."

They continued amongst the shadows. Ade tried to imagine his mother as a politician, but the thought made him laugh.

"What?" Ann insisted.

"Just thinking of you in a government jumper makes me laugh."

Ann stopped walking and turned back toward Ade. "I think I'd look quite fetching. Thank you."

Looking past her, Ade saw the last row of buildings before the open desert. "I'm sure," Ade said, watching a sand tornado swirling through the desert. Then he heard the distant growl of cargo haulers.

Ann turned to see what he was looking at. "It looks worse than it is. And it's under a mile."

Ade looked at her and then back at the desert. "People normally walk this?"

"All the time. When I was a few years younger than you, we walked it twice a week," Ann said, turning and walking toward the sunlight.

Emerging from the shadows, the sun felt hotter than it had previously. The stretch of land between the factories and the transport highway served as a buffer and aided in keeping the factory fans clear of the billowing dust kicked up by the haulers.

Drawing closer to the dust clouds, Ade paused. He trusted his mother, but this was unlike anything he'd ever seen. Golden particles whirled around the highway beneath piercing blue skies and a sun that scorched the planet.

"No turning back now," Ann yelled. "We're almost there."

Ade nodded. "I'm coming."

The noise of the haulers had grown from a distant growl to a roar. Ade scowled under his mask and skeptically continued forward. *I wish we'd taken a transport.*

Sand peppered the lenses of his goggles. It was like the world around him had disappeared. Swirling sand created a haze that reminded Ade of thick tan fog. He focused on the bright color of his mother's scarf. With each step, the roar intensified until they were stopped by a solid red light glowing in the dust. Ade watched the massive, tan, armor-plated trucks speed by between gusts. The noise reminded him of the trains on Cranis.

His mother tapped his shoulder, pointed, and gestured with her hand. "We need to cross this," she yelled.

Ade nodded and looked at the passing trucks. Then he leaned into his mother and pointed. "Those are the new dixothine haulers. I learned about them last week in school. Each one carries enough to power the Labor District for a week," Ade screamed.

"They look like tanks now," Ann yelled.

"That's because the dixothine is extremely volatile until it can be refined."

"I know," Ann yelled as the last truck passed.

Engines faded into the distance, and the light turned green. Crossing the highway, Ade focused on the clearing image in the distance. The dust slowly settled, and the vibrant colors of the market came into view. About five hundred yards from the highway was a large doorway flanked by tall stone walls. It looked like a medieval stronghold that stood just beyond the thatched houses of the city's peasants. He had seen images of it before, but drawing closer, Ade realized it was nothing like the shopping centers on Cranis. Reaching the threshold of the market, Ade removed his face covering and gawked at the shopping mecca. It was more spectacular than he had imagined, and suddenly, the long walk didn't seem so bad. Vibrant, colorful canopies hung over a sea of vendors while shoppers scurried between them like bees collecting pollen. The hum of commerce filled their ears. Ade now understood his mother's scarlet scarf as he observed the people in the market. In stark contrast to himself, shoppers wore decorative jumpsuits embellished with colorful wraps and scarves. Then, his gaze landed on the true gem of the market. Just beyond the vendors in the center of the market was the oasis: water, palm trees, and skimpily-clad humans frolicking in the water.

"Is that why they built here?" Ade asked, pointing at the oasis.

"That and it's close to where things are made. The oasis was why we came here twice a week," Ann smiled.

"Can we go?" Ade asked, a bit too giddily for someone his age.

"After your surprise."

With an expression of wonderment, Ade's head craned from side to side as he looked at each passing vendor and shop. Ade's mouth began watering as the sweet smell of fresh desserts filled his nostrils. Ade's eyes searched for the source of the scent as his stomach grumbled.

Admittedly, Ade was too enamored with his surroundings to notice the large man walking directly toward him. Pain shot down his arm as a broad shoulder knocked him back.

"Watch it, rat," a gravelly voice spat.

"What the heck did you call me?" Ade shouted as he whirled toward the voice.

Momentum brought him to a halt in front of two men, their badges glistening in the sun. Ade froze as the larger of the two drew a wooden club from his belt and stepped toward him. He looked more like a beast than a man. Short, jet-black hair standing still in the wind. His mirrored goggles were bright against dark, tan skin and black stubble. He wore a freshly washed tan uniform and a utility belt filled with gadgets and weaponry. The insignia above his shield read J1A.

The Beast pushed his goggles to his forehead and studied Ade with cold, dark eyes. "Did you just raise your voice at a member of the Special Police, Scarface?"

Abe's mouth was suddenly dry as he struggled to find a response.

"Myers, leave it. We need to get back," the smaller officer interjected.

"This'll only take a minute," The Beast stated.

His mother quickly stepped in between him and the officer.

"Sir," his mother began, "my son simply inquired about what you called him. He's not accustomed to the term rat. Rats are disgusting animals on Cranis."

"They are here too," The Beast sneered. He took another step and leaned forward, looming large over Ade's mother. "I bet you were pretty once." Then he spat in her face.

Abe lunged for him, but his mother caught his arm. The Beast didn't hesitate. Rearing back, he thrust the thick end of the club into Ade's stomach. Pain radiated from his stomach, and his knees weakened as he collapsed onto the sidewalk. Before he could look up, Ade heard his mother.

"You bastard!"

Then he heard a dull thud followed by a choking sound. Ade opened his eyes just in time to see his mother collapse next to him, holding her throat. Then, looking into the shadow of the man standing over him, the club's end came into focus as it settled inches from his nose. Tears pooled in Ade's eyes and streamed down his dirty cheeks.

"I'd suggest you find other places to shop while on Jaber," The Beast hissed. "This place isn't for your kind."

"Myers, enough," his partner scolded.

The Beast huffed and hooked the club back to his utility belt. The shadow of the two men passed over them. Ann rolled onto her stomach and pushed herself to her knees. Gasping for air, she spat blood onto the sidewalk. A rush of adrenaline made Ade's scalp tingle. He quickly rolled onto his knees and removed the lid from his canteen. She raised her hand in a stop motion and held it there as blood dripped from her lip. She wiped her mouth on her sleeve. "I'm fine. You keep that, honey," she said with a slight wheeze.

He felt the need to call for help, but as he looked up, all he saw were purposefully diverted eyes as people quickly walked around them as though they were merely objects in the road. Struggling to his feet, Ade collected himself before helping his mother. "Are you sure you're okay?" he asked, helping her up.

Ann nodded, peered at the passing people, and quickly dusted the sand off her scarlet wrap. It was as if she were horrified that someone might notice the dust on her clothes. Her movements were deliberate yet refined. Then, her attention abruptly switched to Ade.

"Oh my gosh, you," she said, looking him over and dusting his shoulders.

"Mom, I'm fine," Ade barked. A sense of urgency engulfed him. He brushed away her hands. "We should report them! I mean, you can't do-"

"We're not reporting them," she interrupted. She nervously looked for the officers to ensure they were no longer within hearing distance, but they had disappeared into the sea of swarming shoppers. Ade pointed in their direction. "But-"

Ann's eyes shot back to Ade. Her body tensed, and her hands grabbed Ade's arms and pushed them back to his sides. "You can't report something to the same people you are reporting on!" She paused, and her head lowered. "This is Jaber, not Cranis, Ade," she said firmly, "and it's not the same as before the war."

Ade could sense a tone of defeat in her voice. It caused pain in his chest. His lips separated to form a counterargument, but he knew the conversation was over. He clenched his jaw and peered over her at the crowd. “Okay, let’s go home. Can you walk, or do we call a shuttle?”

“No,” Ann insisted. She tugged the day pass out from under her shawl and pointed to a dark orange building with a bright green awning. The large sign below the canopy read Paul’s Offworld Goods. “We get what we came for.”

“But Mom, the man said-”

“The man didn’t know we were paying customers with an order to retrieve. I should have clipped my day pass lower on my jacket.”

The sad determination in his mother’s voice caused his heart to sink into his stomach, and the sadness kindled a fire growing inside him. “That’s no excuse, Mom! Those two were not-”

“Ade, please,” Ann pleaded, looking directly into Ade’s eyes. Scared and desperate, her eyes begged him to let it go.

The anger fumed within, and Ade’s ears turned bright red as more tears rolled down his face. His mother had always joked that he had no fuse. Ade had what doctors called Intermittent Explosive Disorder. Ade had learned to reason with himself to quell the bouts of anger, but the feelings were so strong that his body could not process the emotion and instead produced tears. And so, Ade always cried when he was mad. Growing up with this flaw was brutal, but it forced him to learn to fight at a young age, and eventually, the laughing stopped.

Ade nodded in concession and held her arm as he escorted her toward the store. Her walk was slow but deliberate. She clutched his arm with each step. “It was supposed to be a surprise, but I might as well tell you. I ordered bacon and some of the coffee you always drank on Cranis. I know it’s been hard, and you haven’t felt at home, so I ordered your favorites.”

He glanced at the petite woman holding his arm – the woman who stood between him and a monster. “Mom...” he lost his words but found the ones that mattered. “I love you.”

“I love you too, honey,” she said, patting his arm.

CHAPTER 4 | 5856-W20

Ade bit his tongue, smiled, and nodded. "Yes, Educator Frank. I'd be happy to complete that project." He gave a goofy wave and then punched the disconnect button.

"Thank you for choosing-"

Ade hit the mute button on the pod. "You've got to be kidding me," he scoffed.

Sulking from the halostation pod, he glanced at his mother sipping coffee at the kitchen table. She looked up at him with a smirk on her face. "Good day at school?"

It had been a week since the incident at the market. Neither Ade nor his mother spoke of the attack. He attempted to bring it up the next day, but Ann quickly changed the subject. It seemed she found solace in pretending it didn't happen. Since then, he'd been happy to stay in the confines of the unit and concentrate on his studies. The attack had solidified his purpose. Ade's new goal was to ace the placement test and move back to Cranis as soon as possible. His teacher, however, was making this more difficult than anticipated. It seemed Educator Ruth still held a bitter resentment of his intellect.

"Don't start. I'm doing exactly what you told me to," Ade complained.

Ann didn't say a word. Instead, she shrugged her shoulders and glanced at the halofeed. "Mom, she wants an additional thousand words besides what I'm writing. It's unreasonable," Ade insisted.

"If you break that thing, they won't let you graduate until you pay it off." She took another sip from the cup and peered over the brim at him.

"I didn't hit it hard," Ade argued.

She continued to scrutinize him with the same motherly look.

It was the look she'd used since he was a kid. Slightly pursed lips with raised eyebrows told him he was wrong and intelligent enough to know better.

"Okay, I hit it too hard. But a thousand words! I'm practically teaching the class at this point."

"Nothing wrong with sharing your knowledge. Besides, you said it yourself: the class was too easy."

"Yeah, but she's singling me out."

"What else are you going to do? Drink all my coffee and watch the halofeed all day? It's not like you spend all day cleaning."

Ade sighed and placed his hands on his hips. It was mental chess, and she'd just taken his knight. "Mom, it's not that. I'm super busy. I'm doing my coursework and studying for the placement. It's just not fair. I'm starting to think she's xenophobic."

His mother immediately placed her cup on the table and turned in her chair toward him. "Ade Billings, those thoughts are not welcome in this house," Ann said sternly, her finger wagging with each word. "And before you accuse your teacher of xenophobia, you should know I asked her to give you extra work. Donna is a wonderful woman and certainly not xenophobic. Her son just moved to Cranis!"

Ade shrunk as he stood before her. Physically, he towered over her, but presently, he felt like a small child being scolded. "I'm sorry, mom."

"Good. You should be," Ann said before returning to her cup of coffee.

Ade paused. "But why'd you ask her to give me more work?"

"When I called the school to reinstate you," Ann began. "You were bored, so I asked her to challenge you." She took another drink and glanced at the halofeed while Ade looked at the floor. "So, what is this extra assignment you're glowering about?" Ann asked.

"The events leading up to the war. What she is teaching us is all wrong," Ade began. He couldn't help himself. From his point of view, she was wrong, and he was right, so the complaints rolled quickly from his lips. "She's trying to say Cranis was greedy and no longer wanted the Labor Party to control exports. It's ridiculous. Everybody knows it was because Jaber strong-armed Cranis with the shipping tax and kept us from getting things we needed."

"Is that right?" Ann questioned.

Ade took note of her disapproving tone. "I didn't argue with the teacher. I just said that it differed from what they teach us on Cranis. So now she wants a thousand words on it."

"You know I lived through that, right?" Ann questioned.

Ade stared at her. He knew she was alive during the war. Ethan was born the same year the war began, but imagining her at his age felt foreign. "So, you know what I'm saying. All wrong."

Ann stood silently from the table, walked to the kitchenette, and refilled her cup of coffee. Then, taking a small sip, she leaned against the counter and looked at him. Ade could tell from her expression that she saw him as a child, not a boy on the cusp of becoming a man.

"What?" Ade asked.

"You know there are two sides to every story, right?" Ann asked.

Ade stared at her again. Then, unsure of where she was going with this, he appeased her by nodding in agreement.

Ann lifted the cup to take another drink, paused, and quickly placed the cup on the counter as her free hand shot up to cover her mouth. Her body tensed, and her back arched as a dry, raspy cough escaped her. She held up the opposite hand, indicating to give her a minute as she continued to cough. She righted herself and touched her chest as the fit passed. Then she cleared her throat and retrieved her coffee.

"Are you okay?" Ade asked.

"Sorry, I inhaled my spit," she said.

Ade's face twinged in disgust and disbelief. "That's not a thing."

"It is when you get older," she said, taking a sip. "Anyway, the truth is, the Labor Party raised rates to cover the expense of upgrading their factories, so workers were safe. Cranis saw the tax raise as a threat to their economy and attacked. It was that simple in the end. Granted, there was a lot of bickering leading up to that."

"The Labor Party should have never claimed independence in the first place. They could have worked together," Ade countered.

Ann moved back to the table and sat. She ran a finger around the brim of her coffee mug and glanced at the halofeed. "Physical violence is the result of a weak mind," Ann said.

Ade grimaced. It was something Jack said when he and Ethan fought. After that, he heard it every time he came home with either a black eye or bruised knuckles. His mother utilizing this viewpoint gave her an unfair advantage.

"Imagine you were paid to plant 100 barley plants," Ann said, "but someone thousands of miles away sent you 75 plants and demanded it be done in one day. You could slave all day to accomplish this task and still be short 25 plants. Then, because you were short, the person paying decides to only pay you for planting 50."

Ade didn't see the point of the hypothetical. "Well, that's dumb. First, I'd quit. And second, I'd demand what they owed me. It's their fault for not sending enough plants."

Ann grinned. "In this scenario, you're Jaber, and the employer is Cranis. That's pretty much why the Labor Party split from Cranis."

"That's not what they taught us," Ade interjected.

"Well honey, if two people argue and you only ask one what happened, you'll only learn the other person was wrong."

It took a moment to sink in. Ade had never questioned what was taught to him. He had, as most do, assumed the information to be accurate. However, from what he was hearing, he was being told his teachers were wrong. This contradicted what his parents had hounded him on for many years.

"So don't listen to my teachers?"

Ann spat her sip of coffee back into the cup and looked at him wide-eyed. “Heavens, no!” Ann exclaimed. “I mean, yes. Listen to your teachers. I...I just meant that history has many sides to consider. Each teacher may interpret it differently.”

His mother was backpedaling. Ade withheld a smile. It didn’t happen often, but he took great joy in outsmarting her.

“So, listen to them, but don’t believe everything they say,” Ade responded.

“No! Young man, I meant to get both sides of the story.”

Ade grinned.

“Oh, you little bugger,” Ann scowled. “You know what I mean.”

“Yes, mother. Listen to them, knowing they think they’re right but know they’re wrong,” Ade goaded.

Her face was bright red, and she threw her arms in the air. “Just pass the class. It’s hopeless at this point.”

Ade beamed as he leaned down and kissed her head. “Yes, Mother. I’m going to work on my paper,” he said, turning toward his room.

“Don’t offend the teacher,” Ann called after him.

“Of course, Mother. Donna is a wonderful woman.”

Ade closed the door to his room and grinned. He imagined his mother sitting at the table, scowling over his last remark. *She would have made a good politician. Not today, though.*

CHAPTER 5 | 5856-W21

Ade sat at the kitchen table, skimming his Augmentation Theory 342 course notes. The halofeed chirped in the background, and every few minutes, he would peer up at a story that sparked his interest.

"Special Police Force Commissioner Gordon Paul announced the apprehension of seven Union sympathizers in the Labor District. We have yet to learn if they have direct ties to the organization, but Paul stated their actions posed a severe threat to dixothine refinement and the stability of our economy. In other news, President Hollar-"

"Good," Ade muttered angrily. "I hope they get what they deserve." He shook his head and went back to his notes. Then, a thought entered his mind, and he sighed. *I wonder if the officer thought we were sympathizers.* He looked from his notes to a smiley face he'd drawn in the dust on the housing unit's wall. *Doesn't make it right, though.*

They had been on Jaber for over a month, and the once sparkling white walls now had a golden-brown hue due to accumulating dust. He glanced at his watch and then at his mother's bedroom door. There was an hourlong break before his next class at 10 a.m., and she was still in bed. *Maybe she's finally catching up on some sleep. I'll wake her before my next class.*

Turning back to his studies, he pushed the notes aside and activated his halopad. Opening the textbook, he scrolled to the third chapter. *Augmentation enhancement of a physical being alters the genetic discrepancies passed through generations. It was thought that these enhancements violated the natural order.*

Ade snickered. His father once told him that people on Earth had surgery to change their appearance. When Ade asked why, Jack shrugged his shoulders, winked, and pointed at his face. "I guess they wanted to look like me."

Jack was an average man in both height and width. He was neither attractive nor unattractive. He had a round face similar to Ade's, but it was accented by a neatly trimmed salt and pepper beard and long, thick hair that dusted his shoulders. Jack's most distinguishable feature was a peaked nose with large lumps on the bridge from being repeatedly broken. He had brown eyes that seemed to study everything before them and a belly from too many seconds at the dinner table.

Ade looked down at his lanky frame. He patted his firm stomach and tried to take a drink from an empty cup.

The door to Ann's room opened, and she shuffled her feet as she crossed the room. "Do we have coffee?" she mumbled.

"Yeah, just made it."

Ann looked from Ade to the pot on the kitchen counter. "Looks like you made all of it," she grumbled. "You know we need to make that stretch through next week, right?" she said sternly.

"It's my Cranis coffee. I thought it was a gift," Ade said, pretending to concentrate on his studies.

"A gift that needs to last us until next week," Ann said, pouring a cup for herself. Then, she took a drink and stared at the smiley face drawn in the dust. "Maybe you should be an artist," she said sarcastically.

Ade glanced up at her and smirked. "I thought you wanted me to make a living."

"I'll clean the walls today. You can help me."

"You can't kill Donny. He's my friend," Ade feigned dismay.

She sat the cup on the counter and added freckles to the dust drawing. "You named your dust drawing Donny," Ann said plainly. "You need to get out more."

"That makes two of us," Ade said, looking at the clock. "Are you not going to work again?"

"I'm not feeling the best."

She turned toward him, and Ade's eyes widened as they fell upon the sight of her bare neck. Her neck was a dark blue, purple, and pink palette, all around a yellow spot in the middle.

Upon seeing his reaction, she frantically reached to pull up her scarf but quickly realized she'd forgotten to put it on before leaving her room.

"Mom," Ade gasped.

"It's nothing," she said, backing away and bumping into the kitchen counter. "Don't worry yourself. It looks worse than it feels."

Ade stood from his chair and moved toward her for a closer look.

"I said don't worry," she repeated. She covered her neck and turned away as she sidestepped toward her room.

He took another step forward. Ann quickly spun away from him, which caused her to stagger slightly as she hurried out of the room. The door to her room slammed shut, and Ade stood momentarily, thinking back to the moment at the market. The infuriating thought made it hard to focus.

"Mom," he called after her. He quickly crossed the room and attempted to follow her into the room but found the door was locked.

"Mom," he said again, shaking the locked door. His voice cracked, and he paused to take a breath. "Mom, we need to go to the hospital!" He spoke to the closed door. "Mom!"

The door opened, and she looked up at him. Dark purple rings offset her strikingly blue eyes; she smiled and pushed by him. It looked like she hadn't slept in days.

She had wrapped her neck in the same tan scarf she'd been wearing all week. After becoming accustomed to the heat outside, Ade had thought she was cold in the temperature-controlled housing unit, but now he knew she was hiding the bruise.

"How long has it looked like that?" Ade demanded.

Ann quickly moved across the room to the sink. "I don't know. I didn't even notice your art until today," she said, kneeling before the cabinet below the sink.

Ade stood in disapproval, watching her rummage through the cleaning supplies. He knew she was lying. "Mom, how long has it been like that?" Ade insisted.

"Where did I put those darn dust clothes," she muttered. "Oh, here we go."

She stood, and, as she did, she lost her balance and quickly placed a hand on the sink to sturdy herself. Then she closed the cabinet door with her foot.

Ade rushed to her and grabbed her arm. "Mom, I'm calling a shuttle."

"No, I'm fine. Just stood up too fast. Can you believe how dirty these walls are? Oh..." She looked up at him but immediately looked away. "When did you say your next class started?"

"I'm not going to class. We're going to the hospital."

"No. I'm fine. Maybe I just need more sleep." Ann attempted to pull away, but Ade blocked her path. He always knew her to be a stubborn woman. In part, it was what fueled her through difficult situations. She became hyper-focused on the task before her and obsessed over it until completion.

"Mom, we're going."

"Ade..."

"If you don't, I'm going to the Labor Commission and applying for work as a non-graduate."

Ann's eyes fell to the floor, and she exhaled sharply from her nose. "So, that's how you're going to play this?"

"Someone needs to take care of this family. If it's not you, then it's me."

"Would you even consider letting this go for me?" she said, looking up at him.

Ade could see the fear in her eyes. It was the same pleading look his father burned into his memory.

"I let it go in the market when I shouldn't have. And I'm not losing two parents in one year," he responded firmly.

Ann sighed. "Okay, help me to the chair and call a shuttle."

She shook her head as they slowly crossed the room. "You're as stubborn as your father."

"It runs in the family," Ade responded.

***

Exiting their apartment into the heat of Jaber, Ann leaned into Ade. Her legs wobbled beneath her, and each breath wheezed from her lungs. She tugged the covering from her face as Ade steadied her. He checked his watch and looked at the sky in the distance beyond the Labor District.

"We have to pick up the pace, Mom."

"I can't," Ann said.

He swung her arm over his shoulder. The height difference made it challenging to move swiftly as he leaned down to walk with her. He began taking long, low strides, and her feet dragged in the pebbles. "Mom, can you walk?"

"I'm so tired," she mumbled.

He grabbed both her arms and turned his back toward her. Lifting her arms over his shoulders, he backed into her and lifted her onto his back. Even as petite as she was, he immediately felt a burn in his legs as he stepped forward. He blinked and increased the hauling weight of his leg augmentation. Then, firmly planting his feet, he adjusted his grip on her and hurried down the pebbled path.

The sound of a shuttle was muffled by the crunching of stone under his feet. He looked to the sky and saw the shuttle descending in the distance just beyond the edge of the housing sector. Ade growled in anger. His leg augmentation needed to be calibrated for the 1.5% gravity variance and wasn't as powerful as he needed them to be. Ade blinked and set his legs to sprint. Not paying attention to the ground, Ade overlooked the tortaline ambling across the path until he was about to trip over it. He quickly sidestepped. The additional weight on his back spun him around, and he skidded to a halt. Breathing heavily, his mask sucked into his mouth and billowed out. He took a step toward the tortaline in a motion to kick it but stopped. *Everything here is ridiculous*, he thought. Wildlife in the desert region of Jaber evolved to withstand the harsh environment and constant barrage of sunlight. This meant they were much larger than animals in the cooler regions and often had scales or an exterior shell. Glaring at the giant, shelled reptile, he heard engines rev in the distance. The hair on the back of Ade's neck stood, and he whirled around to watch the shuttle rise into the sky and fly away.

"Fug!" Ade screamed, and he paced in a circle. Then he leaned forward so his mother's weight rested on his back instead of his shoulder. "We missed the shuttle," he huffed.

"That's okay. Let's go home," Ann wheezed.

"Mom, how else can we get to the hospital?"

She peered up and looked for the sun.

"How else?" Ade demanded.

She raised her hand and pointed in the direction of the departed skimmer.

"The boom. Just keep going. You'll see it."

Ade took two deep breaths and began running. Toward the edge of the housing sector, the top of a metal arch could be seen just above the houses. The large burgundy sky arches of the boom train rail could be seen from miles away in the open desert. At the highest point, the arch was six stories from the sandy surface of Jaber. Ade slowed to reposition his mother. His heart sank as he looked at the open desert.

It must be a mile. If not more. "Just a little longer," he said.

Jaber was connected by an extensive system of high-speed rails with stations located throughout the various districts of the planet. The speed of the trains made it possible to travel between the districts in a fraction of the time it would take by skimmer; however, due to the speed of the boom train, these stations were often located outside of populated areas and usually required a shuttle to access them. The Labor District station was the last stop on the line and was purposefully placed away from the Labor District and Market.

Passing the arch base, Ade's eyes traced it into the blue sky and then drifted down to the elevated platform. The station was suspended thirty feet from the desert floor between two large steel arches. The steel was coated with dark red paint, but the color was worn and pitted from years of natural sandblasting. Large steel beams ran every twenty feet on each side of the track and supported a canopy that provided passengers awaiting the train relief from the blistering sun.

Ade's body screamed for rest as he slowed to a stop before the elevator to the platform. To his surprise, he pressed the call button, and the doors immediately slid open.

"Hang on, Mom. We're at the station."

The elevator chimed upon arrival, and the doors slid open. Ade's heart sank as he exited onto the empty platform. He carried his mother to a bench near the track and gently set her down. Ade glanced around the platform. Benches sat just beyond loading zones, and beyond them were information kiosks. Landing pads for shuttle access were at the far edge of the platform beyond the canopy. Ade sat beside her; he could hear her wheezing through her mask. He looked both ways down the track and checked his watch.

"What time does the train get here?"

"Don't know." Her voice was faint and raspy.

"I'll be right back," Ade said. He sprinted to the nearest information kiosk and began swiping through the options. *Forty minutes...* "Mom, the next shuttle is in forty minutes," he shouted. She slightly raised her hand in acknowledgment.

Ade searched the platform until he saw a water machine. He rushed back to her side, sat, and put an arm around her for stability. "Do you want some water?" he asked.

She shook her head, "No. Just sleep."

A knot formed in his stomach as the worry intensified. He

again looked down the track, hoping the train was ahead of schedule. He grabbed Ann's hand. He meant to say something, but the coldness of her skin shocked him. "Mom, your hand is cold!" The severity of the situation set in. It was 106 degrees Fahrenheit in the shade.

"It's cold out here, honey," she mumbled.

What could it be? Ade's mind was racing. "Mom, hold on. I'll get help."

Ade ran back to the kiosk. Frantically searching the screen, he found what he was looking for at the bottom – a red button labeled Report Emergency. Pressing the button, the screen flashed to *Connecting...* Then, a woman popped up on the screen.

"Platform 1316, section A5, state your emergency."

"My mom," Ade pleaded, "We need to get to the hospital."

"Sir, settle down. You can schedule a shuttle at this kiosk, and it'll be there in two minutes. Just use the-"

"I already used our weekly shuttle allotment. We missed it. Can you please send one? She's so cold. I don't think she's breathing properly."

"Sir, what is your mother's name and assigned employer?"

Ade shook his head with confusion. "We need help!"

"Sir, we need to charge the emergency call to her employer since you've already used your shuttle pass. What is her name and-"

Tears of fear and frustration broke loose. "Ann Billings. Diaxo Dynamics," he forced through his lips.

"And what is her position at Diaxo?"

Ade's jaw clenched. "What does that..." He angrily shook his head. "Shipping, now send someone already!"

"Just one moment." The audio was muted, and he could see her speaking into a secondary microphone. She nodded and then turned back toward him. "Sir, EMS will be there in two minutes. Please note that additional charges may occur due to Ann's status as a laborer."

"Just get here," Ade growled, glaring at her through the screen.

"Sir, I do not appreciate your tone. Please stare directly at the screen until the facial recognition protocol has been completed. Your actions will be reported to the Labor Commission."

Without thinking, Ade clenched his fists and slammed them down on the screen, thus causing the image to distort and an alarm to sound.

"One count of destruction of government property has been added," relayed the fuzzy screen. "That is an automatic ten-point deduction on your placement test score results. Please note this may affect your job placement."

"Just send someone!" he screamed.

In his mind, he heard his mother trying to calm him as she did when he was a child, but, looking up, he saw her slumped down on the bench. His heart leaped into his throat. There was a momentary pause as the worst thoughts entered his mind. Then, Ade rushed to his mother. Skidding to her side, he dusted the sand from her face. Her skin appeared ashen, and her lips had a blue hue. He pressed his ear to her mouth and listened as she exhaled a short, shallow breath.

Emergency lights from two skimmers cut through the wispy clouds and descended upon the platform. Ade shielded his eyes as the squeal of the engines cut to a hum and then went silent as they landed.

Ade jumped to his feet and waved his arms frantically. "Over here!" he yelled.

Uniformed men hurried toward them, and Ade knelt again at Ann's side. "Help is here. They're here, Mom."

Footsteps quickened and grew louder before stopping next to him. A level three augment tech and a paramedic knelt on each side of his mother. He could hear them speaking, but the words didn't register.

"Sir!" one yelled into his ear – snapping him from the trance. "We need room to work!" Looking into the paramedic's full-face shield, he saw his distorted reflection. His flushed skin was caked with dust, and his tears had dried in streaks.

"Sir, you need to talk to the officers."

The scene was a blur of movement. Ade slowly backed away from the bench.

"Hey, you! Over here," a familiar voice commanded.

The gravelly voice heightened Ade's senses, bringing the world back into focus. His eyes narrowed on The Beast.

The Beast laughed as their eyes met. "Scarface, I see you've been crying again."

Ade's fists were eager and ready; he only had one thought. It was instinct fueled by rage. "You did this!" He pounced, charging toward the man. It only took five running steps to reach him, but by then, The Beast had already removed his club and raised it to strike. Ade landed on his left foot on the fifth step, cocked his fist, and juked his head to the left. The Beast brought the club down hard to intercept the movement. Rolling his body to the right, Ade dodged the strike, transferred weight to his right foot, and used the power of his leg augmentation to leap into the air. The Beast's missed attack opened up the left side of his face. Ade thrust his fist forward with all the force of his movement, landing a hard, flying punch squarely under The Beast's left eye. The punch spun him and sent his mirrored goggles bouncing across the platform. His muscular frame went limp, and he fell face-first onto the floor. Ade quickly bent down and grabbed a fistful of black hair. "YOU!" he screamed, raising his fist for another strike. A small blinking dart impacted his chest. His eyes shot up to another officer just in time to see him push the button.

CHAPTER 6 | 5856-W21

Ade's eyes fluttered open to a bright autumn sun shining directly into his face. He attempted to raise a hand to shield his eyes, but neither hand would move. A shadow loomed just beyond his peripheral vision and moved closer. Ade tried to stand, but he was held by a force greater than his own. Ade screamed, but the scream was silent. The shadow moved closer. Bright orange leaves swirled around, and the wind pushed the shadow over him. With the shadow came a sharp pinch followed by a burning sensation that spread down his arm to his fingertips. Then he heard his name. "Ade, Ade, calm down. You're waking up."

His eyes burst open to a dingy sleeping pad on a cement slab. The air smelled like urine. Ade looked toward the voice only to see a strange face peering down at his arm through the bars of a cell. The man removed a needle from his arm and let go of his wrist. Ade yanked his arm back through the bars, and his eyes shot past the needle man to a familiar man in a Special Police uniform. "Mom," he gasped as he remembered the platform. Panic took him as he lunged to his feet and grabbed the bars. "My-"

"She's fine," the officer said as he stepped forward. The needle man casually tucked the needle into a small black pouch, nodded to the officer, and hurried away down the hall of cells.

"They put her on oxygen and repaired her AIRE. They'll be releasing her later today."

A sigh of relief escaped Ade, and he closed his eyes and rested his head on one of the cold steel bars of his cage. "She's okay," he exhaled.

"She almost wasn't. If you hadn't called, she wouldn't have survived the wait."

"So, it was her AIRE. I was wondering about that," Ade said.

The officer looked at him, a smile creeping across his face. "Yes, the augment malfunctioned, and she took in too much carbon monoxide."

Ade studied the officer. He was young – likely in his first or second year with the Special Police. Physically, he didn't look much older than Ade, but his eyes carried the burden of a man twice his age. He was shorter than Ade by at least six inches, but his build was more that of an athlete than a scholar. He had a tan square face, a strong jaw, and finely trimmed strawberry blond hair. The nametag on his chest read *Dane 4738926*.

"I figured. She got worse when we went outside. I know they pump oxygen through the vents in the housing units."

"How'd you know that?" Dane asked.

Ade pushed himself back from the bars and glanced around the filthy cell. "Doesn't matter," Ade muttered. "How long am I in here for?"

"I'm here to take you to the hospital to pick up your mom."

Ade's attention returned to Dane, and surprise quickly morphed into suspicion. The obvious question was how or why this man would help after what had occurred, but Dane interjected before Ade's thoughts could manifest.

"I was in the market that day with you and your mom. I saw what Myers did, and I didn't stop him. It wasn't the first time," he peered down at his shoes and shook his head. "I should have done something."

Ade's eyes narrowed on Dane. "I thought you looked familiar."

"Myers is my patrol partner. I didn't choose him."

"He almost killed her," Ade barked.

"And you would've killed him."

"For good reason! He had no reason to do what he did."

"Ade," Dane began, looking up with sympathetic eyes, "I'm not saying I disagree, but we're wasting time here. We should go."

"How, why...why would they just let me go?"

"Myers decided not to report the incident, but you still have to pay for that kiosk."

Puzzled, Ade sized up the man before him. He suspected the officer wasn't being entirely truthful. "Why would he do that?"

"Ade, I said we're wasting-"

"Just tell me," Ade demanded.

"I convinced him not to."

"Why would you do that? You stood by and let it happen. Why now? How do I know this isn't a trick?"

Dane raised his hands, emphasizing his willingness to concede. "Whoa, let's slow it down a bit."

"Well?" Ade asked.

Dane looked down at his utility belt. "Well, I guess we could start with the fact that I'm the one who shot you with the dart. That seems fair."

Ade's face contorted into a snarl. "You!"

Dane shrugged. "I said I was Myers' partner."

"How does that help me trust you?" Ade snapped.

"Well, would a guy trying to trick you openly say he shot you? Besides, I saved your life. If you'd have killed Myers, they'd have executed you."

"Right, because the hero always shoots the guy trying to save his mom," Ade sneered.

The corners of Dane's mouth began to curl into a smirk but quickly dissipated. "Ade, I'm trying to be your friend here."

"Friends don't shoot friends."

"They do on Jaber," Dane quickly retorted. "It's not Cranis, Ade. The rules are different here. Myers could've killed your mother, and nothing would've been done to him."

This was the second time he had been told that this wasn't Cranis. The first time, he hadn't taken it to heart. It seemed like something a mother would say to keep her son safe; however, now it seemed his mom had been telling the truth. Jaber was dangerous. Ade stepped away from the cell door and examined the room behind him. Beyond the stained sleeping pad and the elevated slab it rested on, the only other thing in the room was a cement square in the corner with a toilet seat. Even that had bars just below the seat. He turned to the officer to find he had extended his hand through the bars to offer him a small, folded piece of paper. Ade opened his mouth to speak, but Dane shook his head and raised a finger to his lips. He then pointed up to the light fixture and then to his ear.

Ade glared at him and swiftly snatched the paper from his hand. He stepped back just beyond Dane's reach and unfolded the paper to reveal one sentence. *You got the scar over your eye while playing with your father's tools.*

Ade's eyes widened. Only he and his father knew about this. His father lied to keep them out of trouble. Jack told Ann that Ade had fallen off his swing. "How'd-"

"Your mother will be waiting, Ade." Dane interrupted, shaking his head. Then he mouthed the words- *It's not safe.*

Ade stood contemplating for one last moment before reason prevailed. Nothing made sense, but even he knew his options were limited. "Okay, fine. You win. I trust you."

Dane blinked twice. "Open cell 43," he said. After a few seconds, the heavily barred door slid open with a screech. Dane raised one hand to motion him to step from the cell while simultaneously reaching for his cuffs with his other hand.

"I thought I was free to go?" Ade said, looking at the cuffs.

"I saw what you did to Myers. I'm not taking any chances."

CHAPTER 7 | 5856-W21

The landscape beyond the windows of the endo cruiser slowly changed as they flew west toward the Government District, and the sandy desert beneath them became speckled with wispy shrubbery. With each passing minute, the sun in the rearview mirror lowered in the sky. Ade scowled at Dane. They had been in the cruiser for over two hours, and barely a word was spoken. The questions tormenting Ade's mind remained unanswered, and each time he tried to talk, Dane would clench his jaw, give him a stern look, and shake his head.

Only my dad could have told him that story. I've never told anyone, but that doesn't make sense. How could he have possibly known about that? He's too young to have known Dad while he was on Jaber. Maybe they met on Cranis, but that seems unlikely.

Ade looked back at the arid landscape, and his fingers found their way to the scar on his forehead.

It was late October, and a crisp breeze blew amber leaves into the open door of his father's workshop. The smell of cinnamon and freshly brewed coffee filled the air, and Ade sat in the middle of the room on an old Persian rug, playing with blocks. Most of Ade's fondest memories began as a child in the workshop. Ade craved his father's attention, so he spent hours on that rug waiting for him to play. His favorite activity was skitter racing. Jack had built two skitters, and they would race around the workshop. Ade always won. He knew the skitter was too tiny for his father, but he enjoyed winning. That day, Jack was hosting a dinner for the members of his research team, and Ann and Ethan took the skimmer to the market. Ade had begged his mother to stay behind with his father, and Jack conceded by stating he would watch Ade and the strutten, Ann's specialty, cooking in the oven. Genius, however, didn't wait for a strutten to cook, and Jack hoisted Ade over his shoulder and carried him to the workshop. Ade had no concept of time while in the shop. There were no clocks because Jack felt they were a distraction. Work was never done; it was only paused when other circumstances required his attention.

Then, carried on the wind, came the smell of burning meat. Suddenly, Jack shot up from his stool, cursed under his breath, and bolted past Ade out the door. Turning his attention back to the blocks, Ade carefully stacked one atop another. The smell of burnt meat was overpowered by another, more powerful stench. Ade's eyes began to water. Looking for the source of the scent, he saw smoke rising from his father's workbench. Even at 9, Ade knew the rules: Do not touch his father's tools.

However, a circle of thoughts spun in his developing mind. If he touched the tools, he was in trouble. On the other hand, if his father's work were ruined, there would be no play for the rest of the day. Edging toward the tall table, Ade saw a handheld tool with a spinning tip. The tool's tip rotated so fast it was burning the circuit board beneath it. He reached for the device and paused. All that was needed was to figure out how to turn it off. Ade lifted it from the table. A scorching pain shot down his arm as the overheated tool burnt his flesh. Dropping the instrument, he immediately doubled over in pain. As he did, the spinning end of the device hit the tabletop and flew back toward his face. After that, all Ade remembered was blood. He screamed for his father as blood pulsed from his forehead and ran into his eyes. He heard his father enter the workshop, but no words were spoken. He was lifted into his father's arms and, after a few moments, gently placed into a cold bathtub. Cold water splashed against his skin, and a towel pressed against his forehead.

Ann was hysterical when she returned home. Not only had the strutten been burned beyond an edible state, but her youngest son now had a large gash above his right eye. Ade never really thought his mother believed the bit about falling off the swing, but to this day, only he and his father knew the truth of what happened in the workshop.

Ade sighed and glanced around the rough interior of the endo. Endo cruisers, known colloquially as squads, were exclusively used by police and the military. They were longer and broader than a regular skimmer and had thick, laster-proof plates angling in and out at 45-degree angles, flanking the exterior. This meant anyone dumb enough to fire on one with conventional weaponry was forced to lunge for cover as laster rounds pinged and reflected in unexpected directions. Only an old-fashioned projectile weapon or laster cannon could bring one down. Inside the endo were numerous instrument panels displaying weapons information and flashing coordinates. If the ricocheting blasts didn't get you the onboard weaponry certainly would.

Under other circumstances, Ade might have thought riding in such a vehicle exciting, but today was not that day.

Maybe Dad did work on Jaber, and we didn't know? He was frequently sent away on business trips.

He turned again to the window, and suddenly, his busy mind found a distraction worthy of his attention. His jaw fell slack as they descended into the Government District. It was a shining beacon of man's achievements. Large glass buildings jutted from the planet and kissed the sky as sunlight glistened off their reflective surfaces. The sun would rise or lower depending on the time of day, changing the angle and effect of its reflected glory, but the sun would never set on Jaber. Within a prism of reflecting light, the city glowed eternally. Jack had often taken Ade to the Capital City on Cranis, and Ade often marveled at large steel and glass buildings. But this was far grander than any city on Cranis. And then he saw the city's true treasure in shades of green.

"What is that place?" Ade gasped. In the heart of the city was an enormous forest. The park's edges, framed with red brick, must have spanned a mile in each direction. Grand cement paths cut through the woods, and trees framed ponds and playgrounds. As they drew closer, Ade could see people walking the trails and sitting by the water holding hands. It looked like paradise.

"Pretty impressive, isn't it?" Dane mused. "It's an exact historical replica of Central Park from Earth. All the building architecture in the Capitol Center is based on historic Earth buildings. See that one over there?" Dane pointed at a building shaped like a bullet's tip. Colored glass spiraled up around the building, thinning until it reached the top. "That one was from... let me think. Landen, I believe. It's my favorite." Then he pointed to another. "That's my second. They call it the Freedom Tower. I have no idea why."

Ade just nodded. He was barely able to comprehend what he was seeing. The city bustled with life. Both hover and ground vehicles traversed the roads while people casually strolled the sidewalks, taking in the clean, fresh air.

"How is this possible?" Ade marveled.

"Groundskeepers have watering pipes buried in the soil. Now, if you think that's impressive, you'd be blown away if we flew another seven hours west."

Ade recalled his World Geography class as he considered the distance they'd already traveled. Jaber consisted of four climate zones — desert, semi-arid, temperate, and polar. "The arctic ring?" Ade asked.

"Impressive," Dane nodded, one brow raised in appreciation. "You paid attention in class. But man, it's...." Dane began but quickly trailed off.

"It's what?" Ade asked.

Dane began flipping switches on the instrument panel as the squad lowered into the city. "I hear it's quite cold. That's all."

"Oh. Yeah, I read that," Ade said, looking back at the city.

His eyes fell from the shining buildings to the streets below, and he watched a woman with a small, fluffy dog on a leash. Ade had never seen a dog before. He'd seen pictures and read about them in books, but dogs were endangered. Very few survived the trip from Earth. Scientists tried without success to bioengineer them, but they could never successfully recreate man's best friend. Now, only the most affluent people could afford them.

The endo sped through the city center, and the city's splendor vanished as quickly as it appeared. The grand spectacle quickly morphed into plain, gray industrial buildings. Ade sat back and looked at a small Special Police emblem on the dash.

"Is this normally where he sits?" Ade asked.

"Who?"

"That fugduger you work with."

Dane cocked his head and glanced at Ade. "The what?"

"Fugduger," Ade repeated.

"Oh, I heard you. What is that?"

Ade rolled his eyes. It was like he was talking to his mother. He failed to realize that he was on a new planet, and the slang of Cranis fell upon deaf ears. "It's a bastard, idiot. The worst possible kind of person. Like your partner."

Dane's reserved facade cracked, and he burst into laughter.

"How is that funny?" Ade asked indignantly, somewhat offended. "He put my mom in the hospital. We wouldn't even be here if not for him."

Dane's laughter slowly subsided. "Okay. I can't argue that, but fugduger? Who says that?"

"All of my friends," Ade mumbled, and he looked back out the window.

Dane chuckled a few more times as Ade glared out the window.

"We call them a duxknocker here. Means the same thing," Dane said.

Ade nodded as he watched an ambulance zip past them with lights flashing and sirens blaring. Ade squinted at a large rectangular building in the distance. It was three times the size of the buildings surrounding it and towered into the sky. Skimmers and other transport vehicles lined the lanes leading up to the building, and flashing lights circled the roof, creating a purple halo. A transport would drop from the halo every few seconds and descend to the structure's roof.

"We're almost there," Dane said.

"Why aren't we using the lights?" Ade asked.

"Because you're not dying," Dane said plainly.

Ade shot him a sideways glare, and Dane shrugged his shoulders.

"Well, not at this exact moment anyway," Dane added.

As they drew closer, Ade counted twelve landing areas on the roof of the building- each marked with a large cross and a number painted in the middle. At the foot of the building were six more numbered circles of equal size with runways leading up to them. A road for ground vehicles was off to the south side of the building.

Dane blinked twice and waited for a green light to illuminate on the dashboard. "Grace Reception- picking up one Ann Billings, advise," he said.

Jaw gaping, Ade glanced between the green light and Dane.

There was a brief silence, and then a voice came over the internal speaker of the endo. "Please proceed to runway four and stand by for instructions."

"Roger that, Grace. En route to 4." Dane gently guided the squad toward the ground and pulled up behind three skimmers waiting in line.

"You have a HEP? What level, three?"

"Four," Dane responded.

"Do you all have them?"

"By you, I'm assuming you mean police officers. And yes, we all have them. It's standard issue once cadets graduate reconditioning and go into law enforcement."

They pulled one space forward, and Ade looked out the window at the withered face of an old woman in a bright red skimmer. He tried not to be jealous of Dane. Human Electronic Pairing was the primary focus of his father's work. Ade had known about it since childhood and always wanted it. Commonly referred to as HEP, an electronic pairing mod allows users to interact directly with enabled electronic devices. Most devices were network-enabled, so the user could communicate directly with any network device after creating a secure connection with the device's Knox pin. The technology had improved over the last decade, but slow connection speeds between the implanted transmitter and the device remained an issue.

"Did you hear that the new polymer they're working on would improve interfacing from seconds to milliseconds?"

Dane inched the endo forward. "Yeah, there is quite the fuss about that."

"They say-"

"Hey, I was wondering something," Dane interrupted.

Ade's body tensed as his thoughts went back to the note.

"The scar, why'd you never get it removed?" Dane asked.

Ade's shoulders slumped forward with an exhale, and his eyes fell to his lap.

"Oh, I didn't mean it like that," Dane said quickly. "I just meant that people can get SkinRegen on the open market. It probably would have only taken one sitting on Cranis."

Ade wasn't self-conscious about his scar. His father had cans of SkinRegen lying around his workshop. He could have easily sprayed the wound, which would have healed to new, fresh skin, but the scar was part of him. It had become a special bond between Ade and his father. At first, it was a lesson. His father insisted that Ade keep it to remind him that his actions have consequences. His mother agreed to leave it until Ade turned 18, but by the time his eighteenth birthday arrived, Ade no longer wanted it fixed.

"It reminds me of my dad," Ade sighed. "Mom wants me to get it fixed, too."

"Oh. I get it, but it makes you easily identifiable. If I were you, I'd wear a hat for a while. Myers may have dropped the charges, but he'll kill you if he sees you again."

"Whatever," Ade muttered.

At one point, scars were quite fashionable. Having a body full of scars meant you were important. Only having a few scars meant you lacked anything beyond the base survival augments provided by the government. This was a way people could tell high society from the working class. It didn't matter what you wore — more scars meant more money. Ordinary people couldn't afford advanced augments. The implant fee was more than a laborer's annual salary, let alone the cost of the part itself. This was why SkinRegen wasn't initially popular after its invention. Scientists created it to quickly heal skin after augmentation surgery, but people had become so accustomed to what the scars stood for that nobody wanted it. That was until William the Butcher began targeting people with scars. Over two years, the Butcher killed roughly fifty people and stripped them for parts. Scars quickly became unfashionable as fear spread amongst the elite. Suddenly, surgery scars became rare.

After what seemed like an hour, they finally pulled to the front of the line. "Roger that, Grace. Space H," Dane responded.

The squad floated around the access circle of runway four and landed on space H. Just as they landed, a door opened, and Ade saw his mother being escorted out of the building in a glidechair by a short, plump man in a white jumpsuit. His mother wore only a white hospital cloak with matching slippers. Slumped forward in the chair, her hands rested on a shrink-wrapped package in her lap.

Ade flung open the endo door and rushed toward her. Skidding to a halt before her, he dropped to his knees and embraced her. Only a soft groan escaped her. Then, pulling back, he placed his hands on her shoulders, leaned down, and looked at her. Her eyes were closed, and minimal color had returned to her face.

"She's heavily sedated," the portly man announced.

Ade reached up and placed his hands on her cheeks. Then he leaned in and pressed his forehead to hers. Her skin had a chemical smell and was far cooler than usual.

"I'll never let them do this to you again," Ade whispered.

"Ade," a voice called from behind him.

"What!?" Ade snapped, looking over his shoulder at Dane. He wore a grim look that made him appear older than before. Ade hadn't noticed, but the portly man had left the glidechair to talk to Dane.

"Ade, the orderly needs a word with you," Dane said, looking Ade directly in the eye.

Ade hadn't expected to see her like this. He thought she'd be fully recovered upon their arrival. Ann had always seemed invincible. Seeing her frailty scared him.

"We can't stay here. You'll need to sign her out."

"We need a consenting adult to sign for the charges," a whiny voice added. "Officer Dane stated you're of working age. It needs to be signed before we can let you two go."

Ade stood, leaned forward, and kissed his mother on the head. "Don't worry, Mom. I'll take care of this.

As he turned toward Dane and the orderly, he immediately got the impression that something was wrong. Dane's posture had changed. His stance was rigid, and frown lines spread across his forehead.

"What?" Ade asked.

"We just need your signature," the orderly said, tapping a pen against a clipboard.

"For what?" Ade asked.

There was silence as the orderly looked from Ade toward Officer Dane. Dane gave the orderly a sideways glance.

"Just tell him what you told me," Dane said.

"Well," the orderly began. "We repaired your mother's AIRE to the best of our ability, but we suggest you replace it as soon as possible. It's a very old unit. The replacement parts were not exactly matched, so we can't guarantee the unit's functionality."

Ade winced. He blinked as he processed information that seemed absurd.

"Why not replace it now?" Ade questioned.

The orderly looked again at Dane. “Well, her employer didn’t approve the replacement. They said she had unexcused absences to account for.”

The fear amplified Ade’s anger, and fingernails dug into his palms as his fists clenched. “But it’s a required augmentation,” Ade growled.

“Yes, the government approved the repair. But an upgrade would need to be approved by her employer.”

“But you just said it won’t work!”

The orderly took a step backward and moved slightly behind Dane. “I said we can’t guarantee it. It is currently working.”

Dane stepped in front of the orderly and centered himself on Ade. “Ade, you need to settle down. Just sign so we can go.” Dane spoke firmly. “You can put in a request with the sector governor for a new unit.”

“It’s not right,” Ade huffed.

The orderly remained standing behind Dane. Dane scowled and turned toward him. “Just give me the damn clipboard.”

The orderly handed him a clipboard and a pen without even a blink. “Page five,” he directed.

Ade paced as Dane stepped forward and handed him the clipboard. Snatching it from Dane’s hand, Ade immediately stopped as his eyes landed on a figure at the bottom of the first page.

“What the fug is this! 17,458 drachma?” Ade continued to look over the sheet. “3,687 for scalpel fee? What the hell is a scalpel fee?”

Ade looked at Dane, who looked back at the orderly.

“Oh, that’s the fee for the scalpel they used to cut her skin. It’s right there on line 3B.”

“I see that,” Ade spat. “I thought you said the government approved the repair.”

“Oh, they did. That’s on page two. They covered the parts and the surgeon’s fee. The rest are hospital fees. Unfortunately, the government chose not to do a full reimbursement because the damage was caused by negligence."

Blood rushed to Ade's face, and he reared back and threw the clipboard toward the orderly.

Dane immediately drew his dart gun and aimed it at Ade. "Ade, don't."

Ade's chest raised and lowered with each heavy breath as his death stare alternated between them. "Negligence!" He shouted.

Dane inched toward Ade — the weapon aimed at his chest. "Ade, you attack, and you're back in the cell. You don't sign, and I have to take her to the labor camps to work off the debt. She wouldn't survive the labor camps. You have no choice but to sign. Sign, and we can all go. We can figure it out later."

"Fug!" Ade screamed. His hands fell to his hips. Then he glanced at Dane, stomped to the clipboard, and picked it up. Flipping the pages, he scribbled on page five and threw it back on the ground. "There, let's go." He turned back to his mother and pushed the glide-chair toward the endo.

The orderly rapidly shuffled over to the clipboard, retrieved it, and hurried toward the door. Then he paused in the doorway, dug a bottle of pills from his pocket, and tossed them toward Dane. "Give her two every six hours."

Dane caught the bottle and shook his head. "You people have no soul," Dane muttered.

The orderly closed the door, and the sound of a deadbolt clicked into place.

CHAPTER 8 | 5856-W21

Wooosh, Wooosh, Wooosh, the support arches of the rail zipped by. There were no windows on the boom train, but Ade knew the sound. Ann slept beside him as he obsessively turned the scrap of paper Dane had given him over in his fingers. Ade shifted his weight to one side and stuffed the paper into his pocket. The main cabin of the train was almost empty. Only a few dignitaries traveled at this hour. Even fewer traveled toward the Labor District; however, the economy cabin was full. Officer Dane dropped them off at the train station. He took one look in the economy cabin and insisted accommodations be made for Ann and her guardian. As Dane was a member of the J1A Special Police, the boarding official was happy to comply.

From time to time, Ade would look up to see the more affluent passengers leering back at them while his mother snored. He guessed what they were thinking. *They want to know why we're in the wrong cabin and how long until somebody removes us.* Ade didn't care- the seats were comfortable, with plenty of legroom. He stretched in his chair and yawned. Ade wasn't sure how long he slept in the jail, but it felt like he hadn't stopped moving in days. Ade sighed and rubbed his weary eyes, which caused them to sting from the sweat and sand caked onto his skin. He blinked rapidly, trying to clear his eyes. The augmentation control quickly flashed on and off.

"Greetings, passengers," a soothing female voice said. A woman wearing a blue jumpsuit stood at the front of the cabin, holding a voice booster. "Next stop, Platform 1316 - Labor District in five minutes. Please prepare yourself for a speedy departure. Check under and around your seats for personal items. Anything left on the train will be incinerated upon departure from the gate. You will have fifteen minutes to depart the train and exit the platform before the economy cabin is released." Then she flashed a wide, fake smile, turned, and disappeared behind a blue curtain.

Ade gently shook his mother. She groaned and rolled into him. "Mom, time to get up. He shook her again, and Ann stared back at him through glazed eyes. "Mom, it's time to go."

The train slowed to a stop, and two doors opened. Heat and sun poured into the dimly lit cabin and caused him to wince. Ade hoisted Ann into his arms and cautiously walked down the aisle toward the door. Exiting the temperature-controlled cabin into the heat, what little strength he had left dwindled. He trudged out onto the platform and glanced at the kiosk.

"You've got to be kidding me," Ade murmured wearily, looking at the perfectly functioning kiosk.

"What, honey?" Ann moaned.

"Nothing, Mom. I'll tell you later."

The elevator doors opened to the desert floor. Stepping out into the blazing sun, Ade squinted at an old, battered skimmer that looked like a floating trash can. He took another step forward, and the door of the skimmer creaked and groaned as it opened. A large, burly man leaped from the driver's seat. He waved as if he knew them and began sprinting in their direction. Half asleep and in disbelief, Ade watched the husky man bound forward. He called out and waved again as he ran. Ade glanced over his shoulder and found nobody behind him. He was a peculiar-looking man. He wore brightly colored clothing that hung loose on his large, burly frame and complimented a head and face full of curly red hair. However, the most striking thing about the man was that he wasn't wearing goggles, and his eyes were pitch black. When he reached them, he bent at the waist, put his hands on his knees, and took a couple of heaving breaths. Upon his last deep breath, he shot up and put his hands on his hips. Ade took a quick step backward and needed to adjust to avoid dropping his mother. The man had a fair complexion and angular features that led to a long and bushy beard with braids and beads by his chin. The sides of his head were shaved, and part of his long, wavy hair was pulled back in a ponytail.

"Whoo!" The peculiar man exclaimed. "It's hotter than a dog's tail on fire."

Ade stood staring at the odd, overly large man before him.

"What?" the man asked, looking at Ade. Ade heard his question but was transfixed by his black eyes. "Oh," the man gasped as his eyebrows raised. He blinked twice and looked at Ade with hazel eyes. Then, he winced, squinted, blinked again, and his eyes reverted to black. "Sorry, mate, bright too," he said, pointing at his eyes. "Augments. Built-in eye protection n' sunglasses."

The giant stepped forward and reached out for Ann, but Ade took another step back and bumped into the elevator's closed doors.

"Skittish, eh?" The peculiar man observed. "Makes sense cause of the wringer." He withdrew a step and stroked his long beard. "I guess introductions are in order. Me name's Bill, but me friends call me Floyd. Andy sent me to help when ya got off da train." Then he eyed Ade up and down. "You been drinking enough water?"

Ade's chin pulled in toward his neck as a perplexed look adorned his face.

"Wa-water," Ade stammered. "Who's Andy?"

"Here, I got her, mate," Floyd stepped forward and easily lifted Ann from Ade's arms. Blood rushed back to Ade's hands and made his fingers tingle.

"Oh, yeah. Sorry, I mean Officer Dane. Wanna know what people call him?"

"Dane sent...you?" Ade asked.

Floyd's mustache wiggled as he looked at Ade. "Hmm," Floyd began. "On a different day, I'd think ya judging me appearance. But, ya must be tired from getting tazed and all." Floyd turned and began walking back to his skimmer.

Ade stood for a moment and considered that perhaps he'd fallen asleep on the train and was dreaming. Then he hurried after them.

In haste, Ade failed to notice the power cords running away from the station, and he tripped and stumbled forward.

"Careful there, lad," Floyd said without looking back. "Don't wanna carry two of ya to da skim."

Ade righted himself and stared at him. "Wait, hold on-"

"We all got questions, skipper. Now, be a good lad n' run ahead and open da door. I don't wanna bang Ann's head on Lucy."

Ade used the strength of his leg augments to burst forward and stand between Floyd and his skimmer.

"We're not going anywhere until you tell me who you are and where we're going!"

Floyd stopped and stood looking down his narrow nose at Ade. Ade saw the concerned, puzzled look on his face in the reflection of Floyd's black eyes and tried harder to look intimidating.

"I told ya, mate, Dane sent me to help. I'm here to drive ya home." Floyd looked at Ann and then back to Ade. "I don't think she's ready to trek the desert in this heat. Just me opinion, though."

Ade wanted to maintain his defiance — not to let this strange man dictate what happened to him and his mother, but the scorching sun and his tired body withered his determination. He knew Floyd was right. Plus, Ade didn't think himself capable of carrying her that distance. "Fine, but straight home."

"Yes, sir. No funny business," Floyd said with a wink.

Ade ran ahead of him and opened the passenger door. An old, stale smell wafted from the vehicle, and Ade stuck his head in and glanced around the makeshift skimmer.

"Excuse me, champ," Floyd said.

Ade ducked from the doorway, and Floyd gently sat Ann into the passenger seat. "Looks like you'll be needing to sit on my lap," Floyd said, closing the door. Ade shot him a startled look, and Floyd let out a loud belly laugh. "I'm kidding, kiddo. You get da back seat. You'll be needin' to get in on my side."

Ade already disliked this man.

Floyd circled the car and opened the driver's door. "They call him Andrew. That's his name."

Ade didn't follow. "Who?"

Floyd grinned and pushed the driver's seat forward so Ade could climb back. "Officer Dane. They call him Andrew. I call him Andy." Floyd grinned.

He's so weird. It's like a clown and a pirate had a baby, Ade thought. Ade gave a fake half-smile and crawled into the back. As the weight of the massive man plopped into the front seat, momentum pushed the seat back. Ade let out a yelp as it jammed into his knees.

"Sorry 'bout that, fella. It's a bit cramped for someone your height," Floyd said, flipping switches in a flurry. "Ya ready?"

"I'm-"

The skimmer burst forward, and momentum pushed Ade back into the seat. Then Floyd quickly banked right, and Ade slid across the bench seat. "Belts are required in this skimmer. I busted a few teeth that way."

They quickly banked again, and Ade's knuckles turned white as he gripped the unlatched harness. "Housing unit 582?" Floyd asked over his shoulder.

The harness finally snapped, and Ade glared at him in the rear-view mirror. "Did you steal this heap?"

"Lucy?" Floyd asked. With a confused expression, he turned to look at Ade. "No, I built her. Why?"

"You drive like you're being chased."

Floyd glanced at the open sky before him and then returned to Ade. "Why would someone be chasing us? What'd ya do?"

"It's just an expression. Never mind."

"There's water in the cooler beside ya. Don't worry about me. I have some here," Floyd said, patting a canteen in the middle console. "582?"

"What?" Ade asked.

Floyd peered over his shoulder and furrowed his brow. "Huh,"

Floyd grunted. "Andy said ya were sharp. You must be tired. What's yer housing unit? 582?"

Ade thought for a moment, but no number was coming to mind. "I don't know," Ade muttered under his breath.

"Okay, 582 it is," Floyd repeated.

Ade studied the interior of the skimmer. It looked like Floyd built it from a junk heap and repaired it with mismatched spare parts. Vent tubes hung loosely from the ceiling, and the upholstery was stained and cracked. However, what surprised Ade was the windows' thickness and the engine's smooth purr as it quickly darted through the sky.

"So, like I said, me name's Floyd. Andrew, er, Officer Dane, to the unacquainted, he called me and told me ya had an altercation with good ol' Adam Myers. Man, I'd have loved to see that. Shined him good, I heard," Floyd said, peering out the side window. "Oh, we're here."

The skimmer slowed and descended toward the roof of unit 582. One of the many hanging tubes in the skimmer banged Ade in the face. He just shook his head. *Everything is against me today, even air tubes,* Ade thought.

Ann's eyes opened slightly as the skimmer landed. "Where are we?" she mumbled.

"I reckon yer home," Floyd said. "Well, given I was told da correct address. Yer son was none too helpful," he pointed a thumb over his shoulder at Ade.

Ann sat up and peered out the scratched windows through groggy, squinted eyes. "582?" she asked.

"Well, I'll be!" Floyd exclaimed. "Looks like I've successfully got us home."

"Us?" Ade piped from the back seat.

"Best make sure all yer goggles and such are in place. Winds picked up," Floyd said, leaning across and placing a pair of goggles over Ann's eyes. Ade sat watching him.

Floyd glanced back at Ade. "Any time now, son."

"I'm not your son," Ade grumbled, lifting the goggles over his eyes.

"Aaade stop arrrrguing," Ann slurred.

Floyd took one more look at his passengers and grinned. Then he kicked open the door. The wind rushed in, sending tubes and empty food containers flying through the vehicle. Ade tried to dodge a flying vent, but his harness yanked his body back. A thick, tattooed arm thrust back toward him and caught the tube before it smacked Ade in the face.

"There ya be," Floyd said. An elaborate crest tattooed on Floyd's forearm caught Ade's attention.

"What's that?" Ade asked with a nod to Floyd's arm.

Floyd paused and looked down at what prompted Ade's question. "Oh, that little dandy. That's for another time, friend. Now, remember to hit the lever and slide the seat forward. I'll grab yer mum."

Ade watched as the wind twisted and swirled Floyd's curly red beard. He looked like a wild man, running around the car and opening the passenger door. Ann put her arm around his neck as he lifted her into his arms, and she nuzzled her face into his beard. Ade was baffled by her behavior. Of course, she was drugged, but even in her state, she seemed overly comfortable with this strange man.

Floyd leaned down and looked at Ade through the door. "Come along. Remember, levers at da bottom there, chum."

Ade felt around the crusty fabric until his hand met a metal lever. Then, pushing the seat forward, Ade grabbed his mother's shrink-wrapped clothing and exited the vehicle into the night sun.

"Hey, Ade," Floyd said.

His gaze slowly drifted to Floyd's loose, colorful garments flapping in the wind. "Close the doors, hey. Yer mum's light, but she's not made of feathers," he said, nodding toward the roof access door.

Ade quickly moved around the skimmer, shutting the doors, and hurried to Floyd as he stood waiting by the door.

The housing unit hadn't felt like home until that night. Ade breathed the familiar smells and felt a sense of ease. Floyd followed him in, and Ade closed the door behind them. Floyd crossed the common area without instruction and carried Ann into her room. Puzzled, Ade followed behind him.

"How'd you know this was her room?" he asked as Floyd carefully laid her on the cot.

"This room smells like a girl. Da other smells like dirty laundry," Floyd said, stroking his beard and looking around the room. "Now, I'll leave ya to da undressing. She's a pretty lass, but I'm not one for looking before being invited."

Ade suddenly felt nauseous. "I'm not doing it! And don't talk about my mom like that!"

Floyd shrugged, "Well, at least take off her dirty gown n' tuck her in, yeah?"

Ade looked from Floyd to his mother and then back.

"What, unders is like a swimsuit," Floyd said.

"I think she's fine. Just cover her."

"It's only yer mum," Floyd said, moving around Ade. "I'll do it."

"No," Ade exclaimed. He quickly stepped between Floyd and his mother.

"I'll do it. You can leave now," Ade ordered.

Floyd shrugged and turned his back to them.

"I said leave the room."

Floyd raised his hands and backed out of the room. "Okay, champ. Don't need to be barky."

The door closed, and Ade stood looking at his mother. *There is no way*. He plucked the slippers from her feet and quickly covered her with the cotsheet. He quietly exited the room and gently closed the door until he heard it click. Then he turned to find Floyd sitting at the kitchen table. *Fug, he's still here*.

"Nicely done, sir," Floyd said. He yawned and stretched his

arms wide, revealing more tattoos along his forearms. “My, my, sleep does sound pleasant. I’ll grab me cot from Lucy. You should get some rest, too.”

“Who said you could stay here?” Ade questioned.

Floyd paused. It was obvious he was considering his response. “Caution is an admirable trait. I’ll sleep in Lucy. Then, you and yer mum can talk about it.” He glanced at the smiley face drawn in the dust. “Might be good to have a little help ‘round here.”

“We don’t need your help,” Ade said sharply.

“That guy says different,” Floyd grinned, pointing at the drawing.

Then he lumbered toward the door. “I’ll check back in da morning. Oh, and Ade,” Floyd said, looking back at him.

“What?” Ade snapped.

“Ya might wanna take a shower before sleeping. You smell like the men’s tinkle room.”

CHAPTER 9 | 5856-W21

"Nobody here will miss you!" Ade screamed. His father stood on the edge of a cliff with his back to Ade. Flames from below illuminated his silhouette, and his long hair danced in the wind. "Go!" His father's body tensed, and his shoulders raised and lowered with an exasperated sigh. Slowly turning toward Ade, he stepped forward into the light, and instead of his father, Floyd stood there laughing at him.

Ade awoke to the sound of a booming, roaring laugh. He rolled face down and buried his head in his pillow before releasing a muffled scream. The laughter came again. It was a low, deep belly laugh that echoed off the walls. Ade twirled, yanked the pillow from the bed, and threw it across the room. Before springing from the bed, he blinked and set his AIRE to active mode.

"He's back," Ade scowled.

Marching into the main room to make his displeasure known, Ade stopped dead in his tracks at the sight of them. His mother and Floyd sat together, giggling like schoolchildren. Ann's hand rested on Floyd's shoulder while the other covered her mouth as she laughed. Sitting there laughing, she looked a decade younger than she had only a few hours before. Perhaps it was her smile or the twinkle that had returned to her eye. Ann looked up, and their eyes met. The joy Ade saw flushed the anger from him, and elation took over.

"Oh, he's awake," Ann gasped, and she punched Floyd in the shoulder. "I told you not to wake him!"

Ade rushed across the room and embraced his mother. He felt tears coming as Ann wrapped her arms around him. "You look so much better," Ade grinned.

"You were very brave, honey. William told me all about it," Ann said.

Ade pulled away and wiped his eyes on his sleeve before looking at Floyd. "William? I thought your name was Floyd?"

"Nah, big man, I said me friends call me Floyd. Your mum has always called me by me given name, William. Keeps me on me toes."

"Oh honey, William was your dad's best friend before we moved to Cranis. He's your godfather, you know, the one who sends you gifts on your birthday."

"You mean he's the one who sent me those weird bracelets?"

Her eyes brightened, and she slapped Floyd on the leg. "See! I told you they were weird! You owe me a chocolate bar." She nudged Floyd, "Remember what I like?"

Floyd laughed. "How could I forget? Jack always dragged me with when he bought ya those."

Ann and Floyd's smiles faded a bit at the mention of Jack. Then Ann squeezed Floyd's leg, looked at his face, and smiled. "I expect payment by the end of the day."

"Consider it done," Floyd nodded. Then he turned to Ade. "Ya thought they was weird?"

"Yeah, I never understood why you'd send a boy bracelets. I always figured you thought I was a girl."

Floyd roared with laughter. "Lad doesn't know!" Floyd exclaimed, raising his arm and shaking a wrist full of beaded bracelets.

"These are part of our history, mate. Hopefully, I made up fer it with those leg augments you've been complaining about."

It didn't make much sense to Ade. He had always envisioned Bill as some well-polished jewelry maker with an affinity for exotic metal beads. When he received the leg augmentations, he assumed Bill was a very lucrative jewelry maker. Now, seeing the man before him, he believed his leg augments were stolen.

"Why'd you never come to visit us on Cranis?" Ade asked.

"Long story," Floyd said, with a glance toward Ann. "I'd have liked to."

Ade wrinkled his nose at Floyd's answer. Ann had always spoken of Uncle Bill. Ade had always assumed it was her brother because Jack never mentioned him. Then he thought of the note Dane handed to him.

"So you know Officer Da... Andy?" Ade asked.

"I do. He's me cub," Floyd answered.

"Your what?"

"Me cub. Me son," Floyd said.

Suddenly, the note in the jail made sense, and disappointment overcame him. He thought it was something only he and his father shared. Now Ade knew Jack told this ogre, who told his son.

"Oh. Makes sense," Ade said, oozing disappointment. Then he trudged past them toward the kitchen. "Mom, did you make coffee?"

"Nah, sport, I made you a protein shake," Floyd said.

Ade's shoulders slumped forward, and he looked at Floyd as he pointed toward the refrigerator. "It's in da old icebox there. It's caffeine and breakfast all in one. Brain's not da only muscle needing feeding." Floyd directed his attention back to Ann. "You remember that time by da Oasis? When I dared ya to tip over that one gal sunning herself on the floatie?"

"Oh, that poor girl," Ann giggled. "I had no idea her tan was powder."

"I did," Floyd gibed.

Ade opened the fridge to find a glass of pink sludge. Removing it from the refrigerator as though it would infect him, Ade shook his head in disgust and presented the drink to Ann. "You want me to drink this?"

"I promise, it tastes better than it looks," Ann encouraged. "We both had one."

"It looks like barf!" Ade exclaimed, with a disgusted look on his face.

"It tastes better than barf," Ann reaffirmed.

He took a quick sniff. The aroma was surprisingly pleasant - a mix of nuts, milk, berries, and coffee.

Ade glared at Floyd. "Did you use my coffee in this?"

Floyd looked like a scolded child and quickly looked to Ann for backup.

"Our coffee," Ann corrected. "It's fine. Floyd offered to replace it later today. He will also be staying with us for a while, which will be good. He can visit the market for us and help you study for your placement test. Maybe he can also tell you some stories of us when we were your age."

"I can go to the market, Mom. And I don't need help with the test." Ade eyed Floyd skeptically. *I mean, look at him. He has beads in his beard.* Ade took a drink of the milky concoction. She was right. It didn't taste as bad as it looked.

"He got a 520 on the placement test," Ann said quickly.

The involuntary surprise reaction caused pink goo to spray from Ade's mouth. "Say what!" Ade exclaimed as he wiped his mouth on his sleeve.

"Don't act so surprised, mate," Floyd scoffed, glancing at Ann. "The boy thinks me a dullard."

Ade grabbed a towel from the counter and knelt to clean the floor. *520,* he thought. *That's almost as good as Dad. He could have been an augment tech, a physician...an engineer, even.*

The government placement test was the standardized test given to students upon finishing the general education academy. It tested not only what was learned in school but also creativity and engineering concepts. A 600 was perfect, but no human without an augmentation had ever scored a 600. The average score is around 390. Most people with a 390 get placed in the services sector- shop workers, transport haulers, etc. People who test below 300 are typically assigned military duty, and those below 200 fall into the labor class. On the other hand, a 400 quickly lands you a cushy job in the Government District – usually clerical or education. Four hundred fifty and above gets you a skilled profession...over 500, and you have your pick.

"What did you choose?" Ade enquired.

Floyd shied from the question, but Ann gave him a gentle nudge, "It's okay. Just tell him what you chose. He's not asking why."

Floyd's face contorted, and he looked down at the table. "Ground Operations Attack Tactician Officer," he blurted.

Ade's ears perked, and his eyes widened. He had never met anyone in the war. "You were a GOAT in the war?"

The husky man's posture changed. He leaned forward on the table and clasped his hands. "Yeah, I was in it," he said plainly.

"He was trying to keep his home-" Ann began.

"Did you kill anyone?" Ade interrupted.

"Ade Billings! Have I not taught you any respect?" Ann scolded.

Floyd's eyes squared on Ade. He said nothing, and he didn't have to. Ade saw something similar in The Beast's eyes in the market. The only difference was that there was regret. Ade nervously looked away.

"Apologize, young man," Ann insisted.

"I apologize. I guess it was a dumb question," Ade said quickly.

There was an awkward silence that hung over the room. "It's alright, mate," Floyd said. "I picked it."

Ade looked at Floyd and noticed him staring at the crest tattooed on his forearm. "Jack was always the smart one," Floyd continued.

Ade hesitated for a moment but spoke anyway. "Is that what the tattoo means? Was that your unit?" Ade asked.

"Yeah," Floyd sighed. "The crest was my first unit. Everything else is for me guys. The ones I lost."

Ade marveled at the arm full of tattoos as he watched Floyd's hands fumble with the beads on his wrist. It seemed like he was focusing on each bead as he counted in his head, and, with a breath, he looked up from the beads to Ann and smiled. "Well, best be getting to da market. Seems I got coffee and chocolate to buy. Need anything else?"

The quick shift in Floyd's mood made Ade uncomfortable, and he suddenly realized he felt sorry for Floyd.

Ann's scolding eyes landed on Ade. He had seen this look many times before. It was both a look of disappointment and urgency, and it didn't take a 400-level test score to figure out what she wanted him to do.

"Want help?" Ade forced out.

"I'd rather-"

"It would be good for both of you," Ann interrupted. "Plus, I don't want you to go alone to that place again."

Floyd sighed and gave Ann a disapproving look. Ann countered with a stern look of her own.

"Well," Floyd began, shaking his head and looking at Ade. "The lady of da house has spoken. Grab yer gear."

Instead of walking, Ade saw the housing sector from the air. There was a stillness to the Labor District as the workers slept during the day for their shifts at night. It was amazing how much more he could see from the front seat of Floyd's skimmer: the billowing dust from the transport trucks hurdling their resources toward refinement and the Market District just beyond the highway — commerce signs catching the sun and a flutter of colored canopies in the wind.

"I'm worried about your mum. She's been through a lot."

Floyd's statement hung in the air like a foul smell. Ade closed his eyes and took a deep breath through his nose. Reopening his eyes, they landed on the sky arch in the distance. "What makes you say that?" Ade asked.

The skimmer crossed the dividing highway and pulled to a landing pad off the market. They sat in silence as the engines died. Ade could almost hear the grinding of Floyd's thoughts. Floyd grimaced and looked at his lap.

"I...." Floyd began and trailed off.

"Do you think the AIRE isn't working?" Ade asked nervously.

Floyd focused on the space directly beyond his nose and nodded slightly. "It's not that."

"What then?" Ade asked, becoming annoyed. "She was laughing and joking. She looked normal. Happy, even."

"No, yer right. Just mixing grapes n' tomatoes. You'd know better than me."

What the hell does that mean? Ade could tell Floyd wasn't convinced, but Ade simply couldn't fathom more bad news at this point. He turned his attention back to the market out the window. It didn't look as splendid as the first time he saw it.

"Thinking about getting something for Annie, er, yer mum?"

Ade shook his head and glanced at Floyd. "No, Mom would be mad if I spent money on things we didn't need."

A glower spread across Floyd's weathered face, and he reached over and placed a large, rough hand on Ade's shoulder. Ade watched as his mouth moved slightly as if trying to find words. Then he looked him in the eye and gave a half smile. "You know, you look just like him when we was yer age. Full of piss and rage." Floyd laughed. "Yer old man had that expression when I told him I was enlisting." Floyd released Ade's shoulder and sat back in his seat. "Yer right, Ade. It's probably nothing."

Ade nodded. "Yeah," he said. And, to change the subject, he pulled his goggles down over his eyes. "Let's just get our stuff and get back. I don't want to be here longer than we need to."

CHAPTER 10 | 5856-W22

The minute hand floated over the black clock face. Unobstructed, it continued to circle without care or consequence. One could destroy the device, but what it represented would remain. *If all existence suddenly expired, would time still exist,* Ade pondered as he watched the hands tick past 8 PM. Beyond the gentle tick of the clock, the housing unit was devoid of sound. With each passing day, his mother seemed to be going to bed earlier than the day before. Floyd's remark in the market put him on edge, and paranoia had Ade watching Ann's every move. Besides her early bedtime, she had shown no indication of an ailment. The apartment was spotless, no thanks to either Floyd or himself. Floyd attempted to clean, but Ann often recleaned as soon as he left the unit. What was concerning, though, was her behavior. She was sleeping more and had not returned to work. Ade returned to the list of charges he had received via courier the day before. The total sum made him sick to his stomach. *Even if I did exceptionally well on the placement test, it would take me a year to pay this off.*

The sound of the door startled Ade, and he scowled at Floyd as he lumbered into the unit.

"Mom's trying to sleep," Ade whispered.

Holding two bags in each hand, Floyd grunted and trudged across the gray floor, leaving brown tracks behind him. His colorful clothing was covered in black grime. He set the bags on the kitchen counter and pulled down his dust mask, which revealed a stark contrast between the filthy top half of his head and the clean lower half where the mask had resided.

"Got milk," he said, and he turned, plopped down on his cot, and began removing his boots. "Any leftovers?"

"Nope," Ade answered. "Mom went to bed early. I just had a

ration."

Floyd's face contorted into a look of disgust. "Foul bagged food. Ya know that stuff is good fer thirty years. Plus, it makes you constipated." He kicked off his boots and rubbed his eyes, causing the grime to smear across his face.

Ade was too overwhelmed to laugh and looked from Floyd to his mother's closed door. "She's been sleeping a lot lately. Do you think we should take her back to the hospital? To have them check? Maybe they won't charge as much because they messed up," Ade pondered aloud.

Floyd let out a chuckle and shook his head. "Those people are worse than the thieves stealing augments and selling 'em back to the hospital. Wouldn't surprise me if da hospital bought stolen parts and sold 'em fer a regular price.

Ade's heart sank as he thought of his brother. "Those people aren't all bad. Some do it to survive."

Floyd paused and looked at the floor. "Sorry mate, I didn't mean yer brother."

Ade gave Floyd a sideways glance. He had stopped wondering how he knew everything. It would have been more surprising if he hadn't known about Ethan.

"Besides, Ann's fine. Said so yourself," Floyd affirmed.

Ade sat back in his chair and straightened the stack of papers. "Yeah, I guess. Just worried."

"Let me assure ya, I'm working on some stuff for you and yer mum. If her AIRE starts acting froggy, I know a guy with a jailbroken scanner. We'll get her scanned and put some real fine tech in. No more government parts or hospitals." Then, a great yawn escaped Floyd, and he stretched his arms wide and groaned. "Age comes for us all," he said, standing. "Now, if ya don't mind, I'm gonna shower and hit the rack."

Floyd's words stirred memories, and an epiphany stuck as Ade set the papers on the table. He looked toward his and Ethan's bedroom. *A scanner...*

Jack began his career as an augment technician but was transferred to the Department of Development and Research within the first year. At the age of twenty-five, he was already a project manager. At thirty, he was the youngest division head in history. Jack once told him that a successful man is made from work and dedication. Ade remembered his father's workshop vividly. He would sneak out before bedtime and watch his father work until his mother screamed from the back door. His father preferred working at night. Like a mad scientist, he sat in the center of his dimly lit workshop, tinkering with augmentation parts. There were only two light sources in the shop. A bright LVM light hung above him, spotlighting the man at center stage and an old wood stove that crackled and popped through the night. Ade loved those quiet moments with his father. Just the two of them in their own world. Ade missed that shed more than words could ever describe. It was as if his father's memory lived within those tools. It was heartbreaking when the government cleared out the garage. Jack hadn't even been gone for twenty-four hours when a caravan of suits and soldiers arrived and confiscated Jack's equipment in the interest of national security. They took everything except the light and the wood stove...well, almost everything. An hour after the officer passed along the grievous news, Ade peered out his bedroom window at his father's workshop. It was odd to see the workshop dark at night. Neither he nor Ethan was allowed in the shop without Jack's approval. And yet, there was Ethan. Skulking in the shadows outside the shop, Ethan cautiously approached the door and clumsily dropped the key as he attempted to unlock it. Ten minutes later, he emerged with several boxes on a cart and disappeared back into the shadows. Ade was stunned by the actions of his brother. Less than an hour had passed since they learned of Jack's death. He tried to think the best of his brother, but Ethan wasted no time picking the bones.

After the last government official departed, Ade confronted Ethan over the items removed from the shop. Ethan hung his head and told him they found the stuff in the house. It wasn't until Ethan was arrested that he realized this was a lie. Once again, he thought all the items were confiscated, but then he walked in on Ann as she packed Ethan's things. Ade played dumb, but Ade recognized Jack's scanner when he saw it.

Ade rushed into the bedroom, but his momentum stalled upon seeing the boxes. He stood for a moment, staring at them. *She's probably fine,* he tried to reason. *They know what they're doing.* He turned back toward the door and paused. *But what if she's not? It would be good to know.* He walked to the door and quietly pulled it shut. "If you have the technology to save just one life and don't use it, it's an injustice," Jack once said. *Plus, it's for Mom...Ethan would want me to look.*

He peeled back the tape box by box and sifted through the content. The smell of the clothing brought forth memories, and he was reminded of the time after his surgery. Ethan never left his side; his brother's face was the first he saw when his eyes opened. Ade's fingers landed on something solid packed amongst the clothes. He gripped a short cylindrical object. Pulling it from the box, he unwrapped it and peered at the shiny metallic surface. Ade wasn't sure, but he thought it looked like a forearm augment. He reached back into the box and found several other items stuffed toward the bottom.

Ade hurriedly carried the box to Ethan's cot and dumped the contents. The items tumbled onto the cot, and he swiftly tossed clothing back into the box as he set tools and parts to the side. Ade gasped as he picked up an old T-shirt and instantly recognized the shape beneath. The unit was about a foot wide and nine inches tall. Each end had two rubber-coated handles separated by an LVM screen. Three lenses extend slightly beyond the case in the center of the thin metal casing. He turned the scanner over in his hands. Even though he had seen his father use it, the unit's operation was a mystery. *Okay, so I hold it by the handles and point the lenses at what I'm scanning... but where is the power button?* He ran his finger around the edge of the scanner until he felt a small circular button toward the top right. Ade pressed it. Nothing happened. He hurried to the window and pulled back the blinds. Sunshine poured into the room. Ade waited for a minute and pressed the button again. The screen went from black to a bright blue with a spinning white circle in the middle. Below the process flashed the word *CONNECTING...*

Ade waited impatiently as he watched the circle spin. *Cicero Communications Network* flashed on the screen. Then Ade's eyes grew wide. *Welcome, Jack Billings.* An ellipsis scrolled the bottom, and a green light from the front sensor illuminated his face. A circle returned. *FACIAL RECOGNITION FAILURE. Third attempt failed. System locked. Please contact your administrator.* His heart fell into his stomach, and he grimaced. "Oh, come on," Ade groaned. "That was only one." He held the power button down until it cycled off and on. *System locked. Please contact your administrator.* He sat for a moment staring at the screen, and, without thinking, he angrily whipped the scanner across the room. It skidded across the floor and banged hard against the wall. Ade slumped to the floor. The door to his room flung open, and Floyd stood there filling the doorway, his broad frame squeezed into Ann's pink bathrobe. His fiery eyes scanned the room as his long, wet beard dripped water onto the floor.

"What da hell's going on in here," Floyd exclaimed in a half-whisper.

Ade's eyes quickly darted to the scanner and found it face down under his nightstand.

"I was just unpacking," Ade stammered.

"Bricks?"

"Bricks?" Ade was only half paying attention as he attempted to mask his frustration. Floyd placed his hands on his hips and presented a stern facade, which may have been successful if not for the robe. Then Ade remembered the parts on the cot.

"Are you unpacking bricks?" Floyd repeated.

Ade quickly pushed himself to his feet and stepped to the side to obstruct Floyd's view of the items on the cot. His brother had gone to great lengths to retrieve and hide these items. By no means was Ade going to share his findings with a man he barely knew, especially one squeezed into a woman's bathrobe.

"Why are you wearing my mom's robe?"

Somewhat out of sorts, Floyd quickly pushed down the front of the robe and double-checked to ensure he was covered. "I didn't wanna put my dirties back on."

Ade shook his head. "It's just wrong, Floyd."

Floyd knew when to fold on a losing hand. "Just keep it down. Yer mum's trying to sleep."

"I was just about to go to sleep."

Floyd raised one eyebrow and stared at him.

"I was," Ade repeated.

"Yeah, 'cause we all like doin' a little unpacking right before bed."

Ade's eyes narrowed. He was still perturbed that Floyd was staying with them, and his accusations were unwelcome. "You're not my father, Floyd."

"I'm yer godfather," Floyd countered.

"Who was never around," Ade snapped.

Floyd raised a finger and pointed at Ade but quickly retracted it into a fist and dropped it to his side. Then he nodded, turned, and left the room.

Ade watched the door close and turned back toward the items on the cot. Then he glanced at the scanner under the nightstand. Scampering across the cluttered floor toward it, he carefully slid it from beneath the stand and inspected it for damage. The external case had a slight dent, and the screen remained functional.

That was stupid, Ade thought. *I could try wiping the system cache and reinstalling the software. Perhaps a bios hack. There must be a video on it somewhere. How else would criminals be able to steal them and resell them?*

He paced the room for a moment, moved back to the door, and locked it. He walked a bit longer, sat on the cot, and turned the scanner over in his hands. Ade had very few of his father's things. Opening the drawer to the nightstand, he gently placed the scanner inside and closed the drawer. Laying on the cot, he stared at the ceiling for a moment. *I should just ask her.* Without warning, Ade yawned. *I'll ask her in the morning.* Pulling a cover over himself, he blinked three times, paused, blinked again, and closed his eyes.

***

Ade's eyes shot open to something tipping over in the main room. He heard Floyd mumble a few words before his voice elevated. "Roger that, inform Delta 1 to meet us at extraction point tango." Footsteps ran to his door, and the door made a thud as Floyd tried to open it. With a loud crack, the door flung open. Splinters from the door frame flew into the room, and Floyd burst in. "J1A is comin'. You got two minutes!" Floyd shouted.

Dumbfounded, Ade watched as the man, still wearing a woman's bathrobe, ran to the window and pushed it open. The airlock broke with a pop and then a whoosh of air; he squinted toward the window and saw Floyd throw a backpack out.

"Ade, move," Floyd insisted.

The use of his name created a sense of urgency. Floyd typically called him mate, sport, or some other nickname that fit the situation. Ade quickly adjusted his AIRE and jumped up. "I'll get Mom," he said, darting out of the room.

A loud crack sent the exterior door flying inward as he passed his doorframe. Events suddenly happened in slow motion as his adrenaline surged. Ade flailed as he attempted to stop his forward momentum and retreat toward his room. The open window and door created a tunnel of wind and sand. Four men in all black swept into the unit while loose papers danced in the wind. The swift reversal caused Ade's bare feet to slip beneath him on the slick floor.

"One!" Ade heard a man yell. He struggled to return to his feet, but strong hands shoved him back to the floor.

"Two!"

He heard his mother shriek from within her room. Ade tried to struggle, but the man holding him kneeled hard on his back and neck. His mouth opened to cry out, but his words escaped in a whisper due to the pressure. "Don't hurt her...."

"Open window!"

Then, the howling of the wind stopped. The papers fluttered to the floor under Ade's blurring gaze. His sight started to darken, and his breath became shallow. He felt his arms pulled behind his back as the ties cinched his hands together. The pressure suddenly released, and he gasped for air. Before he could even think, two sets of hands lifted him to his knees. He tried to focus on the soldier walking past him into his bedroom.

"Thirteen feet," the black-clad man yelled. He swung a small handheld device before him. "5...3..." Ade's eyes nervously looked from the back of the man's uniform to a book lying on the floor. Then, the man in black bent over and opened the nightstand drawer. "Bingo," he said, lifting the scanner from the drawer.

CHAPTER 11 | 5856-W22

Life existed in a vacuum devoid of time or sensation. Yanked from the floor by his arms, white noise buds were stuffed in his ears, and a blackout hood was placed over his head. The sun's heat scorched Ade's skin for only a few seconds before being pushed onto a cool metal floor. Ade rolled and impacted a wall as the transport lifted off.

"Where are we going?" Ade asked. His words made no noise, nor was any response heard.

He screamed with all the air in his lungs. Still, no sound was made.

Ade kicked his feet and pushed until his back was against the wall. Then he sat. Only the sensations of his body gave him an indication that time had passed. He shifted back and forth, slumped, straightened his back, and twisted his wrists against the rigid ties. In his mind, days passed as he sat there. Visions of the past and potential future flickered in passing thoughts. Then he gave into the silence. He took a deep breath and wondered if he was dead.

An opposing force caused his body to rock forward, and his thoughts returned to the sensations of his body. He focused on the feeling in his feet and tried to figure out if they were still moving. Then, two hands grabbed his arms. Ade lurched as the hands pulled him from the floor. They dragged him forward, and his feet bounced off a smooth surface. Ade could not feel the sun. There was a slight breeze, but it was neither hot nor cold. Ade found his footing just as they stopped moving and stood still. The breeze was gone. Suddenly, the weight of his body pushed downward as they rose into the sky. Ade knew they were in an elevator, but he had no idea where — they could have been on Cranis for all Ade knew. Ade tapped his foot and counted. *Twenty-three*, he thought. Then, the upward movement stopped.

Walking forward, Ade counted to thirty. They stopped. His arms were released, and he was shoved down into a chair. The ties were cut free. Blood rushed to his fingertips as two hands latched onto his wrists and yanked them forward. Cold metal locked around his wrists. The hood lifted, and Ade winced and squinted at the bright room. Then, the buds were removed from his ears, and he heard very little other than the soldiers shuffling about quietly.

"Wait here," A gruff voice said.

Ade regained focus just as two men in green army fatigues exited through a mirrored door. "What about my mother?" Ade yelled after them. When no response was returned, he frantically looked through the room for any sign of his whereabouts. Like the door, the walls of the large room were mirrored, creating a disorienting effect that seemed to centralize the subject of the room. Ade peered in each direction as his reflection sat in the middle of the room, shackled to a silver, brushed metal table. Uneasily, he shifted back and forth in the chair and stared at his reflection. The boy looking back at him was not the one he remembered. There were no mirrors in the housing unit. His face was thinner than it had been – more defined. He readjusted in the uncomfortable chair.

"I didn't do anything!" Ade yelled. He sat and awaited a response, but none came. He looked again at his reflection. The scar above his eye was more noticeable in the fluorescent light of the room.

"Wait here," Ade grumbled, lifting his wrists chained to the table.

Suddenly, one of the mirrored panels flew open, and a round man in a tweed suit hurried into the room. "I'm so sorry," the man gasped as he waddled across the room toward him. He had a fair complexion, rosy cheeks, and a white mustache with curled tips. He carried a clipboard and halopad under his arm. The man gasped and shook his head as he looked over his shoulder. A boyish-looking man in a blue jumpsuit followed the mustached man into the room.

"Captain Young is behind me," the boy said.

“Thank you, Clark. Go and contact my next appointment. Tell them I’m running behind.”

Clark nodded. “Yes, sir.”

“Oh, and if you see Young, tell him to hurry. This is deplorable,” the tweed-suited man said. He grimaced and looked at Ade’s hands.

“I’m so sorry about this,” he repeated. “You must be hungry and exhausted. Oh, and these!” He reached down and shook the shackles as if appalled by them. “Captain Young!”

A thin soldier wearing holographic fatigues entered with a glidechair and quickly removed the restraints from Ade’s wrists. Ade slowly lifted his freed hands and turned a bewildered look toward the round man.

“There has been a grave mistake. We’ve prepared one of our best suites for you. You’ll be taken there promptly,” said the round man as Captain Young stood silently by the glidechair.

“Where’s my mother?” Ade insisted.

“Oh, your mother. Hmmm...let me see,” the round man answered. He peered down his round nose at the clipboard. His eyes darted back and forth over the paperwork. “Oh, here it is, Ann Billings. She was moved to the Royal Suites in the market while your home was cleaned and sanitized. Oh, it looks to be at our expense as well. Well, our ambassador is generous. But it’s the least we could do after this misunderstanding. I assure you, Mr. Billings. We’ve prepared a luxury suite for you as well. Anything you order from room service is on us.” He looked back up from the board smiling, and from some ingrained reaction, Ade smiled back.

This caused the round man’s smile to widen, and he patted Ade on the arm. “Excellent. Captain Young will escort you to your room.” He pulled a folded menu from under the papers on his clipboard and handed it to Ade.

“Here is our room service menu.”

Ade skeptically accepted the menu and looked back around the room. "I don't understand."

"You can choose whatever you'd like; it will all be covered. Everything is quite delightful. Freshly delivered from Cranis." He pointed at an area on the menu. "I particularly enjoy the captive-raised hen and gravy." He stepped to the side and motioned for Captain Young to bring over the glidechair. Young swiftly obeyed the order, and Ade was left looking between the two men and the chair.

"Please," the round man motioned to the chair. "Captain Young will take you to your room."

"I mean, you're letting me go?"

"Of course!" the round man exclaimed. "The arresting officers simply didn't know who you were! They thought you were a common criminal, not the son of Jack Billings. We were all quite shocked when his scanner came back online. We figured some hooligan had stolen it, not that it was in his family's possession."

"I didn't use it. I didn't know what it was," Ade lied through his teeth.

The man smirked. "It's of no consequence even if you did. Now, please get some rest. One can only imagine the hell you've gone through on this wretched planet."

His words resonated with Ade — *this wretched planet* — and he slowly moved to the glidechair and sat. "Where are we?" Ade asked.

"Oh, how silly of me. In my haste, I failed to introduce myself. I am Abraham Caldwell, Special Advisor and Vice Ambassador to Ambassador Monroe. Monroe apologizes for not being here to greet you. He is on his way back from Cranis as we speak. He will come to visit you as soon as you've rested.

The captain began pushing the chair before Ade could form a sentence.

"Oh, and Ade," Abraham called after him. "Welcome to the Cranis Embassy."

Captain Young wheeled him down a plain white hallway to a reinforced door. The facial scanner passed over Young and turned green.

The captain was a slender man with defined cheekbones and a narrow face. He was shorter than Ade, and his dark skin matched his brown eyes.

The door clicked into the open position, and Young pushed Ade through the security door into a hallway resembling the high-end hotels of Cranis. Ornate gold and royal blue carpet sprawled down a forest green hallway accented with decorative mirrors and polished wood doors. Each door had a flashy gold number on it.

Every year, his father would attend the annual Augmentation Evolution Convention. These conventions took place in the most lavish hotels on Cranis. Jack often called them "a waste of time and resources." However, this never stopped him and his family from enjoying a trip funded by the Cranis Government. Ann, Ade, and Ethan would take in the city's sites and end their days in the hotel pool while Jack attended the convention.

Captain Young stopped and turned the chair to face a door with the number 24. "Can you make it on your own?" the captain asked drily.

Ade pushed himself up out of the chair. "Yes, thank you."

Young nodded and handed him a keycard with the Cranis Government Seal on it. "This will get you into your room. I'm supposed to remind you that everything is paid for. You can call Abraham if you need anything else. His number is on the back of the card," Young said in a monotone. Then, without waiting for a response, Captain Young turned and wheeled the chair down the hall in the direction they came from.

Ade watched as Young's camouflage uniform shifted to match the colors of the hallway, and then his eyes fell to the key in his hand. He turned the keycard over and studied the hologram of a sun and two planets.

Cranis to the rescue. It's about time. Ade thought, lifting the card to the door sensor.

A green light flashed, and the door automatically opened. Ade's jaw hung slack as he stepped into the room. The entire back wall of the suite was one large, fifteen-foot-tall window with an ocean view. Ade took one step onto the white marble floor and marveled at the majesty of the suite. A large, decorative, wooden table sat in the middle of the room, surrounded by five chairs. To the right was a raised floor with a canopied king-size bed and a plush comforter. To the left, three couches surrounded a life-size 3D television. The room sparkled and glistened as the sun refracted through the hundreds of prisms hanging from a chandelier. It was almost too spectacular to comprehend, and, to top it off, a fresh set of clothes had been laid out on the dressing table at the foot of the bed. A wide grin spread across his dirty face as he eyed the bed. Then he charged into the room and leaped into the air before falling onto the soft, pillow-topped mattress. He pulled the comforter around him and inhaled the floral smell of fresh sheets. Even the sheets smelled like home. He closed his eyes, and without the assistance of his augment, he swiftly fell asleep.

***

The following day, Ade awoke to a knock on the suite door. Peering out from beyond the covers, he could see the sun had moved slightly across the ocean. He wasn't sure how long he slept, but it felt like days. Then, casually rolling to the edge of the bed, another knock came at the door.

"I'm coming," he yelled.

Sleepily, he moseyed across the room and opened the door. His heart jumped into his throat as her emerald eyes met his. She had shoulder-length raven hair with the front cut into bangs. Her skin was bronze, and freckles peppered her cheeks.

"Ade Billings?" she inquired.

Ade suddenly felt embarrassed for going to sleep in his dirty street clothes. He ran his hand through his short hair in a feeble attempt to alter his appearance.

She looked from him back to the number on the door.

"Oh, I mean, yes. I'm Ade."

"Excellent," she smiled.

Her smile made him blush.

"The ambassador arrived about an hour ago and wanted to ensure you had a good breakfast before the meeting. We noticed you didn't call in an order last night, so we just made you a little of everything," she said, stepping to the side and revealing a cart full of food.

Ade eyed the food, and his mouth watered. "You made all this?"

"We," she repeated.

Ade swallowed. "Oh, yes, of course. Oh, I'm Ade." As soon as he said it, he wanted to slap himself.

"Well, I sure hope so. Otherwise, I'll have to explain to the ambassador why we gave your food to someone else."

Ade grinned sheepishly.

"Do you mind?" she said, motioning to the room's interior.

"Not at all," Ade said, smiling at her.

She stood for a moment, looking up at him. Ade felt she was the most beautiful woman he'd ever seen. He noticed her hands resting on the cart's handle and looked back into the room.

"Oh," Ade said, quickly stepping to the side.

She pushed the cart into the room by the table, and Ade felt his race. She turned to face him and gave him a knowing look.

"So," she said, "I'll leave you to it. Call the number on the slip when you're done. We'll come back and clean up. Remember, the ambassador said he'd be here at 11 a.m. sharp." She clasped her hands in front of her, rocked a bit, and then walked past him toward the door. Reaching the doorframe, she spun back toward him. "I'm Nadia," she said with a sly grin. "I knew you would ask when you accidentally repeated your name."

The door closed behind her. Ade's heartbeat was heavy in his chest. “Wow,” he gasped. He looked down, noticed his dirty attire, and rushed to a mirror to see his appearance.

CHAPTER 12 | 5856-W22

Ade drummed his fingers impatiently on the wooden table. Then he looked at the old-fashioned clock above the entry door. His father had one of those in his shop. It clicked every second and chimed every hour. The clock in this room, however, was silent. He glanced at it every few minutes as it ticked toward 11 a.m.

He devoured breakfast while looking at the number on the card. Then, he quickly showered and dressed in the stylish jumpsuit laid out for him. It was all black with burgundy trim and a gold zipper. He admired his new look in the mirror while trying to figure out his best angle. Then he rinsed the breakfast plates in the sink, stacked them nicely on the tray, and left a message with food service. Ade anxiously awaited the arrival of Nadia; however, when a knock came at the door, a burly, bearded man came to collect the cart.

I wonder if she was being flirtatious, Ade thought. Since her departure, Ade's thoughts frequently drifted back to her. Replaying their earlier conversation, he cursed his awkwardness. Then, he imagined their subsequent encounter.

Two knocks came, and Ade perked up in his chair. Before he could answer, the door swung open. Captain Young entered the room without waiting for an invitation, eyed Ade briefly, and then searched the room. Once satisfied there was no threat, he took up a position behind Ade.

What does he think? I ate breakfast and laid a trap. Ade thought.

"Clear!" Young yelled.

Young's yard call made Ade flinch in his chair and glare back at the bird-like man behind him.

"You should stand," Young ordered.

Ade stood and smoothed the front of his jumpsuit. Looking back at the door, he found Abraham standing adjacent to the door. He wiggled his shoulders and attempted to stand upright. "I present Ambassador Monroe."

A tall, slender man in an old-fashioned three-piece suit glided into the room. His strides were long and regal, and his leather-bottomed shoes clomped against the marble floor with each step. Ambassador Monroe was clean-shaven with neatly groomed gray hair, black eyebrows, and a tan complexion.

"Mr. Billings," Ambassador Monroe said with a flashy white smile. Monroe stopped just short of Ade and extended his hand. It was considered old-fashioned to shake hands, but Ade extended his hand in return. The ambassador's grip was soft yet firm, and his brown eyes were sharp as he maintained direct eye contact. "I'm Ambassador Monroe. We're honored to have you at the embassy. Please, let's sit," he motioned to the chair Ade had just vacated.

From the corner of his eye, Ade saw Nadia enter the room. She wore a shimmering green dress that accentuated her eyes and caused Ade's heart to leap into his throat. She quietly shut the door behind her and eased onto the bench by the coat rack; however, her stealthy attempt to enter the room had gained Ade's full attention.

Ambassador Monroe peered over at her. "Oh yes, you've met Nadia. Nadia is my assistant. She'll be recording our conversation."

Monroe sat, leaned back in his chair, and crossed his legs. His demeanor exuded confidence. "Please, sit," He repeated.

Ade bumped into the chair as he stepped back to be seated. Nadia glanced up, but he quickly looked away and attempted to focus on the man before him. It was a feeble attempt as his mind was on the woman by the door.

"First, I'd like to apologize for your treatment on Jaber. As a born citizen of Cranis, more care should have been taken on your placement and treatment, especially for the family of Jack Billings. We were lucky that CIU brought you here instead of their other interrogation center. It allowed us to intervene on your family's behalf. Now, we can do our best to make up for this oversight. Let me ask, have you enjoyed your stay thus far?"

"The chair in the mirrored room wasn't very comfortable, but this room is amazing," Ade said with a sly smile.

Ambassador Monroe stared at him for a moment, then turned to Abraham. "Abraham, put in a request with CIU and encourage them to put cushions on the chairs."

"Yes, sir," Abraham replied, scribbling on his halopad.

Ade glanced at Nadia to see if she laughed at his joke. Her lips turned down; she raised one eyebrow. It was clear she was not impressed with his wit.

"And your meal?" Monroe continued.

"Oh, yes." Ade's eyes returned to the ambassador. "Everything has been incredible. The food and the staff are exceptional."

"Wonderful!" Monroe exclaimed cheerfully. "We can't delete the past, but we can fix the future."

Fix the future, Ade thought. "Were you able to look at my mother's AIRE? A member of the Special Police damaged it."

Monroe grimaced and shook his head. "Neanderthals," he muttered. Then he glanced at Abraham. Can you please add a note that Ann Billings needs an AIRE 5 upgrade?"

"They said the parts they repaired it with weren't a match," Ade reiterated.

The ambassador nodded in agreement. "Of course, of course, we will look into it. But, for now, we have her in a luxury suite at the Royal. I'm sure Abraham informed you of this."

Ade nodded. "Oh, and the hospital charged us a bunch of money. They said it was negligence, but it wasn't. She was attacked,"

Monroe frowned, shook his head, sighed, and looked over his shoulder at Abraham. "I'm still dumbfounded by the actions of enforcement agencies on this planet." Then, he returned his attention to Ade. "I'm sure, as a Cranisian, you are equally flabbergasted. It is just appalling."

"Mom said it wasn't like home. I didn't believe it at first," Ade agreed.

"Indeed," Monroe said. "Well, let us move toward restoring the good name of Billings on Cranis and get to the business at hand."

"Business?" Ade asked.

"Yes, Mr. Billings, we must first discuss how you got here."

"I didn't do anything wrong," Ade responded quickly.

"Mr. Billings, you were apprehended by Jaber Special Police because you were in possession of an M356 Augmentation Scanner. As you know, it is a felony for a civilian to possess such equipment."

"I was trying to help my mother, and it was my father's scanner," Ade interjected. "It wasn't stolen."

Monroe gave Ade a sympathetic nod. "We are aware of that fact, but the scanner is property of the Cranis Government. And, until yesterday, that unit was thought to have been stolen and sold on the open market," Monroe stated.

Ade thought of his brother locked away in the labor camps. Then he thought of his mother. Possessing or selling augmentation equipment without a license was illegal, a fact repeated many times during Ethan's trial. Ade knew this. *My mother knew that also.*

His eyes returned to meet the ambassador.

"I'm sure you remember the agents who came to collect your father's things," Monroe continued. "Several items on the manifest were reported as missing, the scanner being one of them."

"My brother," Ade began. "He-"

"We know. Ethan was sentenced for the sale of government equipment. He was apprehended while trying to sell a V7845 Scalpel Set – presumably your father's. They searched your home again, but again, no items were found. It was believed that Ethan had successfully sold the remaining items. But then, the scanner was activated in your bedroom by some miraculous event. And most of the missing inventory was recovered."

Ade's eyes shifted from left to right. "I-Okay, I..." Ade stammered.

"Ade, we don't care about the tools. Perhaps your mother held onto them for sentimental reasons. I'm not concerned with what we found or how it got here. As you said, you were simply trying to help your mother. Water under the bridge. However, what does concern us is what is still missing."

"What do you mean?" Ade asked.

Monroe picked a piece of lint from his shiny trousers and looked at it. Then he flicked it aside, looked toward Ade meaningfully, and clasped his hands. His expression changed as the carefree smile faded. "Ade, your father was very, very important to us. The work he did for the Cranis Government saved thousands of lives. But what he was working on. Now, that was special."

Ade thought for a moment. "The last thing he was working on was pairing. He didn't say anything about a special project."

Monroe reclined in his chair. "That is what I'm referring to. Did you see it being tested?"

Ade's nose wrinkled as his thoughts abruptly turned to the smell of the animals soaked in formaldehyde. "No, the smell was awful."

His father tested interactivity by implanting a transmitting device into dead rats and monitoring the connection speed through soft tissue. He kept these animals in a locked cooler in his shed. Once a week, a truck would come and remove the cooler and replace it with a new one.

The ambassador frowned, and Ade looked from him to Nadia. She sat with her legs crossed, intently listening to the conversation.

"But I overheard him telling my mother that it worked," Ade added, looking back to Monroe. "He said it worked in live rats, and Dad wanted to test it on a larger subject- maybe a clone."

Monroe's eyes widened. "He got it to work! That devil. That's incredible." Monroe shook his head and whistled. "Your father, that man was a genius. We knew he was close. We got that request, right?" Monroe asked over his shoulder.

Abraham flipped through his halopad and nodded. "Yes, sir. It was approved. Oh, a little too late, I'm afraid."

Monroe shook his head. "His work would have changed augmentation as we know it. I think Jack would have wanted that."

Ade furrowed his brow. "Could have? Your scientists can't figure it out?"

"They never had the chance. Jack's work disappeared along with the items recovered last night. He reported that the work was in his home workshop, but it was missing when we came for it."

Ade sat forward in his chair. "Did you ask my mother?"

Monroe nodded and sat forward to mirror Ade's sense of urgency. "We did. And your brother. Neither admitted to knowing its whereabouts. Do you know where he stored his work? We may have overlooked a storage device."

"Everything of importance was in the safe under the desk."

"The safe," Monroe muttered. He looked at Abraham.

Abraham shook his head as he hurriedly swiped at the halopad.

"Just a moment, Mr. Billings." Monroe slowly stood and motioned for Abraham and Young. Abraham had a concerned look as he shuffled toward the ambassador.

The three of them quietly conversed, and Ade leaned forward on the table in an attempt to listen.

Monroe stepped back from the group and turned toward Ade. "Ade, do you mind giving us a moment?"

Ade leaned back in his chair. "Not at all."

Monroe stared at him.

"Oh," Ade said, somewhat confused. "You want me to leave?"

"It will only be a moment," Monroe said, motioning to Nadia. "Nadia, will you keep Mr. Billings company?"

Ade attempted to swallow the lump in his throat and sheepishly followed Nadia into the hall. Once in the hallway, his plans for their subsequent encounter evaporated. Fear silenced him, and he leaned against the wall and studied the top of his shoes.

"Funny, huh?" Nadia smirked.

Ade looked up from his shoes. "What?"

"How you'll talk to the ambassador, but now you get into the hallway with his assistant, and you're as quiet as a mouse," Nadia goaded.

Ade shrugged. He thought he was maintaining a calm, cool appearance, but it seemed she saw right through his nervous facade. He glanced at her and looked back at his shoes.

"You're pretty," Ade mumbled. "You make me nervous."

"Hmm..." Nadia mused. "That surprises me, Ade Billings."

"What part? The-"

The door beside them opened, and Young poked his head into the hall, saving Ade from his awkwardness. "You can come back now."

Nadia's swift, graceful movements cut Ade off from his retreat into the room. "Ade, before you go back in there."

Ade stopped just short of running into her. Only inches separated them. His mouth was dry as he swallowed.

She placed a hand on his arm. "I hope you choose to help us. I think you're pretty, too," Nadia said. Then she turned and entered the room.

Smelling the flowery scent her hair left behind, Ade paused. He felt the thrill of young love, but then her words sank in. *Help us?*

Walking back into the room, he found Ambassador Monroe sitting at the table, intently scrolling through information on a halopad. He didn't look up as Ade entered the room, but he motioned for him to sit back in the chair.

"Please have a seat, Mr. Billings. Apologies for the momentary interruption. We needed to finalize a few items before proceeding."

Ade crossed the room and sat back down. The man with the bushy beard entered the room carrying a tray with two cups of coffee.

He set two identical ornate mugs embellished with the Cranis emblem on the table and hurried out of the room. The aroma wafting from the mug was precisely as Ade remembered from the coffee shops on Cranis. Ambassador Monroe placed the halopad on the table, picked up the coffee, and carefully took a sip. He nodded in approval and set the mug back on the table.

"Ade," Monroe began. The sun over the ocean caused a rippling effect that radiated through the windows. Watching Monroe's stoic expression, his skin appeared to move with the light. Finally, he looked up, and his gaze's intensity made it feel like he was staring into Ade's soul. "I would like to speak plainly. Sometimes, things in life don't make sense until we sit back and look at them with unfiltered eyes. Then, all things become clear. Your father was working on a new encryption algorithm. And, until now, we only knew he was close to a prototype, not that he may have completed the project. We had given up hope of finding Jack's work. That is until you activated his scanner."

"How can I help?" Ade asked, lifting the coffee cup from the table and taking a small sip.

Monroe motioned for Abraham, and Abraham placed his halopad on the table - a contract was displayed on the screen.

"As you see here," Monroe began. "We're prepared to forgive all your debts. This will be done upon agreement to the terms. Upon completing the task, we will release your brother and make arrangements for you and your family to move back to your home on Cranis. You will bypass the placement test and be assigned the job of your choosing. All expenses paid, of course."

Ade's eyes widened. All he wanted was to go home. Now, everything he desired was suddenly placed at his fingertips. *But what do they want in return?* His brows lowered, and he looked from the halopad back at Monroe. "What do you need from me?" Ade asked.

The ambassador smiled. "I'm glad to see that, even after our outrageous oversight, you still want to help your planet. But I suppose we want the same thing – to see Jack's life's work come to fruition. Ade, we knew your father kept the prototype in the safe, but it was empty when recovered."

Ade remembered the night of his father's death and his brother Ethan skulking in the shadows. "You think it was stolen?"

"We know your brother took things from the shop. Did he know the combination?

Ade snickered at the question and shook his head. "No way. Dad didn't tell either of us."

"Do you think it was written down somewhere?"

After watching Ethan sneak away on the night of Jack's death, Ade felt the need to keep something for himself. He could only think of one thing he desired. Ade quietly exited the side door and crept into the dark shed conveniently left unlocked by his brother's carelessness. The moment Ade entered, he wished he hadn't. Tears began trickling down his face as he realized he'd never again see his father in this place. All the fond moments, the simple memories — all within four walls. His first instinct was to run from the pain, but he knew his father's journal was only a few steps away. He took four more steps and looked down at the red leather notebook on the workbench. Jack was rarely without his red notebook. To see him without it made it feel like something was missing. Jack was often found sitting in the den by a fire when he wasn't in his shop, either reading or scribbling in that notebook. Ade slowly approached the bench and picked up the notebook. He turned it over and ran a finger across the inscription stamped into the back cover: *Imagination is only limited by what we think we know*. He had flipped through the pages of that book many times since his father's passing and never found a combination.

Ade looked at the ambassador and shook his head. "He wouldn't have. He didn't trust anyone with his work."

"Curious..." Monroe puzzled. "That means one of two things. Either your father knew his life was in danger and moved his research, or someone-"

"In danger!" Ade exclaimed. "How?"

"We suspect the blast may have been a targeted attack by the Union."

"A targeted attack," Ade repeated. It made no sense to him.

"Perhaps they caught wind of what he was working on for us."

"But the news said it was a dixothine line that was damaged during a firefight with the Union," Ade countered.

"I'm aware of the official record, but I believe it to be more malicious."

Ade sat up straight in his chair, and his eyes darted from left to right.

"Perhaps it was retaliation for his abandonment of their cause. Did you know Jack was Union before the war?" Monroe asked.

Ade's eyes narrowed on Monroe. Being called a Unionist was an extreme insult on Cranis. "You're lying," Ade growled.

Monroe looked back down at his halopad, tapped it, and turned it toward Ade. A man looking much like himself stood with a determined stare, holding a Union sign in front of a factory.

"That's doctored. There is no way. Dad was always Commerce."

"How well do you know William Arfey?"

"Who?"

"I believe he calls himself Floyd," Monroe said, peering back at his halopad. "Police drones spotted him leaving your housing unit the night you were apprehended."

"He's Mom and Dad's friend. Why?"

"Interesting. Your father indicated he had no ties to the Union after leaving Jaber. Your father, Mr. Arfey, and your mother were all Union before the war. Jack left the Union shortly before the war and joined the Commerce Party. He'd been one of our finest ever since."

"My dad was a patriot!" Ade insisted.

Monroe glanced over Ade's shoulder and gave Young a stern look. Then he nodded in agreement. "He was. I'm not questioning his allegiance. Merely he and your mother's choice in friends." Monroe swiped the screen of the halopad, and Ade examined a blurry photo of Floyd taken from a security camera. "That was taken on Cranis. William Arfey is suspected of being a high-ranking officer in the Union," Monroe said, turning the screen of the halopad back toward him. "That photo was taken eight months ago."

Ade's mind reeled. Jack never spoke of politics, but he openly condemned the Union for its actions. He grew up watching his father curse at the sponsored news as it covered Union attacks across Cranis. As such, Ade had learned to hate not just the Union but any that stood with it. "Floyd is Union?" Ade gasped.

"Yes. I am certain of it," Monroe confirmed.

"I can help you catch him."

Monroe smiled and then shook his head. "I appreciate that, but Arfey would never disclose the information we require. He must remain free, for now."

Ade grimaced and nodded his head in agreement.

"We suspect either he or your brother removed the prototype. There was no sign of forced entry. Someone with a key must have opened the door to Jack's workshop, or Arfey manipulated your mother into helping him retrieve it. That is why I believe you are our best option to find it. They will tell you things they would never disclose to us."

Sitting back in the chair, Ade ruminated over Monroe's conclusion. Then, his thoughts drifted to his father. *My father was killed.* His gaze returned to Monroe. "How do we begin?"

"We arrange for you to be taken to the labor camps for two days and housed with your brother. First, find out what he knows. We've offered to commute his sentence should he cooperate, but he has repeatedly refused. After your second day, we will pardon you on the grounds that your brother is already serving a sentence for stealing the found items. You will then return home. If your brother does not disclose the location, question your mother. We know she smuggled the remaining items from Cranis. She either did so at your brother's request or Arfey's. The Union is the only other organization capable of developing that technology, and if they have it, William Arfey will know about it. I suspect Arfey will make contact shortly after your return and attempt to move you to a Union safehouse."

Ade angrily shook his head. "I'll kill that bastard."

Monroe nodded and relaxed in his chair. "You would be doing your country a service, but for now, you are to monitor him and gain intel. Nothing more."

"But, if Mom did help him, will you prosecute her?"

The ambassador smiled. "No, all members of your family will be forgiven of any wrongdoing. It states as much in your contract. It will be concluded that Unionists manipulated them. Only Arfey will be held responsible," Monroe concluded, and he pushed the halopad closer to Ade. "Everything we discussed is in the contract. Upon agreement, you will officially become an employee of the Cranis Government, and we take care of our people."

Ade looked down at the blank line for his signature. *We can go home,* Ade thought. He extended his finger to sign but paused. "What if I can't get the information you need?"

"The contract would be void. However, we will still pay your debts as agreed, and you and your mother can start over on Jaber. As an incentive, I will ensure your mother gets an AIRE 1 replacement for your effort."

Ade didn't blink. He quickly signed his name on the line and pushed the device across the table. "Agreed." Then, he quickly looked around the room. "What if they ask where I was today?"

"Simple. Police records indicate you are at a Cranis Investigations Unit interrogation site. You were interrogated, but you didn't say anything. Tomorrow morning, you will be released to the Jaber Special Police and transported to the labor camp."

"How am I to communicate with you?" Ade questioned.

"We will install a HEP and IVER while you're transferred back. You'll also need to control your temper, so we'll add a Beta blocker, level 2... On second thought, a level 3 would be preferred." Monroe turned back to Abraham. "Switch that to a level 3 Beta."

Ade's eyes lit up. "A HEP! What level?"

"Six," Monroe stated plainly. He stood and extended his hand. "Agent Billings."

Ade shot to his feet and immediately shook the ambassador's hand. A feeling of pride resonated within him upon hearing his new title. *Agent Billings,* Ade thought. *Dad would be proud.*

"Excellent," Monroe grinned with satisfaction. "Captain Young will go over your orientation. Oh, Captain, get him an inmate jumpsuit for the trip. And, Ade, take some time to enjoy a good lunch. Then, you will meet Young and his staff this afternoon for orientation and training. I'll see about getting a technician for the installation."

Monroe turned and started toward the door. His shoes seemed to clomp louder than when he arrived. Abraham hurried to the table and gave Ade a beaming smile as he retrieved the halopad. "Welcome, Agent Billings," Abraham said.

Ade gave him a nod and watched as he and Young followed Monroe out of the room. As the door closed, his eyes landed on Nadia, still sitting on the bench next to the door. She was staring at him, smiling. No woman had ever looked at him that way. Ade stood up straight and pulled his shoulders back. "Would you like to have lunch with me?"

Nadia stood and pushed her emerald dress down over her thighs. "I thought you'd never ask," she grinned.

CHAPTER 13 | 5856-W22

Colors appeared more vibrant, and pleasant scents tickled Ade's nostrils as he strode into the train station from the elevator. He felt taller and more confident, like he'd just received an award and gotten a fantastic haircut on the same day. Ade smiled and nodded at every odd glance as Captain Young escorted him toward the train. There was no thought of the orange jumpsuit nor that he looked like a criminal being escorted through the station. Instead, his thoughts were on the beautiful young woman who laughed at all his jokes.

The embassy exterior was as grand as the interior. Two 25-story glass towers jutted into the blue sky. Small, mirrored triangles angled up the surface of the buildings and reflected the world from different perspectives. The bustling train station was at the structure's base, beneath a sky bridge connecting the towers. People hurried in every which way to and from the train as Ade strutted by them. Seeing Abraham, Ade gave him a mock salute.

"Gentlemen, our gracious ambassador has arranged transport in the presidential cabin. Our best technician is already there preparing. Here is the prisoner transfer order," Abraham said, handing Young an envelope.

Young snatched the envelope from Abraham. "Not the smartest thing. Traipsing him through the station in a jumpsuit," Young grumbled.

Abraham smiled. "It could be all the rage tomorrow. Everyone will want one."

Young looked at the gawking eyes of the people exiting the train. "I guess there have been dumber things," Young conceded.

The presidential cabin was a private car near the train's rear. A luxury car with furnishing matching his hotel room, the maroon walls were accented by light, polished wood. A bed at one end of the cabin had a gold, ornate headboard. Wide recliners sat on the right side of the cabin between windows, and a sizeable halofeed screen was mounted on the opposing wall. A carved wood table, stacked with black rolling totes, was pushed under the halofeed. The technician assembled his station in the middle of the room. Ade stepped over the cords and took a seat by the window.

As the train departed, Ade noticed how quiet the car was compared to the main cabin. There was no rail bounce nor the sound of the arches as they sped across the arid landscape. Ade surmised that custom hydraulics must have been used. He pulled the curtain down and turned his attention toward the technician as he worked to create a sterile installation area. The setup was far more chaotic than Ade was accustomed to. Unorganized cables slithered across the room like entangled snakes, all connecting to a different glowing box. The boxes surrounded a gurney under a bright lamp with an articulating arm.

Jack often talked about the hack job of some technicians compared to others; however, Ade could tell this technician was a master tradesman. His tools and machinery were pristine, and the methodical, purposeful preparation put Ade at ease. *I wonder if he knew my dad.* His thoughts trailed off to the last time he saw his father alive.

One of the technician's machines began to beep. From his time with his father, Ade knew the machine was ready. He pulled back the blind and looked again at the sparse vegetation and sandy landscape. *I can't wait to leave this place,* he thought. *When I do, it'll all be different.* And at that moment, Ade wondered if he was now a man.

"I'm ready. You can lay down on the table," the technician said, motioning to the gurney.

The technician had the face of a Greek philosopher and a crown of white hair wrapped around a forehead that extended almost to the back of his neck.

Ade followed his instructions, laid on the hard gurney, and looked past the bright lights to the gothic pattern on the tin ceiling.

The tech hovered over him and looked down. “I will now induce tranquilization.” Ade nodded. It was not his first augmentation surgery. The technician paused as if he were about to say something, then nodded in return and pressed the button.

***

The powerful desert sun broke through the cracks in the curtains and washed the room in a hue of Orange. Ade slowly sat up and glanced about the dim room until he found the technician sitting quietly in the corner. The technician glanced toward Ade with weary eyes before sighing and looking away. Ade followed his eyes to see what he was looking at but found the technician was staring at the wall.

“Go ahead and try it,” the technician mumbled.

Ade blinked three times quickly in succession, and the interface flashed on and off. He tried again with the same result. “It’s glitching,” Ade said, trying it a third time.

“It’s two rapid blinks now,” the technician stated without looking from the wall. “Basic controls take three. Since you have a Sata and an interface, you can use two. Eye control is the same. You can set it to use three or four blinks, but two is the fastest. Although, I imagine eventually you’ll be able to activate it through cognitive thought.”

“How?” Ade asked.

“I’m merely guessing at this point. Go ahead.”

Ade blinked twice, and a wide grin spread across his face. A transparent, gold interface with white icons appeared in his field of vision. The bottom was a quick start menu with icons for all his current augments in a line. Ade was baffled by the abundance of options. He looked through the transparent interface at the technician. “Why are there so many? My quick-start lists eyes as an option… and storage.” Ade focused on the storage icon, which indicated he had used .003 percent of 1 petabyte. “I have 1 petabyte of storage!”

Closing the interface, Ade awaited an answer from a man with the posture of a defeated athlete, but none came.

"Are you okay?" Ade inquired. "Do you need water?"

"I saw your father speak once," the tech began. "At a conference. He was the keynote. He said we stood on the edge of a cliff overlooking an ocean of possibilities, but we focused too heavily on the other side to see what was just beyond the water's surface. He told us that what we know is comparable to an infant trying to place a square peg into a round hole. I'll admit, I thought him a bit mad at that point. Your father and the other dreamers thinking bigger than their britches, but now I know," he said with a sigh. His eyes drifted to meet Ade. "Your father, he was...well, your father was a visionary," he said, and his eyes returned to the wall.

Ade sat there awkwardly, waiting for the technician to continue, but he instead stared at the wall. Then, thinking he may have missed something, Ade craned his head to get a better look at the wall. After again finding nothing, he broke the silence. "I used to go with him to those," he interjected. "The conferences. We would meet Dad and play at the waterpark in the hotel."

The technician released a single soft chuckle and shook his head. "The waterpark. If you'd paid attention, you might have seen me coming down the slide after too much rum. Those were fun times," he said, looking back at Ade. "Did you even know what he was doing?"

Ade didn't follow and shook his head. "You mean at the conference? I remember sitting in the living room and watching as he practiced his speeches."

"No, no... I mean with you. "

"I don't follow," Ade puzzled.

The technician laughed a bit louder. "That cheeky bugger," he said, shaking his head.

"What?"

The technician finally stood and walked back to the middle of the room.

"Well, I installed the IVER (Internal Voice Electronic Transfer), the AIRE upgrade, and the Beta, but that's it. You already had a HEP, SFA 3, and a Sata 20. All I had to do was activate them."

"That's impossible," Ade blurted.

"Hetiria, as the founders would say," the technician responded. "A new world at your fingertips. Or in your head. Your augments were set to activate in six months. There's probably an admin console within your interface."

Ade quickly guessed they were set to activate on his birthday, but the puzzle of their installation remained. "When were they installed?"

The technician shrugged. "They're unregistered. I couldn't access the interface with my equipment. I'd guess about a year ago from the surrounding tissue."

Ade furrowed his brow and grimaced as he thought. As baffling as the mystery was, his young mind concentrated on one fact alone. His father had given him a gift without him knowing. And it was something he had always wanted. His brow lifted, and the smile returned.

Ade activated the interface and selected the network icon in the top right. "What's the room's password?"

"President," the technician muttered.

Ade gave him a sideways look.

"What? I didn't set it," the technician stated.

Ade entered the password, and network devices populated on the right side of the interface with a green dot indicating a connection. He selected the cabin lights and turned them on. He laughed out loud with excitement, chose the television, turned it on, and changed the channel. "Man, it's fast. What level is this?"

"A level beyond anything we have," the tech sighed. "Looks to be an organic polymer surrounding the casing. It's more gelatinous than the current synthetic coating and looks to have seeped into the surrounding tissue. If this is the case, it may be capable of receiving neurotransmissions. Do you have any lag?"

Ade shook his head and turned on the news. "No, it's instant," Ade said as he looked through the remaining icons.

"I figured from the look of it. Imagine operating without the limitation of eye movement control. The government would-"

"Whoa!" Ade gasped. "I have night vision."

"Doesn't do you much good in the Labor District," the technician said disapprovingly. "Try thinking about selecting an item without using the eye mouse to hover over it."

Ade thought about selecting his SFA, but nothing happened. "Nothing."

The technician grimaced. "Maybe it takes more use to calibrate."

Ade scrolled through the options. "Eye protection, live recording, thermal imaging, and sunglasses," Ade gasped as his eyes turned black, and he smiled as he looked about the room.

The tech shook his head. "I tell you, your-"

"Cover your eyes," Ade exclaimed, and the curtains lifted from the windows, allowing the blinding sun to pour in.

"Ade, please, I can't see," the technician said, shielding his eyes.

Ade lowered the blinds, and his eyes met a stern glare from the technician.

A knock came at the door, and Ade quickly changed his eyes back to normal. Captain Young barged into the room wearing a black uniform. "We're an hour out," he said as his eyes landed on Ade. "Is he done?"

"Do you mind giving us a moment, Captain," the technician asked. "We're still acclimating. I need to-"

"He's either done, or we abort," Young said sternly.

The technician released an exasperated sigh and nodded. "We're done, Captain." Then he turned to Ade. "One quick thing, Ade. I've placed instructions for your augments on your Sata. So, if you don't know how to use something, look there. Oh, and I tweaked your leg augments. They were a bit outdated." Then he looked at Young. "All yours, Captain."

Captain Young glanced from the technician to Ade and back again. "He has leg augments?"

"Yes. Probably a gift from his father," The technician stated.

Ade nodded in agreement.

"And the Sata?"

"He needed it for the HEP. Makes it more functional. I had an extra in my bag. No charge."

Young stared at the technician for a moment and blinked twice. "Comms check, over."

Ade shook his head with surprise as he heard Young's echo in his head. "Whoa," Ade marveled. "I heard you twice!"

"Comms check, over," Young whispered.

This time, a faint whisper came in at normal volume in his mind.

"That's bizarre," Ade said in awe.

"Now you me," Captain Young demanded.

"Select the little radio icon from your quick start. Then highlight transmit, select Captain Young, and speak plainly," the technician added.

Ade selected radio from his menu. "Comms check," Ade repeated.

The captain's face morphed into a scowl as he eyed Ade. Then his eyes darted to the technician. "What did you do?"

The tech just shrugged his shoulders. "I just installed what was given to me. It looks like they're trying out some new tech," he lied.

"Wonderful," Young growled, with a look of disdain. "Now we're giving our best tech to the son of a Union whore."

It took a second for the giddy joy to dissipate and spiteful words to resonate. "What did you say?" Ade's eyes narrowed on the captain.

"You heard me, rat," Young said with a dismissive wave. The

captain's wiry body stood casually, and he turned his attention away from Ade to the tech. "This plan is absurd," Young complained.

Ade jumped to his feet and clenched his fists.

"He's no better than his brother. They should leave his mother to die."

Without thinking, Ade charged. His legs were light and powerful beneath him. Using the same technique as with Myers, He leaped into the air. In a blurred glimpse of movement, the captain drew a knife hidden in his sleeve and slashed into the air. Ade's punch missed, and he felt the blade pierce his skin. Landing, he quickly whirled back toward the captain, only to be punched squarely in the nose. Stunned, Ade staggered back and fell to one knee. He could feel the blood streaming from his nose and cheek and looked down to see blood dripping on the floor. Ade's rage pushed him to his feet, and he readied himself for a second attack.

"Activate your Beta," Captain Young shouted at him.

"It's in your quick start," the tech added.

The captain's posture eased, and he glared at the technician. "You didn't teach him that already!?"

"He doesn't listen," the tech replied.

Confused and bloody, Ade looked between the two and bull-rushed the captain. Young stepped to the side, deflected the attack, and tripped Ade. Ade slid across the floor into the table and knocked over several of the technician's rolling totes.

"Your Beta," The technician repeated. "It's in your menu."

Ade blinked and activated the Beta. He felt his rage dissipate, and his thoughts became clear. "This was what...a test?" he stammered as the tech rushed to him with first aid supplies.

"Make sure he doesn't lose too much blood. We need him to look mistreated, but I still want him to maintain his wits.

The technician held a towel to Ade's nose, which caused pain to shoot behind Ade's eyes.

"Nice move, by the way. Would have worked on most people,"

Captain Young said, walking to the middle of the room. He grabbed a towel from the technician's table and cleaned his knife. "You need to control your anger. Blind rage will get you killed. With the Beta, you'll still feel anger, but the sensation will be dulled at the lower levels. This will allow you to remain calm and think. Level one will calm you. Level five, and you'll feel nothing. Never set your Beta above three. Beyond three, an experienced soldier like Arfey will know."

Ade felt part of his face go numb before the technician seared the wound on his cheek together.

"Done," the tech said. "It'll be sore for about a week. Once you get back, we'll put some regen on it. You'll never know it was there."

Young joined the technician in examining Ade. He now had a large gash that extended from the side of his freshly broken nose up past his cheekbone. Drying blood stuck to his face and soaked into the front of the orange jumpsuit.

"I think that'll do," said Captain Young. "Now, let's go over the plan again."

CHAPTER 14 | 5856-W22

The boom train glided to a stop. Young checked his watch, stood, and crossed the cabin. He pressed a section of the wall panel, and it clicked and opened, revealing an emergency exit hatch. A loud growl penetrated the thick walls of the presidential cabin, and Young awkwardly crouched to look up out the window of the door hatch. Darkness passed over the windows as a large object crossed before the sun. Young twisted the door handle and flung it open. Ade's ears popped, and heat and wind poured into the train car. Young leaned out the door and waved as the growl of the transport's engines echoed through the cabin.

"Closer!" Young yelled.

Ade moved to a window near the hatch and found that the train had stopped high in the air, suspended between the sky arches. They not only hadn't arrived at the station, but they were in the middle of nowhere. A battered prisoner transport hovered from the sky to a position parallel to the train. The transport was a large, boxy craft with round engines affixed to the sides. Unlike modern aircraft, the engines resembled old jet engines and rotated to accommodate movement.

A mechanical clicking sound joined the barrage of noises, and a side door began to lower from the transport. Captain Young gave a thumbs up and stepped back as the thick metal walkway descended into the doorway of the presidential cabin. It made a loud clunk as it impacted the floor. Young grabbed a duffle bag sitting nearby and tossed it out the door.

"Let's go," Young waved at Ade.

Ade glanced at the technician, who sat off to the side with his hands covering his ears. The technician looked back at Ade, and his eyes became stern. He mouthed one sentence. Ade stared at him, hoping he would repeat what was said, but the technician nodded and looked away.

"I said let's go," Young repeated.

Both confused and apprehensive, Ade stood and looked from the technician to Young. "Now?"

Young scowled. "Yes, Ade. Now!"

Ade felt like he had forgotten something. He looked about the cabin, and his gaze returned to the technician. It stalled there for a moment, hoping the technician would look back. When his stare was not met, Ade walked toward the door. Reaching Young, he peered out the door at the walkway and transport. The condition of the prisoner transport and the height made Ade feel uncomfortable. The carrier had laster round scorching on its body and mismatching metal plates covering the siding. The walkway looked heavy but was missing rivets in several empty holes.

Ade made the mistake of looking down as he inched toward the doorway.

"Go!" Young yelled over the wind.

Ade gave him an uneasy look. "Where are we?"

The captain smiled. "Stop stalling."

Unwilling to admit fear, Ade shook his head and took a slow, steady step out of the train. It was sturdier than he'd imagined, and, gaining confidence, he took another step forward. A gust of wind caught him, and his arms shot out to balance. He froze and looked through the small gap separating the train and transport at the miles of sand dunes. Then he swallowed and concentrated on the doorway of the carrier. Taking three quick steps, he jumped forward into the transport. The smell of chemical cleaner burned his nostrils the moment he stepped inside. The interior of the carrier was as lackluster as the exterior. There were no windows. It was simply a steel box with benches on opposing walls. Young walked around him into the transport and grabbed the duffle bag before sitting on the bench to Ade's right.

"Why stop in the middle of nowhere?" Ade questioned.

"Changing the plan. I don't want to risk you being seen exiting the train. You might want to step forward," Young said without looking at him. "Close the outer door."

The platform began wheezing as it rose back into position, and Ade moved to the bench across from Young and sat. The interior of the transport darkened as the door closed. A loud click sealed the door, and it was pitch black. A red light flickered on above them as the engines revved. They rocked slightly as the transport began to move.

"We've got about ten minutes before we reach the precinct," Young informed him.

Ade nodded.

"You remember the plan?" Young asked.

"It's pretty simple."

"Sometimes simple is the hardest."

Ade rolled his eyes.

"You need to take this seriously," Young scolded.

Ade glared at him. "I am."

"Listen and report. That's it. Remember, we don't need any spy stuff. Just ask about your dad's work. Tell them you're curious-"

"I know. We covered this twice," Ade groaned.

Young shook his head and smirked. "Meat."

Ade cocked his head. "What?"

"That's what we called guys like you during the war."

"I don't get it."

Young chuckled. "Neither did they."

"Whatever."

Young sighed and looked away for a moment. "Meat is what we called the guys who thought they knew it all and didn't listen during the briefing. They didn't admit they were afraid and charged into battle as if they'd win the war themselves. We had to walk over their dead bodies. What I'm saying is, don't mask fear with arrogance."

Ade eyed Captain Young with curiosity but quickly looked away as Young's attention returned to him.

"You know, I was your age when I joined," Young continued. "I thought I was a man, but when I killed a man, I realized I was just a boy. That's one thing I'll give the Labor Party. They didn't send fresh meat into the meat grinder."

Ade gave him a sideways glance and pretended not to be interested — even though he hung on every word. "What's it like?" He asked.

Young sat upright and smirked. "Ah, the question everyone wants to know about. You know, some guys take offense to that question. They're afraid to face the demon. It's like they're calling a ghost. For me, it was work. We trained to kill, and it's what we did. What's it like, though? I guess it depends on the person and the situation. At times, I felt like a god and at others a monster."

"Why a monster?"

"Because..." Young's eyes settled on the floor. "When you shoot down a man and the rest of his family watches, it doesn't matter if you were ordered to do it. It makes you realize you're the monster under the bed. You..." Young trailed off again. Then he paused and refocused on Ade. "What's important is that everybody fights for a different reason. It doesn't mean either of us is right or wrong. On any day, it's either kill or be killed. We have our side, and Arfey has his."

Ade nodded. It wasn't the revelation he hoped for.

Young checked his watch, reached under his seat, and pulled a black sack from his bag. "Put this on." He tossed the covering across the transport. "I'll also need to cuff you."

"Is this necessary?" Ade asked, holding the sack in his hand.

"Standard procedure, Agent Billings. If we don't follow it, they'll suspect something is off. We'd risk blowing your cover on a technicality."

Ade reluctantly pulled the sack over his head and extended his hands for the cuffs. The ties zipped tight around his wrist. "Remember what I said. Use your Beta to remain calm. You were interrogated by CIU and said nothing. When you get information relevant to the mission, relay it on your communicator. If you are compromised, contact us immediately. We will extract you. Do you have any questions?"

Without the ability to see, his mind raced between topics, but no one question came to mind. "No, sir," Ade said, and as he said it, he realized how strange the formality sounded coming from him.

"My name's Chad," Young said. "I work for a living."

Uncertain of what that meant, Ade remained silent as the transport pulled to a stop, and the pressure in the cabin changed again as the door opened. "On your feet, prisoner," Young barked.

Disorientated under the dark hood, Ade stumbled as he rose. A firm hand grabbed him by the arm. "Now walk."

They quickly passed from heat into a quiet, cool building.

"Are we there?" Ade asked.

The guiding hand released his arm. A bright light flashed behind his eyes as a sharp pain shot down his cheeks, and his nose began to bleed again. Dazed from the punch, Ade staggered but was caught and held upright.

"You speak when spoken to, inmate."

Ade opened his mouth to curse at Young, but the ding of an elevator silenced him. Young dragged him forward, and a click preceded the doors closing.

Ade felt his stomach drop as the elevator rose. *Why does it matter if I can see things,* Ade wondered. Then he remembered his new augments. Blinking twice, he accessed the interface, navigated to quick start, and selected thermal imaging. The world around him appeared in green, red, yellow, purple, orange, pink, and blue hues. He saw Young's wiry frame standing beside him, holding his arm. The elevator stopped, and the doors opened to two men. Even though distorted by the colors of the thermal image, Ade knew the two men before a word was spoken.

"Is this him?" Officer Myers grunted.

Young shoved Ade out of the elevator. "One Ade Billings for transport."

Ade quickly deactivated his eye mod as Myers reached for the sack, lifted the covering, and tossed it to the floor. As their eyes met, Myers let out a loud laugh. "Scarface, I see you got an upgrade. Oh, that's a fresh one!" Myers winked at Captain Young.

"He got mouthy," Young stated.

The Beast let out another laugh. "Got what he had coming. Don't worry; we'll treat him equally well."

Young didn't flinch. "I expect nothing less from the J1A, but remember, he's scheduled to arrive at the labor camps later today."

Officer Dane stepped between Ade and Myers and grabbed Ade's arm. "We've got it from here."

Young blinked twice and nodded. "Case note: Prisoner transferred to Jaber Special Police at 0940."

As Dane led him away from the elevator, Ade looked back at Young's interaction with Myers. Then he glanced at Dane. "Why is it always you two?" he grumbled.

Dane looked around the empty hallway, peeked back at Myers, and leaned in. "Dad asked me to look out for you."

Ade cocked his head and glowered at Dane. "Well, you've done a bang-up job so far," he said sarcastically.

"Not like you make it easy," Dane said plainly.

The conversation behind them ceased, and Myers' quickened pace echoed through the empty hall as he ran up behind them. He latched onto Ade's other arm and squeezed like a vise. The excessive grip made it feel as though his arm was a balloon on the verge of exploding. Ade's anger began to simmer, and he blinked and set his Beta to level one.

The air became warmer, and Ade could hear engines as they approached a door at the end of the hall. Myers yanked the door open, and the trio exited the building into a garage filled with police vehicles. The smell of rotting garbage and engine fumes filled the air. Traversing the rows, Ade looked out the opening of the garage at the open desert. The hair on the back of his neck stood, and sweat ran down the small of his back. He knew the plan, but, as of that moment, he had no control over what happened next.

Dane released Ade's arm and stepped to the door of his endo. It was the same cruiser Ade had become familiar with the last time he was a guest of the JIA. Dane opened the rear door, and Myers shoved Ade into the backseat. "Don't get too comfortable, rat," Myers spat and slammed the door shut.

Ade watched through the dirty window as Dane squared on Myers. "What are you doing?" Dane scolded.

Dane followed Myers around the endo to the driver's door.

"I'll take it from here," Myers huffed, opening the door.

Dane shoved it shut. "Prisoner transport is a two-officer job per regulations," Dane insisted. "I'm driving."

Myers looked through the window at Ade and shrugged. "Suit yourself."

The endo skimmer dipped as Myers heaved his body into the passenger seat. He threw an elbow back at the steel grate separating the front seat from the back. "If you start begging now, I might even untie your hands and give you a fighting chance."

Ade saw the sneer on Myers' face from his peripheral vision but didn't look directly at him. Instead, he looked out the window and remained silent. Officer Dane slid in easily with barely a rock from the hovercraft and looked from Myers to Ade and back to Myers. "Am I missing something here, Myers?" Dane asked.

"We need to make a stop."

Closing the door, Dane shook his head and ignited the endo's engine. "No. We have orders to take him directly to the platform. Labor Marshals will be waiting."

"I'm your superior, Junior Officer Dane," The Beast huffed. "We stop."

There was an awkward silence as Dane glared across the front seat at Myers.

"We stop, or you get out," Myers ordered.

Dane glanced over his shoulder at Ade, then looked out the window at the rolling sand beyond. "Fine. Have it your way," Dane said.

"Thatta boy. We'll make a man out of you," Myers laughed.

The squad shot out of the garage like a ball being fired from a cannon. When Dane cleared the precinct air space, he banked and dove toward the desert. Ade watched as the squad turned away from the giant arches of the boom train. The endo sped low over the dunes and created a cyclone of sand behind it. "Around here is just fine," The Beast grinned. Then, without warning, Dane slammed on the brake and lowered the squad to hover over a large dune.

"Good enough, Senior Officer Myers?" Dane inquired.

The Beast patted Dane on the shoulder and looked back at Ade. "Sorry rat, don't have enough time to uncuff you." Myers slid on a pair of brass knuckles and tapped on the cage. "You can try kicking, though," he said with a grin. "Keep it running. This won't take long."

"No, it won't," Dane agreed.

The Beast kicked open the door, and the vehicle tipped as his weight transferred to the sand. He stepped away from the squad, threw two quick punches at the air, and laughed.

"Oh, Myers! One thing," Dane called after him. The Beast turned his monstrous frame back toward the door and crouched down to look at Dane just in time to see Andrew swiftly draw his sidearm and fire one round into his chest.

Ade sat motionless; his wide eyes focused on the lastergun beyond the grate, and time slowed as Ade's eyes shifted from the gun barrel to Myers as his body collapsed upon the drifting sand.

You got the scar over your eye because you were playing with your dad's work tools.

Dane sat petrified with the gun still pointed out the open door.

"Andrew," Ade said in a whisper.

"Can you see him?" Andrew asked.

Ade scooted across the squeaky, plastic-lined seat and looked through the window at Myers's lifeless body. "He's not moving."

Dane slowly lowered the lastergun and placed it on the seat beside him. Minutes before, the same seat had been occupied by a man. Andrew removed his earpiece, tossed it onto the floor, and looked over his shoulder at Ade. "How'd you know my name?"

"Your father told me," Ade said quietly. He felt a dull sense of fear, but his heart rate remained normal, and his thoughts were lucid. "Or should I say Andy?"

Andrew nodded and turned his eyes to the horizon. "We need to get out of here. They'll be looking for us soon." Andrew crawled across the seat and leaned out to grab the passenger door. He paused as he looked down at the red, blood-stained sand beneath his former partner and then slammed the door shut.

Returning to his seat, he sat quietly for a moment. "He had a family...Hard to believe. I don't think he'll be missed by anyone else. Maybe not even them." And then, without warning, Dane looked up, grabbed the controls, and punched it. The skimmer jolted forward and pinned Ade to the seat as they sped toward the clouds. "We have to meet my father. We're already past due."

Ade's ears perked, and his stomach tightened. "We're meeting Floyd?"

"Yeah," Andrew said, banking the skimmer to the left and pointing the nose back toward the sand. "This didn't go as planned."

Ade looked out the window and saw a dull, dark object sitting atop a dune. Ade instantly recognized it as the pile of scrap Floyd lovingly referred to as Lucy. They slowed as they drew closer, and Andrew flipped the emergency lights on and off twice.

"What are you doing?"

"Letting him know he doesn't have to shoot us down."

The squad landed beside Floyd's skimmer, and Andrew killed the engines. Andrew took one careful look around the vehicle's interior and then ripped the Special Police insignia off his uniform and tossed it onto the seat. Then he looked back at Ade. "Are you ready?"

Ade nodded. Before Andrew could exit the skimmer, the back door flung open, and looking down on him were the black eyes of William "Floyd" Arfey.

"Let's get those cuffs off ya," Floyd said, leaning in with a large pair of shears. Ade's numb hands burned hot as the cuffs were cut free. He clenched and released a fist as he tried to regain feeling.

"Ya can do that in Lucy, yeah? We're in da middle of an escape."

A soft breeze brushed his skin as he stepped out onto the sand. Floyd gave him a firm pat on the shoulder. "Looks like ya can take a licking. Don't worry, you'll be pretty again," Floyd said with a grin. Then his eyes drifted to Andrew, and his smile faded. He gave a quick look back at Ade. "Get in da back of Lucy. You know the latch."

Ade nodded, and Floyd gave him a half-distracted smile. "Good to have ya back, chum."

Floyd casually walked toward Andrew, who stood just beyond the police skimmer looking at the desert. Ade opened the heavy door of Lucy and slid into the backseat while watching their interaction. He realized he wasn't enraged upon his first encounter with Floyd. On the contrary, oddly, he felt a sense of relief. Upon realizing this, anger came quickly. His jaw clenched, and he took a breath through his nose. He blinked and set his Beta to three. Calming, Ade sat back and glanced around the cluttered back seat. It was dirtier than it had been previously. Along with the empty bottles and hanging tubes, there were four large, tan bags stacked on the seat beside him. They looked like military bags — the kind soldiers packed for deployment.

Floyd's flailing arms caught Ade's attention. The thick windows and siding made the pitted skimmer soundproof, but from the look of it, Floyd was giving Andrew an earful. Then Floyd grabbed Andrew, yanked him forward, and embraced him. Andrew just stood there motionless in Floyd's embrace. Ade felt awkward watching the exchange and looked back to the bags. Floyd had scribbled his name on the side of each bag with a black writing device. His father used to scribble in a notebook, but, for the most part, nobody handwrote anything. He studied the slanted curvy text until a warm wind swept through the skimmer, and Ade looked up at Andrew as he slid into the front seat and closed the door behind him. Then Floyd joined them. Floyd immediately ignited the engines, yanked the skimmer off the desert floor, and catapulted it into the sky. No words were exchanged as Ade sat quietly in the back.

He glanced at Floyd's overly large shoulders and was reminded of Myers. *He was more than a man...he was a mountain. And yet, he crumbled with one round to the chest. I wonder if my father knew. The moment before the blast took him.*

"We should make contact. Tell them 2 plus 1," Andrew said. "Plus, we need a debrief before proceeding."

Floyd made a face like a foul smell was wafting in the front seat. Then he looked at his son and shook his head. "When'd ya become all procedure and paperwork? Better to ask fer forgiveness than permission on this one," Floyd responded.

Andrew's head slowly turned toward his father. "Are you saying this was an unsanctioned op? Em didn't approve?"

Floyd glimpsed at the scolding look of his son twice before shrugging his shoulders again. "Wasn't a hundred. I approved it. Short notice."

"Dad!" Andrew exclaimed. "I blew my cover for this!"

"Saved his life too. Don't forget," Floyd said with a backward nod.

"He wouldn't have been in that situation if you didn't have me watching him."

"Maybe, maybe not. Ya knows them J1A boys hate da Labor District," Floyd replied.

Andrew glanced at Ade and shook his head. "Dad, they'll throw us in the brig for this."

"Who is them?" Ade asked, looking at Floyd's reflection in the rearview.

"You're joking," Andrew spat. "You didn't even tell him we were Union?"

"Didn' come up in regular conversation," Floyd said. Then he looked over his shoulder at Ade. "We're with da Union." Then he looked back out the front window. "There, he knows now," Floyd said, winking at Ade in the mirror. "Wait," Floyd turned his attention to Andrew. "I don't have yer clothes."

Andrew's look hardened. "We're getting ahead of ourselves, Father. We need a debrief."

The playful eyes reflected in the rearview mirror dulled, and Floyd nodded in agreement. The skimmer slowed and descended toward the desert floor. Gliding to a stop, Floyd turned in his seat to face Ade. "Ade," Floyd began. "Before we go further, I'm gonna need to tell ya a few things. We-"

"Why were they holding you?" Andrew interrupted. "CIU held you for over 48 hours. I know what they do. People don't usually get released back to the J1A."

Ade looked between the two inquiring faces peering back at him. Captain Young had prepared him for such a conversation, but the temperature in the enclosed skimmer began to rise as they awaited an answer. Ade looked down at the blood on his jumpsuit. "They kept asking about Dad's work. Wanted to know why we still had his stuff."

"Those bloody vultures," Floyd hissed.

"What did you say?" Andrew insisted.

"I lied. I told them I brought the stuff and was going to sell it."

"Why'd they sweat you then?" Andrew followed.

"Huh?" Ade asked.

"Why'd they keep ya and ruff ya up," Floyd interjected.

"Oh," Ade responded. "They said I wasn't telling them everything. That some of Dad's stuff was still missing."

"What stuff?"

"How should I know? I didn't bring it. Mom packed it. I just told them I brought everything they found."

Floyd cursed under his breath. "But they believed ya? That Ann wasn't involved?"

"I think so," Ade replied.

Floyd clenched his jaws and looked back out the window at the desert.

"We can't," Andrew said, looking at Floyd. "When they find Myers, it'll be the first place they go. We can't go back now." Floyd looked his son in the eye and gave a slight nod.

"Hopefully, they believed him," Andrew finished. Then he turned back to Ade. "Anything else? Did you tell them about Dad or me?"

Ade shook his head. "They asked if anybody else contacted us about the parts. I said no. That's it."

Andrew continued to stare at Ade — to study his every movement.

"What? I don't know anything!" Ade exclaimed. "I didn't even know you were Union."

"Well, we know one more thing about ya," Floyd said, returning to his seat. "We know ya can take a beatin'. So, da plan then?" he looked toward Andrew.

"Yeah. Let's go home." Andy said.

"Home?" Ade asked.

Floyd punched the throttle, and Lucy launched back into the sky. Before Ade could even blink, they were back among the clouds.

"Da plan is to get ya somewhere safe," Floyd finally answered. "So, I'm taking ya to da safest place I know."

Ade sat quietly in the back seat while watching the clouds. Young had told him not to force conversation. He said forcing an exchange is the fastest way to place your target on guard. But Ade's curiosity got the better of him. "So where are we going?"

Floyd glanced in the mirror and then quickly turned to Andrew.

"What about yer clothes?"

"You got extra?" Andy asked.

"Pfft... They'd be huge." Floyd said.

Andrew shrugged. "Better than nothing."

It was quiet for a moment. Floyd kept looking at Andrew, but Andrew continued to look out the window.

"Ya did what you had to, son. It's not easy," Floyd said.

"Maybe," Andrew muttered. "Maybe not. Either way, we're short an asset in the J1A."

"We'll manage," Floyd insisted.

Ade looked back at the sun. They were heading directly west. *I can't imagine the Government District is safe.* He then considered what was beyond the government center and recalled his conversation with Andy.

He leaned forward and stuck his head into the front seat. "So, we're going somewhere safe that needs special clothes — the polar ring?"

Both Andy and Floyd looked at him as he perched between them.

Floyd grinned. "None other, me friend."

"I hear it's cold there," Ade said.

Andrew's stoic facade cracked, and he shook his head and smiled. "Cheeky bastard."

"Told ya he was smart," Floyd said.

CHAPTER 15 | 5856-W23

Ade awoke to the glow of vivid colors dancing across the dark sky. The purple, blue, and green of the aurora borealis radiated onto the ceiling of the skimmer, and shadows played within their midst. He slowly rose from the seat and raised his hand into the floating light. Rotating it, he watched the movement of the colors as they painted his skin. The vast expanse of the polar ring reminded Ade of a frozen desert — dunes of snow drifted like white sand and stretched as far as he could see in the glow of the borealis. He searched the snow for signs of life but saw nothing but frozen tundra.

"Are we almost there?" Ade asked with a yawn.

"Welcome back, sleepin' beauty," Floyd said. "Yeah, we're a couple minutes out."

"And those?" Ade asked, pointing to the glowing lights in the sky.

"We call it the western lights," Andrew called over his shoulder. "It's something of a natural wonder."

"How cold is it out there?

"Oh, about negative forty," Floyd said plainly. "I got ya a parka and snow pants. There in me bags. As for the rest of yer duds, I'll talk with Aunt Em right off and get ya squared away. You'll like her. She's a feisty one."

The skimmer banked slightly and slowed to a hover. Ade peered out the window but saw nothing except the empty white canvas of the arctic floor.

Lucy began to descend, and Ade's first thought was they'd have to walk to their destination in inhuman conditions. Then, a loud crack echoed below them. Ade watched as the icy floor of the planet began to move. The light from the borealis disappeared into a gap widening below them. Ade got as close as he could to the window and looked down into the widening hole. A red circle radiated far within the opening, and Ade watched it grow as the skimmer drifted past the planet's crust and descended toward a dimly lit platform. The skimmer closed within inches of the landing pad, and the opening above them made a loud, repeating clunking noise as it began to close. The skimmer gently landed on the platform, and Floyd killed the engines. Within the red light, Ade could only see about ten feet. Beyond that was a mystery. Andrew unbuckled his safety harness and turned in his seat. His face eerily half illuminated, he peered at Ade as the mechanical doors banged shut and omitted a hissing noise.

"That's the airlock. You might want to shield your eyes," Andrew said, pulling a bag from the pile on the seat.

"I what?"

It was like his mother had called to wake him just before flipping the light switch. Ade winced and squinted as a massive hangar bay came into focus. All around their landing area were old fighting craft parked on elevated platforms. Their windows were frosted from the cold, and icicles hung from the wings; they looked like they hadn't moved in years. Ade recognized some fighters from popular war movies and games and others from his history classes on Cranis. These were the far inferior craft the Labor Party deployed to defend against the invasion. Slower and less maneuverable than the Cranis fighters, Cranis quickly achieved air superiority.

"Grab da top bag there," Floyd said, turning in his seat. "Bag right next to yer noggin. Ade pulled the bag onto his lap. The contents were soft and fluffy. He pulled an oversized jacket from within and looked at Floyd.

"Is this a tent?"

"Nah mate, it's me jacket. Yours must be in da other bag," Floyd said.

Ade stuffed the jacket back in and handed the bag to Floyd.

"No jacket in this bag," Andrew said.

Floyd pulled the bag from Andrew's lap and replaced it with his pack.

"Wear that. I'll get me other bag."

Ade pulled a colorful lime-green parka lined with thick brown fur from the bag and wrapped it around him. Leaning to his side, Ade struggled to pull on the puffy pants, and sweat formed on his brow.

Andrew looked back and let out a laugh. "You look like a little boy in his father's jacket," he mocked.

Floyd nudged Andrew playfully. "Careful there, sapling, you'll look worse."

"What about you?" Andy asked Floyd.

Floyd shrugged. "Looks like I'm going in style," Floyd kicked open the door, and Andrew whirled in his seat to watch him exit into the icy air.

"Dad," Andrew gasped.

Floyd leaned back into the doorway, looking like a crazed bull about to charge. Warm air exited like smoke from his nostrils, creating icicles in his beard.

"Feels like home," Floyd said with a wink.

"You're mad," Ade said, shaking his head and blowing warm air into his hands.

"I agree with Ade," Andrew added, quickly zipping his jacket.

"Enough, chatty Kathy," Floyd said, pulling bags from the back. "We got work to do."

For the first time, Ade stepped from the vehicle into real snow. It crunched under his feet, and he lifted one foot and examined his footprint. Looking up, he found Floyd and Andy were already crossing the hangar.

The eerie silence of the large hangar was unnerving. The only sound was their footsteps. Ade yanked the hood over his head as he eyed the battered aircraft. Frozen in time, they served as tombstones for a lost war.

"Where is everyone?" Ade said, catching up to them.

"Down in the crypt. I like it up here, though. Can't spoil Lucy," Floyd said.

At that moment, Ade wouldn't have cared what anyone liked, let alone William Arfey. His toes had gone numb.

"Where's that?" Ade chattered.

Floyd pointed at a small door at the end of the hangar. The potential for warmth caused Ade to sprint forward. Reaching the door, he quickly yanked it open and bound into a dark room. Sensing his movement, lights flickered as they illuminated. Sadly, it was only slightly warmer inside the room. Ade billowed warm air from his lungs as he studied the room. It was an oddly large circular room without decorations or decor. Desperately looking around, he did not see another door or buttons to push. The fleeting hope for warmth faded. Floyd and Andrew entered the chamber and joined him in the middle of the room.

"It seems like I've been gone a lifetime," Andrew mused.

"For justice, we remain!" Floyd shouted.

Ade glared at Floyd. "Can we just-"

The bright white light turned amber, and the room began moving. It was a slow descent while something above them ground and hissed.

"You'll be warm soon," Floyd grinned.

Ade tried to gauge how long they stood in the center, but after a few minutes, he lost count. All he knew was that it was becoming warmer, and for that, he was grateful. Their descent slowed, and the grinding noise became a groan and fell silent as the chamber jerked to a stop. The walls around them slowly turned as one panel slid behind the other. A splinter of light shone through and continued to widen. Heat rushed into the room, but Ade's attention was no longer on the chill of his bones. As the walls parted, another hangar came into view. Twice the size of the previous hangar, light glistened off rows of modern war machines. Both ground and aircraft sat flanking two taxiways that led directly to the room they stood in. Then, Ade realized they were standing not in a room but in a large elevator. The hanger was relatively quiet at this hour, with only a few men and women leisurely walking amongst machines checking their armament. They wore drab stone-blue jumpsuits and paid no attention to the elevator as the doors locked into the open position. Then his eyes lifted from the hangar floor up the carved rock walls until they fell upon two massive, double-barreled machine guns with both barrels pointing directly at the elevator opening.

"Come on, sport. Now that it's warm, maybe ya can carry a bag," Floyd said.

Ade eyed the guns as he slowly moved toward the bags and lifted one over each shoulder.

Noticing Ade fixating on the weaponry, Floyd chuckled. "Nah, mate, we're not going to shoot ya on your first day. We're civilized and such," he said with a wink.

Ade caught something moving in his peripheral vision and turned toward a small hovercart speeding toward the elevator. The cart stopped just short of the elevator, and a tall, athletic woman jumped from the seat and ran to Floyd. Floyd dropped his bags and caught her as she leaped into his arms.

Somewhat uncomfortably, Ade averted his eyes.

Andrew patted him on the shoulder as he passed him. "You get used to it."

"I doubt it," Ade grumbled, and he followed Andrew to the hovercart and tossed the bag onto the flatbed.

"So, this is your godson?" A female voice asked.

Ade turned and stood eye-to-eye with the woman. She had a flat face with full lips and a round nose. Her brown skin glowed in the hangar light, and her large golden eyes smiled until they saw the condition of Ade's bruised and bloody face. "Oh, my goodness! Are you okay?" She gasped.

"I'm fine," Ade said, looking away.

"Now honey, ya know I'm not his official godfather. It was never made official," Floyd said plainly.

The woman wasn't listening as she took Ade's face in her hands and examined the damage. "We can fix this. You'll be good as new."

"Do you have the two-way?" Floyd asked her.

"Aren't you going to introduce me?"

"Of course, my love. Ade, this is Tonja. Tonja, Ade. The two-way?" Floyd repeated.

She released his face and wrapped her arms around him. "Oh, it's so nice to finally meet you. Floyd's talked about you for years. He's very proud."

Floyd anxiously paced as he waited for Tonja. She held him like he was her son, and Ade felt awkward in her strong embrace. He was in the den of the enemy — the group he learned to hate. And she was hugging him.

"You too," he muttered.

"The two-way, hun. It's important," Floyd demanded.

Tonja released Ade, removed a small handheld radio, and tossed it to Floyd.

"Have ya seen Em?" Floyd asked, punching numbers into the handheld.

"Command center, as usual. You know she never sleeps."

Determined, Floyd plugged one ear to minimize the noise from the hangar, lifted the communicator to the other, and walked away from the group.

Tonja placed her hands on her solid hips and smiled at Ade, "So, how do you like your leg augments? Did you know those are military grade?"

Andrew approached with his arms stretched wide. "What, no love for your son?"

Tonja grinned and happily embraced Andrew. "Of course, silly, but this one here needs attention first. He's quite the mess," she said, nodding toward Ade.

"You don't even know the half of it," Andrew mocked.

Ade's lips parted to return his jest, but Tonja's attention quickly returned to him.

"So, the augments. Do you like your legs?"

Ade thought of what the tech on the train had said about them. "They're good. Working great."

"Oh good! Floyd worked so hard to get those for you. Hmm... Maybe we can give them a firmware upgrade. I can scan you and take a look."

Ade's heart jumped in his chest. "Oh, no. I love them the way they are."

"Oh, you," Tonja said with a wide grin. "Your mom must be so proud."

Ade glanced past her at Floyd as he paced back and forth.

"What exactly is going on here?" Ade said, looking back at her.

"Oh, he's just calling Em, our president."

"No, I mean here," Ade said, motioning toward the hangar.

"Oh! They didn't tell you?" Tonja asked with a disapproving look toward Andrew.

"I said the same thing, but then he fell asleep," Andrew shrugged.

"Okay, well, it's a bit of a doozy," Tonja began. "Where to start? You know about the war, right?"

Ade nodded. *Everybody knows about the war,* he thought.

"Well, when the first Commerce troops were deployed to Jaber, they hit us hard and fast. Labor troops didn't even have time to mobilize. Most of the infantrymen worked in the factories, and that's what they targeted first. With all the men inside the factories, all they had to do was wait for our soldiers as they ran out to fight. They didn't even have weapons. But those Commerce boys shot them down. I bet they didn't teach you that part."

Lies. "No, certainly not," he said disapprovingly.

"They knew how to hurt us. Do you remember how quickly the capital fell? I bet they told you it was because we were so weak by comparison. That was malarky. When they took the factories, we abandoned the capital and relocated our headquarters to the place nobody wanted to go." She smiled as she looked up at the walls of the hangar. "This was a top-secret research facility before the war."

"But how'd you get all these machines? I thought you only had old stuff," Ade asked.

"Ha," Tonja laughed. "All those superior aircraft they said we didn't have. That's laughable. All their weapons were manufactured on Jaber. Like we wouldn't keep any for ourselves. We'd have won the war if it hadn't been for the surprise attack. After the factories, Marshall knew we wouldn't win, so he ordered two-thirds of the force to retreat here. The remainder of the military were sent to defend five bases."

"What about the Battle of Falling Rock?"

"Oh yes. That was just a distraction. Some of our best men launched a counter-offensive. We lost some of our greatest fighters there."

This was nothing like what Ade was taught in school. According to the history books, the entire Labor Army was wiped out. They called the War of Worlds a swift, decisive victory won by intelligence and overwhelming force.

"Anyway, we'll get it back. We're like a sleeping bear. Just waiting for the right time."

Standing in the large hangar, surrounded by weaponry, it was hard for Ade to dispute her story, but still, one part didn't make sense.

"But it's been twenty years. Why wait so long?" Ade responded.

"Because a sleeping bear knows the right time to awake from hibernation," she recited.

Ade furrowed his brow. "What's a bear?"

Tonja paused for a moment. "You know, I'm not sure. Some Earth animal, I'd guess. It's what the president says."

"So, the Union is basically the Labor Party?"

Tonja looked proud. Like a mother who had just taught their

child something profound. “Yep, we just call ourselves the Union now.”

Just beyond her shoulder, Ade saw Floyd stuff the two-way into his pocket and shuffle back toward them.

“I couldn’t get ahold of Em, but Wallace said they’d assemble a team,” Floyd informed them without making eye contact. Then he cursed under his breath. “It should be my team,” he muttered.

Tonja stepped before him and slowly raised a hand to his face like she was attempting to calm a wild dog. “Shhh,” she whispered. “You can’t take back Jaber on your own. And you’re needed here.”

Floyd leaned his head into her hand, and she began gently stroking his beard. Finally, his shoulders relaxed, and he peered down at her.

“I need you,” Tonja continued.

Floyd gently nodded and reached for her hand. Their fingers intertwined.

“I know, Tonj.”

Ade felt a pang of guilt in his stomach and turned away from the tender moment. *Remember, Ade. Remember. They are the enemy,* he scolded himself.

CHAPTER 16 | 5856-W23

Cool vented air fluffed Ade's hair as the passenger elevator descended deeper into the planet. Ade studied the facility map on the wall of the elevator. The Union stronghold had grown from its time as a research facility and was now more like an underground city. The original facility consisted of the upper and lower hangar with a wing off the far end of the lower hangar with several rooms. New construction began off to the right side of the lower hangar and went straight down. Access to the lower levels was either by elevator or staircase. There were fifteen sub-levels. 1-5 housed government offices, a retail level with shops, a health and wellness center, a medical center, and a cafeteria level. Level 6 was the maintenance floor, and 7-15 were housing. As such, Ade was happy to take the elevator. The door opened to a rough, dim, carved-rock hallway.

Floyd stepped from the elevator and took a deep breath. "Ah, I missed that smell."

The air had a musty scent. Ade inhaled, wrinkled his nose, and looked from left to right at the timber support beams lining the red stone hallway. Above him, silver venting whistled as air flowed from the vents. The only light source was a string of dim bulbs running down the middle of the hall and sagging between wood support beams.

Floyd turned right and walked down the hall. Andrew patted Ade on the back as he hurried around him and ran past Floyd. The lights dimmed, became brighter, and then returned to normal.

"No worries. Someone must be whipping up a cocktail er something. We bank fuel cells at night, so we have extra energy should we need it. Doesn't leave much for frivolity," Floyd said.

"I made cookies earlier," Tonja chirped.

"Only the best for our reternin' heroes. Hear that, Ade? Cookies," Floyd said.

Ade hadn't a clue what they were talking about. He followed Floyd through the cave and ducked whenever Floyd did. The hallway made a ninety-degree left turn. Ade counted 16 doors thus far. A man in a maroon jumpsuit with a gold star on the chest walked toward them. Unlike Floyd, he had short, quaffed hair and a small patch of blond hair on his chin. The man grinned as he approached.

"Colonel Cole," Floyd acknowledged with a mock salute.

"Good to have you back, general," Cole said.

The narrow passage caused them to hug the wall as they passed each other. Ade glanced back to the man and then counted door seventeen.

"It goes in a square. Hard to get lost after a few too many at da pub. Just remember floor 13, room 1317. Here we go," Floyd said, stopping before a splintered wood door. "Home sweet home."

Floyd pushed the door open, and a sugary smell drifted into the hallway. Ade followed his nose into the apartment's entryway, and his eyes widened. The housing units were surprisingly homey. Unlike the hallway, the apartment had walls painted with bright, vibrant colors. Oil paintings hung on the colorful walls, and patterned carpets covered the floor. Just beyond the entry was a large room, with a kitchen area off to the left with a sturdy wood dining table and a living room with plush seating and a halovision to the right. On the back wall were four doorways to separate rooms.

"You can take the room on the far right. I made up the bed for you." Tonja said as she helped Floyd with his bags.

Ade dropped the bag he was carrying and gawked at the paintings. "A bed," he repeated.

Tonja stopped helping and looked at him with a motherly look of disappointment. "Mr. Billings, you think we'd make you sleep on the floor?"

Ade didn't know if it was a trick question and shrugged. "I

don't know. We only had cots. And that was a house."

Floyd chuckled. "You gotta watch this one. He's a wee bit cheeky. Oh, Andrew, give Monsieur Billings some of yer clothes for da night and show him da bathroom and his room. You know, da one with the nicely made bed just for him." He winked at Ade. "We'll get ya some clothes in the morning."

Andrew crossed the room, studying Ade as he walked over. "I think I have some longer pants; might still be too short," Andrew said, eyeing Ade's long legs. "Meh, they'll do for a day. Do you need my help finding the room? It's right there," Andrew nodded over his shoulder.

"It's called manners," Floyd interjected.

"No. I'll be okay," Ade answered.

"Good. I'll get you some clothes," Andrew answered.

Ade casually walked to the corner room, examining the thickly painted wall art. He had only seen art in museums – never in an individual home. He stepped into the room in the corner. Although simple, the space contained everything a person would need. A small bed in one corner was covered by a hand-sewn quilt and a nightstand beside it. Atop the nightstand sat a lamp with a floral lampshade and a thick book. On the opposite wall was a battered wood dresser. Unlike the main room, this room had white wallpaper with burgundy diamonds. Ade glanced about the room until his eyes landed on a painting above the bed. He slowly gravitated toward the image as tears began forming in his eyes.

A knock came at the door, and it creaked open behind him.

"Here you go," Andrew said.

Ade didn't turn to face him.

There was silence, and Ade could feel him staring at the back of his head.

"Ah, Okay," Andrew said, entering the room. "I'll leave the clothing on the bed?"

"Yeah...thanks," Ade managed. "I just need a minute."

"Okay. But Mom made cookies. You should get to them before

Dad does."

The door gently clicked shut behind him. The paint strokes sunk into his mind. A barley field washed orange by the setting sun. He closed his eyes but could only see his father's face. He reopened his eyes and took another step toward the painting. It had a heavy, purposeful stroke and vibrant colors layered over muted brows. Watching the sunset with his father was a memory he cherished. It was never the same night, but they made a point to go once a week. This memory was how many of his nightmares began, with Ade and his father sitting on the hood of their skimmer while watching the sun wash an orangish glow over barley fields. Then, in a flash, it was night, and they stood in the driveway in the pouring rain. His father paused before opening the door to the skimmer. Then he'd look back at Ade. His eyes pleaded for forgiveness as cutting words spewed from Ade's lips.

His breath quickening, he abruptly turned away and sat on the bed. Ade took a deep breath and focused on the sound of the air coming from the vents. He blinked to access his interface and set the Beta to maximum output. The anxiety dissipated, and a lulling numbness washed over him. His thoughts became clear. Looking back at the painting, he felt nothing. Then, Ade turned away and noted the message displayed within the interface. *Network Connection Available* flashed repeatedly. He selected the communication device. A repeating green ellipsis scrolled across the bottom, and several networks appeared. He chose the first one on the list, and it prompted a network password. Ade tried the second, third, and so on. Each network initiated a security key. Ade stared at his hands. *Great. I'm trapped.*

Another knock came. "Yeah," Ade responded.

"Ade honey, would you like a snack before bed?"

"Yeah. Be right out." Ade stood and looked back at the painting. Then he looked away and adjusted the Beta to level three. A tinge of sorrow returned, but the aching had subsided. He took another deep breath in through the nose and out through the mouth like Captain Young had shown him.

Exiting the room, all eyes turned to him as if he were emerging from behind a velvet curtain.

Tonja gasped. "Oh honey, are you okay?"

They were all sitting around the table with a plate stacked full of small, round, tan food. The smell made Ade's stomach growl.

"Long day," he muttered.

Ade sat down at the table with them and looked at the food. They looked like some sort of bread with brown teardrops protruding from the dough.

"What are they?" Ade asked.

Tonja giggled and plucked one from the plate. "I can't believe your mother never made cookies. They're best when they're fresh," she said, taking a bite.

Andrew snatched two off the plate. "Synthetic milk would top the cake," he said.

Floyd slowly reached for the plate while eyeing his wife. "It's open season now, yeah?"

Tonja raised an eyebrow at Floyd. "Only if you don't eat the whole plate."

"Yes, ma'am," Floyd said, grabbing four.

"Floyd!" Tonja scolded.

Floyd sat one down in front of Ade and shrugged his shoulders. "What, just grabbing one for me mate. He might be nervous about digging in. Believe ya mean the icing on da cake, Andy."

"Oh. Same thing," Andy said, shoving a cookie in.

Floyd looked Ade up and down. "Your mum never made ya chocolate chip cookies, eh? It's a Jabber specialty."

Ade plucked the cookie from the table and sniffed it. He could smell the sugar and nibbled the edge. His eyes lit up. The sweet dough and chocolate delight washed over him, and his stomach growled for more.

The trio broke out in laughter. "Looks like Ade approves of yer bakin', honey," Floyd smiled. "Speaking of, what'd you think?"

Ade grabbed two more from the plate. He suddenly felt the hunger of a wild animal and ate half a cookie in one bite.

"Maybe he didn't notice yet," Tonja said.

"I saw him looking at da ones out here. He noticed," Floyd said.

Ade studied the wood grain of the table. "You mean the painting. How'd you know?"

"Yer mum told me about how you and yer dad would go watch da sunset. I painted it myself. Thought you'd like it. Make ya feel at home."

Ade focused on the taste of the cookie and shoved the other half in his mouth. "It's good," he said, crumbs flying from his mouth.

Andrew laughed. "Art's clearly not Ade's thing," Andrew said, covering his mouth.

"Floyd is pretty incredible with those paints," Tonja added. "It doesn't matter if you like art. It's pretty."

Ade jammed another cookie in his mouth and nodded. "Drink?" he mumbled.

Tonja quickly hurried away from the table and patted Ade on the shoulder as she passed. She moved with the grace of a dancer. Even with the small space in the kitchen, Tonja managed to maneuver between them without disturbing a single hair. She removed a large container with white fluid from the cooling unit and beckoned to Andrew, who opened the cupboard behind him.

"Sure, you get the milk for him." Andrew scoffed.

"You can go to the market and get more. We're on a budget around here, and Ade's our guest," Tonja responded.

Andrew placed four small drinking glasses on the table, and Tonja poured the odd liquid.

Ade devoured the remainder of the cookie and gulped down the silky white liquid. It was like goat milk but left an odd residue in his mouth. He ran his tongue over his teeth and nodded. Then he gave them a half smile, stood, wiped his hands on his trousers, and looked toward his room. "Do you have the-"

"Oh," Tonja exclaimed. Before I forget. I want you to have something," Tonja pointed at Floyd and then to a bookshelf in the back of the room. Floyd followed her eyes to the shelf and then tried to follow the direction of her pointing finger. "Your other left, darling."

Floyd seemingly touched each book on the shelf before his fingers landed on the correct one, and Tonja rewarded his efforts with a smile and nod.

"I'd like you to have something from Earth," Tonja grinned.

Floyd pulled a book from the shelf, crossed the room, and handed it to her.

"Not me. Him, silly."

Floyd grunted and smiled. "Of course, honey."

Floyd handed Ade the book, and he looked down at the tattered red cover with gold lettering. *Fahrenheit 451*, he read. He turned it over and fanned the tan pages. "What language is this?"

"It's American English." Tonja stepped forward and flipped the book back to the first page. "There is the scan code. Andy, can you get the network..." Then she paused. "Oh wait..." She looked from Ade to Floyd and then to Ade. "You don't have a Sata yet, do you?"

Ade swallowed, looked between the two, and shook his head.

"Well, hang onto it anyway. You'll be able to read it soon enough."

The hair on his neck stood as his eyes fell to the book. There was only one reason he'd need to know the network password; if not for Tonja's interruption, he was about to ask for it. His cover would've been blown by stupidity. In his introspection, Ade failed to realize all eyes were on him.

"Oh, don't be upset. It's just a book," Tonja gasped.

Ade turned the book over in his hands. "Thanks. Mom would have enjoyed this."

Floyd stepped forward and placed a hand on Ade's shoulder. Unable to control his reaction, Ade flinched and stepped back.

"Easy, big guy," Floyd said, raising his hands. "Yer safe now."

Ade avoided eye contact and shook his head. "It's not that. It's... It's been a lot. I think I'm going to get some sleep. Thank you again," he said, holding up the book. Then, he turned and retreated to his room.

Floyd took a step after him.

"Leave him be, Bill," Tonja instructed.

"Yer mum's gonna be okay, Ade. I promise," Floyd called after him.

Without looking back, Ade closed the door to the room. He sat on the bed and stared at the book. *Stupid, so stupid, Ade*. Ade rolled onto his back and lay in the bed. He stared at the ceiling as the mattress formed to him. Then he half-turned and flipped the switch on the lamp. The room was black, with only a sliver of light under the door. Ade switched to sleep mode, rolled on his side, and stared into the darkness.

CHAPTER 17 | 5856-W23

In complete darkness, Ade felt his eyelids open and close. It was an odd sensation — looking but not seeing. He had never been in total darkness. Then Ade blinked and activated his interface. It was 7:32 AM.

He selected his SFA and activated night vision, but the darkness remained. Furrowing his brow, he tried thermal instead, and heat appeared around him in different colors. He reached for the lamp and flipped the switch. Deactivating thermal, Ade sat in bed and glanced over his shoulder at the painting. Ade couldn't help but feel it was taunting him to drift back into a nightmare. He turned and focused on his interface as he scrolled through the listed networks. Now he knew why it was illegal for civilians to own this augmentation. With a hacker, he could control every network-enabled device in the bunker, including the large cannons looming over the elevator. The thought of that much power caused him to cringe.

Ade crawled from the bed and quietly dressed in the clothing Andrew had given him. As expected, the hem of the pants dangled two inches above his feet. Ade sighed again, pulled on a thick pair of socks, and tucked the short pants into them before tugging on his boots. *I wonder if there are still cookies....*

The dwelling was quiet as the steel door creaked open. Ade quickly went to the kitchen and looked down at the empty plate. He was reminded of the awful things Floyd made for breakfast and promptly began rummaging through the icebox.

"Morning, sunshine."

Ade jerked and slammed his head on the lid of the icebox.

"Easy, killer," Floyd said, walking up behind him and activating the coffee pod. "A war on appliances ends in defeat."

Ade shook his head as he rubbed the sore spot.

"Hungry?" Floyd asked.

Ade's stomach growled. "Are there more cookies?"

Floyd grinned. "Nah, mate, fresh cookies don't last long around here."

"I don't want a shake," Ade said, looking back into the icebox.

"How about bacon, eggs, and pancakes?"

Ade's ears perked, and he closed the icebox and turned toward Floyd.

"Let me get some joe, and we'll hit the cafeteria."

The term cafeteria reminded Ade of the school lunches on Cranis, and he glanced back down at the icebox.

"It's good. Trust me. They make daily runs to da farms out east. Nothin' keeps people happy like good food."

Without intending to, Ade scowled at Floyd. He and his mother had been surviving on rations. They ate the sludge provided for them while terrorists made daily runs for fresh produce.

"What? I need me coffee," Floyd said.

Another door creaked open, and Ade looked toward the back wall to see Andrew stroll into the kitchen. Ade did a double take — he had never seen Andrew in regular clothing. He wore gray sweatpants and a khaki field jacket. His hair was slightly amess, unlike the typical slicked style of the Special Police. His cheeks rosy and his eyes sharp, he patted Ade on the shoulder and sat at the table.

"I haven't slept that well in months," he said, relaxing into the chair.

"Ade here is ready for breakfast, you?" Floyd asked, pouring a cup of coffee.

"What about Mom?"

"Tonj is gonna need some sleep. She was up pretty late-"

"Stop. Don't need to hear it," Andrew said.

Floyd patted Andrew on the back with his bear-sized hand. "Son, love is a beautiful thing."

Andrew's face contorted into disgust, and he slapped his father's hand away. "Let's just get breakfast. I'll grab a plate for Mom."

"Let me finish me cup! You know da rules. Besides, you can't flirt with Dionna no more. She took a suiter while you was gone."

Andrew looked around the table for something to throw, but only the glass plate remained. "Would you stop with that? I was ten. She gave me extra eggs."

Floyd downed the cup and grinned. "Well, you ain't ten no more. Lucky if she gives you eggs at all."

"You're lucky mom is asleep. I'd throw this dish at you," Andrew said, picking up the plate.

"You know that's your mum's favorite plate. I'd have to whoop ya for that."

"You could try, old man."

Floyd looked at Ade while pointing at Andrew. "You believe this little...No respect for one's elders. Didn't raise 'em right, apparently."

Andrew stood and put his arm around his father's shoulders. Even as a man, Andrew looked like a boy standing next to Floyd. "You know I love you. I can't help you got old."

Andrew quickly side-stepped, crouched into a fighter's stance, and prepared for an attack.

"At ease, captain," Floyd said, turning toward the apartment door. "Our guest needs food. He was already sniffing about for more cookies."

"Oh," Andrew said, standing straight. "Those didn't last long."

Navigating back toward the elevator, Ade wondered how long it must have taken to construct such a stronghold. Having no practical experience in digging or building, Ade imagined it took decades.

They stopped before the elevator doors, and Andrew hit the call button. "So, you feeling any better? Sleep well?"

Ade shrugged his shoulders. "Yeah, pretty well, I guess." He'd been so concerned with food that he'd forgotten the retreat to his room.

"You worried about yer mum?" Floyd asked.

"Yeah," Ade lied. He hadn't considered it. He wasn't worried about her. He knew Cranis would care for her in his absence, but he imagined she would be worried sick. "Did you tell her where I am?"

"She hasn't made contact yet. We sent a courier with word you was okay."

Ade nodded.

The doors chimed and opened. Ade stepped in and pressed the button for the cafeteria.

"Lad already knows," Floyd said to Andrew.

"It's on the map," Ade said.

Floyd looked past Ade at the map on the wall as they ascended. He tilted his head and nodded. "Ah, a map."

Andrew burst out laughing. "You didn't notice, did you?"

"Is it new?" Floyd asked.

"It's been there for over a year. It was there before my deployment," Andrew said. "He never notices signs. Just ignores them."

The elevator slowed to a stop, and Ade thought he heard birds chirping. When the doors opened, Ade's senses were overwhelmed by a bevy of mouthwatering smells wafting in the air and the echo of a thousand voices.

A sea of tables sat before him, swarmed with people. Brighter than most other areas in the underground complex, Ade froze at the sight of the crowded room. He had previously assumed the Union consisted of a few hundred soldiers, but after seeing this, Ade thought the number must be in the thousands.

"Come along. Ya can marvel as we eat."

The cafeteria was easily the size of the first hangar. A large white and tan open room with various food vendors lining the exterior walls. In the middle were hundreds of long tables with bench seating. They weaved through the tables of prying eyes toward a line leading to a vendor boasting 24-Hour Breakfast on a banner. As they approached the back of the line, waiting people stepped aside and ushered them toward the front.

Andrew nudged him, "You're already a celebrity."

"They don't do this for Floyd?"

"Nah, Dad would wait. Says a good leader waits like the lowest soldier. By now, they know he won't skip the line."

Ade nervously glanced up at the soldiers as they bypassed the line. Smiles, an occasional nod, and several looks of curiosity met his eyes. *If only they knew the truth.*

"Why am I a celebrity?"

Andrew stopped, and Ade almost ran into him. "Are you kidding?" He gasped, turning to face Ade. "Your dad was a founding member of the Union. He protested with Marshal Lando. His photo is literally on the wall over there," Andrew said, pointing across the room.

Mouth gaping, Ade turned and looked up at a large photo on the far wall. Once again, a young man looking very much like Ade stood holding a picket sign next to a man that history books vilified on Cranis. "I knew he grew up here, but he never mentioned the Union."

"Yeah. Helps you look like him."

Ade mulled this over as they continued to the front of the line. *My father knew Marshal Lando*. Ade glanced back at the photo.

As they reached the food vendor, a murmur spread through the cafeteria. And the soldiers sitting at the tables began springing to their feet. Ade glanced at the empty plate in his hands as his stomach groaned. Then he looked back at the room.

"Attention! Make way for President Miller!" A voice shouted from across the room.

"At ease," a commanding female voice sounded.

Floyd joined them, nudged Ade, and nodded toward the woman in the middle of a small entourage. "Aunt Em always knows how to make an entrance."

She took long, purposeful strides. Her eyes were poised and

focused. Halfway through the room, there was no mistaking her trajectory. She was walking straight toward Floyd.

Floyd casually turned toward her as she approached, and the people around them moved away like water poured into a pool of oil.

"Mornin', Em," Floyd greeted her with a two-finger salute. "Come for some breakfast?"

She planted both feet firmly and stared him directly in the eye. She was a tall, thin woman with short brown hair sprinkled with silver. Her nose was long, and her cheekbones were high.

"Address me as President Miller," She fumed.

Floyd glanced at Andrew and then furrowed his brow and met her glare. "What's this about?" Floyd placed his hands on his hips and cocked his head. "You miffed?"

The once boisterous cafeteria was silent. Ade glanced from her to the soldiers in the room but immediately looked away as all eyes lay upon them.

"You...I can't even begin to fathom. You..." Her face grew red. "In my office in five!"

She stepped forward. Their faces were only inches apart. Ade may not have heard her whisper if not for the extreme quiet.

"Now give me a proper salute and call me President Miller. That's an order."

Floyd snapped to attention and raised a firm, sharp salute to the corner of his brow. "Yes, President Miller. Five minutes, ma'am."

He maintained his salute until she and her entourage were halfway back through the cafeteria. Then his hand slowly lowered to his side, and he looked at Andrew. "Well, ya were right. She's pissed. We'd best get it to go."

Ade felt his stomach turn as his mind began racing. *What if it's not them? What if they saw me in the connection interface? What if-*

"The lady's talking to ya, Ade," Floyd called.

Ade's mouth was dry. Half paying attention, he pointed to what looked like a pancake. The old woman behind the counter rolled the cake around a piece of meat, repeated the process, and handed the dish to Ade. She didn't immediately let go of the plate. The wrinkles around her mouth turned upward, and her knowing eyes glistened. "You look just like him," Dionna said.

CHAPTER 18 | 5856-W23

Two rigid-looking men wearing maroon and gold jumpsuits stood flanking the thick metal door of the president's office. Their lasterguns slung before them, they stared straight forward at the wall of the reception office. Ade shoveled his lukewarm breakfast into his mouth while looking from the guards to the receptionist and then to the maroon and gold banners hanging from the room's ceiling. Ade had never been to a politician's office, but the white walls and the patterned maroon carpet were what he'd have imagined the room to look like. The only picture on the wall was a stoic painting of President Miller leaning on a desk. Ade wondered if Floyd painted that one too.

Floyd finished half of his breakfast and held up the plate. "You gents get breakfast?"

The two guards exchanged a glance.

"Listen, I know there's two more of ya past that door and a ceiling cannon that'd blow me in half. If yer hungry, grab it while it's still warm."

"General, sir. No disrespect, but Royal Guard are prohibited from eating or leaving their post."

Floyd looked from them to the plate and shrugged. Then he tossed it into the garbage beside the bench on which they sat.

"Suit yourself," Floyd mumbled.

Ade finished his breakfast and licked his lips. A full stomach had been a passing memory. Feeling satisfied, he stood, stretched, walked to the trash, and tossed the plate.

"Hey, mister. That's a perfectly good plate you tossed," Floyd objected.

Ade stiffened and looked at the plate in the garbage. It was right above the one Floyd just threw away. The door swung open behind him, and Ade whirled around to see a young woman in green fatigues.

"The president will see you now," the woman stated.

Floyd stood and ruffled Ade's hair. "I'm just messing' with ya."

Fugduger, Ade thought, watching Floyd pass through the doors.

The trio passed the first set of doors into a small security passageway. Two more guards pushed open the next set of doors. Floyd paused and looked back at Ade. "Alright, this is gonna be a bit o' pageantry. Just do what we do." Floyd stood erect with his shoulders thrown back and marched through the doorway. Andrew fell in behind him in the same manner, and Ade attempted a similar, yet slightly awkward, march into the room.

Large glowing chandeliers hung from a high ceiling. Like the previous room, it, too, was decorated in crimson and gold. A red carpet ran down the middle of the room and led to a desk carved from stone. President Miller stood as they approached and circled to the front of the desk. Floyd stopped just short of her and snapped a sharp salute. She placed her hands on her hips and glared at him.

"I gave you specific orders."

"President Miller, permission to stand at ease?" Floyd asked.

"Denied," Miller barked. "Captain, stand next to your father." She pointed to the floor, and Andrew took two quick diagonal steps forward and saluted. "Captain Andrew Arfey reporting as ordered."

"You two." She paced before them. "In what – strike that – who..." She struggled to maintain composure as she seethed. "You put us all in danger! You two," she snapped. Looking back at Ade, her eyes softened before narrowing on Floyd. "Bringing him here was a risk; we're not yet ready." She paced for a moment and centered back on Floyd. "At ease."

Floyd and Andrew dropped their salutes and placed their hands behind their backs.

"Explain," Miller demanded.

"They was takin' him to the camps," Floyd responded.

"That's none of our concern," Miller said sharply.

"He wouldn't have made it. A J1A officer intended to kill him before he arrived," Andrew added.

Her features sharpened. "So, you kill the J1A Officer and bring their prisoner here? Directly after he's been interrogated by CIU." She shook her head.

"Ma'am, we performed a field interrogation and deemed him no danger to the cause," Andrew interjected.

"You did what?" President Miller fumed.

Floyd gave his son a sideways glance and began laughing. At first, it was a chuckle and then a hearty belly laugh that echoed through the chamber.

Both Andrew and President Miller looked at him as if he were a madman.

"What's so damn funny?" Miller exclaimed.

Floyd began laughing harder. "A field interrogation," he spewed between cackles. He laughed so hard that Ade thought he was about to fall over.

Miller looked at Andrew, and he shrugged. Whatever the joke was, it was only funny to Floyd.

His laughter subsided, and he wiped his eyes on his sleeves.

"Can you please enlighten us as to why you were laughing," Miller said drily.

Floyd's outburst seemed to ease the tension in the room. He took a few deep breaths and slapped his leg hard before standing upright.

"Sorry, mum. Me son did a field interrogation. I was there. It was stupefying." And with that, the laughter began again.

Andrew's jaw went slack, and President Miller shook her head.

"General William Floyd Arfey, this is serious," she said, attempting to suppress a smile.

Ade observed the diffusion of President Miller by her general's outrageous laughter. Ade had thought Floyd's erratic behavior and manner of dress was all part of his eccentric personality, but now he wondered if it was as calculated as his laughter. If so, Floyd was as intelligent as his mother led him to believe. If he was, this made him more dangerous than Ade had initially anticipated.

Floyd's laughter subsided, and he faced the president. "It is serious, Em. We need to get his mum out."

"Yes, I saw the request from Wallace," Miller said. Then she looked beyond Floyd at Ade. "He doesn't know, then?"

Ade opened his mouth to speak, but Floyd quickly interjected.

"No. CIU interrogated him, and he lied to cover for his mum. He didn't know anything about da parts."

"Is this true?" Miller asked, looking at Ade.

"I knew they were there. I saw Mom pack them, but I didn't know what she packed," Ade admitted.

President Miller nodded her head and began to pace. Her hands clasped behind her back, she leaned slightly forward as she walked. "What game is she playing? Why risk bringing them here? Did you know about the tools?" She asked Floyd.

"No, mum. She didn't mention it."

"She probably just packed them for my brother," Ade blurted, stepping forward.

Miller nodded, walked around her desk, and stood with her back to them while peering at a banner hanging from the ceiling. "Perhaps. Either way, we don't know her motive. But we also know Cranis didn't find Jack's work. She stood for a moment in silence. "General, prepare your men. You go for extraction tomorrow morning. I'll send down the order." She turned back to them in calm reverence. Her hands clasped at her waist. "You were right. We need his mother. We must do what we can to prevent Cranis from discovering whatever technological advancement Jack worked on. If it's this important to them, it's more important to us. Deploy a recon unit ASAP. You and your men are to follow and extract the asset. We need to know what she brought to Jaber.

The Union doesn't have the prototype. Floyd doesn't know, Ade realized.

If you can, sweep the house for anything important—notebooks, ledgers, anything that might give us the edge," Miller continued. "I'm sure CIU already swept the house, so look for anything hidden. Take Mr. Billings with you. Perhaps the two of you can convince her the device is safer in our care.

Ade felt a surge of excitement. He could potentially rule out both Floyd and his mother. He had always suspected it was Ethan. If he could confirm that his mother doesn't know the location, Ade could connect to the network and have Floyd apprehended.

"Yes, ma'am," Ade grinned.

"No," Floyd interjected. "Ade stays here."

"It's not up for debate, General."

Ade's mind raced. "President Miller's right. Some things are hidden. My father's journal, for example. You'll need me."

"No. It's probably a trap. I'm not takin' a civy into an ambush. He stays," Floyd insisted.

"I'm not asking, General. Your concern has been noted. Mr. Billings will retrieve the journal, help extract information, and ensure his mother returns with you. After not telling you about the equipment, I'm not certain your bond is as strong as you suggest."

"But-"

"You're dismissed, William. Make sure he gets a vest and a helmet."

The room was still as Floyd looked from the president to Ade. He grimaced. "Yes, ma'am." Saluting again, he turned and stormed toward the door.

Ade did his best imitation of Floyd's salute. "Thank you, ma'am."

The glint in her eye suggested she enjoyed her authority over Floyd. "Get out of here before I change my mind," she said with a dismissive wave.

He turned and took long, swift strides to catch Floyd and Andrew.

As the elevator doors closed, Andrew patted Ade on the back. "Member of the Union for one day and going on a mission."

Floyd shot Andrew a sideways glare. "Don't encourage him."

"They won't even know we're there,' Andrew said. "He'll be fine."

Floyd growled. "They'll be either watching or guarding her by now. We just got him out n' we're taking him back. He'll be fine," Floyd huffed. He shook his head and stared at the elevator door. "Reckless. We shoulda just gone back. At least then we'd had surprise."

The elevator doors slid open, and bright white light filled the elevator. Floyd's determined stride carried him into the wellness center. The room had a running track around the exterior, two basketball courts, a tennis court, a swimming pool, a sauna, and a weightlifting area in the far corner. Long and rectangular, the light blue room had large steel beams scattered between courts supporting the ceiling. Andrew and Ade hurried out of the elevator, trying to keep pace with Floyd's swift, angry strides.

They have a gymnasium? The halls are barely big enough to walk through, and then this, Ade thought. Ade lagged a bit behind as he tried to comprehend how they could accomplish all of this inside a cave system. Meanwhile, Floyd continued across the court toward the weightlifting area where a group of surly-looking men were exercising.

"At ease, men," he shouted before reaching them.

Ade hurried to catch up. His shoes squeaked on the hardwood floor, leaving black marks on the polished wood surface.

Each man would have been indistinguishable if not for their hair color and slightly different features. In a way, they all looked like slightly smaller versions of Floyd. They had long, wily beards, tattoos, and bulging muscles. Even their haircuts were the same — long hair on top with closely shaved sides.

"Luger," Andrew chirped, and he ran toward the group.

One of the men with a black beard smiled and opened his arms. The two men embraced and excitedly patted each other on the back.

"Man, you look like one of those fancy lads," Luger grinned.

"Give it time, and I'll look like you roughnecks again," Andrew said, placing a hand on the back of Luger's head and shaking it.

"Focus, gents," Floyd commanded. "We've got orders."

A general excitement washed over the group, and they hurriedly exited their weight stations and huddled around Floyd.

"Don't get too excited. It's recon and extraction. Stealth is our objective," Floyd continued.

A couple of the men grumbled. "No contact," one of them complained.

"Nope. No killin' this time, boys. Well, not unless things go sideways."

Floyd kneeled in the middle of the huddled men, removed a marker from his pocket, and began drawing the basic layout of the housing sector on the floor.

"There is a service alley there," Andrew added.

Floyd plucked a handkerchief from a different pocket, swiped away part of the drawing, and added an alley.

"There we go," Floyd said, looking up at his men. We split into two teams. Team Bravo — Luger team leader with Wench, Knowles, Rohland, and Ruiz. Team Alpha — Me, Arfey, Bonta, Numa, and Zorin. Luger, you'll position yer men in these locations." He placed an X in each location. "We need to know if Cranis is watching da target house, how many are watching, and da location of the asset. Yere not to make contact or engage. Team Alpha, da extraction team, will contact Bravo when on da ground 22-4 at 1000 hours. When Alpha makes contact with da asset, Bravo moves to defensive positions here, here, and here," Floyd said, circling areas on the map. "Copy?"

“Copy that, general. We’ll take care of it,” Luger said.

CHAPTER 19 | 5856-W23

"But you just got back!" Tonja roared.

"Honey, it's a quick extraction. We'll be back tomorrow night."

"No! Have someone else go! Why is it always you? And Andrew! Don't get me started!"

Ade had seen his parents fight before, but it was usually one-sided. Ann would get upset, and Jack would concede without much argument. It wasn't that she was always right. It was more that Jack didn't want to waste time arguing. Floyd and Tonja were more evenly paired. Tonja stomped her foot to emphasize her stance, and Floyd rested his hands on his hips and leaned into the argument.

Andrew tapped Ade on the shoulder and nodded toward the door. Ade bobbed his head in agreement.

"We're going to the range," Andrew shouted.

"Be back by supper! I've worked all day on it! Floyd, you tell him," Tonja insisted.

"Listen to yer mum."

"Yep," Andrew said, and the two of them quickly exited into the hallway.

After the shouting match, it was nice to have some quiet. Ade could tell Andrew felt the same as neither spoke until they were in the elevator.

"You ever fire a lastergun?" Andrew asked.

"No. I've never fired anything."

"Well, you're in for a treat. I used to go there whenever they'd fight. I was a marksman by fifteen. Don't get me wrong. They love each other, but they're two completely different people. You may have noticed."

As Ade listened to the argument, he felt terrible for Tonja. She was a lovely woman, and Ade wondered if she knew who her husband really was.

"Yeah, your mom is really nice," Ade muttered.

"Ha," Andrew laughed. "Don't let her fool you. Mom is the alpha in the family. Dad just plays the part. He's a big softie."

Ade gave him a quick sideways glance. "But he's a general in the Union?"

"It's just the role he plays. Dad wasn't meant to be a soldier. It's just how he ended up. You should see him with babies. It's ridiculous."

Ade couldn't fathom Floyd in the manner Andy was describing. He briefly thought back to their encounters and shrugged. "Guess I'll take your word for it."

The doors opened to the hangar, and Andrew smiled at him. "His heart is bigger than his brain, trust me."

"Mom says he's pretty smart," Ade countered.

"Exactly," Andrew grinned.

Ade's attention turned from the conversation to the fighters and tanks as they traversed the hangar. The smell of dixothine filled the air. He had only seen pictures of the fighting craft. As he passed, he examined their dull metal exterior. They didn't look as flashy as the photos but were larger than he imagined. Some square and some cylindrical, each was equipped with different weaponry to suit their specific function. He thought of what he had learned in history. The mere existence of these weapons proved that what he learned in class was only part of the truth. Cranis didn't have the superiority they claimed. They exited the hangar into a long hallway. Halfway down, they stopped at a grated window with a bald, wrinkly man eating a pastry at a desk. His eyes lit up as he saw Andrew, and he wiped crumbs from his scruffy chin.

"Walter!" Andrew exclaimed. "They still have you in the cage?"

The old man stood, and more crumbs fell from his shirt. He grinned. "You've been asking me that since you were thirteen."

"I'm just surprised you're not relaxing in the colony by now."

"I belong here. Gives me purpose. I know every gun coming out of here and every soldier's preference."

Andrew leaned against the grate. "Oh yeah? Try this one, old friend. My mate here has never shot before. Can you set him up with the laster I learned on?"

There was silence for a moment as the old man rubbed his chin. Then his grin widened. "MPL40. Thought you had me," he goaded. "That's still your weapon of choice."

Ade was only half listening to the conversation. His thoughts were on the future — what his life would be like after this mission. *I want to work in the same field as Dad, or maybe weapons development.* He imagined his brother and mother sitting around a table laughing as Ade talked about his day. Then Nadia came in and kissed him on the head before joining them at the table.

"MPL40," Andrew said, handing Ade the lastergun. "What are you grinning at?"

"Oh, nothing," Ade said, rejoining reality.

Ade took the foreign object and rolled it over in his palm. Polished steel with a thick plastic grip. He held it out with one hand and pointed it down the hallway.

"Never point the gun unless you're ready to pull the trigger," Andrew instructed.

Ade quickly lowered the weapon. Having never held a gun, he did not know the proper etiquette.

"Listen to Andy. He's got the best weapon scores in the Union," Walter said.

"Keep sweet-talking me, Walter, and I'll have to take you out for dinner."

"Don't be barking up trees now that Dionna has a suiter. You could bring me more of these snack bars, though," he said, shaking a half-empty box of granola bars.

Andrew grinned and shook his head. "Even you, Walter. I'm

disappointed."

Walter smiled and shrugged.

"Range is the next room over," Andrew said, nodding toward the door.

Both nervous and excited at the notion of firing a gun, Ade grabbed the handle and found the door was locked.

"Patience, Ade, geez," Andrew scoffed. "Walter?" A loud buzzing was heard, and Andrew looked at Ade.

Ade yanked open the door and entered a long, narrow room with targets on a pulley system at the far end. Ade immediately stepped to the line and pointed the gun at the target.

"You're not in the movies. Use both hands. Only shoot one-handed if you have to. Stand facing the target with your legs slightly spread. Bend a bit at the knees and hold the gun in front of you with two hands. Two gives you better stability and helps you aim."

Ade placed his second hand around the grip and looked at the man-shaped silhouette.

"Just line up the three glowing dots. Then, when they're in perfect alignment, you're sighted in."

Ade quickly lined up the sight and pulled the trigger, but nothing happened.

He pulled the trigger again as Andrew started laughing.

Ade looked at the weapon in his hands and then at Andrew. "What?"

Andrew handed him a square black object. "You need to insert the battery pack first."

Ade glowered at his laughter and snatched the battery. "Where?"

"The slot in front of the trigger. The arrows on the battery indicate which way is up. You can figure that out, right?"

Ade orientated the arrow and slammed it into the weapon. "Anything else you're leaving out?"

"See the light by the trigger? The red one?"

Ade nodded.

"Press it to release the safety. Then you're ready to fire."

Ade pointed the weapon back down range. He pressed the button by the trigger and aligned the sight. Then he pulled the trigger. Within a blink, there was a burning hole in the bottom right of the target.

"Not bad. Try exhaling and using only the tip of your finger to pull the trigger. You jerked that one a bit."

Once again, Ade aimed at the target. He inhaled, exhaled, and pressed the trigger with the tip of his finger. He opened his eyes to see a second hole burning in the center of the target.

"Whoo, that a boy! Center mass," Andrew cheered. "Go ahead and keep firing."

The Beta held the adrenaline surge in check, but the feeling of power was undeniable. Ade pointed again down range and squeezed off five rounds. All rounds impacted different areas of the target, but he didn't miss once. He couldn't help but smile. *Okay. I'm going for weapons.* Ade glanced from the gun to Andrew and was suddenly reminded of the moment in the patrol car. His smile faded as Andrew stepped beside him and raised his weapon to fire.

"Andrew..."

Andrew turned his head toward Ade, his weapon still in the ready position. "Yeah?"

"Thanks for...you know."

Andrew glanced at Ade and quickly looked away. Then he exhaled through his nose and gave a slight nod. "It was either you or him. I chose you. Plus," he said, looking down the weapon's barrel at his target, "I hated him too."

He began firing, and Ade's jaw dropped as he watched the center of the target disappear. Then, Ade looked at his target peppered with random holes.

"You're good," Ade marveled.

Andrew shrugged. "Like I said, Mom and Dad fought a lot." He pointed the lastergun higher and began boring a hole into the head of the target.

Ade tried the same and grimaced as he shot his target in the ear.

"You'll get it," Andrew said, patting him on the back. "Want another target?"

Ade became a bobblehead, and Andrew chuckled. "Yeah, it's pretty fun."

***

The morning was eerily quiet in Floyd's home. Tonja made breakfast before they awoke and barely said a word after. Ade could feel the tension as Floyd kissed her on the cheek and told her they'd be back in a bit. Ade and Andrew waited in the hall as Floyd stopped in the doorway and looked back at his wife. Without a word, they exchanged a look, and Floyd exited the entryway and closed the door.

Floyd trudged before them as he led them to the elevator. His steps were heavier than usual, and his shoulders slumped forward. Ade considered saying something and looked to Andrew, who shook his head.

They ascended in silence. Floyd's manner, combined with the uncertainty of the mission, made Ade nervous. Then, as the elevator slowed, Ade heard voices. The doors opened to people rushing through the main hangar. Soldiers shouted at one another while dixothine lines were attached to aircraft and laster cannons equipped with batteries. They dodged fuel lines like hopscotch as they weaved between soldiers and aircraft across the hangar. Ade found it odd that the soldiers practically ignored them instead of stopping to salute them like before.

"What in da hell is going on here?" Floyd shouted.

A soldier looking much younger than Ade sprinted up to them. "General Arfey, Miller called ahead. You've got three air support fighters, and your team is outfitted and in the hauler. We'll be ready to launch in fifteen minutes."

"Bloody hell," Floyd growled. "Have da fighters stand down. It's a fuging extraction, not an assault."

"Your recon unit reported suspicious activity in the extraction zone. So, the president ordered more firepower," the young man said hesitantly.

Floyd looked about the hangar, threw his shoulders back, and began to yell. "This is General Arfey—Commander of da assault force. Everybody stand down. We aren't rolling heavy on this one."

A momentary silence fell upon the room before a murmur of confused chatter ensued.

"But President-" The young soldier began.

"I'm the onsite commander. That's an order," Floyd barked.

"Yes, sir. Understood."

The soldier sprinted off in the opposite direction. Floyd blinked and accessed his comms. Alpha Team, dis is one. Change of plans. I'm going in light. Take da day off and be with your families."

Once again, they entered the hall just beyond the hangar, but instead of continuing to the range, they entered the first door to the armory. Inside were racks filled with weaponry and shelving units overflowing with uniforms, knives, helmets, and other assorted battle gear. Off to the right, a short, broad, young woman with rosy cheeks and thin lips stood before a table of equipment studying a clipboard.

Floyd approached, and she looked up and nodded. She was about the same age as Ade. Dressed in fatigues, she had a strong jaw and narrow eyes. "I've got your normal kit prepared, general," she said, patting a large bag on the table.

"Good. We're also needin' a full kit, size small, long," Floyd said, opening the bag.

She marked it on the clipboard and looked at Andrew. "Long time, Captain. See, you've gained weight. Should I mark you down for a medium wide?"

"I see you've gotten shorter, Amanda," Andrew sneered. "And no, a medium regular is fine."

Amanda grinned. "Welcome back, Andy. What would you like?"

"I'll take a full kit, standard layout, but add an MPL40 with two packs. He'll also need an MPL40 with two," he said, nodding at Ade.

"Roger that," Amanda said, noting it on the clipboard.

The young woman disappeared into the stacks as Floyd organized his kit. Then he shot a look of disapproval at Andrew. "We're arming the kid?"

Ade furrowed his brow and scowled at Floyd, but Floyd didn't notice.

"I taught him last night. He's pretty good. And we may need an extra gun if we're rolling light."

Floyd grunted an acknowledgment and went back to his gear. "All right. He's yer responsibility."

Floyd hoisted a long, high-caliber lastergun equipped with a scope from the table and slung it around his back. Then he grabbed an old-fashioned pistol from the table and stuffed it in his pants.

Ade gaped at the sight of the chrome wheel gun. It was the same gun he'd seen in old cowboy movies. He didn't even think they were real.

"I prefer da old projectile handgun," Floyd said, noticing Ade's look. "Creates more fear. Wounds don't cauterize. Plus, no network interface."

A thud drew Ade's attention, and he watched Amanda standing on her tiptoes, pulling gear from a high shelf. For some reason, watching her made him think about Nadia. She tugged another bag and let it fall to the floor. Then, she shuffled back with a bag in each hand. Reaching the table, she grunted, slung them onto the surface, and stood momentarily, catching her breath.

Andrew smirked as he opened the bag. "Quit hitting the gym?"

"Shut up, Andy," she huffed.

"You look good, though," Andrew said with a wink. "Out of shape, but good."

Amanda scowled at him. "You looked better with that wispy patch of hair you called a beard."

Ade laughed. He didn't know how bad it was, but he imagined long, thin, sparse hair on Andrew's face.

"Cool it," Floyd barked. "We leave in five."

Amanda quickly skirted away from Andrew and presented her clipboard to Floyd. "General, I need a signature for you and your team's gear.

"My team," Floyd mocked. He hastily signed and tossed the pen and clipboard on the table. Then he grabbed his gear and walked away. "We're taking Lucy. Be in da upper hangar in ten."

Andrew hurriedly pulled the assault vest over his head and strapped it around his torso. Ade dug through the bag, removed the same vest, and mimicked Andrew.

"What's eating the general?" Amanda asked when Floyd was out of earshot.

Andrew shrugged, clipped a holster to his belt, and snapped the bottom strap around his leg. "Could be a couple of things. Mom wasn't happy, for starters."

"They're at it again?" Amanda asked.

"Yep. Same old."

They don't cauterize. Ade felt a chill run down his spine. "What does a projectile gun shoot?"

"Bullets," Amanda said.

"A piece of metal," Andrew added. "Really nasty. Dad has the bullets made special."

"A piece of metal," Ade repeated. "So, they bleed all over like the movies?" He lifted the MPL40 from the desk and holstered it like Andrew. The thought of it seemed barbaric.

"Just like the movies," Andrew confirmed. "Except worse in

real life." Andrew removed the last item from the bag and wrapped the dust scarf around his neck. Looking at Amanda, he folded the bag three times and lifted it from the table. "So, want to hit the gym with me after we're back?" he asked her.

"I didn't sign out the bag," Amanda stated.

"You don't trust me?"

"You cheated off me in school."

Andrew rolled his eyes. Ade didn't notice right away, but Andrew was blushing.

"Amanda, I'm asking you to trust me with this very important green bag."

"Okay, but if you lose it, you owe me dinner. And I get to choose where," Amanda said.

Andrew grinned, and suddenly, Ade felt awkward. They were just standing there smiling at each other. "I'm going to go," Ade interrupted. "Your dad said ten minutes."

"Oh," Andrew said, checking his watch. "Yeah." He smiled again at Amanda. "Gotta go."

"Move it or lose it, captain," Amanda goaded.

Andrew and Ade hurried across the hangar. Andrew glanced back twice with a stupid grin plastered on his face. Ade knew the feeling, and it made him miss Nadia.

CHAPTER 20 | 5856-W24

The sun's heat through the window was a welcome change to the cold darkness of the polar ring. Floyd slowed the skimmer to a crawl and landed between two parked tankers on the edge of the factory sector. The dust settled as they sat in silence.

Peering through scratched windows, tension oozed as they scanned the landscape for anyone who may have observed their arrival. Finally, after five minutes of unnerving quiet, Floyd pointed to the duffle bag on the seat by Ade. "Pass out da ponchos."

Ade dug into the bag and removed three tan ponchos. They looked like the attire seen in the open desert worn by goat herders, but they also cleverly concealed the weaponry of the wearer.

"Mine smells like armpit," Andrew said in disgust.

Ade laughed, then immediately covered his mouth as Floyd shot a cautioning look over his shoulder.

"Don't forget this is a tactical mission," Floyd warned. "Armpit smell will blend right in."

Then he blinked twice. "Bravo, this is Alpha 1. How are we looking?"

Ade wished he could hear the response.

"Roger that. We're heading on foot," Floyd responded. Pulling the poncho over his head, he turned to look at them. "Bravo confirms clean landing. No bogeys. We're clear to move."

"What's a boogey?" Ade puzzled, and with that, Andrew laughed and earned another stern look from Floyd.

"I'll leave ya in da car if you can't take this seriously," Floyd snapped at Andrew. "Bogey, not boogey. It's a hostile or enemy. Bravo says we're clear."

Ade nodded.

"On me," Floyd said, kicking the door open.

The three exited the skimmer onto the shadowed walkways of the factory sector. Even in the shadow, the day's heat caused Ade to gasp for air. The warmth he had been appreciating was now stifling. Perspiration dripped like a broken faucet, and Ade wiped the sweat from his forehead and traced the tactical belt under the poncho until his hand landed on the canteen.

"Remain close but stay far enough apart to avoid suspicion," Floyd whispered.

Ade wondered how three goat herders walking together in the factory sector wasn't already suspicious, but he thought it best not to ask.

Exiting the factory sector into the direct sun, the rays beat against their thick ponchos as they moved toward the housing sector and Ade's home. Ade recalled how quiet it was during the day, but the silence was unnerving in the current situation. Floyd motioned with his hand for them to stop. Then, he scanned their surroundings. "Bravo One, come in, over," Floyd whispered. "Do you see anyone?"

Ade quickly looked at Andrew to see what was going on. Andrew looked nervously up at the roofs of the buildings, his hand clearly resting on his weapon under his poncho. Ade quickly felt for the grip of his pistol. "Roger that," Floyd answered. "Me either. It's just too quiet."

"It's daytime," Ade interjected, but Floyd quickly shushed him.

"Bravo, move to defensive positions and prep fer hot extract."

Ade didn't follow the jargon, but it was easy to surmise that Floyd was expecting a fight. Floyd glanced back at them and waved his hand forward. The rocks on the path seemed louder than before as they crunched underfoot. Ade slowed as the others continued. Lowering his head until the poncho's hood concealed his eyes, Ade blinked twice, connected to the open network, and selected his IVER. "I'm in the housing sector. Don't shoot me."

Floyd's eyes darted around as if alerted by the sound, and

Ade's heart pounded in his chest. Floyd's eyes landed on him, and he furrowed his brow. Ade quickly increased his pace to rejoin Floyd and Andrew.

When they reached Ade's home, Floyd made a circular motion above his head and crouched by the wall of the house. Andrew fell in behind him, and Ade followed. "Bravo, is da perimeter still clear?"

Ade looked around at the houses simmering in the heat and wondered if goat herders huddled next to buildings. Then, Floyd looked back at them and whispered, "Clear."

They walked around the house to the front door, and Floyd knocked five times. The door flung open almost immediately, and Ann stood there wild-eyed, looking around and beyond Floyd. Then, when she saw Ade, Ann bolted forward and hugged him.

"Oh, my dear boy she cooed as she rocked back and forth while holding him.

She leaned back and examined him. "You're poor squishy face. They already delivered some SkinRegen. I'm just glad you're home."

Ade marveled at her flushed cheeks and sparkling blue eyes. She looked just like she did before the market. "You look..."

"I'm fine. Just fine," Ann exclaimed. "There's nothing wrong with my AIRE."

"We need to get inside, Ann," Floyd insisted.

Movement from within the house drew Ade's attention, and his hand shot toward the handle of his pistol. Then his hair tingled, and tension eased as Nadia rushed up behind Ann. Her green eyes sparkled in the sun.

"We were so worried about you," Nadia exclaimed.

His mother stepped aside and allowed Nadia to embrace him. Completely dumbfounded, his arms hung at his sides. She kissed him on the cheek and stepped back.

"Inside," Floyd repeated, ushering them inward.

Nadia grabbed his hand and led him into the main room. Their fingers intertwined, and he opened his mouth to speak, but his jaw hung slack as he watched his mother jump into Floyd's arms.

"Thank you for getting him," she cooed. Then, with a curious look, she released him and stepped back. "What do you have under there?"

"Yeah, I wondered that too," Nadia added. "You look like a bunch of goat herders." She laughed.

Floyd stepped away from Ann without answering her question and stood eyeing Nadia. "Ade, who's this?"

Ann ran up behind Nadia and placed her hands on Nadia's shoulders. Her eyes scolded Floyd for his tone. "You behave. This is Ade's girlfriend from school. She came by after Ade didn't return to class, and we worried together."

"You know her?" Floyd asked Ade with a sideways glance.

"She's my girlfriend," Ade repeated.

Ann looked past them at Andrew, and her eyebrows raised. "Is this? No, he's so big!"

Floyd held up a hand and stepped between Andrew and Ann. "We got no time fer reunions, Ann. If ya got any more of Jack's stuff hidden, ya need to grab it. We're leaving in ten and ain't comin' back."

Ann's eyes narrowed on Floyd, and her body tensed. She crossed her arms. "I didn't cooperate with them, Floyd, if that's what you're thinking."

Floyd's grave expression turned curious. "What'dya mean?"

"CIU, I didn't say anything. That's not why they released him."

"Released him? They was gonna kill him!" Floyd roared.

"Kill him! They said it was a misunderstanding," Ann yelled back.

"Misunderstanding my backside. They was taking him to da camps. They'd have killed him if we didn't hijack da transport!"

The color drained from Ann's face. Her eyes darted around the room. "You what?" she gasped.

"You didn't get me message? We sent a currier." Floyd's brow lowered over his eyes, and his mustache twitched.

"Not from you! A member of the embassy came by. They said Ade was being released and credited our account for the misunderstanding."

Floyd's eyes widened as they darted about the room. He dashed across the room and looked out the window. The rigidity in his swift, deliberate movements fueled panic. A feeling of peril washed over the room before Floyd said a word. "Bravo, prepare to engage. It's a trap. Say again, prepare to go hot."

"What's going on here!" Ann exclaimed.

Floyd removed his poncho and returned to the middle of the room. "Andy, take up an overwatch on da roof."

Without question, Andy threw off his poncho and ran toward the roof access door.

"William?" Ann asked.

Floyd turned and planted his feet. "They lied to you. Grab the stuff ya hid. We leave in three. Ade-" Floyd paused, held up a finger, and tilted his head. "Say again, Bravo."

In one quick movement, Floyd spun the long lastergun to his front and gripped the handle. "Roger."

"How long?" Ade asked.

"Five minutes. Maybe less," Floyd answered. Then he looked at Nadia. "You should go."

Nadia turned and threw herself into Ade's arms. This time, he embraced her as she pressed her lips against his, and as quick as it had happened, she pulled back from his arms and moved toward the door.

"Be careful out there," Ann called after her.

Nadia glanced back as she pulled open the door and gave a timid nod. Her dark hair danced in the wind, and then she was gone.

Floyd pressed the charge button on his weapon and released the safety. "Ade, go grab the journal." Then, Floyd's fierce eyes turned to Ann. "Ann, things, now!"

Ann ran from the room, and Ade felt his muscles tense as his fingers fumbled for the handle of his gun. *Maybe they didn't get my message*... He stood frozen in the middle of the room. And then, without warning, Captain Young's voice sounded on his communicator.

"Ade, this is Young. As soon as the man on the roof returns, suggest an escape route out your mother's window into the alley. Continue one block east away from the house. There you will find Nadia. She has a hovercraft. Insist she comes back with you. I repeat, make sure Nadia is with you. She will assist in your extraction. Out."

"Ade, the journal," Floyd barked.

Ade rushed into his room and began fumbling through the books scattered across the floor. *Why didn't I clean this?*

Floyd rushed past him and leaned against the wall by the window. "Fug!" he screamed.

Ade jumped and whirled toward him. "They found Lucy," Floyd scowled. He spun, slid on a knee to the center of the window, and opened it. The wind turned the pages of the books on the floor as Floyd raised his lastergun and aimed it out the window. "All teams. Engage." And he fired his weapon.

A deafening blast shook the home, and windows shattered, raining down shards of glass on Floyd. Lasterfire erupted all around them. Rounds hissed and popped as they scorched the walls. Ade dropped to his stomach and buried his head in his hands. A large hand grabbed the back of Ade's vest, and he glanced up to see Floyd dragging him toward the main room. Ade pushed himself to his feet just before Floyd kicked over their table and shoved him behind it. Ann dove for cover beside Ade, and her large bag clanked off the floor. The roof access door swung open, and Andrew sprinted past them to a shattered window and began firing. "We're pinned!" Andrew screamed over the commotion.

Andrew ducked behind the windowsill as the lasterfire ripped through the home. Andrew looked desperately at Floyd. Floyd nodded and looked at Ann.

"Is that the stuff?"

Her eyes peeled open, she nodded rapidly.

"Slide it to me," Floyd ordered.

She slid the bag across the floor, and Floyd snatched it up, pulled a grenade from his vest, armed it, and dropped it in the bag. Then, rearing back, he heaved the bag out an open window.

"What are you-" Ann shrieked, but her scream was cut short.

The grenade exploded, and shards of augmentation parts shot through the air. The lasterfire lulled for a moment, and Ade peeked over the table to look out the smoldering window. His eyes widened as Captain Young stepped from behind a neighboring house and aimed his weapon. A laster round zinged high over Ade's head. He ducked back behind the table as rounds ignited the kitchen cabinets.

"What about the alley?" Ade yelled over the commotion. "It's out Mom's window!"

Floyd glanced toward Ann's room. His eyes returned to Ade, and he placed his hand over his mouth and yelled into it. Bravo, Bravo 1, service alley behind the house, advise."

Seconds passed like minutes as the rounds penetrated the walls, burning holes through the cinder.

"Keep low and go! Bravo, retrograde!" Floyd pulled another grenade from his vest and tossed it toward the destroyed window. It popped, and red smoke billowed through the destroyed housing unit. Ade and his mother scampered from behind the table and fell in behind Floyd and Andrew as they bounded into Ann's room and stacked against the wall beside the shattered window. Floyd cautiously peered out.

Lasterfire increased behind them. "Let's move," Floyd said, hopping the windowsill into the alley.

The narrow back alley, trapped between buildings, radiated heat. The sand pathways served only as utility access to water and air systems for the houses; however, many homes found the alley useful for discarding unwanted items like old chairs and cooling units.

The passage barely fit the four of them as they crouched behind a sand-blasted air control unit.

Floyd pointed toward the end of the alley. “We move as one. I’ll take point. Andrew, watch da rooftops. Ade, watch our six — behind us. Once we reach da road, we run. When that happens, don’t look back. Only look at da back of da person in front of you.”

They took swift, cautious steps with a slight pause behind anything that could provide cover should they be caught in an ambush. Floyd’s pistol swept before them like a metal detector, searching for prey. Nearing the end of the alley, movement caught Floyd’s attention. Sand kicked into the air as he dashed to the right, lowered to his knee, and took aim. Ann lunged forward and shoved the barrel of the weapon into the sand.

“Don’t,” Ann yelled at Floyd.

Ann stood and cautiously approached a person hiding behind a cooler box. She approached as though it was a cornered animal. “Nadia, is that you? It’s okay. You can come out.”

Nadia’s frightened eyes peered over the box. “Oh, honey, it’s okay,” Ann said calmly, moving forward and holding out her hand.

“Ann, we have to keep moving,” Floyd whispered.

“We’re not leaving her in this mess! Honey, come with us. It’s not safe.”

“We’re not-” Floyd attempted.

“We are, and that’s final,” Ann ordered. “Nadia, honey, you need to come with us.”

“But my skimmer?” Nadia pointed to a hovercraft parked across the road.

Floyd’s eyes widened. “Fine. She comes. Nadia, I need your fob.”

Nadia trembled as she slowly raised her hand and presented Floyd with the fob. He snatched it from her as a laster round zipped past Ade’s head. Without thinking, Ade spun toward the blast’s origin, raised his weapon, and fired two rounds toward the silhouetted figure on the roof above them. In slow motion, the rifle fell from the man’s hands as his arms flung back and his body fell forward. Ade watched in horror as the lifeless body fell into the alley. Behind him, Ade heard the commotion of movement, and he turned to find Floyd rushing toward a son who now only had one arm. Ade froze as Floyd scooped the convulsing body from the sand. His vision became blurry as he looked from Andrew to the disjointed body lying on the alley floor. Ade heard his name, but it didn't register until his mother's blurred face obstructed his view.

He heard his name again, distant and muffled. Then, his eyes focused on his mother, and the shouting around him became clear. He shook his head and looked from her to Floyd as he sprinted toward Nadia's skimmer with Andrew in his arms. Then, his eyes settled on Nadia. Her lips moved without sound.

"Ade, we need to go."

***

"Roger that, control. Fifteen minutes out," Floyd responded.

As the hovercraft descended deeper into the darkness, Ade wondered if Andrew was about to die. His breath was shallow as he lay motionless across Ade and Nadia's laps. The danger of his objective wormed through Ade's mind as he looked from Nadia to the charred nub of Andrew's arm. Ade tried to close his eyes, but each time, he saw the soldier's silhouette as his laster round ripped through him. *I wonder if he had kids.* The thought made him wince. He remembered the officer who delivered the news of his father. He felt the sorrow in his chest, but he also felt numb. He blinked and deactivated his Beta. Tears immediately began to stream down his dirty cheeks. Nadia reached for Ade's hand. Their fingers naturally entwined, and she pulled his hand to her chest. She gently guided his face with her other hand until their eyes met. Ade saw sympathy in her green gaze. "Just focus on me," she whispered, resting her head on his shoulder. "It wasn't your fault."

Ade found no relief in her words. He was now a killer. A reel of images flickered in his mind. Floyd, the soldier, Andrew, and his father. A sickening feeling joined his dread. *I failed to find Dad's journal.*

"You're still tense. I mean it. Not your fault."

"It's not just that," Ade whispered.

"What?"

"I forgot something," Ade said.

"What?" she whispered.

"My dad's journal," he whispered.

"Is it important?" Nadia whispered back.

"It's the last thing I have of his."

The skimmer was quiet for a moment. Most of the ride had been this way. Questions remained as each reflected on the events that had just transpired.

"If it's important, it'll be safe," Nadia said, patting his hand.

"How's he doing?" Floyd called from the front.

Ade jerked at the sound of Floyd's voice. "He's..." Ade began. "He-" Ade's voice cracked as he sniffled and began to cry.

Floyd turned to look at him.

"He's asleep," Nadia answered.

Floyd looked from her to his son and then turned back in his seat. His broad shoulders slowly raised and lowered as he took a breath to center himself.

Nadia turned and placed her lips by Ade's ear. "Activate your Beta. Set it to four. They won't be able to tell. They'll just think you're upset."

Ade sniffled, nodded, and accessed his interface. The calming effect poured over him like cool water on a hot day. He took a breath and wiped his eyes on his shirt. "Thanks," Ade mumbled.

Looking back at Andrew, Ade placed a hand on his forehead. "You're going..." He stopped his sentence. "Floyd, he's burning up," Ade stated.

Suddenly, Nadia gasped. "And his breath is quickening!"

Floyd did a double take over his shoulder.

The hovercraft surged forward as Floyd pushed it to top speed. "Union control. Incoming craft requesting emergency elevator access. Clearance code Alpha 1 Sierra 12 Yankee 6, repeat Alpha 1 Sierra 12 Yankee 6. Five minutes out." There was a brief pause. "Roger that. Request a crash cart along with medical. Emergency response 1. Repeat, Response 1."

Floyd looked back at Andrew and then at Ade. "Hold onto him. We're coming in hot."

Floyd maintained speed and tilted the nose of the hovercraft into a dive. The velocity pushed them back into their seats, and the hull cracked and groaned under pressure. Nadia's hand found Ade's, and she squeezed. "It's not a fighter," she gasped.

Ade saw the snow splinter in the distance. It slowly cracked as the hangar doors opened. The metal exterior of the vehicle began to rattle.

"Slow down!" Nadia screamed.

Ade's body tensed as he watched them plummet toward the small opening.

"William!" Ann screamed, and, with that, Ade closed his eyes and braced for impact.

A rush of air whooshed past the vehicle, and Ade's entire body sank as his heart and lungs felt like they were pushed up toward his throat. He was tipped back in his seat, and suddenly, the vehicle slowed. Ade opened his eyes just in time to see the elevator doors part and the craft hover and land within. The red lights illuminated everything around them, and the elevator descended before the doors had time to close. Ade quickly unlocked his harness and tried to find Andrew's pulse. Blinding light filled the elevator. Still adjusted to the dark, Ade shielded his eyes as the skimmer's doors were jerked open, and Andrew was pulled from his lap. Grief-stricken wails echoed through the elevator, and Ade saw Tonja being held back as her son was carried away on a stretcher. Floyd sprung from the driver's seat and ran to her. He fought through her flailing arms to embrace her. Tonja's hands turned to fists as she brought them down hard on Floyd's back.

"You...You promised to take care of him," she wailed. "You promised!" She fought to break his embrace but buried her head into his shoulder as they collapsed to the floor.

Still seated in the back with Nadia, Ade watched the events unfold through the front window. Ann had initially rushed from the vehicle to help but now stood watching with her arms wrapped around herself in a protective hug.

"Do they have it," Nadia asked.

Ade shook his head. "No. And the rest of the stuff mom had was blown up."

"How?"

"Floyd blew it up."

"Oh," Nadia sighed. "Proves she knows something."

Ade stared out the window and nodded. "Maybe. I don't know."

Nadia squeezed his hand. "We need to convince her to tell us. It's for her own good. Convince her, and we can all go home."

Ade looked into Nadia's soft eyes. She placed a hand on his face. "If we do this, I'm going back to Cranis also."

Looking at her, he thought of the man falling from the rooftop. He placed his hand on hers and nodded. "Okay," he said and forced a smile.

CHAPTER 21 | 5856-W24

Ade sat quietly in the corner of Andrew's hospital room. Once Andrew was stable, the arguing between Floyd and Tonja amplified until Tonja slapped Floyd across the face and stormed out of the room. After that, Ade was left alone with his thoughts while Andrew slept. For a few moments, the quiet was nice. But then his thoughts began tormenting him. He thought of the man on the roof. The silhouette crumpled to the ground in the bat of an eye. How easy it was to end a man's life. Ade cringed and shifted in the chair. He tried to focus on Nadia and how his hand felt in hers, but each time he relaxed, he saw the silhouette of a man. *It's not your fault.* He blinked twice and adjusted to max output. He eased back in the chair and glanced through the display options. Ade looked at the top row. Thus far, he'd only selected network and the quick access on the bottom. He focused on an icon of a crown. Ade selected the crown, and a box appeared on the bottom of the display, prompting an admin password.

"My dad used to tell me never to play with his guns," Andrew said in a raspy voice.

Ade quickly decreased the Beta and closed the interface. He found he was grinning as he looked up at Andrew.

"He told me about your scar to scare me," Andrew finished.

Ade stood and walked next to the bed. "Did it work?"

He let out a soft chuckle. "For a few years."

"Need anything, water?"

Andrew nodded and scanned the room. Then he motioned to a water pitcher and a glass on a table near the bed. Retrieving the glass, Ade filled it and offered it to Andrew. Without thinking, Andrew lifted his short, bandaged nub and winced in pain. He took a few breaths and looked at where an arm had been.

"It still feels like I could wiggle my fingers." Andrew shook his head and grabbed the glass with his remaining hand. "You know. After my dad told me that story, I always imagined your face to be far worse than it is," he said before taking a drink.

Unbeknownst to Ade, being around Andrew set him at ease. He felt an instant bond with him.

"I can't imagine yours was ever good," Ade responded.

Andrew spit the water back into the glass. "Wow, make fun of a guy who just got his arm shot off."

"The new one will be better. You'll probably shoot off the other arm just to match," Ade smiled.

Andrew let out a loud laugh and then cringed. "Don't...it hurts to laugh." He adjusted his position in the bed and leaned onto a pillow. "You're right. I'll get a prosthetic. It'll be better than the real thing. Plus, the ladies love a prosthetic. Not that you have anything to worry about."

Ade gave a somewhat guilty smile and moved back to the chair. "Amanda might like the new look."

Andrew nodded and sighed. "Yeah, I guess dinner will have to wait a bit."

In another life, they may have been best friends. An uneasy feeling befell Ade as he watched Andrew take a drink of water.

"It's weird, right? The fact that my parents never mentioned you or Floyd to me. I mean, Mom mentioned Uncle Bill, but she never told me anything about him."

"Oh, you don't know the half of it," Andrew said, taking a sip. "My mom hates your mom. And your dad hated my dad...even though they were all friends once. Come to think of it. That probably means we're destined to be great friends or mortal enemies."

Ade shrugged, prepared a fake grin, and looked back up. "Who says I don't hate you already?"

Andrew laughed again and winced in pain. "I said stop it."

Ade maintained his fake grin, but underneath, he felt a sick pang of guilt in his stomach. They sat for a moment in silence until the moment passed.

"But why, why do they hate each other?"

"It makes sense you wouldn't know. Your parents probably didn't always argue about it like mine. Dad would never admit it, but I think he had a thing for your mom back in the day. That and they talked on the halopad all the time. Well, at least until about a year ago. Then it stopped."

"They what? When? I never saw her talking to anyone."

Floyd stepped into the room, and Tonja rushed past him to Andrew's bedside. She brushed the hair from Andrew's face and kissed his forehead. Even from where Ade was sitting, he could tell she was on the verge of tears.

Floyd sat in the chair beside Ade. "Good to see him awake n' smiling."

Ade nodded and stared blankly at Andrew.

"Aunt Em wants to see ya," Floyd added. "Lieutenant Cooper will take ya there. Once yer done, you'll get yer new livin' quarters with your mum and girlfriend." He leaned over and patted Ade on the shoulder. Then he stood and joined Tonja by the bed.

As Ade rose, Andrew peeked through the crack between his parents and gave him a nod. Ade returned the gesture and exited the room to find a familiar face waiting for him. He paused, smiled at her, and looked past her. Finding nobody else, he looked down to see her glaring at him.

"Hey Amanda, is Lieutenant Cooper coming back?" Ade asked.

Her glare narrowed. "I'm the LT."

"Oh!" Ade responded, somewhat baffled. "No, I mean, of course you are. I mean, you're a Lieutenant; yes, I knew that. It's just... You know women aren't allowed in the military on Cranis."

"Survival of the species. Keep the breeders safe," she scowled. "You'd think they'd be past that crap by now."

"Yeah, it's dumb," Ade back peddled. "Women are awesome.

My mom could've been a soldier."

She cocked her head and gave him a wry look. "You mean the woman who helped start the Union?"

Ade stood and stared at her. "What?"

She rolled her eyes. "What, they don't teach history on Cranis? Never mind. The president's waiting."

With that, she turned and walked away. Ade needed to take long, uncomfortable strides to keep up with her short, swift pace. Then, looking down at her, he banged his head on a light.

"Hey, do you know what Em wants to see me about? Floyd didn't say."

"I'm not at liberty to say. President Miller made the request. That's all you need to know. Oh, and President Miller is a woman. Try not to act too surprised," Amanda scoffed.

"We've already met." Ade felt relieved when they turned the corner and came to the elevator. "What floor is this?"

"Five. Medical," she replied, pointing to a large five painted on the wall.

Ade nodded. He knew but was trying to change the subject. The doors slid open, and they entered in unison, which caused them to bump together as they attempted to squeeze through the door. Then they slid apart and stood awkwardly on opposite sides of the elevator, waiting for the doors to close. Ade glanced at her and looked her up and down.

"What?" Cooper asked, with her eyes straight forward.

"Oh, nothing."

"Don't give me that. I don't need to look at you to know it's something."

"You should visit Andy. It would cheer him up."

Her stony expression broke into a small smile. "Did he say that?"

Ade shrugged. "Not directly."

The doors slid open to an armed guard.

"I plan on visiting later today," she said, exiting into the reception area. Ade followed her and glanced at the garbage where he'd tossed his breakfast plate. When he looked back, he found Amanda talking to the receptionist. She looked back at him and rolled her eyes.

"Right through those doors. I'll be waiting."

"You're not coming?"

"You're a big boy. You don't need a chaperone," She smirked.

Ade looked from her to the door and tried to remember the sequence of stopping, saluting, and talking.

"Am I supposed to salute?" Ade asked.

Amanda scowled at him. "You're not in our military. You just walk in. Now. She's waiting."

Once again, he found himself before President Miller's sharp eyes. She stood as he entered the room, and with each step, he felt scrutinized beneath her gaze. When he stopped walking, he stood awkwardly, contemplating what to do with his hands. She leaned forward on the desk and stared at him.

"Did you get the book?" Miller asked.

Ade's eyes fell to the floor.

"I thought not."

"Everything happened so fast. I couldn't find it," Ade stated.

"Indeed. It seems you and our men walked directly into a trap. Although, what strikes me as strange is how rapidly they arrived at the target house. Almost like they knew you were there."

Ade froze. Maintaining eye contact, he clenched his jaw and let it relax as he considered a response, but before he could respond, President Miller continued. "My thought is-"

"They bugged the house," Ade interrupted.

"Perhaps, but Floyd's team swept the area for outgoing transmissions. None reported. However, just before you arrived at your mom's house, a military-grade communicator pinged the tower in the Labor District."

Ade stared at her. He was unaware they could track secured

transmissions. The revelation aggravated him.

"Let me ask you this," The President continued. "How well do you know this girl you brought with you?"

"My girlfriend," Ade stammered. "You think she had something to do with it?"

"Your thoughts, not mine. I simply asked how well you knew her. We ran her prints and confirmed she is registered at your school. But it's possible she was planted there from the beginning. A new boy in class, lost, with no friends on a new planet. It makes sense you'd quickly fall for such a pretty girl."

Ade felt his pulse increase. He then realized his Beta was reduced, and she was looking directly at him. It felt like the temperature in the room was swiftly rising.

"It's not her. Her grandfather died in the invasion. She even talked about trying to join the Union," Ade lied.

"That is exactly what a spy would tell you."

Her stare bore into him. It was as if she was looking into his mind and reading his inner thoughts.

"It's not her," Ade repeated. "Perhaps someone was watching the house? A drone or camera, or something."

"How can you be certain? Perhaps she was that person," Miller argued.

Ade felt as if he were backed into a corner. His eyes narrowed, and his face became warm. *How dare you question me after what you did.*

"Because I have more reason to hate the Union than she does. How dare you hang my dad's picture in the cafeteria!"

Their eyes locked.

"Your dad. Now he knew hate."

"He hated the Union."

"It certainly appeared that way," Miller replied.

"And you killed him." Ade stood staring at her. He didn't realize the weight of his words until their echo faded into the room's depths.

Miller's gaze narrowed on him. "I don't know who told you that, but they lied to you, Ade. Jack wanted to leave Cranis, and they killed him."

"That's ridiculous. He was their top engineer," Ade snapped.

"And they killed him," she repeated.

Ade flung his arm across her desk, knocking several items to the floor. "You're lying," he growled.

She didn't flinch. From his peripheral, he saw her hand move under the desk. Then he heard the doors behind him burst open. Ade whirled on his heels toward two men rapidly crossing the room with lasterguns aimed at his chest.

"On your knees!" one yelled.

Ade's eyes widened, and his hands shot into the air.

"I suggest you go peacefully, Ade," Miller said. "Go peacefully, and I'll assume this outburst was part of a misunderstanding. Fight, and I'll assume you're with the enemy."

Ade looked back at her as he lowered to his knees.

"You are an intelligent young man, but your temper may prohibit you from becoming a great man."

"Place your hands behind your head," the guard ordered.

That was stupid, he thought as he interlocked his fingers behind his head. The guard yanked his hands behind his back and zipped the cuffs into place. Ade suddenly realized that all the moments he regretted were due to his rage.

"Mr. Billings, I want you to think about one thing. If your father's research was so important to Cranis, why did he work on it at home? Wouldn't they want to protect something that valuable?"

Ade's eyes darted back and forth as he contemplated her question.

"Guard, escort Mr. Billings to main holding. Get him a meal and a proper mattress. If he tries anything, disregard my order and act as you see fit."

CHAPTER 22 | 5856-W24

Ade had always thought of his parents as two separate people. They were rarely together. Even when they were together, they appeared more like business associates than man and wife. As such, affection between a man and woman was unfamiliar to Ade. He had been infatuated with this or that pretty girl over the years but never felt protective of anyone besides his mother. Jack often traveled for work, and even at home, he spent most of his free time in the workshop. As a result, Ade grew up only truly knowing his mother. She often said the world's problems are only solved by genius, which is a lonely pursuit. Without men like his father, humankind would have been extinguished from existence. It was difficult for Ade to understand why his father was absent for what were, in a young boy's mind, all the moments of importance. He and his brother shared that fate, but their emotional response differed entirely. Ade sought those moments with his father. He craved them. Meanwhile, his brother Ethan seemed to push them away entirely.

Perhaps it was because Ade wanted to be like his father while Ethan wanted the opposite. Ade studied hard in school and strove to get the best grades, while Ethan barely did enough to pass. Not because he needed help understanding the concepts. Each assignment Ethan handed in received a perfect score. It was just that he turned in so few of them. In a way, Ade thought this was how Ethan tried to get back at their father — by failing to live up to his expectations. Nothing had felt as real for Ade as the moments spent with his father. It provided a feeling of completeness unparalleled by any other. That is until Nadia reached over and took his hand within hers. He lashed out to protect her, and now doubt had been planted in his mind.

His heart sank, and he looked around the cage with the barred wall. The dark, quiet cell left him trapped in his mind. Only a single bulb hung outside the cell. He may have only been there for hours, but they dragged on like days. He recalled the awful sound of bones breaking as the soldier fell into the alley. He shook the memory from his thoughts and concentrated on Nadia. He had only dreamed of being with a woman like her. Self-doubt stirred his thoughts. *What if Nadia is playing me?* He cringed at the thought. To him, it made more sense that the Union was the enemy. They were a group of terrorists. *Father always cursed them on the news. It wouldn't make sense if he were one of them, but why did he always work from home? Maybe he was just testing things to take to work.* Ade rolled away from the dim light and stared at the wall. *I need to talk to her.* The uncertainty was driving him mad. He accessed his interface and set his Beta to max output. *Just for a little while,* he thought. A sense of ease engulfed him, and he felt numb. He relaxed into the mattress. *Even their jail mattress is more comfortable than my cot.* Then he looked again at the box with the crown. *That must be the admin console.* He selected it again and watched the box pop up. *Admin Password... Did my dad put this here, or is it only for the install technician?* He entered his father's name, and it turned red. He entered his birthday — again red. He tried his mother's birthday and received the same result. Frustrated, he accessed his memory storage instead.

Floyd's footsteps pounded down the quiet hall and announced his presence far before reaching Ade's cell.

Ade exited his display. Swinging his legs over the side of the bed, he placed his bare feet on the stone floor. Then he ran his fingers through his thick hair and felt the area under his cheek where Captain Young slashed him with a knife. Ade prodded the soft, fresh skin before his hands fell back to his lap. The steps ceased, and Ade looked through the bars at Floyd. Floyd looked down at him and then casually leaned against the bars.

"Yer mum is okay. They gave her and yer lady friend a suite on level nine. Did they feed ya?"

Ade nodded.

"Good. Em gave orders to treat ya well," Floyd said.

"How's Andrew?"

"He's gettin' his fancy robot arm, so he's happy. They took him to Prosthetics before I came here."

Ade nodded and looked back to the floor. His eyes traced the lines made by carving the stone. He wiggled his toes. It was odd how warm it was beneath the frozen landscape above them.

"So, ya went a bit mad when Em questioned ya about yer lady."

Ade intentionally avoided eye contact.

"Ya mean what ya said? You think we killed Jack?"

Ade thought about the outcasts in school. They always stood defiant before everything and everyone who followed the rules. They always had half-shaved heads and shouted at the news as they ignored the teacher's instruction. Ade was always annoyed with their constant interruptions in class. He often wished they'd drop out of school and join the labor force.

"You're all alike. You are always blaming somebody else for your actions. It doesn't matter if you killed him or someone else killed him. He died because of the Union. It's your fault either way."

"Yer father set da meeting! He wanted to talk to us!" Floyd exclaimed.

"The news said the Union caused the blast," Ade said. "For all I know, you were the one who caused it."

Floyd's weathered face glowered, and he stared at Ade. His casual lean against the bars tensed as he pulled back and squared on him. He pointed and leaned his face close to the bars. "I'll give you that once," he spat. "Once!" He wiped the spit from his beard. "You don't think I mourn him! I think about him every day!" He began pacing the bars like a caged tiger, then abruptly stopped and stared at Ade. "All he wanted was for ya to be safe. That's why he called me."

Ade could feel Floyd's glare. He tugged on a loose thread from the mattress, and the seam unraveled. "And now he's dead," Ade sighed, looking back at the floor. "And I'm in a jail cell."

Floyd's long shadow crossed the floor numerous times before it stopped, and Ade heard a deep sigh.

"I can prove it. Ya can check me comms logs. I'd have never hurt a hair on that man's head."

"But why would Dad call you? Why not just have Mom call? Andy said you two talked all the time." Ade turned to look at Floyd. "Funny though, I never saw her on the halopad, Floyd."

"That's not important, Ade."

"Tell me when."

"Let it go."

As he looked at Floyd dancing around the subject, Ade thought of the painting hanging in his room. "No way," Ade whispered.

"What?"

"You talked when Dad and I went to watch the sunset." He and his father had gone to watch the sunset at least once a week. It became a ritual after his mother encouraged them to spend time together outside the workshop. He had always been grateful for those moments. *Maybe it was all a ruse to allow her time to call Floyd.*

"Your mum and I was always friends."

Ade was numb. He knew he should be mad, but he was calm. "Did Dad know?"

"Yer dad n' I had a complicated relationship."

"So, no. Dad didn't know." Ade turned his back on Floyd. "William, go. This conversation is over. Stop trying to help me."

Floyd stepped back from the cells at the sound of his name. A look of disappointment washed over him. He opened his mouth to speak but quickly closed it and nodded. But before edging out of view, he looked back over his shoulder. "I'll talk to Em. Ya may not want me help, but I made Jack a promise."

Ade listened to Floyd's footsteps fade as he trudged away. He slumped back onto the bed and turned toward the wall. *I want to go home.* He blinked to activate his breathing mod and quickly drifted to sleep.

***

Ade stirred and opened his eyes. The sun broke through green leaves, and light rays flickered on his mother's sandy blonde curls. She sat against the base of a schmekle tree while his father lay in the grass with his head in Ann's lap. Ann stroked Jack's hair, pushing it off his forehead. He could hear his brother, Ethan, playing in the field. Ade stood and strolled from beneath the tree to look out at the endless fields of green.

His father saw it first. He sat up, peering into the clouds. Ade heard it before he saw it. A screeching noise descended upon the quiet field — at first faint and then steadily growing louder. Ade looked to the sound to see a burning fighter hurtling toward them. His father reached for him.

Ade jerked awake. "Dad!" His eyes searched the dim cell for his father but landed on Lieutenant Cooper and two armed guards. The heavy door creaked on its hinges as she pulled the door open.

"You know, I planned something witty as I walked down here. You kind of ruined it," Amanda said, stepping into the cell.

Ade sat there staring at her. It didn't seem real. He could almost smell the burning dixothine from his dream.

"Ade," she said, snapping her finger.

His attention focused on her crinkled nose, and he rubbed the sleepiness from his eyes. "I'm up," he grumbled.

"Miller wants to see you again."

"Fug," Ade groaned, rolling his eyes.

She held out a pair of cuffs and pointed to them. "Now, be a good boy and hold out your hands."

Ade held out his hands without complaint or pause, and Amanda fastened the cuffs.

"Good. Do you want breakfast? The general put in the order,"

Amanda said.

Ade rolled his eyes again at the mention of Floyd. “I don’t want anything from that man.”

“If it weren’t for him, you’d still be in the cell. He went to the president on your behalf.”

“He doesn’t care about me. They want my dad’s work. That’s all anybody wants.”

She pursed her lips and then grinned. “Not true. I want the bacon you won’t eat.” She patted him on the chest, turned, and exited the cell.

Ade shook his head as two guards flanked him and escorted him down the dim hall after her.

Cooper slowed her typically brisk pace as Ade struggled not to hit his head on every obstacle hanging from the ceiling. He had yet to shake the dream that awoke him. He replayed it as they walked. In the wake of last night’s conversation, Ade knew it had meaning, but what it meant remained a mystery. *Perhaps it was a metaphor*. The one person he trusted betrayed the person he admired the most. *Maybe the plane was Floyd*. They stopped at the end of a hall and turned to face an unfamiliar red door. Amanda stepped forward, pushed it open, and entered the room. Ade’s eyes widened, and he gulped at what was beyond the door. One of the guards tried leading him in. When Ade didn’t move, the other pushed him into the room. In the center of the room was Ade’s doom — a large augmentation scanner that hummed and flashed as a technician calibrated the unit. It had two arms that moved vertically around a platform with an X in the middle. Several cords ran from the machine to a large box resembling an old-fashioned arcade machine.

Ade imagined the noose cinching around his neck as the platform gave way, and the last thing he heard was his strangled breath escaping him. He looked around the room for a way to escape. It was a small room — only one exit directly behind him. Amanda joined the technician as the guards stood in the doorway.

"We're ready," The technician stated.

"President's orders. We need to scan you," Amanda said, pointing at the X on the floor. Stand there, and the machine will rotate around you."

Ade didn't move. He stared at the spot marked on the floor. It didn't matter what or who he believed. If they scanned him, he was dead. "What is this thing?"

With a look of disdain, Amanda beckoned him forward. "You know what it is, Ade. Just step forward."

Ade glanced back over his shoulder at the guards.

"On the X," the guard ordered.

When he was young, his mother sang him the same song every night. It was an old song from Earth that had carried across the galaxy to tuck him in at night. She perched on the edge of the bed, lovingly stroking his hair as she sang. Ade didn't know why this was the time to remember that song. It seemed like his mind was trying to force him to focus and think.

Ade shuffled forward as the song looped in his mind. Eyes darting around the room, he inched closer to the scanner until one foot was on the platform. "Are you sure this thing is safe?"

"Step on the X, Ade. It's safe," Amanda said, growing impatient.

"It looks ancient. I read this model causes cancer."

"Just step on the X!" a guard barked.

"I thought you didn't know what it was," Amanda countered.

Ade heard the unmistakable sound of the illustrious General Arfey approaching. Floyd marched down the hall and into the room. Ade's eyes remained focused on the wall as he stopped somewhere behind him.

"What's all the yelling?" Floyd inquired.

Ade didn't flinch and continued to stare straight ahead.

"Your boy is afraid of the scanner," Amanda said, nodding toward Ade. "He thinks it'll cause cancer."

"Well, that's just rubbish," Floyd huffed as he walked around the machine and looked Ade in the eye. "What-" he began but quickly stopped himself. Floyd glanced at Cooper and then back to Ade. His eyes fell to the X on the floor, and he shook his head. "Here, let me take over," Floyd said, motioning to the controls.

Floyd brushed past Ade, and his large frame forced the two women away from the monitor as he edged in front of them. "Ade, did you get breakfast?"

Ade didn't speak.

Cooper shook her head. "No, he refused."

Floyd studied the screen for a moment and looked back at them. "He refused bacon?" Then he looked at Ade. "You refused bacon? I had it flown in for ya," Floyd said, shaking his head. Then he glanced back at the screen, paused, and looked at Amanda and the technician. "Why don't ya go grab some breakfast? Get some of that bacon before it goes cold. I'll take care of this."

"You're the boss," Amanda shrugged.

The technician looked from Floyd to the machine and back at Floyd.

"I was using this here machine before ya was even born. Go with the LT. that's an order."

The technician saluted, and Floyd returned a two-finger salute.

As the technician and Amanda passed the guards, Floyd pressed two buttons on the screen, the scanner's lights changed color, and an electrical hum surged through the old wiring.

Ade stood perfectly still.

"Yous can wait in the hall. I think yer making him nervous. Plus, I can handle him if he gets froggy," Floyd ordered the guards.

Ade clenched his jaw.

The two men exited without question, and the red door latched shut.

"Ade, yer gonna have to step on that platform. President's orders. We need to log a scan before ya see her. Trust me."

Ade continued to stand there.

"Ade, you gotta get scanned. If you don't step forward, I'll have to call the guards back, and they'll put you there. We don't want that."

"I'd like to see them try," Ade said dryly.

"Deactivate your Beta or turn it down," Floyd sighed.

Ade's eyes grew wide. *Fug.* He knew as soon as Floyd said it. He forgot to decrease the level.

"Once, Jack and I had a field trip in school. We was outside da Labor District in the desert lookin' at the water converters. Being kids, we decided to catch desert creatures and have them fight. I went and found the biggest scorpio I could find. I thought without a doubt that anything your dad found would lose. And then he came back with this little two-headed lizard, and I laughed. We dug a hole in the sand and threw them both in. My scorpio kept jabbing that lizard, and I kept rooting, thinkin' I was winning as that darn lizard just kept running in circles. My scorpio musta jabbed that thing twenty times, but it kept running. Finally, my scorpio got tired and just walked away. My hootin' stopped as it settled into the sand, but that darn lizard kept running. Then, when it seemed it ended in a draw, that lizard attacked my scorpio and tore its darn tail off. I'd never seen anything like it. And Jack, Jack just started laughing. Ade, I know you're da lizard. Now step on the damn scanner so we can move on."

Ade blinked and set his Beta to 3. Suddenly, he felt more like the scorpio. Ade had been careless and let his guard down. The lizard knew he was immune to the venom of the scorpion's sting, so he waited until it was time to strike. Ade may have been the lizard, but he lost the element of surprise when Floyd looked him in the eye.

"What if I said you were wrong?" Ade asked.

"I've looked enough young men in the eye while a Beta was active. I'd call ya a liar."

Ade exhaled. His fate was sealed. He stepped forward onto the X and looked at the wall. The arm of the scanner glowed blue as it rotated around his body and stopped above him before slowly beginning its descent back toward its starting position. Ade trembled. After experiencing the Beta at its maximum level, Beta 3 felt inadequate for this tense situation. Then he began to shiver. It was as if the temperature had dropped ten degrees while he stood there.

The room became silent as the arm of the machine settled to the floor and deactivated. Ade didn't even look back to see Floyd's reaction.

He stood in unnerving silence, waiting for Floyd to say something. Instead, all that he heard was a tapping on the screen. Then Floyd's footsteps approached. They sounded quieter than usual as he walked up behind Ade. Ade reluctantly turned to face him and looked up at the sullen features of Floyd. Floyd drew a large knife from his belt, and Ade tensed and closed his eyes.

"Give me your wrists," Floyd said.

Ade cringed and slowly raised his hands.

Floyd quickly sliced one restraint. Ade's eyes shot open in disbelief as Floyd twirled the knife over in his fingers and cut the other hand free.

Floyd's expression was stone, and his shoulders slumped forward. "We're going to see Em. Leave yer Beta at 3. That's the max ya can go without anyone knowing." Floyd crossed the room, pushed the door open, and exited the hallway. Ade followed at his heels, and the two guards fell in behind them. The nervous anguish of wondering what came next ate at him. He had been scanned. And yet he walked free. His hands swung freely at his sides.

Behind him, Ade could hear the two guards whispering.

"I heard they tracked them."

"No, that's impossible."

"It's what I heard. One or two days, max."

"Do we evacuate?"

"They've already started moving the machinery. I don't know if we're leaving."

"So, we're going to fight?"

"I think so."

Floyd stopped in his tracks. And Ade nearly ran into him.

"I think he heard us."

"Yes, I can hear ya," Floyd blared as he turned toward the soldiers.

Ade ducked and jumped to the side. He was getting used to seeing Floyd this way — jaw clenched, brow lowered, and nostrils flaring.

"Let me ask ya boys this. Did you join the Union to fight?" Floyd said, approaching the soldiers.

Their heels snapped together, and the duo saluted and spoke in unison. "Yes, sir. To fight for what was once ours."

"I didn't ask ya to repeat our damn propaganda. I asked ya if you joined to fight," Floyd snapped.

They stood stupefied by his question. Then, one piped up. "Yes, sir!

Floyd took a step forward. "What's yer name?"

"Private Colbert, sir."

Floyd's eyes drifted up and to the left. "Yer mum and dad were Union, yeah?"

"Yes, General, both officers."

Floyd looked back at him, and Ade saw an expression he'd not seen before. His jaw was set, and his brow stiff above slightly wide eyes. Floyd appeared both angry and disappointed at the same time.

"We all think we're one thing till we figure out we're another," Floyd said, turning back to the soldiers. "I didn't join to fight. I joined fer a friend. I joined because her father was killed by a government that didn't protect its people." He looked back at Ade. "Ann Billings believed all people deserved the right to be safe. And I believed in her." Then Floyd squared on the soldiers. "We're not here to get back what we lost. We're here to make it better than it ever was. I want ya to think about that. We're gonna find a fight, and it'll be soon. And when we find that fight, yer gonna have to kill or be killed. Thinking you want to fight is different than being forced to." Again, he looked to Ade. "He's the only one of ya that knows what it's like ta be forced to fight. And he killed a man to save me son. So, do I think we're ready? I think we'll only know that when da enemy is knocking on da door, and yer only option is to fight or flee. I trained ya to the best of me ability, but when the time comes, it's yer trigger to pull. You have to decide if your home is worth fighting for. I want ya to think about that before the time comes. You two are dismissed." With that, Floyd turned and continued down the hall.

Ade's eyes followed him, and he looked at the two soldiers. Dumbfounded, they glanced at each other. Then, one looked at Ade in awe while the other shook his head.

"Was that a pep talk?" the smaller soldiers asked.

"You saved Captain Arfey," The other marveled.

Ade glared at them, turned, and hurried after Floyd.

When he caught up to him, he walked beside him. Neither said a word as they entered the elevator. Ade turned, glanced down the empty hall, and realized he could have run. There were no armed soldiers to stop him. Instead, he followed Floyd into the elevator.

The doors closed, and as the elevator began to rise, Floyd hit the hold button, bringing the elevator to a stuttering halt.

"Ya didn't run. Thought you would," Floyd said.

"There's nowhere to go."

"Did ya tell 'em we were coming?" Floyd asked.

"Who?"

Floyd stepped from Ade's side and confronted him. "Don't play dumb. Not now."

"No, I didn't. I swear," Ade insisted.

"They installed a Beta, a military-grade AIRE, a Sata 20, SFA, and an Iver. All standard for a field operative. Did I miss anything?"

Ade looked from Floyd's fierce eyes to the floor. *I'm the scorpion*. "HEP," Ade muttered. "It was a birthday present."

"Bloody hell," Floyd gasped. "It didn't show on the scan!"

"Dad's work. New coating."

"Almighty," Floyd gasped. "And the rest?"

"Dad installed the Sata and SFA; the legs are from you, and the rest was Cranis."

"Does you mum-"

"She doesn't know. About any of it."

Floyd's brow furrowed, and his eyes narrowed on Ade. "I'm gonna ask one more time. Did ya tell them we was coming?"

"No! I couldn't. I haven't even been able to network!"

Floyd looked away. With his hands on his hips, he tapped his foot. Then, his eyes returned to Ade. "If I find out yer lying to me..."

"I swear. It all happened too fast. I tried when they were shooting but couldn't get through."

Floyd grimaced, and his mouth opened to continue his questions, but then he blinked twice. His eyes glanced at the elevator stop button and then at his watch. "Secure, just having a chat. There in a wink." Floyd clenched his jaw and looked back to the button. He released the stop button and stood back beside Ade. "We're movin'. Over and out." Exiting his comms, he glanced at Ade. "This stays between us. I replaced yer scan. Anyone else finds out, and I won't have to kill ya. They will."

The doors slid open to four men with rifles aimed at the door. Without a thought, Ade ducked behind Floyd.

"At ease," Floyd said, slowly raising his hands. "We're all on the same team."

"The fire is smokey," A guard stated.

"It burns my eyes," Floyd responded. And the four soldiers lowered their weapons.

Ade peeked around Floyd, looking for fire as the two soldiers in the middle stepped back, allowing access to the presidential suite. "We thought maybe you had some trouble."

Floyd chuckled. "Nah. No trouble at all. I just had a word with me mate. He gotta bit carried away last time," Floyd said, exiting the elevator.

Ade followed closely behind.

"Don't do stuff like that. Makes ya look guilty," Floyd whispered, pushing the doors to the presidential suite open.

"I just reacted. I-"

Ade's mouth gaped as the room's commotion buzzed in his ears. It had only been a short time, but the quiet presidential chamber had transformed into a war room. A red carpet split the room, and workstations flanked the carpet leading to the president's desk.

Halo monitors now lit the previously dim room. In addition, the wall on the left side of the room displayed live video feeds from around the compound.

"What happened?" Ade asked, baffled.

"Em wanted this setup as a control center in case of a siege. It's safer here than in da hangar."

Ade glanced around the room but didn't see the president. "Where's the president?"

"Just follow my lead," Floyd responded as they stood before her desk.

The massive Union banner behind her desk extended from the floor to the ceiling. Ade stared at it while waiting. Then, the banner began to move. Floyd slid his feet together and saluted as President Miller pushed the banner aside and emerged through a narrow passage in the wall.

She waved dismissively at Floyd's salute and eased into the chair behind the desk. "At ease, Floyd."

Her previously razor-sharp eyes seemed dulled by the dark circles framing them. Ade surveilled the room around them, not eager to look her in the eyes after their last encounter.

"Well?" She asked — straight to the point.

"He's clear, jus da legs I got em for his birthday. Still think he could be useful."

She nodded and began clearing a space on the desk. "Maybe.

Only time will tell." She reached into a drawer and retrieved a bottle of brown liquid and two glasses. Then she glanced at Ade and grabbed one more glass. She poured some brown liquid into each and pushed two across the desk. "You know about the other two?"

"Yes, mum. Heard this morning. Both clear."

She nodded again, lifted her glass to Floyd, and took a swig. A shudder surged through her, and she winced as her lips puckered. "Desperate times, General."

Floyd took a step forward, raised the glass to the President, and dumped the contents of the glass down his throat in one gulp. "Indeed, mum." He set the glass back on the table and looked at Ade.

Hesitantly, Ade lifted the glass and sniffed the foul odor.

"Drink it, lad. It'll put hair on all your man bits. Maybe yer back too."

Ade cringed and looked from the president to Floyd.

Floyd winked at him.

Ade had never tasted alcohol. Jack forbade it — he insisted it "Dulled our greatest weapon." Ade had always been curious about the effects. He knew firsthand that Ethan partook. However, a boy's first drink seemed like something a son should experience with his father — a rite of passage. He downed the drink, gasped, cringed, and set the glass on the desk. His insides became warm, and he withheld a curse.

"I don't need more hair," Ade coughed.

Floyd grinned and looked back to the president. "See, even now, we can have a little fun."

"You must sleep like a baby," Miller said. She shook her head and refilled two of the glasses. "Where are we at?"

Floyd grabbed the drink and repeated the process. Compared to the President's face, it was almost like he was drinking water. "We're at phase two, bravo."

"Troops ready?"

"We're ready, mum."

Taken aback, Ade looked at Floyd. He was missing something

important. Ade thought about two soldiers in the hallway.

"You disagree?" Miller asked.

Lost in his thoughts, Ade didn't realize she was talking to him until the silence forced him to look toward her curious eyes.

"Oh, yes. I mean, no. Are we getting attacked?"

"We," the president repeated. "Interesting, you'd say we."

His head a bit light from the drink, Ade stared at her for a moment. "Is that a yes? Did they follow us? Shouldn't we be evacuating? My mom, Nadia?"

Her hands clasped before her. "We cannot do a mass evacuation. As far as we know, they do not know our exact location. Your trio is clean, so we imagine they followed you. Since only one craft was seen entering our airspace, you lost them before arriving at the base. This means they only know our general whereabouts. If we evacuate everyone, they'll have no doubt as to our position."

"But they're coming," Ade persisted.

"Yeah, mate, they're sniffing like a horny dog. They'll find us eventually," Floyd said.

Ade sat erect in his chair and looked between them. They looked far too comfortable in the face of an imminent attack. Then he thought about the soldiers escorting him. *There is no way. They'll be slaughtered.*

"William thinks you could be useful, but we never got to finish our conversation."

Ade glanced at Floyd. "Floyd said he came to meet my dad. But I know it was a Union bomb that killed him. It doesn't make sense."

Her eyes remained focused on his every move. Then she shook her head. "Oh, my dear boy. You've got a lot to learn about power. They show and tell you whatever supports their narrative. It's the same with JSN here. They make you think we're the bad guys, but Cranis took our home. Not because we're evil or we planned to invade. They took our home for a resource – so they could hold the power. We're the bad guys because that's what they've taught you your entire life. It's not complicated. If you'd never seen the sky and I told you every day it was green, you'd believe me. Why? Because, first, you don't know any better, and second, you don't have a reason not to trust me. Jack knew there would always be war here. People will forever fight over things they determine are valuable. Silly that nobody listened. Things may have been different if we had. If he hadn't left." She looked at the table and ran a finger around the lip of her empty glass.

Ade hung his head. "I wish he was here." Then he shook his head and looked at Miller. "I spent my whole life thinking he hated you, and now you're telling me he was union," Ade said plainly. "He said it every time the Union was mentioned on the halofeed."

President Miller sighed, and a grin curled her lips. "He was quite verbal about his dissatisfaction with our antics. He contacted me many times over the years. His greatest fear was that our tactics would put you in danger. Just about everything that man did was to protect you. I think that's why he was trying to leave Cranis. He knew they were coming for him."

"He-" Ade began to object, but his thoughts drifted, and his eyes fell to the desk.

His father was working in the shed that rainy night. He'd said there were important things to finish up for work before Ade's match. So, Ade sat quietly before a chessboard, studying potential strategies. It was his father that taught him the game. Jack said it was a game as old as human existence — that entire wars were waged with pieces on a board, not with people. At a quarter to seven, Ade dressed in the suit his father helped him purchase and sat waiting with his mother. The nerves set in as it drew closer to the time to leave. Ade had never won a championship. It wasn't for lack of knowledge of chess theory. It had more to do with patience. His opponents' slow, second-guessing play would easily frustrate him and throw him off his game. However, with age and practice, Ade believed this was the night to overcome his previous failures. Just as Ade was about to check his watch, he saw his father burst into the house. Ade took a deep breath and stood. His father brushed past him and frantically shuffled through things in the front closet. He tucked a jacket under his arm and lifted his work bag from the closet.

Ade's eyes narrowed on him. "Dad, we're going to be late!"

Jack paused and looked from Ade to Ann. "I can't. I have work; it's on the other side of town. Can you get a cab?"

Ann put her hands on her hips. "It's the championship match, Jack."

"I'm sorry. I must go," Jack stated.

Jack moved to kiss Ann on the cheek, but she pulled away. He stood for a moment staring at her, then turned his frantic gaze toward Ade. "Ade, I left my notebook in the workshop. Can you grab it and bring it in?"

"Don't you dare," Ade hissed.

Jack looked between them, sucked in his lips, and exhaled through his nose. His eyes fell to the floor, and he nodded. "I have to go. I love you both."

Neither returned the sentiment as he turned and hurried out the door.

Ade had been too angry to notice then, but Jack never said I love you — a fact he overlooked until now. He never cried after the death of his father. However, as he sat before President Miller, tears began streaming down his face.

"Jack made contact a week before his death. He offered intelligence in trade for asylum and arranged a meeting with Floyd to organize an extraction for his family," Miller said.

Ade sucked in air and looked up at the ceiling. Then, exhaling, he bit his lip and looked back at President Miller. "Did Mom know about this?"

"Jack asked that we keep our dealing private until all terms were in place. She didn't know," Miller answered.

Ade leaned forward in the chair and stared at the floor. He could feel them both looking at him, and he looked up at the empty glass and then at the bottle. President Miller poured another drink and pushed it across the desk toward him. He reached for it and quickly downed the contents. It burned going down his throat, and he suddenly felt lightheaded.

Floyd extended a hand to place on Ade's back. "Ade, I know yer confused, but-"

"It's fine, Floyd. It's like you so eloquently stated. They haven't found us yet," Miller interrupted.

"Em, it ain't that. I think-"

"We all need to think. I, too, would find it difficult to trust the word of someone who imprisoned me. But, Ade, I assure you that this is accurate. I can provide the call logs for further evidence, but you must decide for yourself the truth you chose to believe," The president said, standing. "I will need to know soon. If you decide we are your enemy, I don't wish to worry about you while preparing our defense. An enemy outside is better than an enemy within."

She stood and turned to walk away, then paused and returned to Ade. "One thing," Miller began.

"Yes, ma'am," Ade said quietly.

"What did your father say about us?"

Ade paused, glanced around the room filled with war, and recalled their conversation after watching breaking news about a military convoy attacked by Union troops. "He said a sense of entitlement misguided you, and you fought for something that wasn't great to begin with."

President Miller let out an amused laugh. "God, I admired that man. And to think, Marshal wanted to make him his number two."

She walked back toward the long banner and disappeared behind it. Ade sat for a moment, considering her words. "I need to speak to my mother."

CHAPTER 23 | 5856-W24

When Ade was young, his best friend's name was Connor. Connor was a husky boy with duck lips, large wandering eyes, and a shaved head. Jack disapproved of the friendship, as Connor was not one to elicit intelligent thought — or so Jack said. Ann and Jack argued this point repeatedly as Connor would run through the house, knocking things over while they played good guys and Unionists. Ade was always the smartest kid in class. It didn't matter if Connor was on the opposite side of the spectrum. Once, on a warm summer day, they raced into the house; Ade was pursuing the Union scum and launched a barrage of foam bullets at his enemy. One such shot happened to impact a hand-thrown pot from Jaber and initiated a reaction that led gravity to pull the pot toward its demise. Although simple in its craftsmanship, it had been a gift to Ann from her father. Jack was furious, and as he stood fuming, Connor stepped forward and took the blame.

Ade stood beside Floyd and stared at the elevator doors, thinking of his childhood friend. *If only I had someone to trust.*

The elevator chimed, and the doors opened to the smug sneer of Lt. Amanda Cooper.

"Didn't get arrested this time, huh?"

"Leave da lad alone," Floyd ordered. "He's had a rough go. Escort him to his mum's new flat. You know where?"

"Yes, General."

"Ade, I'll look in on ya later. Yeah?"

Ade nodded. He only heard half of what Floyd said.

Floyd and Amanda traded spots, and a brief silence forced Ade to look at Amanda.

She raised one eyebrow and pursed her lips. "You cost me twenty drachma."

"Huh?"

"After that stunt with the scanner, I bet the other two you'd get arrested again. I lost."

"Oh," Ade muttered.

"Jeez. It was just a joke," she said, rolling her eyes.

They stood in silence, descending underground. Ade felt his stomach in knots. Nothing added up correctly. His father worked through every significant event in Ade's life. *But who was he working for — Cranis or himself?* Ade had always assumed Jack hated the Union because he constantly complained about them. He would have never thought that Jack's verbal slander was directed at the group's leadership rather than their antics. *If they're telling the truth, then what? Cranis lied? Maybe they didn't know. Nadia wouldn't know. But can I trust her? Is everything I think and know wrong?*

The doors opened, and Ade followed Amanda from the elevator.

"So, you saved Andy's life?" Cooper inquired.

Ade heard words, but they did not register. "What?"

"You saved Andy's life," Cooper repeated.

"Oh. Not really."

Ade tried not to think about it. His thoughts were already spiraling, but in a blink, there was the soldier's silhouette.

Amanda slowed until they were walking side by side. He knew she was looking at him but pretended he didn't notice.

"Looking at you, I'd never guess you were capable of it."

He gave her a quick sideways glance. "I don't want to talk about it."

Amanda shrugged. "In training, they gave us mind exercises. They may be able to help you."

"I doubt it," Ade said dismissively.

"Maybe. Talk about it then. I'm a good listener. I was first in my class..."

Do I confront Mom about Floyd? Would it do any good? May-

be she's still Union. But why bring the tools? So Cranis wouldn't get them?

"Ade?"

He looked up as she stopped and pointed to a door. "Home sweet home," Amanda chimed.

He brushed past her and quickly closed the door behind him without a pause.

"You're welcome," he heard through the door.

The room was familiar yet entirely different. It had the same basic layout as Floyd's home but lacked the personal features and warmth that make a place home. Ade looked around the empty dwelling. He circled through the main room and peered into the back rooms. The only evidence of their occupation were unmade beds and clothing folded atop the dressers. His mother's scarlet scarf was at the top of one of the piles. He entered the room and stood silently observing the room's contents. *I wonder if she smuggled anything else here, maybe in her pockets. She wouldn't have time to hide it well.*

He carefully lifted things from the pile of clothing, checking pockets. Finding nothing, he glanced back around the room. Ade moved to the bed and dropped to his knees. He lifted the mattress and searched for anything hidden between the mattress and the spring. Then he leaned forward, fell onto his hands, and looked under the bed.

The dwelling door creaked open on rusty hinges, and laughter filled the home. Ade lurched back from the bed and, in doing so, lost his balance and fell into the nightstand. He saw the lamp fall in slow motion. He winced just as it crashed to the floor. It only took one breath, and his mother was hovering over him. He didn't need to look up to know she was there. She had always been there during these moments.

His first instinct was to clean up the mess, so he reached for a large piece of glass.

"Don't," his mother warned.

Ade's hand stopped just shy of the jagged ceramic. With a deep sigh, he sat back on his heels and stared at the broken shards.

"I think I saw a broom in that room by the bathrooms," said Nadia.

Ade's eyes shot up from the pile to see Nadia peering over his mother's shoulder. His face turned red, and he looked back at the mess.

"I'll go grab it," Nadia added.

Ade listened to her steps as she crossed the room and reopened the creaky door.

"Ade, what's going on? Are you -"

"Mom, I need to ask you something. It's important."

The room became silent, and as their eyes met, Ann took a step back, stood in the doorway, and crossed her arms. "Go ahead."

"Was Dad Union?"

Ann sighed and looked at the floor. "Is that why you got so angry?"

"She said Dad called a week before he died."

"I didn't know anything about that," Ann replied.

"Well, was he?"

Ann shook her head. "It's not that simple, Ade."

Ade glowered at the broken glass. "Mom, I just need to know the truth."

"What was that?" came Nadia's sweet voice.

Ade's eyes shot up from the pile, and he watched Nadia cross the room.

"Oh, nothing, honey," Ann stated. "Just family stuff."

Ade clenched his jaw. Frustration swelled at her deflection.

She stepped around Ann, crouched, and placed her hand on Ade's arm. Their eyes locked. Then, she gave him a slight nod as if a silent understanding had been made.

"I'll clean this up," she said. Then she turned her head and spoke over her shoulder. "I don't know how you could ever keep a clean home with this one around. My parents couldn't stand one minute with a mess like this in the house," Nadia said, and she stood and began sweeping up the mess. "I mean, with everything Ade told me, he and Jack must have made quite the mess," Nadia continued.

"Our house was always clean. I made sure of it," Ann objected.

Ade looked at Nadia as she knelt and swept the last bits of broken glass into a dustpan.

Nadia stood and smiled. "Of course, Mrs. Billings. It just seems like there'd always be a bunch of sciencey stuff around. Ade told me Jack was pretty important. Always working on stuff."

"Not inside the house. I made Jack keep that stuff outside."

Nadia took a moment to consider this while playfully swinging the broom in a pendulum motion. "Even the important stuff?"

"Everything. No exceptions. He-"

Then why bring his stuff here? Ade became bitter as she talked about his father. *Maybe things would have been different if he had been allowed in the house.*

"Even the prototype?" Ade interrupted.

"The what? Ade, I-"

"Why bring dad's stuff then? You didn't even want it in the house."

Ann's brow raised as her eyes became wide, then quickly narrowed. "That woman," Ann scowled, and her eyes darted back to him.

"Mom, I know."

"Know, know what exactly?" Ann demanded.

"I know you talked to Floyd every time Dad and I went to watch the sunset. Explains why you never wanted to come with us."

Ann's jaw dropped. "That's not fair! Your father despised..." She stopped, pressed a finger to her lips, and shook her head. Ade could see the tears forming in her eyes. "Floyd is my friend. He was always there for me."

"Is that why you brought Dad's stuff? To give to Floyd," Ade followed.

"No! I brought those for Ethan. Once he gets released."

"What about the prototype?"

Ann's arms flew into the air in a moment of exasperation. "Everyone's asking about this stupid prototype. I don't know. Okay. Your father barely talked to me. You probably know more than I do!"

"That makes no sense," Ade fumed. "Fine, was Dad-" He stopped and glanced at Nadia. "Was any more of Dad's stuff brought here?"

"Why do you care so much? You knew those things were in the boxes. So why does it matter now?"

Ade thought she was too smart for her own good, and he shook his head. "Because, Mom," Ade said, vexed.

"You just want something of your father's? Is that it?" Nadia asked.

Mom's not the only one, Ade thought. "Yes."

His mother's eyes softened. Then she closed her eyes and shook her head. Tears traced her cheekbones and pooled at her jaw before falling to the floor. "I'm sorry, honey. Everything I had was in the bag Floyd threw. There's nothing left."

Ade hung his head. *She doesn't know about the prototype.* He began pacing while looking at his feet. Stopping before his mother, he placed a hand on her shoulder. "It's okay, Mom. I'm sorry."

Her teary eyes met his, and she nodded. "Me too."

"I need to clear my head," Ade said. "I'm going to go for a walk."

"Do what you need to, honey," Ann sniffed. "I'll make some coffee for when you get back."

"I'll go with you," Nadia interjected.

"Oh, honey. Ade might want some-"

"It's fine, Mom," Ade interrupted.

When they entered the hall, and the door closed, Nadia turned to face him. Before he could speak a word, her soft lips pressed against his. Ade's racing thoughts were too scattered to comprehend her actions, and he stood there.

Then, she stepped back to look him in the eye. "Then it's your brother."

"Maybe it was destroyed."

Nadia nodded in agreement. "Maybe, but either way, it's not here."

"Can you contact Captain Young?" Nadia asked.

Ade shook his head. "I don't have the network password."

"It's fine. There is an escape tube. It's at the back of the armory. We just need to get-"

"Nadia, I need to-" Movement down the hall caught Ade's attention.

"Oye, waiting for me in the hall, are ya?"

His booming voice caused Ade to lurch and step on Nadia's foot. She winced, then tensed at the sight of Floyd. Then she took a breath, released his hand, and stepped away. "Hi, Floyd," she chirped.

"Sorry for da interruption, but I need to talk to yer feller."

"Oh," Nadia said, somewhat disappointed. "Will you be long? Ade was going to take me for cake."

"I do believe da cafeteria is closed, love. More pressing matters than cake at da moment. Why don't ya see to Ann? Tell her we're gonna be evacuating soon. Make sure you two is ready."

"We're evacuating?" Nadia questioned.

"Yep, our friends to da east are paying us a visit. No need to be frightened. We got a plan. Now go tell Ann," Floyd said, shushing her away.

Nadia looked between Ade and Floyd, nodded, and entered the apartment. The door closed, leaving Ade and Floyd alone in the dimly lit hall. Ade kicked at the floor as he waited for Floyd to speak. Then they spoke at once.

"I-"

"Time-"

"Sorry," Ade said.

"Time's up. President needs ta know."

Ade glanced up at him and quickly looked away. Floyd had covered for him, and it was difficult to understand why. "Andrew said Dad hated you."

Floyd sighed and placed his hand on his hips. "He didn't agree with me joinin' da military."

"Why?"

"He wanted me to come with. Leave it all and move to Cranis."

"Why didn't you?"

"Cause this is me home. I told him that. He told me I was throwing me life away. We got into a dandy of an argument, and he gave me an ultimatum — come with or lose me best friend. I think he was just scared. But yer dad," Floyd said with a soft chuckle. "He always stuck to his word."

"But why you? That night. Why?"

"Jack and Em never saw eye to eye. I think he knew I'd do my best to keep ya safe. At least, that's what I was hopin' he was thinking. Who knows. Ol' Jack was always three steps ahead. Till it caught up to him."

Ade was silent. He glanced back toward the door.

"I'd never hurt ya, Ade. When Jack learned he was gonna be a father, he made me promise I'd always look after yous. Then when-" Floyd paused, grimaced, and shook his head. "Hasn't been a real easy job. You kids kinda dig a deep hole."

"That's why you covered for me?" Ade asked, avoiding eye contact.

"After all ya said, I figured they'd filled yer head with nonsense. Prolly offered ya all kinds of goodies. Plus, help yer mum. It's what they do."

Ade's eyes darted to Floyd.

"Yeah, figured. So, what they want in return? Jack's research?" Floyd asked.

Ade looked away. "Yeah," he mumbled.

Floyd nodded. "Any luck? It seems if ol' Jack wanted someone to have it woulda been found already."

Ade shook his head. "You don't have it, and Mom doesn't know about it."

Floyd grimaced. "I gotta ask one more time. Did ya lead em to us?"

Ade thought of the communication with Young and then Nadia. *But they scanned her*. "No. I didn't."

Floyd contemplated Ade's response and nodded his head. "Okay, so, what's it gonna be? Heads er tails?"

Looking at Floyd, Ade was reminded of his father. Physically, the two were nothing alike, but the fatherly look in Floyd's eyes was familiar. It made Ade miss Jack. "Floyd, what happened that night?"

Floyd sighed. "Ade, ya don't wanna know. Trust me."

"I need to."

Floyd breathed through his nose while stroking his beard. Then his hands dropped to his side. "I guess ya deserve da truth. Well, the plan was to meet in a public place. So, we chose da square in the market. We got there three hours early — me team and me. We swept da block and set up a perimeter. Then I waited by da fountain. Jack was running a bit late, so I had me boys do another security sweep. The square was secure. Then ol' Jack floats up in his skimmer n' all hell breaks loose. He didn' even make it from da skimmer. Da damn thing exploded when he opened the door." Floyd hung his head and took a deep, stuttered breath. "It was like they was watching. I run to Jack and...and he's already gone. Then CIU is on us. They musta followed him cause I didn't even blink, and they was firing. CIU didn't' care. They fired on everyone in da market. It was a bloody massacre. Only me and two of me guys made it out." Floyd paused, looked away, and sniffed. His eyes were glossy as he looked back at Ade. "I did what I could. Wasn't enough."

They stood in silence. Ade bit at his lip and wiped away tears with his sleeve. "Floyd, what do I do now?"

Floyd shrugged his shoulders. "I guess it depends on how this goes. We've been fighting fer so long. Sometimes, ya forget what peace feels like. Jack was right. Maybe ignorance is bliss. Maybe ya go back and tell 'em it was destroyed. Live a good life-" Suddenly, Floyd looked at his watch and blinked twice. "Roger that, Union." He pulled his shoulders back and stood straight. "Well, that was faster than anticipated. It's time."

"Time for what?" Ade whimpered.

In a blink, the lights shut off. Red lights illuminated in their place, and static hissed over the speakers of the communication system. "Threat condition Zulu. All soldiers report to battle stations. All nonessential personnel report to hangar section F. I repeat, Threat condition Zulu. Enemy inbound. This is not a drill."

A loud, wavering siren followed and bounced off the rock walls

"Time fer that," Floyd yelled over the noise.

The door to the housing unit swung open. Ann and Nadia rushed into the hallway. The dim red light cast eerie shadows upon Ann's angular face. More doors began opening, and half-dressed soldiers sprinted down the hall past them. Ann's mouth hung open as she glanced from soldier to soldier as they hustled by. Ade caught a glint of light in her right eye as she swallowed and looked up at him.

"They're here," she gasped.

"Afraid so," Floyd said. "Go grab yer things. There's a good chance we ain't comin' back."

CHAPTER 24 | 5856-W24

Ade saw more people in the hallways between the housing area and the elevator than he had for the entirety of his stay. A nervous energy permeated the narrow quarters as Floyd led them through the hall toward the elevator. Ade glanced back at Nadia, and his eyes drifted down to a young boy carrying a striped sack. He clutched the bag tight to his chest while holding his mother's hand. As odd as it seemed, Ade had never stopped to consider other families lived here also. Then he ran into Floyd's back. He shook his head and looked past Floyd at the mass of people stagnant in the hall leading to the elevator.

"Take the stairs, ya lazy arses," Floyd yelled.

Frightened eyes shot back toward them, and a murmur passed between those waiting. Slowly, the line began moving, and they ambled with the group toward the elevator.

The elevator doors parted, and soldiers cleared a path for someone much shorter than the average human adult.

A rumble shook the stone beneath Ade's feet, and the lights flickered. Ade tensed as Nadia grabbed his arm. Then, the world around him shook again, and small pieces of rock fell from the ceiling.

"Bloody hell, they're probing," Floyd cussed.

Amanda pushed her way through the frightened crowd. Her face was flushed. "Sir, we need-"

"Ya need to take 'em to the evacuation point. Send 'em with me wife."

Amanda shook her head. Another explosion shook the cave, and it was pitch black for a moment. The lights flickered back on, but the blast silenced the siren.

"President Miller has ordered you to the command center. I'm to escort you there now."

Floyd shook his head and looked at the soldiers cowering around the elevator. “Everyone take da stairs. Report to yer stations. That’s an order,” Floyd roared, and the hall quickly began to clear as people hurried to the stairwell.

“General, I need you to-”

“Take ‘em. That’s an order, Lieutenant.”

Amanda scowled at him. “We’re to report back to command immediately. President’s orders.”

“Fine. Take them with ya. They can evacuate with da command group. Tell Em I’m joining me men.”

Amanda winced at his words. It was clear she was unhappy with his decision.

Another blast shook the stronghold, and dust fell around them. The sound caused all but one to flinch and crouch. Floyd stood firm, looking at Amanda. “Lieutenant, are we good?”

“Yes, sir,” Amanda glowered.

The rumbling above them intensified. Ade fought the urge to cower and lay on the floor.

“Buggers are ramping up. Floyd said with a glance at the ceiling.” Then he looked down at Ade. “We’re safe. Enough rock to keep em out. Only worry is the roof of da upper hanger.”

Ade began to stand, but another blast froze him in his crouched position. Then Floyd looked him square in the eye. “Take care of yer mum. I gotta get to work.” Then he winked and ran toward the stairs.

Ade watched Floyd disappear into the stairwell and felt a twinge in his stomach. For some reason, this moment reminded him of the last time he saw his father. Then, a small hand grabbed his shirt and yanked him toward the elevator.

“Let’s go!” Cooper yelled.

Nadia caught him as he stumbled. Then, regaining his footing, they followed the short strides of Cooper. The elevator door immediately opened, and the four of them entered.

"What's happening? Why the command center?" Ade asked.

"Because we're being bombed, dummy," Amanda said.

Ade glared at her. "I know that! But what-"

"You'll know when we get there!"

Ade glanced toward Nadia. There was a joy in her eyes that baffled him.

The elevator door slid open to a platoon of soldiers guarding the entrance to the presidential suite. It reminded Ade of ferling insects on Cranis. He'd watched a documentary in his world biology class. When in danger, ferlings all swarmed to the exterior of the nest. When an ant tried to invade, the swarm attacked in unison before the queen could be harmed.

I don't want to be the ant closest to the queen, Ade thought.

Cooper pushed open the familiar doors of the presidential suite. Ade expected the same chaos they experienced in the halls. Instead, the suite was eerily quiet as the soldiers in the room gathered around a wall of screens, each streaming video feeds from around the compound. However, with numerous screens, every set of eyes was transfixed on a single black monitor in the top right corner. Cooper quickly gravitated toward the group and stood at the back on her tiptoes.

Ade looked at the people hypnotized by the screen and leaned toward Nadia. "What are they looking at?"

"The upper hangar is a decoy," Nadia whispered. "They're probably hoping we'll find it and think the base is abandoned. Which one is the president?"

Ade looked again at the people in the room. "I don't see her," he said, craning his neck from side to side.

Suddenly, there was a flash on the black screen, and the group gasped as a vibration rippled through the room. Ade looked up at the ceiling as the blast's concussion seemed farther off than before.

"This room is reinforced. Probably why they put the command center here," Nadia observed.

Ade gave her a sideways glance. *How did she know I was just wondering that?*

Then there was silence. Each passing second felt like a minute. Ade, too, had become transfixed by the black screen as they waited for what came next.

A hand gripped his shoulder. Thinking it was Nadia, Ade reached up and held it.

"I'm sorry for all of this," Ann said.

Surprised by his mother's voice, his eyes shot over his shoulder at his mother standing next to President Miller.

He patted her hand. "Not your fault. Never was," Ade said.

"What's behind the flag?" Nadia asked.

Ade hadn't realized she'd been watching the room while he watched the screens.

Miller's eyes narrowed on Nadia as if her question was offensive. "Why aren't you on the transport with the other civilians?"

Nadia shrunk before Miller's gaze and looked to Ann for help.

"Floyd told us to go with the girl," Ann replied. "He said we should evacuate with the command unit."

"Is that so?" Miller mused, clasping her hands behind her back. She raised an eyebrow and tilted her head to the left. "Floyd and I do not always agree on protocol, yet here you are. I suggest you keep your questions to a minimum."

Nadia lowered her gaze and looked at the floor. "I'm sorry, Madam President. I was just worried we'd get trapped in here."

Miller's judgmental gaze remained on Nadia until the prolonged silence called attention to the fact the bombing had stopped.

"Maybe they're out of bombs," Ade heard a soldier mumble.

Miller whirled to look at the screens while intently listening to the silence. "Everyone to your stations," She yelled. We will only have seconds if they don't take the bait."

Without pause or argument, the group quickly dispersed throughout the room.

"Mr. Billings," President Miller began, turning back to Ade. "Floyd thinks you'd be good in either tech or intelligence. So, for now, I'll assign you to tech. Please join Captain Kramer at his station."

Ann nodded in agreement.

Dumbfounded, Ade furrowed his brow. "I-"

"He's right over there," Miller continued, pointing to a husky man with thinning brown hair and a bushy beard.

Ade glanced toward the man and looked back at the president.

"Everyone in this room has a job. You are no exception, Mr. Billings."

He could feel Nadia's eyes on him. "Yes, ma'am."

"Nadia, watch the monitors. Report the minute they breach the hangar roof."

"Yes, ma'am," Nadia said quickly.

"Mum! Dozer inbound!" A woman screamed from across the room.

Miller's eyes remained on Ade. "How long?"

"Two minutes!"

"Prepare for breach," Miller said. Then she turned back to the room.

Ade had never seen such calm resolve in the face of danger. It was hard for him not to respect her at that moment.

"Long live the Union!" she shouted.

As the words passed the president's lips, they were silenced by a loud blast. A shockwave rippled under their feet, and the lights flickered. As they did, the black monitor in the corner lit up. Numerous spotlights illuminated the fighter craft graveyard.

"President!" Ade yelled. "They've breached the upper hangar!"

Specks of dust and dirt distorted the view from the lens, but a section of the hanger's roof door had been blown open. Beams of light shined through the massive opening and searched the hangar floor as snow poured down on chunks of the destroyed ceiling. Ade squinted as he watched a dozen black dots falling amongst the spotlights. At first, he thought they were falling debris, but parachutes ballooned as they passed the roof access doors, and the dots slowly floated to the floor. He looked back at Nadia. She had a slight smirk as she watched Cranis troops land and begin sweeping the hangar. Then he looked at his mother. Her face bore the horror of the potential conflict. She unknowingly chewed on her bottom lip as her eyes darted about the screen, watching the troops. Then, he met President Miller's watchful gaze, and she motioned for him to join Captain Kramer.

"Colonel Cole, how big is the breach?" Miller called.

"About twenty meters," Cole shouted. "Big enough for a Dozer."

"Prepare for defensive measures," she ordered. "Prepare surface to air for strike."

Ade dodged cables while joining Kramer at his station. Kramer had five screens, and the middle screen displayed the main feed from the hangar. Ade leaned over his shoulder, looking for the wiry frame of Captain Young.

"Little space, please. Trying to work," Kramer scoffed.

Kramer was a younger man who resembled a much older man. He had wire-rim glasses that sat low on his nose and a thin mustache hair that accumulated anxious sweat on his top lip.

Ade took a step back while his eyes remained glued to the screen.

"Lieutenant Zane, standby on gun doors. Captain Kramer, pull all remaining feeds from Hangar 1 and put them on the main display. Colonel Cole, prepare to fire." Miller barked orders in succession.

Kramer's fingers began hammering the keys, and monitors began cycling through static and images of the Cranis troops weaving through the rubble. Without sound, Ade watched as the soldiers motioned to each other and methodically moved through the hangar. As a soldier approached the elevator access door, Ade felt the air leave the room.

"Ma'am. Three craft holding above the hangar," Zane yelled.

A soldier around the same age as Captain Young held out a device that illuminated his face and pointed it at the door. The soldiers behind him stopped and took a knee. Then his lips moved. Slowly, deliberately, the soldier eyed the area around the door. Then he focused on the door, raised one arm, and circled in the air. All the soldiers in the hangar moved toward him and pointed their weapons at the door.

"They know," someone said in a hushed voice.

"Mum, aircraft breaking holding pattern and beginning descent," Zane said.

"Artillery, open the gun doors. All units, prepare to fire on my command," Miller ordered.

Ade's gaze broke from the screen to watch Miller stalk between stations. Her hands clasped behind her back, she took long, confident strides. She didn't make eye contact with anyone. Her thoughts were not in the moment but in the future — five steps beyond her current move.

Turning back to Kramer's station, Ade watched three fighters circling the hole in the hangar ceiling. The large dozer slowly passed between them and continued to the hangar floor. The soldiers by the door started to scatter and take up positions behind the large scarps that had fallen from the ceiling. The dozer was a beastly machine of war. Created shortly after the first war, they served as both troop carriers and tanks. Like an endo, the angular side hull had numerous refraction points. Protruding from the nose of the craft was a canon, and jutting from the top and flanks were domed turrets with large caliber lasterguns.

"Fire!" The president bellowed.

Ade's eyes darted from screen to screen, watching the Cranis troops unknowingly walking into the Union's trap.

"I said fire, damn it!" The president yelled, storming up behind Colonel Cole.

The colonel's fingers flew across the keyboard, and he hit the enter key hard at the end of each string. His eyes grew wide with terror. He re-keyed the command. His head shook in frustration, and he repeatedly pressed the final key. Ade looked back to the screen. Nothing happened.

"Air defenses are down," Cole gasped. "It says they're offline!"

President Miller whirled away from the Cole toward Kramer.

"Kramer, report!" Miller demanded.

"Guns offline," Zane shouted.

Kramer's stubby fingers blurred as they typed commands.

Ade glanced back to the monitor and watched the dozer as the stability legs impacted the hangar floor.

"Tech!" Miller screamed.

Kramer flinched, but after that, his body remained still. Only his fingers moved as his eyes focused on the screen. "They're not offline!" he yelled desperately. "I can ping them."

"Then fix it! We're out of time!" Miller shouted.

Beads of sweat formed on the bald spot of Kramer's head. Thinking he had a duty to help, Ade tried to encourage Kramer.

"You can do this, Kramer. Just-"

"Shut the fug up," Kramer spat. His intense eyes focused on the strings of passing commands. "They're back up!"

"Fire!" Miller yelled.

Ade's eyes snapped back to the screens as the dozer prepared to fire. When nothing happened, he looked back at the technician. Any resolve Kramer may have mustered had now shattered as his mouth gaped at the screen before him.

"Kramer!" The president screamed.

His fingers slowed to a stop. "They're gone. They're-" He turned in his chair and looked up at the president. His face was as white as snow.

President Miller moved as if in a trance. Slowly edging toward Kramer's station, her eye twitched as her gaze broke through the lines of code, seeing their true meaning. "They're on our network," Miller said. "That's impossible." There was a long pause. Her eyes drifted through the room and focused on the gold and maroon flag hanging at the back of the room.

"Reboot the network!"

All eyes turned toward Kramer.

"But if we-" Kramer interjected.

A blast louder than any previous shook the room.

"Reboot it now!" Miller ordered.

Kramer held down three keys on the board until the screens flickered off and back onto a spinning circle. His eyes never left the screen, and Ade heard him mumbling as dust fell from the ceiling.

"We need men on all guns—manual override. Manual override on all weapons systems," Miller yelled.

Kramer glanced at Ade as he hovered over the technician's shoulder. His blue eyes were hollow and lifeless. "We're all dead."

"We can't send the order until the network is back online," Cole said.

A set of hands pushed Ade to the side, and his foot caught a cable, and he stumbled to the floor as President Miller rushed past him.

She grabbed Kramer's shoulder and spun him toward her. Miller reared back and slapped Kramer in the face. Kramer's head snapped to the side, and when his eyes returned to meet the president, they were alive.

"We can save ourselves, but we need you," Miller shouted.

Kramer's lips pressed together as he stared at her. Then, a bulb of hope illuminated behind his fragile eyes. He whirled back around in his chair and sat poised to type. "Five minutes."

"We need it now!" The president growled.

"Yes, ma'am!" The monitors flickered as the meek man quickly went to work.

President Miller looked about the room at each of her soldiers. Her eyes landed on Ade but quickly moved past him to Ann. Then, without pause, she crossed the room toward Ade's mother. Ade suddenly felt short of breath. Without thinking, he leaped to his feet and sprinted toward Ann. Intercepting the president's path, he planted his feet firmly between Miller and his mother.

"No. She can't," Ade insisted.

"Will you go?" Miller asked, looking past Ade.

Ade could never explain it, but his mother moved with a silent grace unbeknownst to anyone around her. He hadn't even noticed, but Ann had moved around him. He saw her from his peripheral vision as she moved to join Miller. Ann placed a hand on Miller's shoulder and looked back at Ade. Her soft and vulnerable eyes looked back at him, and then, like flipping a switch, they became cold. The sudden change caused Ade to tense.

"I can go," a voice heralded from across the room.

An eager Lt. Cooper sprinted up and skidded to a halt beside Ade.

"Cooper, back to your-"

"I will inform General Arfey and rejoin the men. I'm more familiar with the base. It will be faster."

"The answer is no, Cooper. We need you here." Miller said.

Ade's pleading eyes look back at Miller. Miller's jaw clenched, and she averted her gaze back at Ann.

"Just relay my message and come directly back. You understand," Miller ordered.

Ann nodded. She began to move but hesitated. Then, without looking back, she ran toward the door.

A thousand moments flashed before Ade's eyes. He wanted to call out — to insist she stay. Instead, he stood silently watching her go.

Miller whirled back to the room. "Kramer, where are we?"

The door closed behind his mother, and Ade turned to find Cooper standing before him. Ade sighed and nodded. Cooper sucked in her lips, nodded in return, and hurried back to her station.

"Kramer! Are we-"

The monitoring station powered back on, displaying images from across the compound.

"Systems coming back online," Kramer shouted.

Another shockwave shook the room. As soldiers cowered, Ade saw Nadia standing upright, watching the live feed. He moved in behind her and leaned in to see what she was looking at.

"Whatever happens, follow my lead, okay?" Nadia whispered.

Ade didn't follow. Then he saw what Nadia was looking at. The main elevator door was blown open, and a team of soldiers circled the elevator.

"They're in the elevator!" Ade yelled back at the room.

"Cole, fire!" The president repeated.

Cole angrily shook his head as he typed. "They're still loading the configuration."

"Kramer, how long?" The president called.

Ade heard the hope draining from her voice. She stood in the center of the room between the stations. Her hands were on her hips, and her narrow shoulders slumped forward as her eyes focused on a spot six inches beyond her toes.

"Union, dis is Viper 1. Do you read," Floyd said in a whisper.

Miller's head snapped up.

Floyd's whisper brought forth excitement, and cheers echoed through the room.

Ade spun back toward the monitors. A video feed in the top row shook as the camera turned and settled on Floyd's face. Ade heard the commotion behind him as Miller quickly moved through the room.

"Viper 1! They were on our network. The guns are down," Miller relayed.

Floyd nodded. He held the camera just inches from his face, and it shook slightly from adrenaline. "And here I thought ya took a nap," Floyd grinned. "Ann relayed the message. I've moved me men into da maintenance stairwell. Since yer running da show, give the word, and we'll take out these blokes fixing to blow our elevator."

Ade looked from Floyd's image back to the president, and all eyes were upon her as she leaned over the communications officer.

"Floyd, there are six total in the elevator. Three on the perimeter and three setting the charges. Take those bastards out," she fumed.

The video spun around, and a gloved hand covered the lens until it was affixed to Floyd's chest. "Roger that, mum."

A maintenance hatch slowly pushed open, revealing the back of a Cranis soldier. The camera turned to the dark stairwell, and Floyd's arm could be seen giving signals just beyond the top of the video feed. Then, the video returned to the back of the Cranis Soldier.

Nadia's hand slipped into Ade's and squeezed. His hand was limp within hers; she gasped as Floyd slowly opened the metal access door.

"Behind you," she whispered.

The elevator and part of the hangar beyond came into view. The relics of war sat crumbled beneath fallen rubble. Lights angled in from all directions, and snow glistened as it fell through the hole in the ceiling.

There were more than six, Ade thought.

Floyd shoved the access door open and leaped into the elevator. Floyd swung his lastergun before him with precision in a flurry of movement. He fired three quick, deadly shots. Ade shuddered as laster rounds terminated the lives of three enemy soldiers. He wanted to look away but was drawn to the violence. To the left of Floyd's video feed, two Cranis soldiers spun and aimed at Floyd. Ade's heart skipped. But, before their aim found its target, two of Floyd's soldiers brushed past him with weapons aimed, and with three quick shots, the final Cranis soldiers fell to the floor. The camera bounced as Floyd bound forward and slid toward the explosive device in the middle of the elevator. He rapidly removed several colored wires from the explosives and lifted it from the floor. The image blurred, spun, and slid toward a large piece of the hangar ceiling. Floyd took a deep breath and exhaled an expletive. "Bravo team, this is Viper 1. On those guns yet?"

"Zane?" Miller shouted.

The camera flipped as Floyd pressed his back against a large chunk of rubble and displayed the destroyed door of the open elevator as laster rounds zipped past him and bore into the elevator wall. In the corner of Floyd's feed, a member of his team was cut down by enemy fire while attempting to exit the hatch into the elevator.

"Guns back online," Zane relayed.

"Viper team, do not advance," Floyd screamed into the microphone. "Bravo team!"

Four consecutive blasts rippled through the compound. Three hangar cameras went black, and a murmur swept through the control room.

"Bravo team!" Floyd repeated.

Ade anxiously waited for a return from Bravo Team, but none came. Instead, Floyd's camera feed slumped closer to the ground as the rounds zipping by him intensified.

"Hangar guns destroyed!" Zane shouted.

"Floyd, get your men out of there," Miller ordered. "The hangar is lost."

Floyd lifted the disarmed explosive to his chest.

"Floyd!" Miller barked.

Floyd fumbled with something in his other hand and began taping a grenade to the explosive. He pressed the edge of the tape to ensure it remained in place, peeked over the rubble, and pulled the pin. The camera spun as Floyd stood and whirled toward the enemy. The destroyed hangar came into view and revealed an entire regiment of Cranis soldiers. Floyd launched the improvised explosive into the air, and a round zipped past the camera. The image spun and fell, looking up at the hangar ceiling.

The shadows of men were briefly cast upon the walls as the explosion ripped through the hangar. Silence fell like a dense fog as the room watched the smoke cross the camera's lens. There was no movement. Two Union soldiers rushed into the frame, kneeling over Floyd. One quickly blinked while the other pressed his hands near the camera's lens.

"Union, this is Viper 2. Need medical. Viper 1 down. Send-"

The soldier speaking yanked up his lastergun and began to fire as the other soldier grabbed Floyd by the feet and dragged him toward the elevator maintenance door. Then the camera tumbled and turned back to the hangar. The first round hit Viper 2 in the shoulder and spun him around. Then, a second round hit him in the back, and he fell to the ground. The feed flipped back to the ceiling and moved toward the back of the elevator. It shook and went black as Floyd was pulled through the opening, and the maintenance hatch slammed shut.

"Union, Viper 3."

Ade watched Floyd's feed bounce as he was carried down the steps away from the elevator.

"Go Viper 3," Miller responded.

"Permission to initiate hellfire."

Ade turned away from the monitors to look at the president. President Miller stood upright and stared at the microphone. Then she looked at the many eyes awaiting her order. She slowly leaned down to the microphone. "All units initiate Lando Protocol Delta. I repeat, Delta. Viper 3, stand by for hellfire."

"Roger that," Viper 3 responded.

"And Viper 3, make sure you're clear before initiation."

"Roger."

Miller looked at the men and women in the room. She nodded, and chaos filled the room as soldiers rushed in different directions while trying to collect their gear.

His mouth gaping, Ade looked around the room and then at Nadia. He realized he was gripping her hand tightly. "I think we're evacuating," Ade said.

Nadia stood transfixed by the remaining monitors. Her brow was low over her eyes as she glowered at the screens.

"Nadia," Ade repeated.

"What?" she snapped.

Ade released her hand and took a step back. She looked like a wild animal about to attack. Her lips parted, but then she looked at the room and pressed them tightly together. Nadia stepped in close enough so only Ade could hear.

"Remember what side you're on." Then she stepped in close and buried her head in his chest. "I'm just scared," Nadia whimpered.

Ade moved one hand to place on her back but let it fall to his side.

"Miller said to give you these," Cooper said, dropping a pile of clothing onto the floor beside them. "You'll evacuate with the command unit."

Ade glanced down at Nadia and then at Cooper.

"Now would be good," Cooper scowled toward Nadia.

"What about my mother?"

"I'm going to find her," Cooper said, moving toward the door.

"Cooper," Ade called. He wiggled free from Nadia's grasp and took a step after her.

Cooper glanced back, nodded, and exited the room without pause. Ade watched Cooper disappear and turned back to Nadia.

"She'll be safe. No matter what. I promise," Nadia assured him. "Just remember, follow my lead."

CHAPTER 25 | 5856-W25

Ade had only seen snow once before on Cranis, and that was at an indoor recreation park that used machines to create an artificial winter wonderland. The park's most notable attraction was the ice-flier hill, with white-capped trees and snowmen. At Ann's insistence, Ade attempted to slide down the hill once. To be more accurate, he only slid part of the way down. Most of his trip was either tumbling or rolling. When he returned to his mother with snow melting under his jacket and stuck to his eyelashes, Ade vowed never to be where there was snow again.

Ade slid the heavy, fur-lined parka over his shoulders and pulled the zipper to his chin. As if the fear of their current situation wasn't enough, it was amplified by the fear of going outside. He swung his arms around, testing his mobility.

Remember what I said?" Nadia asked, looking up at him.

Ade nodded as he stuffed his hands into a pair of mittens, two sizes too small for his hands. "Your lead."

Nadia gave a half nod in return. "Wait for the other soldiers to leave. Then we follow. We want to be last." she said softly.

A large explosion rattled the room, and workstations tipped and crashed to the floor. Ade felt a sense of urgency to move, but Nadia just looked at him and remained crouched while pretending to tie her boot.

"They've breached the elevator!" Miller yelled. "Ade Billings, let's move!" Ade stood and looked at the empty room. Only President Miller remained. Standing beside the banner behind her desk, she waved for them to hurry. Nadia glanced over her shoulder. "Last one out. How noble," she grumbled. Then she stood and ran across the room. Ade followed, and the president pulled the banner aside as they approached. Ade matched Nadia's stride as they ascended the narrow path toward the surface. He focused on her movement – the rise and fall of her shoulders. His lungs burned, and the hair in his nose froze.

The tunnel lights dimmed and faded behind him as they ran. Nadia's silhouette pushed forward, illuminated by the radiance of the aurora borealis. The light danced and swayed on the tunnel walls as they closed in on the exit. Ade's footing began to dig in and slip with each step, and he looked down at the trampled white powder beneath his feet. Then, in a breath, they exited into the frozen desert. The wind hit him like a bucket of ice water, and Ade tucked his face into the neck of his jacket. The aurora reflected off the snow and illuminated the endless drifts of snow. Freezing temperatures gave him pause, and he stopped to catch his breath.

President Miller rushed past him toward a group of soldiers standing fifty yards from the entrance. At first, he didn't see it, but next to the soldiers was a white airbus camouflaged amongst the snow. The engines of the airbus fired, and a cloud of smoke rose into the sky.

The thought of shelter set his feet back in motion, but a hand grabbed his jacket and pulled him back. He turned, and Nadia tucked into him. He felt her warmth against his chest, and her breath warmed his face.

"When it happens, run back to the tunnel," she whispered.

"When what-" Ade heard a gentle hiss in the distance. It came from the horizon like a storm blowing in from the sea.

"Ade, run!" President Miller shouted.

Ade flinched, and Nadia's grip on him tightened. "Not yet."

Soldiers piled into the bus while the president's arms slowly fell to her sides as she watched them. The hiss intensified, and he and the president looked to the sky. His nightmares became a reality as a fighter craft bulleted toward them.

"Go! Take off now! The rest of you, with me!" President Miller screamed.

Ade's attention shot back to the bus as the doors closed, and it slowly lifted from the ground. President Miller led her group to a ridge of jagged rocks protruding from the snow. Her remaining soldiers rallied around her and took up a defensive position. Ade looked back at the fighter as it banked and prepared for an attack run. The bus's engines groaned as the pilot gave them full power. *They're not going to make it,* Ade thought.

"Fire," President Miller commanded. Then, red laster rounds traced into the purple sky.

"Now!" Nadia exclaimed.

She released him and dashed back toward the tunnel while Ade watched the events in disbelief. He raised his arms and started waving at the descending fighter. "Abandon attack," he screamed, running toward the airbus. Two missiles dropped from the belly of the fighter and hurtled forward. The airbus banked, and the engines roared for more power. "No!" The explosion lifted Ade from his feet and sent him flying backward. A light flashed behind his eyelids as his body impacted the tundra, and he slid back toward the tunnel.

His eyes opened to Nadia looking down at him. The aurora behind her was darkened by smoke, and a flickering fire lit her face. She screamed his name and tugged at his jacket. A ringing in his ears muffled all sounds around him. Pushing himself to his knees, he felt a wet warmth on his face and ran his fingers across his cheek. Retracting his hand, he placed the bloody white glove before his eyes. His hand returned to his head, and he winced as his finger fell upon an open gash above his right ear. He slowly turned back toward the bus. All that remained was a pile of burning scrap smoldering in the snow. Smoke from the explosion painted the white canvas black and billowed across the drifts. Holding his breath, he exhaled as the president and her men rose to their feet. A few of them sprinted through the smoke toward the wreckage while the others gathered around Miller.

Nadia pulled Ade to his feet and led him back toward the tunnel. Muffled shouts filled the air behind them. Nadia increased her pace, and Ade slowed to look back. She gave his arm a hefty yank, and the two fell together into the tunnel's opening.

Ade heard more shouting. He rolled away from Nadia and tried to sit up, but she yanked him back down. His vision blurred as blood ran from his gash into his eyes. He wiped his face on the sleeve of his jacket and looked at Nadia. Her hood had fallen from her head and rested on her shoulders. Ade gasped as he saw her black hair matted to her cheek with blood.

"Your-"

"It's your blood, not mine," Nadia said quickly.

She unzipped and removed her jacket. Reaching for her boot, she unsheathed a black knife and stabbed it through the bottom of her shirt. Ripping a strip from the bottom of her shirt, Nadia began wrapping the cloth around Ade's head. He winced as she touched an area near the fresh would. She didn't pause at his reaction and tucked the remainder of the strip into the makeshift bandage. Then Nadia inspected her work and covered Ade's head with his hood.

The ringing in his ears subsided, and the commotion beyond the cave became clear. Miller shouted at her men as the ominous sound of the fighter returned.

Nadia closed her jacket and pulled on the hood. "Stay down and follow me," she said without looking at him. On her elbows, she crawled back toward the opening. The descending fighter created a sense of impending doom. Ade hurried to the entrance and looked out as a burst of fire rained down on Miller's position. The fighter soared overhead, and Miller's outfit returned fire. It appeared hopeless as the red laster rounds trailed harmlessly behind the speedy aircraft. The screeching of the fighter faded into the distance and revealed the deep growl of a descending dozer. There was a brief moment when the only noise came from the dozer. Then, shooting resumed, and the sound of the guns echoed through the tunnel. The bright red rounds created a strobe light effect on the smoke surrounding Miller, and her soldiers existed in a glow of continuous lasterfire. The dozer bore down from the sky like a predator swooping to eliminate its prey. Rounds deflected off the heavy armor, and then the dozer opened fire. Ade watched in horror at the brutality of men. Men and women fell lifeless to the snow as the large caliber rounds pinned down Miller's small force. It was like watching a grown man beating a child. The small band of soldiers stood no chance against the monster of progress. And yet, they stood in defiance.

"Why don't they retreat?" Ade pleaded.

"Because rats lack common sense," Nadia spat.

Ade winced at her words.

"If the dozer stopped firing, they could surrender!" Ade exclaimed.

"This is war, Ade. People die," Nadia said, watching the events unfold.

The dozer's legs extended from the belly of the craft and sank into the snow as the beefy vehicle landed. The larger exterior guns continued to fire as the side doors opened. Even in the low light, Ade recognized Captain Young as soon as his feet planted in the snow. He moved as if the rounds could not touch him. Ducking and skirting, he darted between streaks of red as if guided by an otherworldly presence. Ade blinked and activated his thermal vision. The glowing figures dashed across the cool blue earth. Rounds zipped through the air at an enemy dancing, step by step, closer to Miller's positions.

Ade's nervous gaze shifted from the battle to Nadia and back again. He watched as Young's soldiers overwhelmed the small Union force. President Miller screamed over the commotion for her soldiers to fall back, but Young and his men pinned down each position. Only a handful of Union troops remained. Ade felt bile form in his throat as he watched President Miller crawl to one of her fallen soldiers and pull the lastergun from his hand. He looked away and deactivated his thermal vision. With all the noise, Ade didn't hear the returning fighter until it roared over their position.

"Cease fire!" Young shouted.

Ade looked back to see Miller standing upright as her men

huddled by her feet. Young took a step forward, and he and Ade watched in amazement as Miller carefully raised the lastergun and aimed it at the fighter. Then, she let out a war cry that pierced the darkness and fired. Captain Young's lips moved, and the fighter banked and turned away from the battle.

Miller continued to fire until the lastergun in her hand only clicked when she pulled the trigger. Then, the gun dropped to her side and fell from her hand to the snow.

"Surrender," Young shouted.

Miller took a breath. She pulled her shoulders back and glared across the battlefield at Young. "Death before dishonor!" she screamed.

Captain Young hung his head and looked at the black snow beneath his boots. Then he peered back at her. "It doesn't have to be like this."

"Better to die in battle than be tried and executed for defending my home," Miller responded.

Young nodded his head. "So be it," he stated. Then, to the fighter above: "Sierra 1 reengage."

With each breath, the fighter's engines rumbled across the snow and grew louder. With tear-filled eyes, Ade tried to focus on the figures standing, one by one, next to President Miller. Suddenly, a loud cry filled the night sky. Mouths wide, teeth snarling, rounds from the guns of Union soldiers lit the dark sky as the fighter entered a dive.

The roar of the fighter's engines shook Ade's teeth, and as it opened fire, he closed his eyes.

Within a second, the sound of the fighter tailed off into the distance, and then there was silence. The snow crunched under Nadia as she rose to her feet. The cold became an afterthought. Ade squeezed his eyelids tight and took rapid breaths as grief and guilt collided within him.

"It's clear. You can get up now," Nadia said softly.

His eyes fluttered open to Nadia standing over him. Fearful of looking toward the battle, he looked back into the tunnel and watched Nadia's shadow flicker on the stone ceiling. *If only this were the reality that existed.*

"Ade, let's go," Nadia ordered.

A slideshow of images flipped in his mind's eye – a barrage of faces, all staring directly into his soul. A faint thudding sound drifted up the tunnel, and a warm breeze ruffled the fur on his jacket. Then, a blast shook the earth. The tunnel walls cracked as the explosion pushed warm air, dust, and metal cracking sounds into the tundra.

"Move!" Nadia screamed.

The urgency of her tone forced Ade to his feet. Then, he saw a glow of orange from deep within the cave. Another explosion shook the ground. Nadia grabbed him by his arm and yanked him from the mouth of the cave into the snow.

"Over here," Nadia yelled as they sprinted toward Young and his men. The snow beneath their feet began to crack, shift, and flow backward. Nadia staggered sideways. Her grip on Ade's arm tightened, and as she fell, she pulled Ade down with her. Ade quickly adjusted his leg augmentation as they struggled to their feet. He grabbed Nadia's hand and lunged forward. The forceful momentum yanked her, and she stumbled. The rumble behind them grew louder as another bomb erupted. Ade looked back at Nadia, and his windburned face turned as white as the landscape.

With each explosion, the collapsing base pulled the ground above into a gaping hole.

He pulled Nadia back to her feet and wrapped his arm around her waist.

"Just kick your feet," Ade ordered, and he sprang forward. Landing ten feet beyond the tunnel, he adjusted his grip on Nadia and jumped again. The snow moved in a current as an avalanche fell into the crater behind him. The dozer's engines roared as it pushed upward and retracted its legs. Ade and Nadia landed and tumbled into the rushing show. He fought to stand, but snow pulled him down. He grabbed Nadia with both hands and pushed with all his might. They barely moved as the snow carried them toward the collapsed base. Only inches off the surface, the dozer hovered toward them. The pilot hit the forward stop and fired the rear engines. The nose drifted away from them as the rear of the tank swung in their direction.

"Grab my hand!" Young called.

Young leaned forward from a side door as two men held him in place. The gap closed between them. Nadia's grip on him tightened. Ade reached out. Six feet separated them. Then five feet. Ade couldn't jump. *I need more,* Ade thought. He deactivated the Beta, and fear took over. He dug his feet in and pushed upward. Ade's palm landed on Young's forearm.

"I got them. Move!" Young yelled.

The engines rumbled, and the dozer drifted away, dragging them across the snow. Ade closed his eyes and focused on his grip on Nadia. Several hands grabbed his jacket and slid him from the snow onto a smooth, hard surface. The noise of the engines dulled to a hum as the door clicked into place. Ade opened his eyes to the orange glow of the dozer interior. Captain Young crouched next to him, and Nadia rolled from his side. Flat on her back, she took deep breaths and released them in a long exhale.

"You okay?" Young asked.

Ade couldn't bring himself to look Young in the eye. His chest felt tight, and he struggled to breathe. A metallic taste formed in his mouth, and his stomach twinged. Bile crept up the back of his throat. He pinched his lips together, but his body convulsed. And he rolled and forcefully expelled the contents of his stomach.

Ade heard a few of the men laugh, and his ears burned red. He inhaled deeply through his nose and spat out the putrid taste in his mouth. His body shook from the cold. For some reason, he thought of the trip to the snow park. Then he thought of his mother and began to cry.

"She's okay, Ade. I promise," Nadia whispered. She rubbed his back. “She got out.”

His mind was racing. It bounced from thought to thought. The ache in his chest was unbearable. Ade shook his head and pulled away from her. *Cooper, Kramer, Miller....so many.*

“And that’s why women and children don’t fight wars,” one of the soldiers mocked.

Ade whirled toward the men.

“She was braver than all you cowards,” Ade snarled.

The laughter abruptly ceased, and all eyes turned toward him. An uneasy silence drifted through the dozer as Ade’s contempt met the scorn of Young’s soldiers. Captain Young waved a dismissive hand before placing it on Ade’s shoulder.

“I will not argue that.” Then he looked at his men. “She died a warrior’s death. We should all be so lucky.”

“Luck? She’d have been lucky to hit anything the way she was shooting,” someone shouted.

The men roared with laughter, and Ade’s tear-filled eyes shot toward the grinning face of the soldier closest to him. He had a youthful, tan face with white goggle lines around his eyes. Ade’s legs tensed, and he clenched his fist. It didn’t matter who said it. The boy continued to laugh. Ade lunged forward and threw a hard cross at the soldier’s face. The punch landed with a thwap, and he and the soldier tumbled to the floor. Ade quickly rose to his knees and drew back his fist. Two strong hands grabbed Ade’s jacket and yanked him backward. Ade fell, rolled, and threw another punch at whoever pulled him. His fist missed as Young ducked to the side and shoved him down again.

“Lock it up,” Young yelled. “All of you!” The dozer fell silent. “And you,” Captain Young fumed, turning to Ade. “Activate your Beta.”

Ade’s chest heaved as he glared at Young. Again, Nadia placed her hand on his back. He flinched at her touch but didn’t avert his eyes from Young.

"We're safe now. You can relax," Nadia whispered into his ear.

Her words bounced in his head. *Safe, I haven't been safe since I got here.* He blinked and set his Beta to 5.

"I know you've been through a lot. I admired her, too." Young said, kneeling beside Ade. "But you hit another one of my men, and I won't protect you. You copy?"

The Beta calmed him, and he looked from Young to the swelling face of the soldier he assaulted. Then he nodded. Young stood and turned back toward his men. "Back on your leash." Young barked. He paused as he looked at each man. "Nobody is to touch him. Understood? He risked his life; we would not have achieved this victory without him. Without him, none of this would have happened. You copy?"

There was a grumble amongst the men. "I said, you copy?" Young shouted.

"Yes, sir," returned loud and in unison.

"Now, get some rest. We have a long day ahead." Young looked at his watch. "Debrief at Camp Snoopy in 6 hours."

With the Beta active, Ade's emotions drained from within, and his thoughts became still like water in a pond. He watched Young stride to the corner of the troop carrier and recline in a cargo net as if it were a hammock. Then, with no argument and very few words, his soldiers followed suit. Ade thought about President Miller. She also had the respect of her people — even Floyd. However, it seemed like a different kind of leadership.

He felt Nadia's finger return to his hair while her other hand massaged his neck.

"Why don't you lean back and put your head in my lap," she said softly.

Because rats lack common sense, Ade thought of her words.

"I'm fine," Ade said.

She scooted around him and placed her hand on Ade's face. Ade winced as she touched the fresh cut on his head.

"Oh," she said, somewhat startled. "Let me look at this." She slowly removed the makeshift bandage from his head and leaned in close.

Ade stared at the floor. She leaned back and glanced around the cabin until she saw a soldier digging through his bag.

"You," she said sharply.

The soldier looked up and then looked side to side.

"Yeah, you. Give me your med kit."

Ade glanced up at a paper-thin soldier with a round face. Dumfounded, the soldier looked from Nadia to Captain Young. Young's hat was over his eyes, and his hands rested on his chest. He lifted one hand and waved it slightly.

"You better do as she says," Young mumbled.

Without a blink, the soldier returned to his bag and tossed a silver package to Nadia. She plucked it from the air, opened the container, and removed tweezers, a disinfectant towel, and a bottle of SkinRegen.

"Hold still," she said. She held the tweezers in one hand and the towel in the other.

A sharp pain spread from his skull down his jaw, and she pressed a cool towel against his head. Nadia held out the tweezers and dropped a chunk of metal. It rattled as it hit the floor, and Ade looked down at a piece of the airbus. She dropped the tweezers, grabbed the SkinRegen, and began shaking it. "She left quite the impression on you."

Ade thought about Floyd and his advice. "I know she was the enemy, but she was...." Ade trailed off. "Well, you know. You saw it."

"Maybe I would feel different if I knew her better," Nadia began. "But the Union killed some of my friends on Cranis. It's hard to get past that."

Ade nodded and thought of his father.

"I said hold still," Nadia repeated.

Ade stopped nodding and looked at Young. "I've never seen

anything like that. What he did out there. It was like the rounds searched for him but couldn't find him," Ade murmured.

"You mean Young?"

"Yeah," Ade said.

"There is a story about that. I've heard it so often that I wonder if it's even true, but the men love telling it. Near the end of the war, Young's team got intel that the remainder of Jaber's Army was at a stronghold in the mountains. So, they went to see if the intel was good. Young was a Sergeant at the time. They went up that mountain, and sure enough, the rats were up there. They took out half of Young's team before they could get their lasterguns ready to fire. Young's captain ordered the team to move forward and engage while he and his Lieutenant stayed back. Young didn't listen. He told his men to retreat while he covered them. Four hours later, he wandered down the mountain covered in blood and punched his captain in the face."

"Didn't that lead to the Battle of Falling Rock?"

"Wow. Mr. Billings knows his history," Nadia answered.

"I watched the movie. Thought the guy was named Tatum, not Young."

"I thought you were more of a book guy," Nadia said as she removed the towel and sprayed his head with SkinRegen.

Added shrugged. "Depends."

The wound sizzled and popped above his ear as the skin began to form.

"Tatum wrote the book. He was one of Young's men. His dad was a representative. He got the captain to drop the charges. It pretty much made Young an instant hero. Do you want me to get the other scars?"

"Leave the one above my eye. The others can go."

Ade heard a hiss and felt the cold sensation of the SkinRegen. It began cold and then quickly became warm.

"Can't believe that's him," Ade said.

"Yeah," she said, snapping the cap back onto the bottle. "In the flesh, sleeping in a net on a transport. Life of glamor."

Ade looked at her delicate features glowing in the light. "What happened back there? How did they find us?"

Nadia gave him a motherly smile while running her fingers over the scar above his eye. "You'll have to ask Captain Young. Now, try to sleep. It's going to be a full day tomorrow."

"I'm not tired."

Nadia moved behind him, and he felt a slight pinch on his neck. He quickly became lightheaded. His thoughts spiraled as Nadia lowered his head into her lap. Then Nadia stroked his hair and began to sing softly.

Oh where, oh where have our boys been?
They've gone to hell and come back again.
The angels fly, and our thoughts begin
To remember those who brought peace again.

CHAPTER 26 | 5856-W25

Drops of blood fell from the sky like heavy rain. Ade peered through the drops at the shadowy figure looming beyond. With each step, the dark figure grew more prominent. Fear burrowed like a parasite into his mind. His instinct was to run, but his feet would not move. He stood paralyzed as the shadow moved between the drops toward him. He felt cold exuding from the creature, and his breath billowed before him. He heard Nadia's voice crying for help in the distance. The shadow drew closer. Ade tried to turn but was held in place by an unseen force. Captain Young sprinted up from behind him and pulled his sidearm. He fired two rounds that zipped past Ade's ear. Spinning back to see the impact of the shots, he looked up at the bloodied face of President Miller. His reflection quivered in her all-black eyes. "It's either you or her!" She screamed.

"Ade, wake up."

He jolted up, gasped, and rubbed his eyes before looking around at the sleeping soldiers. The interior of the dozer remained the amber color it had been previously, but it seemed hotter and stuffier than before. It smelled of men, sweat, and urine. Ade scrunched his nose at the realization that he, too, was contributing to the foul odor.

"You were dreaming," Nadia said.

He sat and ran his hand over the fresh skin above his ear. A few inches lower, and he'd be missing an ear. A few inches to the left, and he'd be dead. He blinked and decreased his Beta. The longer he left his Beta active, the less human he felt.

"How much longer?" he asked. He still felt partially asleep.

"Not much. Young said twenty minutes about ten minutes ago," Nadia replied.

Ade looked about the dozer but, in doing so, found Captain

Young was not in the cabin. "Where is he?"

No answer was returned, and Ade glanced over his shoulder at Nadia. He quickly averted his eyes as she pulled her outer shirt over her shoulders. Ade glanced around to ensure nobody was looking and then looked back at her. All that remained was a tight undershirt that clung to her skin. She arched her back, stretched out her arms, and groaned softly. Ade quickly looked away.

"You can look," Nadia said. "I'm still dressed. You could look even if I weren't."

Ade wondered if he was awake or still dreaming.

"You should kiss me. Before the neanderthals wake up."

He glanced back at her and quickly looked away. *Rats*, Ade thought, and he shook his head. His thoughts blurred, and the previous night felt like part of the dream. It felt distant, like a past life. He yawned. He was still groggy, and his head felt heavy.

She placed a hand on his shoulder and slid it down his back. He looked back at the corner where Young had been sleeping.

"Where's Young?"

"Who?"

Ade furrowed his brow at her answer and looked back at her. As soon as their eyes met, she removed her undershirt. He was unable to avert his eyes as they fell upon her. He had never seen a woman before.

"Nadia, I..."

"I want you to look."

Nadia grabbed his hand and slowly placed it on her torso. He tried to focus on her eyes, and she guided his hand upward. A soldier behind him groaned. Yanking his hand away, he fumbled with his jacket. His attention turned to the cabin of sleeping soldiers, and he quickly removed the coat to cover her. Ade draped it over her shoulders.

"You don't need to protect me," she said.

Ade shook his head and grimaced. "Not here. It's not right."

She laughed at him. "You're funny." She shoved the jacket back at him, kneeled, and shuffled closer.

Ade looked away. The sound of grinding metal echoed through the cabin as the legs of the dozer extended for landing. Men stirred, and Ade looked back at Nadia.

Her emerald eyes met him briefly, and she looked away and reached for her shirt. "I didn't realize my man was so chivalrous."

"Nadia, I-" Ade stopped at the sound of footsteps and looked back at Captain Young.

Young averted his eyes as Nadia pulled the shirt back over her head. Then, once Nadia was dressed, Young kneeled beside Ade and placed a hand on his shoulder.

"You remember Abraham?" Young said plainly.

Ade nodded.

"It's all going to happen very fast. All I'm saying is don't be who they want you to be. Be yourself," Young said.

"What does that mean?"

The transport door hissed and lowered to the tarmac. Standing there amongst the people awaiting their arrival was Abraham.

"You'll know soon enough," Young answered.

The door cracked as it hit the paved surface, and Ade flinched. He cringed, shook his head, and scowled at Abraham, shuffling up the ramp toward him.

Young nodded as Abraham approached. "He's going to take you back to the embassy. Nadia, do you remember your way around the base? Hasn't changed since you were stationed here."

"Hard to forget," Nadia deadpanned.

"Good. I'll find you after I get these clowns debriefed."

A soldier behind Young scoffed, and the captain released Ade's shoulder and turned back to his men.

"If we're clowns, then you're the ringmaster," one of the men heckled.

Young raised one finger and waved it before him. Then he

stopped and placed the same finger on his chin. "On second thought, I take it back. You all are my clowns, but Private Patrick," he said, pointing at a peaked-faced boy. "He is my idiot."

The dozer erupted with laughter, and Ade winced. *They act as though nothing happened. And now they laugh*, Ade thought.

"Mr. Billings," Abraham chirped.

Ade looked at the sweaty, winded man.

"Mr. Billings," Abraham repeated, panting. "I'm so glad you are okay. That was quite harrowing in the Labor District and the Polar Ring! One can only imagine what you went through." He took a deep breath. "I mean to have you back safe with us away from those, those... animals."

Ade's brow lowered, and a spiteful remark stalled as he remembered his place.

"Yeah, it's been a lot," Ade mumbled.

"He was very heroic," Nadia interjected. She moved around him and stood between them. "He saved my life." She looked back at Ade with a humble smile and adoring eyes. "We're lucky to have him."

"Oh yes, indeed, indeed," Abraham said, wiping his forehead with his sleeve.

The soldiers began exiting, and their large backpacks bumped them as they passed. Abraham attempted to continue speaking as he stepped to the side, but each time he opened his mouth, another bag would glance off him and push him further away from the door. Captain Young followed at the end of the line and tipped his hat slightly as he passed Abraham.

Ade waited until the soldiers had descended the ramp. "Have you heard anything about the other soldiers, Floyd, or my mother?"

Abraham's chipper disposition faltered, and he scrunched his nose. "They are being tracked but have not yet been captured. More got out than anticipated. Your mother is with them. We have not yet engaged to ensure her safety."

"I told you. She is safe. I promised, and I meant it," Nadia added.

Ade sighed and looked beyond the stuffy interior of the dozer. "Can we get off this thing?" Ade asked, brushing the dust from his pants.

"Of course," Abraham grinned. "No reason to delay. It does smell a bit, ah... lived in."

Ade brushed past Abraham and hurried down the ramp. From the sun's position, Ade assumed they were still west of the embassy. The tundra's short pines surrounded the airfield's exterior, and crisp, cool air filled his lungs. Abraham's cologne was more noticeable as he approached and stood beside Ade.

"The Ambassador has ordered you back immediately. He lent us the luxury cruiser to make our travels more enjoyable."

Nadia glowered at Abraham. "It can wait," She insisted. I'd like to take Ade to the cantina. Get some food. We've barely had time to breathe."

"I completely understand, but I must insist. President Hollar is flying in today," Abraham stated.

Nadia's eyes widened as she stood staring at Abraham in disbelief. "He's coming here?"

"Yes. I was in the room with the Ambassador when it was announced. He will be here this afternoon."

Ade remembered the media frenzy around President Hollar's election. He was young, handsome, and brilliant. His company built the Star Liner that transported people between planets. Before the Star Liner, it took days to traverse the distance. Hollar's transport cut the trip down to a few hours. Ann detested Hollar and his politics. Meanwhile, Jack just shrugged and talked about the benefits of Hollar's research grants. At the time, all Ade knew was that he was young compared to previous presidents, and much to Ade's chagrin, every girl in school had a crush on him.

"Whatever," Ade huffed. "He's an empty suit." Ade had yet to learn if this was true. He never paid much attention to politics, but his mother said it frequently while watching the news. Abraham's jaw fell slack, and Nadia's eyes narrowed. Ade turned toward the sun and closed his eyes, pretending not to notice their displeasure.

"Mr. Billings, freedom has allowed you your words, but I ask you to show restraint when meeting with the president. He is, after all, coming from Cranis to meet you."

Ade's chin lowered, and he slowly opened his eyes. He drew a slow breath and looked past the runway at the horizon. A loud bang came from within the dozer, and Ade flinched. He immediately thought of Miller and her men.

Shaking his head, he turned toward Abraham. "Why would he come here to see me?"

Meeting the mythic President Hollar made little sense to Ade. President Hollar was a celebrity. Except for his mother and a few outliers, most Cranisians loved and adored Hollar.

"Why, Mr. Billings, you're a hero of Cranis. It's all over the news. How a young, dashing man infiltrated the Union and took down their defenses for a Cranis attack. You're all the talk back on Cranis.

Took down their defenses?

"But I didn't-"

"I don't think he's had time to process it all yet," Nadia interrupted.

Flustered, he looked between them. "What do you mean took down their defenses?"

Abraham's eyes shifted awkwardly from Ade to Nadia as he looked for answers. "You...ah. I was told you were responsible for-"

"He was," Nadia affirmed. She slid into him and wrapped her arms around his waist.

Ade shook his head and grimaced. "It doesn't make sense."

Nadia grinned. "You're a hero, Ade. Enjoy it."

When he first saw her, Ade felt it was love at first sight. Now, her words only aided in churning his inner turmoil. *I need to think. I need space. Fug. I don't know what I need.* He awkwardly patted

Nadia's back and stepped away from her toward Abraham. Ade felt the need to be away from her. Nadia's affection was only clouding his thoughts.

"We should go then. I'll need some time to myself before meeting President Hollar."

Abraham's round face expanded as a toothy grin lifted his rosy cheeks. He did a half bow and waved toward a glistening aircraft parked on the tarmac. Just looking at it caused Ade to squint and shield his eyes. It was white with a silver stripe running down the middle, leading to a blue Cranis flag near the back of the craft.

"After you, sir," Abraham said.

Nadia grabbed his hand and squeezed. Ade paused. Her eyes and mouth smiled, but her expression was unnerving. "It's not goodbye. I'll see you later. Don't worry. I'll be there. After it's done, we can go home."

Ade nodded. He gave a sheepish smile and squeezed her hand. Then he walked away. *Perhaps she does love me.* He shook the thought from his mind and began counting his steps. His pace increased as he put space between himself and Abraham. *I hope my mother and Floyd are okay.*

As he approached the cruiser, a man in a crisp blue and white officer's uniform exited down the ramp, took one step to the side, and rendered a sharp salute.

"Honor to have you aboard, sir," the man said as Ade passed him.

Ade gave him a quick two-finger salute and hurried up the ramp. The interior decor was the same as the presidential cabin on the train — plush seating and the latest halo tech.

"Welcome, Ade Billings. Hero of Cranis," a voice chimed over a speaker. Please make yourself comfortable. An attendant will be with you shortly."

The conflicting emotions inside him began to swell. He felt the need to either scream or cry. Abraham huffed up the ramp behind him.

"You, oh youth," Abraham gasped.

Ade stared at a photo of President Hollar on the cabin wall. It reminded him of Miller's painting. Then he took a deep breath as the door to the aircraft closed.

"We can take off as soon as you're seated," the pilot stated.

"Prepare for takeoff. We'll only be a moment," Abraham responded with a dismissive wave.

Ade shook his head as the officer disappeared into the cockpit. "Abraham, why am I a hero of Cranis? I didn't do anything."

A familiar-looking boy in a blue jumpsuit entered the main cabin from behind a gold curtain, quickly sat, and buckled the belt. Ade eyed him while trying to remember his face. Then he shook his head and glowered at Abraham. "Abraham?"

The cabin was silent for a moment. "I think what we know and what you think may very well be different, Mr. Billings," Abraham said, plopping down in a cushy chair.

"That doesn't make any sense."

"I assure you, Mr. Billings. Your courage will be rewarded in spades."

Abraham's beaming grin aggravated him.

"I don't want anything else," Ade snapped. "I just want what we agreed to."

"You will appreciate this surprise. I can assure you."

"You know me better than I know myself," Ade spat.

"I may not know you at all, frankly. But I know what awaits you."

Ade winced. He just wanted to go home. "What?"

"Alas, it is not for me to ruin the surprise. Now, please do sit. We're on a schedule," Abraham said, looking at his watch. Then he glanced at the boy. "Clark, I'll take a scotch as soon as we're airborne. Also, get Mr. Billings whatever he desires." Then he looked back at Ade.

Not one muscle moved as he stared down at Abraham. In return, Abraham's annoying smile grew wider. "A warrior's grit, eh? I'd expect nothing less from the hero of Cranis."

"I'm not," Ade began to object. He placed his hands on his hips and shook his head in disgust. "Fine, if I sit, will you tell me why people say that?"

"Certainly," Abraham chirped. "It's a deal."

Ade moved to a seat across from Abraham and sat. "Okay, why-"

"Seatbelt, please."

Ade rolled his eyes and dug into the seat for the belt. Then, clicking the clasp, he looked back at Abraham and threw his hands in the air. "There, happy?"

"Indeed," Abraham said. "Captain, we're ready."

The engines fired, and the cruiser began to move.

"So?" Ade demanded. "Why am I a hero?"

"Where to begin," Abraham pondered aloud. "Well, from Young and Nadia's reports, you infiltrated the enemy stronghold, gained their trust, and allowed us to find and destroy the enemy."

"How did I do that?"

"You contacted us upon your return to the Labor District. This was key as it allowed more time to deploy the strike team. Then you helped Nadia sneak the hacker into the enemy compound."

"Hacker?"

"Yes, the skimmer."

Ade cocked his head and glanced from side to side. "You mean Nadia's skimmer. The one we took back from the Labor District?"

Abraham grinned. "The exact one. Once it was within the compound, it hacked their network. We just needed to get close enough to connect. Then we took it over entirely."

Ade sat forward in his chair and wiped his sweaty palms on his pants. Then he shook his head. "No, I mean, how? How could I?" he said in disbelief. "I didn't know about the hacker."

Abraham waived at a Clark. "I'll have that scotch now. And you?" he asked Ade.

Ade's eyes shifted from left to right, and he shook his head. "I didn't know," he repeated.

"He'll have water for now," Abraham said to Clark.

Clark quickly exited, and Abraham examined his fingernails before his attention returned to Ade. "We know. But you were key in getting it there."

Ade thought of the chaos in the command center as the Union's defenses failed. Then, he thought of Floyd and the IED. "I was just doing what I was told," he said in disbelief.

"Precisely. A good soldier."

His words landed like a blow to the abdomen, and Ade recoiled back into his seat.

Clark returned and handed Abraham a glass filled with a brown liquid. The smell immediately took Ade back to his meeting with President Miller and sickened him. Abraham's eyes lit up, and he took a long sniff of the contents.

"Ah, only top shelf on this plane," Abraham said. "Are you sure you don't want one?" Abraham asked again.

Ade shook his head as Clark placed a water by his seat.

"Oh, you're no fun," he said while taking a drink.

Ade shuddered. *If what Abraham said is true, then I'm the reason Miller is dead.*

"Plus, we knew your mother was likely a sympathizer due to her communication with William Arfey. We figured the Union would try to extract her, so we had Nadia play the part of the distraught girlfriend. A task she was giddy to accomplish."

Ade rocked forward and placed his head in his hands. He glanced up as Abraham downed the remainder of the scotch and waved at Clark. "You really must try this. It's delightful."

The cabin began to spin. President Miller, Kramer, and countless others were dead. Then he thought of the silhouette on the roof,

Andrew reaching for the glass, and Floyd being carried from the elevator. The room became sweltering.

Ade unbuckled his harness and stood. His legs felt wobbly beneath him. He needed air. Maybe water. Anything.

"Dear boy, you must sit," Abraham insisted.

He reached for the water and knocked it off the table. "I," Ade swallowed. He took one step and staggered. "I just need to think." He turned away from Abraham and looked at the picture of Hollar on the back wall. Suddenly, he felt as though he couldn't breathe. His eyes began to well up, and the cabin started fading in and out. He took another step while attempting to increase his Beta, and the cabin went black.

***

Opening his eyes, he looked up at Abraham's sweaty, bloated face. At first, he didn't know if he was moving or if Abraham was swaying. He attempted to sit up and felt a pinch in his forearm. Looking down, he saw a needle taped to his skin. His eyes traced a clear tube from the needle to a bag of liquid hanging from a metal post. He shifted his weight to the other arm and gradually pushed himself up in the reclined chair. His head throbbed, and Ade ran his hand through his hair until it landed upon a considerable lump.

"You went down pretty hard. Hit your head on the arm of the chair," Abraham informed him.

Ade lifted the arm with the needle and looked at him.

"Oh yes. We thought you were dehydrated. Hence your collapse. Oh," Abraham said, waving a hand. Clark appeared from behind Abraham and knelt next to Ade. He extended a hand with two white capsules and then presented a glass of water.

"For the swelling and redness. We can't have you looking beat up," Abraham said.

Ade took the two pills, threw them in his mouth, and chased

them down with the glass of water.

"Thank you," Ade said to the Clark.

Clark stared at him with an odd look of disdain in his eyes. He smiled when he noticed Abraham watching him.

"Will you need anything else, sir?" the young man asked flatly.

Abraham's eyes drifted from Clark to Ade. For a second, Ade thought he saw contempt. The look was gone in a blink, and Abraham flashed a wide, toothy grin. "Another scotch, Clark. Oh, and can you remove that needle? Looks as though he's recovered."

"Of course, sir," Clark said quickly, and he knelt back down and yanked away the tape holding the needle in place.

Ade winced, and Clark removed the needle and let the blood run down Ade's arm.

Ade's brow lowered into a scowl as Clark turned to leave the room. Then he watched Abraham as he waddled across the cabin, sipping his glass of scotch. Ade wondered if he'd only imagined the break in character. *A wolf in sheep's clothing, snake in the grass... what's the expression?*

"Don't forget the scotch," Abraham called. Then he smiled and looked at the empty glass. "Only the best on this plane." Abruptly, Abraham sidestepped and pointed toward the window. "If you'd like to see something impressive, look out the window. We'll be landing soon."

As the cruiser banked, the rays of reflected light scattered throughout the cabin. Ade leaned in his seat and peered out at the glistening towers of the embassy. His gaze traced down the glass exterior to a crowd of people gathered at the foot of the building. He could not read the hoisted signs, but the crowd's excitement was clearly visible as they waved flags and pumped their fists.

"Do they think we're Hollar?" Ade asked, glancing at Abraham.

Abraham chuckled. His gleefully rosy cheeks bounced with each laugh. He leaned into the window and pointed to a small group of people separated from the crowd. As Ade's eyes landed on them, he instantly recognized President Hollar standing in the middle. His perfectly quaffed hair rustled in the breeze as his shiny new suit reflected the afternoon sun. Hollar waved at the cruiser, gave two thumbs up, and returned to the crowd. A distant cheer could be heard.

"Are we landing in that?" Ade groaned.

Abraham laughed again. "Heavens, no! We can't present our hero looking like this," he said, motioning to Ade. "We'll be landing on the roof. You'll have time to rest and eat before the ceremony."

"What ceremony?" Ade asked.

"Dear boy," Abraham said, shaking his head. "The Medal of Freedom, of course."

Ade eyed him. Abraham looked like he had eaten the last cookie and was savoring the taste.

"Doesn't Young have enough medals? From what I hear, you should just put his face on bits." Abraham omitted a loud, ridiculous cackle. His presence was growing more aggravating with each passing second.

"What's so funny?" Ade glared at him.

"Oh," Abraham gasped, pulling a handkerchief from his pocket and wiping sweat from his brow. "The ceremony is for you."

Ade just stared at him.

The Medal of Freedom was the highest honor the government could bestow on a soldier or civilian. Ade remembered the last time he saw it awarded. It stood out in his mind. He and Ethan sat on the floor playing with army men while his mother and father sat on the couch. Jack made them pause their playing and use their "Don't find me voice" while it was awarded. Ade didn't understand the importance of such a thing but remembered his father's words. "If I play my cards right, I'll have one of those." Ade didn't know why Jack would want one, but after that day, Ade dreamed of getting one too.

The cruiser hovered and slowly lowered until it softly kissed the landing platform. Ade rose to his feet as the airlock broke and filled the cabin with warm, fresh air and the cheerful chants of those far below. Ade quickly moved toward the door. He felt the need to be free of Abraham. But, before reaching the door, the pilot rushed from the cockpit and stood between Ade and the door. Ade took a deep, exasperated breath and looked back at Abraham to find him blushing even more than usual. His cheeks were red, and sweat formed under his wide eyes.

"Um, Ade. Yes. Absolutely," Abraham said, blinking twice. "It seems plans have changed," Abraham gulped. "The president wants to meet you before the ceremony."

Ade closed his eyes and shook his head. "When?" he moaned.

"Oh, well. He's on his way up now," Abraham said with a nervous smile.

Ade took an exasperated breath and shook his head. "Now?"

"Um, yes. Maybe we should sit."

Ade trudged back toward the middle of the cabin as several pairs of boots thundered up the ramp. Five men in matching black jumpsuits entered the cruiser. Their flat black suits had shiny burgundy accents on the collar and sleeves. They took up positions in each corner of the room. The fifth man walked to the middle of the room and eyed Ade skeptically.

Their physical appearance was practically identical. Light tan skin and chiseled features beneath a finely groomed head of sandy blond hair. Ade eyed each of the men in the corners before meeting the gaze of the man before him.

"Ade Billings," The man in the middle asked.

Why do they look the same? Ade pondered. He glanced back at Abraham. Abraham looked as though he was about to pass out.

"Are you Ade Billings?" He repeated.

"He is," Abraham burped.

The man in the middle studied Ade from head to toe. "Do you have any weapons on you?"

Ade's jaw clenched. "Do I look like-"

"I'll need to search you."

"I don't-"

"That won't be necessary, General," Hollar said. "He's one of our nation's greatest heroes, after all."

Ade saw Hollar enter the cabin, and the men in the four corners snapped their heels together and rendered a salute.

Hollar strolled across the room toward Ade. A blinding, white grin spread across his face. He wore an old-timey three-piece suit that appeared either black or gray, depending on his movement. He stopped directly before Ade and extended his hand. For some reason, Ade stood in awe. It made no sense at the moment. Yet the regal air of power and influence wafted off him like his expensive cologne. Ade looked down at his hand locked in a handshake with the president. He hadn't even realized he'd extended his hand until it was firmly gripped and shaken with vigor.

Then, the president released Ade's hand and patted him on the shoulder. "You honor us all," Hollar mused.

Then he stepped back, waved his finger in a circle at Ade, and peered back at a unique man standing in the doorway of the cruiser. "Gustof, we need our new hero ready to meet the world in a few hours." Then he returned to Ade, patted him on the shoulder again, and exited the cruiser.

As the president and his men exited, the distinctive, lanky man in a flashy gold suit strutted across the cabin and studied Ade's appearance. Ade wondered how he overlooked this bizarre man standing in the doorway.

"Lots of work to do. Please follow me, Mr. Billings. We have a suite prepared."

As swiftly as he arrived, the lanky man turned and disembarked the cruiser.

Ade watched the man leave. *Young was right,* Ade thought. The sound of Abraham heaving drew his attention. He glanced over his shoulder at Abraham. His face was scarlet as he peeked at Ade from the garbage can. Then he gave a guilty grin and wiped his mouth on his sleeve. “Only the good stuff,” he panted.

This is too bizarre for a dream, Ade thought.

Behind Abraham, Clark stood holding a glass of water and a bottle of pills while waiting for Abraham to finish. Ade shook his head and turned to follow the flashy man in gold.

Gustof's suit glistened in the sun. Ade paused as he looked beyond the roof of the building at the ocean. From sand to ice to water, events occurred so rapidly that he barely had time to comprehend them. And now he had returned to where his time as a spy began.

“Come along,” Gustof beckoned.

Ade's senses heightened, and his hair tingled. He glanced behind him, but nobody was there.

“Mr. Billings,” Gustof called again.

Ade joined Gustof by a gold-plated elevator with the Cranis emblem etched in the door. He could not help but think of the elevator in the Union stronghold. Two doors with the same function, yet so different by comparison. This door was extravagant beyond reason. It slid open, and Ade walked into the mirrored elevator interior and looked at an unfamiliar face looking back at him. He saw a man resembling the boy he was just a moment ago. He had dark sunken eyes and patches of stubble surrounding fresh skin on his face. His shaggy hair was matted to his head with blood and framed his imperfections. The gold door closed, and the elevator descended into the embassy. He hadn't realized it, but he had not seen his reflection since he left here. There were no gold elevators or flashy decorations in the Union stronghold. Everything they had was utilitarian. Their lives were invested in one thing – reclaiming Jaber. The elevator doors slid open behind him.

“This way, sir.”

Ade looked at the reflection of the lanky man. Gustof had a long, thin face, a pale complexion, and long blond hair on half his head – the other half was shaved, as were his face and eyebrows. There was no reason to hate this man, and yet he did. Ade didn't realize his stare lingered until the elevator doors began to close, and Gustof held out his arm to keep them open.

"I don't mean to bother you, sir, but it's right across the hall," Gustof said, pointing at the door.

Ade's eyes lowered from the reflection, and he turned toward him.

"Sorry. Long day," Ade grumbled.

Exiting the elevator, it felt like he'd traveled back in time. The smell of freshly cleaned carpets filled his nostrils. The lanky man opened the door to the suite, and Ade brushed past him into the room. The room was identical to the one he occupied during his last stay at the embassy. It was unnerving to stand in a room that felt foreign yet familiar. A click from the door closing caused Ade to lurch. He glanced back to ensure Gustof wasn't pointing a lastergun at him. Then Ade hung his head and thought about the last time he stood here. He was so sure he was doing the right thing.

Ade felt Gustof watching him, and he slowly walked to the table in the middle of the room and ran his fingers across the smooth surface of the wood. A grooming kit sat on the end of the table by a chair with a drop cloth draped over it. Just beyond the table was a flashy suit like President Hollar's on a mannequin.

"Have a seat," Gustof said, lifting the drop cloth from the chair.

Ade wondered what Floyd would think of all this. He looked around the room and held back tears. Then, he nodded, sat, and stared out the window at the ocean. The lanky man draped the cloth around him and taped it to his neck.

His thoughts drifted to his childhood home, but his thoughts were scattered. Ade's gaze dropped to his hands, and he examined the dirt under his nails. He thought of how his mother would scold him for such filth. His breath quickened, and he focused on the sound of the scissors. Floyd's laugh entered his thoughts. Then, the faceless man appeared and morphed into President Miller. He felt his muscles clench as his mind reeled. His eyes shot to the table, looking for a distraction. His stare befell a familiar object. Aggressively shaking his head, Ade stood, yanked the cloth away from his neck, and threw it to the floor. His skin crawled. He wanted to be outside himself.

"Go," he commanded.

Gustof stood looking at him.

Ade lifted the chair and slammed it back to the floor. "I said go!"

The lanky man stepped back and placed the scissors on the table. "I will let the president know you needed a moment," he said. Then he slowly backed out of the room as if preparing to dodge some thrown object.

The second the door closed, Ade stepped up to the table and ran his finger over the inscription stamped into the red leather of his father's journal. Ade yanked off his clothing and threw items about the room. He began pacing. Then he stormed toward the shower.

He cranked the water to cold and let the cool water wash over him. Then, whenever a thought entered his mind, he scrubbed a limb until it burned red. When he had scoured his entire body clean, he turned off the water and leaned against the cool marble wall. He was unable to control his thoughts. They bounced like a batted ball between Cranis and the Union. Ade hammered his hand on the marble and pushed open the shower door. He centered himself before the mirror above the vanity and scowled at his reflection. He hated the image in the mirror. It was not him. The man he looked at was a stranger. He ran to the table, snatched electronic hair clippers from the grooming kit, and returned to the mirror. Without pause, he clicked the button and shaved his head. Wet clumps of hair fell into the sink with each swipe, and his movements became more determined. When there was no more hair to shave, he ran his hand over his prickly scalp and looked again at the reflection in the mirror. The boy was gone, and the battered, tired man remained. He reared back and threw a fist at his reflection. The mirror cracked and splintered. A crippling sorrow swallowed him like quicksand, and he sank to the floor and wept. He gasped for air between sobs. His hand began to throb, and Ade looked at the blood dripping from his knuckles to the floor. Then, he looked at his bruised, naked body in a mirror shard and laughed hysterically.

A knock sounded at the door, and Ade's laughter trailed into silence. Another knock came, and Ade rolled away from the sound and pulled a towel over him like a blanket. The marble floor was cold against his skin and reminded him of the stone walls of Floyd's home. He listened for another knock that never came and thought of Floyd's rugged face looking through the bars at him.

The door opened, and Captain Young entered with his usual casual saunter.

"Ade, everything okay?"

Young's keen eyes glanced about the room and met Ade through the half-open bathroom door. Ade abruptly looked away as if he wasn't watching.

"Ah, there you are." His steps grew louder and were accompanied by something that sounded like a pocket full of change clinking together. Then, finally, the clinking stopped, and the bathroom door moved on its hinges. Ade half rolled and looked up at the man looming over him. He was dressed in a royal blue suit with a gold sash draped over his chest with countless decorative medals pinned to it. His shoes were like a black mirror. "What are you doing on the floor?" Young asked.

"I..." Ade didn't know what excuse would work. "I was hot. The floor-"

"Is cold," Young said, looking from the mirror to Ade's bloody hand.

Ade nodded.

"It's funny. You get used to the cold being over there. When you're there, you never think you'll adjust to the cold and crave warmth, but when you leave, it's always too hot."

"Yeah, I guess."

"I'm surprised you adapted so quickly."

Ade remained silent, and Captain Young shifted his weight from one leg to the other.

"Nadia mentioned you stayed with Floyd while down there. It must have taken real restraint – living with the enemy."

"It was fine," Ade sighed. He pushed himself to a seated position against the vanity and adjusted his towel. This was a conversation he didn't want to have. "I should-"

"You know, I met Floyd once. At the end of the war," Young began. "He was in the hangar with what was left of his men. They had just come from the battlefield after surrendering at the Battle of Falling Rock. I remember looking at him and thinking he looked like a Viking, so I asked the floor commander who he was. When I heard his name... Man, I'd never felt so intimidated. The war was short, but I can't tell you the number of times we heard his name. It was like he was everywhere."

Ade recalled the first time he saw Floyd. The large man with a fiery red beard and black eyes sprinted from his floating trash can to help them. Even at that moment, Ade never felt threatened by Floyd. To think that a decorated warrior like Young stood in awe of him felt surreal.

"He fought at Falling Rock?" Ade asked.

Young nodded. "That man is what all the stories are about. Floyd and his men held off an entire army for over six hours." He paused for a moment as his thoughts drifted. "I lost a lot of friends because of that man. But when I saw him in that hangar, I couldn't help but respect him. It was like seeing Achilles sitting with his men after a battle. I guess what I'm trying to say is sometimes we tend to view the enemy differently at certain times. You may have hated him for what he did to your father, but it's natural to feel otherwise after spending time with him. You know what I mean?"

Ade rubbed his weary face and looked at Young. Young's eyes looked softer than they had previously. Ade paused, wondering if he knew, then looked beyond him at the robe hanging on the bathroom door. “Can you toss me that?”

Young glanced over his shoulder at the robe.

“Not hot anymore?” Young asked.

Ade shook his head as Young tossed the robe to him.

Ade pulled the robe over his shoulders and wrapped it around him before standing. He felt Young’s knowing gaze burning a hole in him as if pushing his soul to scream. Ade took a deep breath. He attempted to close his eyes to clear his thoughts, but as soon as he did so, President Miller’s face appeared and forced him from the darkness.

“Why do you keep deactivating your Beta?” Young asked.

Ade studied the puddle of blood he’d left on the tile floor. “Makes me feel less human.”

Young nodded. “Sometimes it’s good to feel pain. Now is not the time, though.”

Ade absently nodded and examined the grout between the tiles.

“Do you remember why you began this journey?”

“Of course I do,” Ade said quickly.

“Do you still want revenge?” Young questioned.

Ade turned his gaze from the floor and glared at Young. His heart and his mind provided two different answers to the question.

He knew Young was beating around the bush at something, but Ade wasn’t biting. It was too late. Miller was dead. His mother and Floyd were in the wind, and Ade was solely to blame. The burden of this thought crushed him. He hoped Floyd and his mother would understand his motives, but something inside told him they never would.

“Can you move?” Ade said, standing before Young in the doorway.

Young moved from the doorway, and Ade pushed past him into the main room.

“You know,” Young called after him. “Sometimes, when we win, we actually lose. And we don’t even know we’ve lost until it’s too late. So, I'll ask you again. Do you still want revenge?"

Ade walked to the table and looked down at the journal. The pain swelled within, and he blinked twice and set his Beta to maximum output. Within seconds, he was completely calm. He felt his heart rate slow in his chest, and the pain subsided to a dull annoyance in the back of his mind.

He gazed across the room at Young. "There are no winners in war—only life and death. I will have revenge — one day. Now, if you don't mind. I don't want you standing there while I change."

Young eyed him for a moment. "One day, the Beta won't be enough. You must learn to let people help you."

"Not today," Ade muttered.

"Ade, you-"

"You are dismissed, Captain."

Young stood watching as Ade examined the contents of the grooming kit. Then he took an exasperated breath and looked at the floor. "I'll let Gustoff know his services are no longer required."

"Please do," Ade said passively.

Ade listened to Young's footsteps and waited until they disappeared beyond the closed door. He peered about the empty room and let the robe slip off his lean shoulders to the floor. In the grooming kit, he found a bottle of SkinRegen. He wiped the blood from his hand and sprayed the wound. It immediately began to scab over, and Ade watched as it dried and the scab flaked away, revealing fresh skin. Brushing away the flakes, he walked to the mannequin and examined the suit. Piece by piece, Ade lifted each outfit layer and covered himself with the fabric of lies. Then, he raised his father's journal from the table, and it slid into a pocket. Finally, tightening the cloth noose around his neck, Ade walked to the mirror and examined his appearance.

He thought of what Floyd had said before the attack. "Is it better to live an elegant lie or be truthful and suffer the consequences," Ade muttered.

He tugged the cuffs of his shirt beyond the jacket and wiggled his shoulders. Even dulled by the Beta, he knew the lie would torment his soul until his last breath was drawn. He blinked again and attempted to adjust his Beta but found he'd already set it to maximum output. "Fug," he exhaled. "I need a drink."

From his interface, he accessed the guest network and selected *Directory*. Then, scrolling through options, he found *Room Service*, but a knock at the door interrupted him.

"What?" he yelled, closing the interface.

The door pushed open, and Young re-entered the room. Ade rolled his eyes.

"What-"

"Clear," Young called, and before Ade could argue, Ambassador Monroe sashayed into the room.

Monroe looked even more pompous than Ade remembered. With his shoulders thrown back and nose in the air, Monroe crossed the room toward Ade with a pleased grin. He, too, wore a classic suit, but he had a large royal blue sash across his chest.

"Mr. Billings, your efforts far exceeded our expectations," Monroe beamed. He stopped just short of Ade and extended his hand. Ade returned the gesture, and Monroe shook his hand and glanced back at Young. "Look at him. So dapper." His grin returned to Ade. Our young hero returned a man."

Monroe abruptly dropped the handshake and motioned to the chair. "Please, let's sit for a moment."

Ade shook his head. "I'd rather stand."

Monroe maintained his cheerful disposition. "Of course. Well, now, as you know, you are being awarded the Medal of Freedom. Quite extraordinary for a man your age. But, before the festivities, I want you to know that I am a man of my word. I will say it was not an easy task. Strings needed to be pulled, but it is only right a hero of Cranis is awarded with those dearest by his side."

Ade frowned. Nadia was the last person he wanted to see.

Monroe rocked on his heels with excitement. "That is why I requested a presidential pardon for brother."

Ade's eyes widened, and his jaw hung loosely from his face.

"Bring him in," Monroe beckoned.

Ade watched in disbelief as a man Ade barely recognized entered the room. Ethan was a splinter of a man. Razor thin with gaunt features and dark tan skin wrapped tight around the bone.

"I will give you some time to catch up," Monroe beamed. "I'll return in a few hours to escort you to the ceremony. I'd suggest some food, but not drink. We need our hero sharp," he said with a wink. Then he stood staring at Ade.

Ade glanced at Monroe, but his attention quickly returned to Ethan. His breath quickened. Seeing him brought both joy and sorrow. Ethan now seemed much older than the meager two years separating them. Ade had never imagined what it was like in the labor camps, but seeing the gaunt man before him made Ade realize it was hell.

Monroe's grin faded, and he glanced at Young. "I thought he'd appreciate my gesture."

"I believe he's in shock, sir," Young replied.

Young's response drew Ade's attention back to Monroe, and his words finally registered. "Oh, yes. Thank you. It is greatly appreciated." Ade felt like a puppet dangling from two strings

"Indeed," Monroe said with a grin. He clapped his hands together. "Please do get something to eat. It appears your brother could use a good meal."

CHAPTER 27 | 5856-W25

The latch clicked, and the two of them stood in silence. Ethan stood staring blankly at something at the back of the room, and Ade turned and saw a pale green chair near the window. Looking back at his brother, his stare seemed to penetrate the chair and extend beyond the realm of human vision. Ade took a step and bent forward at the waist until his face was within Ethan's line of sight.

"Thirty seconds," Ethan muttered.

Ade furrowed his brow and stood. *Thirty seconds? What's in thirty seconds?* Standing there watching his brother, Ethan's right brow raised and lowered as he stared. *They've broken him.* If not for his augments, Ade was certain the same would have happened to him. His shoulders slumped as he considered a course of action. Then he leaned back into Ethan's line of sight.

"Ethan, it's me, Ade. You're safe."

Ethan blinked and looked his brother in the eye. The blank stare was gone, and his mind returned to the present. "It hasn't been that long," Ethan said.

Ethan approached and placed a hand on Ade's shoulder. Then he pulled him in and wrapped his arms around his younger brother. Ade buried his face in Ethan's bony shoulder and deactivated his Beta. Tears broke free and dampened Ethan's brown jumpsuit.

"You're here," Ade sputtered.

Ethan squeezed him tight. "Thanks to you, I'm guessing."

Ade's nose rubbed the course jumpsuit fabric as he nodded. Ethan pulled back and placed his hands on Ade's shoulders. Ethan's keen eyes examined Ade from head to toe and then glanced around the room.

"I see you've gone and done something impulsive again,"

Ethan said, his eyes returning to Ade.

"I really did."

"What happened?"

Ade shook his head, stepped back, and dried his eyes on his sleeve. He sniffled and sucked in his lips. "Mom was sick. I tried to use Dad's scanner, but they tracked me."

"Is she okay?"

"Yeah. She got out."

"What do you mean, she got out?" Ethan demanded.

"After the attack, before the explosion, she got out. Abraham said."

Ethan's eyes widened, and the white made them look larger because of his dark, tan skin. "Attack? Abraham? Ade, you're not making sense."

Ade activated his Beta and took a breath. As his thoughts cleared, he looked at his brother. "We should sit."

"Ade, what did you do?"

Ade moved back to the table, sat, and motioned to a chair.

Ethan reluctantly joined Ade at the table while eyeing him curiously. "Ade, I'm serious. I'm starting to worry."

Ade nodded. "After you were convicted, Mother and I struggled to afford the house..." He started from the beginning and dove into the events that led him to this moment. Ade spoke calmly and with precise details of the events. He recalled the events with The Beast and his demise by Floyd's son. Then he continued through the Labor District, the ambush and his shooting of a Cranisian soldier, Nadia, and so on until his breakdown only minutes before. Ethan sat quietly listening. He did not interrupt as he often did when they were children. Instead, he concentrated on Ade's words and occasionally nodded or winced at the tale. When Ade finished, he sat erect in the chair, nodded, and wiped his sweaty palms on the jumpsuit pants.

Ethan stood and placed his hands on his hips. He looked down at Ade, raised an eyebrow, and shook his head. "And you're sure Mom is okay?"

"She is. They can't harm her. It's part of our agreement."

Ethan took a deep breath, turned, and walked to the wall of windows.

A deafening silence befell the room as Ade awaited a response from his brother. It was unlike Ethan not to have a reaction of some sort. He was not as quick as Ade but usually had something within a second or two. With a blink, Ade increased his Beta and stood. The silhouette of Ethan's skeletal frame appeared both fragile and ominous against the clear blue sky.

Ade crossed the room to stand beside Ethan and look at the ocean. *It's like everything on this planet is vast and dangerous.* On Cranis, Ade loved their trips to the beach. They basked in the sun while swimming in the surf and playing hoverdisc. This ocean felt like a vast body of water with danger lurking beneath the churning surface.

"I understand," Ethan finally stated. "I don't agree with your actions, but I understand. It's just, Ade, there is so much you don't know."

Ade's eyes remained on the waves, and he nodded. "You knew about Floyd calling Mom?"

"Yeah, I knew."

"Figures," Ade said with a sideways glance.

"You don't understand it like I do. Floyd was their best friend — her and Dad. Dad was able to leave things behind and move on. Mom couldn't."

"Did you know they were both in the Union?"

"I suspected. Dad put on a good show, but I found some old pictures."

Ade watched a wave come in from the ocean. It grew and foamed and then crashed into the rocks of the shoreline.

"I guess it doesn't matter, anyway," Ade stated.

"Are you using the Beta?"

"Yeah."

"I can tell. You seem detached compared to normal. Normally, your emotions are on your sleeve."

"It helps. I don't like it all the time. It makes me feel like I'm piloting a robot instead of my own body."

Ethan snickered and turned away from the window. "Maybe if you'd had it earlier, you'd have been more levelheaded and not tried to use Dad's scanner. Amateur move, Ade. Everyone knows it uses facial recognition."

Ade shrugged. "You said it yourself. There's a lot I don't know."

Ethan cracked a small smile and looked at his brother. "You have no idea."

"Why did you keep Dad's stuff?" Ade asked, observing his brother closely. "You said they confiscated it all, but then I saw Mom packing it when we moved. We wouldn't be here if it weren't for that."

"There's my little brother," Ethan deadpanned.

"I'm serious."

"Active Dad's interface."

The hair on Ade's neck stood, and he looked back at the empty room. He had not mentioned their father's work for fear of the room being bugged.

"It's fine. I scanned the room for audio and video surveillance. I knew before you said anything. You're connected to the network."

"You what?" Ade gasped. *He can scan the network? How?*

Ethan frowned and shook his head. "Save the questions. Just do as I say. Then I'll answer all your questions."

Ade had never been one to do what Ethan told him. Generally, he rejected this as a point of principle, but Ade blinked twice.

"Okay, now what?" Ade asked.

"Go to the crown."

Ade's eyes shot toward his brother as his mouth gaped. He struggled to make sense of it. *How does he know? Are they all the same?*

"Have you accessed it yet? It's the big crown in the corner."

Ade gawked at his brother through the amber interface, stared at him for a second longer, and then selected the crown. Again, the same password screen popped up on his screen.

"I tried this before. It needs a password-"

"Checkmate," Ethan said.

Ade stood dumbfounded.

"If it had gone as planned, it would have activated on your birthday. Then, there were clues on your SATA that would have led you to the password. Dad thought it would be fun to watch."

"Ethan, what-"

"Checkmate," Ethan repeated. "Enter it now."

There were too many questions, and Ade's mouth was dry from hanging open. He slowly entered the password. On the last keystroke, the interface disappeared. Ade stopped breathing. The word loading appeared and flashed to *Online Connected*. A new, deep red interface appeared. New icons displayed shortcuts to his mods with a simplified adjustment setting. Several new icons replaced the area where the crown had been — a circle with a slash, a lightning bolt, and a power symbol. However, the most staggering difference between the interfaces was the list of auto-connected devices displayed on the right of the interface. Ade selected the devices and began scrolling through the list. *Sentry Gun, Jail Access,* and *Drone Deploy* passed his vision. He shook his head as the green dot beside each entry indicated he was connected.

"I don't understand. It says I'm connected to the sentry gun," Ade puzzled.

"Try selecting it," Ethan instructed.

Before Ade could highlight the gun, it had been selected, and a mini screen popped up in his display with a view of the main entrance. Ade paused. He blinked to close the interface. *Open interface*, Ade thought. The interface reappeared, and Ade's breath quickened. *Select sentry door guns.* A video feed displayed with a crosshair was in the middle of the screen, and below the feed was a list of commands: *pan, zoom, tilt, and fire*. Ade selected the pan feature and moved the gun slightly to the left. As the camera moved, Ade flinched.

"Ethan, I-"

"Can you control the gun?"

Ade slowly nodded while the color drained from his face.

"There's hope after all," Ethan grinned.

In disbelief, Ade shook his head. "I can interface by thought," he gasped.

Ethan's brow lifted, and then he paused and nodded. "Huh, I wasn't sure it would work."

"How?" Ade muttered.

"Dad figured out neuro transmitting into the interface console. He found synthetic wouldn't allow transfer. It had to be organic. He also found that using the host's DNA to create the polymer allowed an instantaneous thought/action connection."

"This is crazy," Ade said.

"It's Dad's life's work," Ethan stated.

"But what is it? A hacker?"

"It's more like an admin console," Ethan began. "It overrides and connects to any available network and the connected devices. You won't need the network to connect to the device if you're within range. The interface will override security protocols and connect you."

"Why would Dad make this?"

"To save lives, Ade. It's that simple. Remember the boy that fell off the roof of the school?"

Ade vaguely remembered the news story. "The one who died?"

Ethan nodded. When the paramedics arrived, their tools failed to connect to the network. If they had, it might have saved his life."

Ade frowned and looked back through the list of options. Guns, electrical, transportation, and communications, he could either control or disable everything connected to the network just by thinking about it. Ade cringed. Ethan's example made sense, but Jack must have known the dangers of creating such a device. "You could destroy a city with this," Ade mumbled.

Ethan's eyes turned cold, and Ade shuddered under his gaze. It felt like he was looking into the eyes of his father. "Dad knew what it was capable of. He didn't mean it to be used for war. That's why he didn't want either side to have it. He knew they'd just use it to kill each other. That's why he gave it to you."

"Did Mom know?"

"Only Dad and I knew," Ethan answered.

"But how? You were never in Dad's shop. You never spoke," Ade questioned.

"We talked all the time. When you were young, you got so jealous if we did things. So, we figured out our own way, and it stuck."

It was like hearing Jack was in the Union all over again. It was hard for Ade to believe, and the thought felt utterly wrong. *That makes no sense. I never saw them together. But he had the password, and he scanned the network.* "Did he give you one too?"

"I volunteered for the first build. Mine can only scan and connect to open devices. I can't connect to secure devices. Dad found it was necessary to bypass encryption because mine wouldn't connect to anything. Everything is encrypted now."

Ade searched for answers as he recalled their shared past. Then Ethan's words settled in amongst his spiraling thoughts.

"You volunteered? But I didn't even know!"

Ethan withdrew into a memory and smiled. "You were always a bit too trusting when it came to Dad. He didn't think you were ready, so we installed it with an activation timer. Dad wanted to wait and ask, but he was worried someone was coming for his work. I thought he was paranoid... Turns out he was right."

We... I wasn't his favorite son. It was Ethan. The thought stung.

"But why not replace yours then? Since he chose you."

"It's not that simple," Ethan answered. "The organic polymer fuses with the surrounding tissue. It cannot be removed without serious damage."

Ade's hand slid up the exterior of his suit and felt the bulge from his father's journal. Then, he quickly reached inside the jacket and presented it to Ethan. "I guess he'd have wanted you to have that."

Ethan's eyes softened, and he looked to the floor and shook his head. "Still sore about us spending time together, huh? No, he wanted you to have that, Ade. He loved us both."

"Just take it."

The look of compassion vanished in a blink, and Ethan's brow lowered. "You should deactivate your Beta. You're almost not human."

"I'm thinking clearly."

Ethan threw his hands in the air and turned away from his brother. He took a few steps away and whirled back toward Ade. "You know that's why I was mean to you! I loved him and could never spend time with him because you were too jealous. You wanted all his attention, and he was so busy with you and his work that he barely had time for us. That's why Mom talked to Floyd, and that's why I tried to make your life miserable."

Ade stood staring at his brother. With a deep breath, Ade decreased his Beta.

"You were the baby," Ethan ranted. "Even Mom spent more time with you. And where was I? Off on my own. At some point, you must face the fact that you are responsible for things too, Ade."

Ade bit his lower lip. His brother's words stirred a pot of boiling emotions. He thought back to his childhood. All the memories of time in the city with his father, in his shop, watching the sunset, the beach – Ethan was never around. "Now is not the time for this," Ade said. "It's too much."

"You have everything Dad ever worked for inside your head. You have to let the past go. It's what Dad would have wanted, Ade."

Ade hung his head, and tears broke free. He nodded in agreement. "It is."

"Good," Ethan said, placing a consoling hand on Ade's shoulder. “We’ve both been through a lot. Dad hoped this would bring us together — not push us apart.”

Ade nodded and glanced up at Ethan with teary eyes.

“Go ahead,” Ethan said, “but don’t set it to max. Use your brain instead.”

Ade set his Beta and paused for it to take effect. “Okay, what do we do?”

“We start by teaching you what’s in your head. Maybe then we can get out of this mess. But, before that, we should get some food. I’m starving.”

CHAPTER 28 | 5856-W25

Crumbs fell from Ethan's lips as he chewed with his mouth open. Ade sat stupefied as he watched his brother devour the last corn muffin. Ade tried to remember their last meal together as a family. It had been rare and only occurred at the insistence of Ann. It was usually just the three of them when they were young, as Jack often took his meal to the workshop. Later, it was just Ade and his mother, as Ethan was often out with his friends. The last family meal he could remember was Founders Day. Founders Day celebrated the first settlement on planet Cranis. Ann spent most of the day in the kitchen while Jack watched the halovision. It was the only day of the year Jack didn't work. He sat in his favorite beat-up burgundy chair and complained all day that athletes contributed nothing to society beyond a distraction that interfered with the progression of our species. And yet, there he sat. On their last Founders Day as a family, Jack complained about sports, Ann complained because Jack wasn't helping in the kitchen, Ethan complained that he was stuck at home, and Ade sat across from his father, pretending not to enjoy the game. By the time they finally sat to eat as a family, the tension caused them to eat in silence. Both Jack and Ethan ate with their mouths open, and the sound of chewing played like two dueling pianos. Halfway through the meal, Ann stood, scolded them for their poor manners, and exited the room. The moment she left, Ethan stood and ran out the door. Jack shrugged, asked Ade to pass the strutten, and suggested they work in the shop after the meal.

Ade cringed as he remembered this. Then he watched his brother wipe his mouth and lean back in the chair.

"I'm probably going to regret eating that much," Ethan

groaned. "So, did you successfully control every networked device on the floor?"

"A guy was waiting for the elevator. Every time it stopped, I sent it to a different floor. I think he was pissed after the third time."

Ethan let out a single laugh. "The most advanced technology in either world and you're playing pranks."

"Better than firing off a few rounds at the entry checkpoint."

"Less conspicuous, at least," Ethan agreed. "Anything else?"

"I disabled the network on the floor below us for three seconds."

"Wow, you're a wild man."

Ade smiled. "I saw a guy on the security feed turn in a circle with confusion."

"You hacked the security system?" Ethan said with a look of disapproval.

Ade looked sheepishly at his brother and shrugged. Then his brother started laughing.

"You fugduger," Ade scoffed. "I thought I did something wrong!"

"Takes one to know one," Ethan responded.

A knock came at the door, and Abraham burst into the room before Ade could respond. His face was bright red. It looked as though he had run a mile before opening the door. Ade scowled at his presence. "It's only been an hour and a half, Abraham. Monroe said-"

"My apologies," Abraham wheezed. "Ambassador Monroe wanted to be here for this momentous occasion, but he is busy with President Hollar."

"What is it, Abraham?" Ade said with annoyance.

"Bring her in."

Ann was escorted in by two soldiers. Her hands were shackled at her waist; she wore a new tan jumpsuit. Her skin was red from windburn, and her eyes appeared more gray than blue as they locked onto Ade. Her expression was as cold as the Polar Ring, and a shiver ran down Ade's spine. Ethan jumped to his feet and stepped toward her, but a soldier motioned for him to halt. Ade swallowed and looked away from her and toward Abraham.

Abraham struggled to remove an envelope stamped with the Cranis seal from his pocket. He fumbled with the envelope and removed a letter. Clearing his throat, Abraham attempted to stand straight.

"On behalf of Ambassador Monroe and authorized by President Hollar, we, the people of Cranis, do hereby pardon Ann Billings and release her into the custody of Ade Billings. Upon completion of the ceremony, Ann, Ade, and Ethan Billings will be transported to Cranis and awarded the remaining items in the agreed terms. We thank Ade Billings for his service to our beloved home. Signed James Arden Monroe, Ambassador of Jaber." Then he folded the paper, stuffed it in the envelope, and motioned to Ann's shackles. "Guard, please remove the restraints."

Ade did not dare look at his mother. He could feel her wrathful gaze upon him. Instead, he stood and watched Abraham scuttle across the floor and stand before him. "The award letter," Abraham said. "Thank you for your service."

The sweat on Ade's hand soaked into the paper as he accepted it. It seemed odd that after everything they gave him a piece of paper.

"You're welcome," Ade mumbled. Even the words coming from his lips made him cringe in the presence of his mother.

"I'll be back in a bit. I need to freshen up and change into a ceremony suit," Abraham stated.

Abraham's words took a moment to sink in as Ade looked at him, nodded, and then looked at him again. "I thought we had three hours? It's only been one and a half."

"Oh yes, well, Hollar bumped up the time of the ceremony. Due to recent events, several small skirmishes have taken place. Hollar would like to see them quelled and return to Cranis to deal with an unlikely group of protestors," Abraham said, patting Ade on the shoulders with both hands. Then he turned and walked toward the door. "Crazy to think there are pro-Unionists on Cranis. My, how the crazies come out of the woodwork."

The door closed behind Abraham and his entourage.

Ann huffed. "What a pig of a man." She took a step, then quickened her pace as she crossed the room and embraced Ethan. They held each other as Ade stood awkwardly off to the side.

As they parted, Ann sniffed and wiggled her shoulders as she cleared a few tears with her fingers. Then she looked at Ade. There was no love in her eyes. No emotion whatsoever. Ade was taken aback.

"Are you okay?" she asked plainly.

Ade thought of the time he fell from the tree. She came running to him, concern in her eyes, but the moment he admitted to being okay, the fire ignited. He never made that mistake again.

"No," Ade said. "What happened to the others?"

Ann's cheekbone twitched, and her breath quickened. Her eyes began to well up, and she blinked rapidly while holding back her tears. Then she looked toward the window and walked away.

"Mom-"

"Don't," Ethan said, placing a hand on his chest. He stepped in close to Ade and leaned in. "I may understand why you did it, but she will take more time."

Ethan followed Ann to the window and put his arm around her. She leaned into him and began to weep. Ade suddenly didn't know what to do with his hands as he stood there watching them. He fumbled with the buttons on his jackets and then stuffed his hands in his pants pockets. Minutes passed as he stood there waiting. Ade heard them whispering and strained to listen to what they were saying without resorting to his augmentations. Growing impatient, he took a small step toward them but stopped as his mother looked at him. She glanced back at Ethan, nodded, and began walking toward him. Her expression changed three times in the ten steps it took to join him by the table. It morphed between compassion, indifference, and then anger. Anger is what met him at the table.

"I know why you did it, but how could you?" Ann said. Her voice was steady but an octave higher than usual. "They were good people, Ade. They took us in."

"I didn't know that when I made the deal. I thought we were Cranisians."

Ann hung her head. Her chest raised and lowered with each long, deep breath. Then she placed her hands on her hips and shook her head. "Ethan said as much."

"What happened to the others?"

Ann said nothing. Her eyes remained on the floor. Ade saw her hands squeezing her hips.

"Mom?" Ade asked, quietly.

She took a breath and shook her head again. Ann didn't look up at him. Then she spoke just slightly louder than a whisper. "Most escaped – Cooper, Luger, and Andrew. Floyd and I were captured."

Ade gaped, and it felt like the weight of his heart multiplied by three. He glanced at his brother. Ethan was again staring through the wall, intently looking at something in his interface. "What?" Ade stammered. "Where is he?"

Ann sniffled and looked away from the floor to the window. Ade could see the fear in her red eyes. She swallowed and sucked in her lips. "I don't know. They separated us."

"They haven't logged him as a prisoner on the public records. I can't access the other documents," Ethan said. "Ade, access the Central Holding Network and look for the booking computer. They should have a log on there."

A single knock came at the door, and, without pause, Abraham scurried in with Clark at his heels.

"We're not ready, Abraham," Ade scowled.

"No matter," Abraham said. "It's time. The ceremony is set to begin shortly." Then he looked back at Clark and extended his hand. "Kerchief." Clark dug in his inner pocket and removed a handkerchief.

Abraham wiped the sweat from his brow and tossed the cloth back at Clark.

"We need more time, Abraham. My mother-"

"A pardon can be rescinded just as easily as given," Abraham seethed. His brow lowered over his narrow eyes.

There it is, Ade thought. The forced chipper persona cracked and confirmed Ade's suspicions. He had never liked Abraham, but now he detested him. He glanced at his mother and then at Ethan. Ethan nodded and looked to the door.

"It's fine. You know what to do," Ethan said, nodding toward the door.

"Fine," Ade huffed. "We'll go."

Abraham's grin returned. "Wonderful. Follow me. We will need to take the service elevator. Oh," Abraham paused. "You do look quite dapper, by the way." Then he headed for the door.

Clark looked at Ann and Ethan and then back toward Abraham. He gave them a nod and followed.

Ade glowered at Abraham's back as he opened the door. "Find Floyd," Ann whispered. "He's here somewhere." He glanced at Ann as she stepped beside him. Her skin was paler than usual, and frown lines sunk deep into her face. He met her fearful gaze, and she tugged on his coat to keep him from leaving the room. Ade opened his interface and accessed the Central Holding Network. There he found the booking computer and selected it. There was a slight pause and a blinking red dot beside the device. Then the dot turned green and displayed the booking computer console.

"The door is this way, Mr. Billings," Abraham grumbled.

"Just a second. Forgot something, Ade said, turning to Ethan.

Ann grabbed Ade's hand. "Hurry," she whispered.

Ade wiggled his fingers to loosen her grip. He began toggling tabs until he landed on the prisoner log. Ade nervously licked his lips as he scanned the names.

"Ade, he is-"

"Ethan, I can't find Floyd."

The words escaped his lips just as his mother squeezed his hand.

"Find who?" Abraham chimed.

Ade whirled around to find Abraham standing within arm's reach. The effectiveness of his Beta seemed to diminish. Fear, uncertainty, and rage swelled in a blink as he stared at Abraham's smug grin.

"Oh, mister scowly face, it was only a question, but I do believe you said Floyd."

Perhaps his body was becoming accustomed to the effects of the Beta, or maybe it was just that Ade had hit a tipping point, but Abraham's arrogance pushed Ade over the ledge.

"Where is he?" Ade demanded.

Ann gasped.

Abraham grinned. "Oh yes, the antagonist to our hero."

"Tell me."

"And ruin the surprise? Oh, no, Mr. Billings. Besides, the Ambassador would never forgive me. Now, let's go. You're testing my patience."

Ade thought of Floyd smiling. Then he remembered seeing him in the feed as his soldiers carried him away. His mother's hand clenched his tightly. A wave of emotions crashed down on him at once, and Ade quickly deactivated the floor's communication network. Then, he selected the folding blinds and set them to close over the wall of windows.

Abraham looked over Ade's shoulder as the blinds clicked and closed over the window. "Well, that's a neat trick," Abraham said with a curious look at Ade. Then, a look of recognition befell his eyes. "A neat trick indeed."

Ade killed the lights, and the room became pitch black. Then, activating thermal vision, he watched as Abraham stumbled back, trying to feel his way around in the dark while Clark stood still near the door.

"Mr. Billings, I...I...You can leave. You have everything you wanted." The timber in his voice shifted. "Young! Anyone-"

"Where is he, Abraham? Tell me now!"

Abraham twirled, and his movements became more frantic. He swung his arms wildly, attempting to counter anything approaching. "I... Please, Ade. I'm-"

"Just tell him!" Ann shouted.

Ade clicked the lights back, and Abraham froze. Then, slowly, Abraham turned his head toward Ade. "I'll pay you. I-"

In a blur, Clark rushed forward, reached into his pocket, and lunged toward Abraham. Ade tensed and, by reflex, bent at the knees, preparing to counter. Then Clark thrust his hand into the small of Abraham's back. A long exhale preceded Abraham's eyes rolling toward the top of his head before he collapsed to the floor.

Ade's eyes shot to the item in Clark's hands. He held a small silver object about the size of an old-fashioned pen. At one end were two metal prongs and a red button at the other.

"You disgust me," Clark snarled. And then he spat on Abraham's motionless body.

Ade set his legs to combat, clenched his fists, and killed the lights. Before he could attack, a single word ceased his advance.

"Union," Clark said. "I'm Union." Watching his movements in thermal, Clark stood straight, placed the weapon back in his jacket pocket, and raised his hands. "I'm guessing you can see me."

Turning the lights back on, Ade eyed the curious young man.

"My name's not Clark. It's Gunner."

Gunner circled to Abraham's feet. "He's going to be heavy."

"Is he-" Ann gasped.

"Knocked out. He'll be fine."

"How do we know you are Union?" Ade asked skeptically.

"You told my sister to go visit Andrew in the hospital. She told me they planned a date," Gunner replied. Then he knelt, grabbed

Abraham by his feet, and dragged him toward the bathroom. "Little help please."

Ethan hurried around and lifted by the shoulders.

"Did you kill the comms too? If so, you should reactivate them. People will notice if you don't," Gunner huffed.

Ade immediately enabled the network and watched as Ethan and Gunner placed Abraham on the bathroom floor and closed the door.

"Is Amanda okay?" Gunner asked.

"She was with the group that escaped," Ann stated.

Gunner nodded and gave her a slight grin. "That's good. One less thing to worry about. "So, what the hell just happened? How did you get the network password? I've been trying for months."

Ade gave Ethan a quick look. "I have a hacker," Ethan blurted. "We hacked the network, and he's using his interface to control network devices."

Ann glowered at each of her sons and then looked at Gunner. "We need to find Floyd. Can you help?"

Gunner placed his hands on his hips and studied the three of them before shaking his head. "I thought he was with them?" He asked Ann.

Ann dropped her gaze and shook her head. Then, her eyes narrowed and returned to Gunner. "We just need to find Floyd and get out of here. Can you help us or not?"

The young man stood for a moment without an answer and then nodded. "The General is at the ceremony. They're planning on making an example of him. We had a plan, but they moved up the time."

Ade felt panic crawl up his back and into his mind. *Make an example of him*. "They're going to kill him," he muttered.

Ann's breath quickened. She looked up at the ceiling and took one step forward, then she turned and took another step. It was as if she couldn't decide on a direction. She shook her head as if baffled by an unsolvable riddle. "What if...What if Ade does the same thing? The same thing he did here. What if he turns out the lights, and you zap the guard with that, that thing."

"Too many guards," Gunner stated. "And you can't kill the lights. It's in the Atrium. All-natural light."

"Well, what were you going to do?" Ethan asked.

"My job was to gain intel on the layout and let them in. That's it."

"Well, what were they going to do?" Ade followed.

"If you think we will do what they were planning, the answer is no. We don't have the weaponry or manpower. And I can't get you weapons. I don't have clearance."

"We stall until they get here," Ann stated.

Gunner shook his head and glanced back at the door and then up at the old clock on the wall. "We're already stalling."

Weapons, Ade thought. He remembered his disgust when Floyd tucked the old wheel gun into his pants. Then he remembered what he said right after he did it. *Plus, no network interface*. "We only need one gun."

A gaggle of confused eyes landed on Ade all at once. "I disable all but one gun. We take Hollar hostage and have them release Floyd. Then we go back to the roof and leave on the cruiser. We take Hollar with us. Nobody will risk his life."

The four of them looked at each other while considering this option. "It seems like the best option," Gunner nodded.

"Are you sure you can do it?" Ethan asked.

"I'm positive," Ade responded.

CHAPTER 29 | 5856-W25

The polished gold door slid open to a hallway made of glass. Rays of sunlight refracted between panes, making it appear like one was looking through a prism. The silhouette of a familiar man walked toward them. Ade squinted and looked past Young at the crowd in a glass room surrounded by vegetation. It reminded Ade of the park in the Government District. Trees were scattered around the large, open space with bushes and flowers. Yet, from this distance, the vegetation looked foreign — otherworldly.

"It's about time," Young called as he approached.

Drawing closer, Young's keen eyes darted between them, and his expression became stern.

"What happened to Abraham?" Young demanded.

"The adrenaline wore off," Gunner answered. "He drank half a bottle of scotch on the cruiser. Hit him like a rogue wave."

Young's eyebrows raised and then lowered over a vindictive smile. "I'll take them from here," he said, looking at Gunner. "Let Abraham know his actions will have consequences."

Gunner gave a sheepish nod. "Sir, I'd like to attend the ceremony."

Young gave him a quick, decisive response: "You best see to your superior. You may soon be his successor."

Gunner gave another nod and stepped back into the elevator. "Yes, sir. Thank you, sir."

The golden doors closed, and Young grinned. Then he looked at Ade. "You look better. Beta set to full?"

"No, three," Ade answered.

"Good. It seems having family nearby has helped. Are you ready? The president has already started."

"I need a moment with my family."

"Ade, we need to-" Young began with a look of disapproval.

"This is important. I must ensure my family is in check before we go in. Mainly my mother. We didn't have much time after her arrival."

Young looked past Ade toward Ann. Then he pressed his lips together and nodded. "Okay. I'll be down the hall by the atrium. But Ade, five minutes. They're already yelling on my comms."

Ade nodded in agreement. "Five."

"Ade, I'm serious."

"I know."

Young gave him a stern look, turned, and walked back toward the atrium. Ade watched until he could no longer hear Young's medals clanking on his chest and turned toward Ann and his brother.

"Ethan, you need to get the gun," Ade whispered. "Without Gunner, it has to be you."

"I'll get the gun," Ann said.

"They'll be watching you. Ethan doesn't look like a threat."

"It's true," Ethan agreed. "I don't appreciate it, but it's true."

"Just look like you do when you scan the network and look broken. Stand off to the side near a guard. I'll deactivate all network devices. When this happens, make your move. I'll create a diversion to draw their attention."

"What about me?" Ann asked.

"If Ethan fails, it's on you to either help him or get a gun. When I activate your weapon, fire a shot in the air and then go for Hollar. You may have to shoot one of his guards."

"We should just shoot Hollar," Ann interjected.

Ade and Ethan looked at each other before looking at their mother. Then Ade shook his head. "No, we need him. He's the only one that guarantees we all make it out. Maybe Monroe, but Hollar for sure."

"Hollar will have his security detail. Along with the embassy guard," Ethan said.

"Good. When we take Hollar, we each take a gun. We may need them for the way out," Ann added.

"Ade, he's waiving at you," Ethan said.

Ade glanced down the hall at Young. "Now, Ade," Young said over comms.

"Okay," Ade responded. Then, he turned back to his family. "We're going to be okay."

It was as much to reassure himself as the others. Then, he took a deep breath and started his journey toward redemption. With each step, the commotion from within the atrium grew louder. Ade had been so focused on Floyd that he failed to realize the enormity of the situation. This ceremony would air on every halostation across Cranis. Millions of people would be tuned in — all awaiting his arrival.

Beyond the glass barrier, people stood shoulder to shoulder. His gaze traced the outlines of their raised hands until it reached the stage where Hollar's words flew with spit into the crowd. Then his heart stopped as he saw Floyd. Off to the left of President Hollar, Floyd stood between two guards. His hands were bound to a chain cuffed to his ankles, and his shoulders slumped forward as his head hung in defeat.

Every hero has a villain. Which you are depends on the side you've chosen, Ade thought. Ade felt Young studying him, but he didn't look away from Floyd. He felt both sickened and enraged by his actions. *I'm the villain,* Ade thought.

"Ade!" Young snapped.

Ade's attention didn't break from Floyd.

"You've got to be kidding me," Young grumbled. "You're not ready for this."

Ade answered without thinking. "I'm ready."

"No, Ade. You're not. You're looking at Floyd like he's a damn chained puppy."

"I said I'm ready," Ade repeated.

"Ade, listen. You don't understand. You need-"

"I already know," Ade interrupted. "They're making an example of him." Then he brushed past Young, pushed open the door, and entered the atrium.

The glass barrier had muffled the commotion of the audience, but now it consumed him. Overwhelming his senses, Ade suddenly felt trapped amongst the masses. He felt sweat forming on his brow. He closed his eyes, increased his Beta, and stood still. He took deep breaths and concentrated on the feeling of the air leaving his body.

Suddenly, there was a shift in the room's energy, and a murmur rippled through the crowd. Ade opened his eyes and looked up at the people staring at him and parting as they cleared a path toward the stage. Then he saw Nadia standing next to President Hollar, pointing at him.

"Ladies and gentlemen," President Hollar called. "Please join me in welcoming Cranis' newest hero, Ade Billings."

Applause erupted, and Ade gave a slight, awkward wave as he walked toward the stage. The audience reached out to pat him and repeated congratulatory remarks came from all directions. Ade looked up at the sun breaking through the leaves of the trees and thought of his father. Then he focused on the stage. All eyes were upon him as he walked, all except for Floyd. Floyd's gaze remained at his feet, and his shoulders lowered and raised slowly with each deep breath. He glanced at Nadia and quickly looked away. She looked every part the ecstatic girlfriend. Her hands clutched at her chest; she momentarily broke her clasp to wave and then returned them to her bosom. Ade knew she was playing him after the assault on the Union's base when he felt the prick on his neck. The bit after he awoke just solidified her desperate attempt to maintain control. Ade felt the dull pang of anger. As he neared the stage, camera drones zipped around him. *There are too many,* he thought. A camera centered on his approach, and it dawned on him that his demeanor was unlike those he saw accepting the award previously. Ade forced a smile and waved at the audience.

Then he leaped onto the stage and extended a hand for Hollar to shake. Amused, Hollar shook it vigorously and raised it into the air. Eating it up, the crowd cheered louder.

"I love you, Ade Billings!" Ade heard Nadia shout.

He could feel her eyes on his back. He didn't glance back. He focused on the plan and nodded at his brother as Young escorted Ethan and his mother onto the stage.

Hollar dropped his arms and released Ade's hand. The crowd began to hush. Hollar moved back behind the podium and rested a hand on each side. He paused and looked out at the silenced crowd. Ade looked back at his family and watched Young leave them and walk across the stage to stand by Ambassador Monroe. Monroe nodded as their eyes met, and Ade returned a simple nod and looked back at the audience. *Fug,* Ade thought. *I hope Young didn't bring his knife.*

"Our forefathers came here to preserve mankind's place in the universe," Hollar began. "To give us a fresh start — a new beginning. A place to celebrate our achievements while honoring the past. However, it didn't take long for some to lose sight of that. Greed spread amongst them like the plague, and with that plague came the Labor Party. When the Labor Party claimed humankind's most valuable resource as their own, they failed to realize our forefathers' sacrifice. They did not respect what was given to them. They only thought of themselves. Peace and prosperity for one people — that was the dream of our forefathers. One people. We are an endangered species, my friends. And we are on borrowed time."

Ade glanced at Young and then looked over his shoulder at Ethan. Ethan stared straight forward as if oblivious to the world around him. His arms hung loosely at his sides, but at Ade's glance, he motioned to the guard at his side by making a fist and pointing with his thumb. The guard to Ethan's left was young. His face was still pitted with acne scars, and a wispy mustache decorated his upper lip. *Good choice,* Ade thought.

"The Union sought to ruin the revitalization of our species.

They destroyed transportation, interrupted technological advances, and killed innocent people as they slept. Well, today, today I can say that the plague has been eradicated! The Union lives no more!"

The cheers and the forceful jest of Hollar's voice faded into a murmur. Ade now knew the evil in the heart of humankind. It stemmed from an unspoken hatred deep within the soul. His eyes drifted to Floyd. *Is hatred taught by those we trust, or is it something we develop on our own?* He hadn't previously noticed Floyd's face and arms were covered with fresh bruises, and dried blood stained his orange beard. Floyd's brow slowly rose, and his eyes met Ade. The fight was gone from Floyd's eyes, and with it, the glimmer of hope. They stared at each other, and all Ade could think was *run*. He looked away and shook these thoughts from his mind. *Focus*. He pulled up all network devices and glanced again at Ethan.

Ade jerked as President Hollar slammed his fist onto the podium. The crowd roared its approval and drew Ade's attention to the beaming grin of Hollar. Hollar half turned toward him and applauded. Then his grin turned vindictive, and he shook one finger at Ade. Then Hollar turned his gaze toward Floyd. "What you see here is the Union's last hope. Its champion. This man led numerous attacks on Cranis. He killed hundreds of innocent people. He, dear people, is an instrument of violence," Hollar preached.

The crowd began chanting almost in unison. "Kill, kill, kill...."

Hollar raised his hands for quiet, and the crowd complied. Slowly lowering his hands, Hollar placed one hand on the podium and reached inside his jacket. The steel of Floyd's revolver glistened as he withdrew it and raised it in the air. The crowd gasped at the sight of the archaic weapon.

Ade tensed at the sight of the wheel gun. *Off network weapon.*

"He used this very weapon to strike fear into his enemy. A savage weapon. A relic of an uncivilized time."

His mind spun. An off-network weapon foiled his plan. *Network, local, devices, weaponry. Disable all.* Ade clicked the button and glanced back at the guard near Ethan. The light near the weapon's trigger went from green to red.

"This is the man that stands before you today. Did you know our dear hero's father was one of his many victims? He likely used this monstrosity to end his life," Hollar said, shaking the gun in the air. Then he fell silent, lowered the pistol, and placed it on the podium. A collective gasp rippled through the crowd, followed by murmurs of chatter. Then someone screamed. "Kill the bastard!"

The Beta wasn't enough. Ade felt his pulse in his ears. He frantically looked around the room to see if any of the soldiers had noticed. *One had to. They can't all be mesmerized by Hollar*. He met the gaze of one soldier and smiled and nodded. The soldier immediately turned his attention back to Hollar. Ade followed his eyes back to Hollar and then drifted down to the gun on the podium. *I need to get that gun.*

Hollar turned and nodded at Ade. "When we first met Ade, we knew he would become an asset to Cranis. So much promise and potential. The son of the legendary Jack Billings. And on that day, we made him a promise we will now fulfill. As our hero, it is only right to grant Ade Billings the revenge he desperately desires. Today, Ade Billings is given the privilege of executing William Arfey."

Hysteria swept the room. Ade thought he misheard Hollar. Then the guards flanking Floyd seized his arms while another removed the shackles from his feet and disconnected them from his wrists. A large metal platform was rolled onto the stage. The soldier wheeling it stopped behind Floyd and pressed a button on the side. The box lowered over the wheels, and four stability legs dropped on each side. An arm with a galvanized cable telescoped upward and extended horizontally until the nose hung over the middle of the platform. The soldier approached Ade and handed him a remote with one button.

The chant resumed — *kill, kill, kill*. Events occurred in stop motion. Ade could hear his mother pleading and screaming as the guards restrained her.

Ade's eyes were saucers as they looked from the button in the soldier's hand to the gun on the podium.

Young stepped forward, snatched the remote from the soldier, and stood before Ade. Behind Young, the guards forced Floyd onto the platform and secured the noose around his thick neck. A tight grip clamped around Ade's wrist, and Young firmly pressed the remote into his palm. Ade looked down at the remote and slowly lifted his gaze toward Young.

"I tried to warn you," Young said. "Turn your Beta down to one, pause, and set it to max. You'll get a brief moment of euphoria to collect yourself," Young instructed.

Ade followed Young's instructions, and the emotions drained from him.

"Next time, ask for help," Young said, walking back toward Monroe.

The two guards flaking Floyd stepped down from the platform. Floyd's head hung low, then his eyes lifted from the floor and locked onto Ade.

"I loved yer father like he was me brother."

"Lies!" Hollar screamed.

Floyd turned a fierce glare toward Hollar. "You killed him!" Floyd roared. "Everything you know is a lie!" He screamed at the audience.

"You lie with your last breath," Hollar growled. "Rats have no dignity. Mr. Billings, exact your revenge," Hollar said with a wave.

Seconds felt like minutes. The camera drones hovered around them, awaiting the glory of gore. The chanting grew louder.

Floyd clenched his jaw.

Ade's finger hovered over the button. He thought about Floyd's dumb grin as he sprinted toward them in the sand.

"I didn't do what they say!" Ade yelled over the crowd at Floyd. Then he paused, took a breath, and activated the sprinklers in the garden. Confusion erupted as sprinklers soaked the audience. And then, with another click, he disabled all outbound communication.

Without another thought, Ade lunged for the gun on the podium. Events blurred before his eyes as his hand grasped the wooden handle. A hand landed on Ade's shoulder and shoved him. He stumbled back with the gun in his hand, skidded to a halt, rightened himself, and aimed it at President Hollar.

Two guards lunged for President Hollar as a third raised his weapon and aimed it at Ade.

Ade yanked the gun toward one of the lunging guards, closed his eyes, and pulled the trigger. Only a metallic click came from the gun. His eyes shot open, and he pulled the trigger again — another click. *Fug*. The soldier taking aim did the same. Then he looked at the weapon and saw the red light. The soldier slammed the connect button. Hollar quickly disappeared into the crowd in the arms of two soldiers. Ade looked back at Ethan as he struggled to wrench the gun away from the scrappy soldier. Ann jumped on the soldier's back in an attempt to help, and all three toppled off the stage into a cluster of shrubbery.

Then Ade caught movement out of the corner of his eye. He ducked just as the butt of a rifle thrust toward his face. Grabbing for it, Ade gripped the barrel and stock. His hand and fingers brushed those of the attacking soldier, and then each yanked on the rifle. When neither gave, Ade leaned back, jumped, and kicked as hard as he could. The force of the blow sent the soldier tumbling across the stage, and Ade landed flat on his back with the rifle in his hands. His first thought was Hollar. *Network, local, security, lockdown, all.*

Shouting and cursing joined the audience's screams as people moved in all directions. Ade rolled onto his stomach and tried to stand. In a blink, he was rolling across the stage with a soldier on top of him. He maintained his grip on the rifle as the soldier tried to rip the gun from Ade's grasp. Ade wrenched the weapon back, and the air was pushed from his lungs as an impact cracked his ribs. Ade tried to roll away. *Network, ping closest device, activate.* Hands grabbed at his back. He swung his legs while turning onto his back, blindly pointing the weapon, and fired. A crack echoed through the atrium as the laster round shattered the ceiling, and Ade opened his eyes in time to see glass raining down on the atrium.

Another blur of movement approached, and more pain shot down his spine as a boot impacted his side. Ade contorted and drew his legs in as he fumbled with the weapon.

Then, a tan mass impacted the dark object standing over him.

"Ade, do it!"

He recognized the sound of Ethan's voice. *Ping nearby, 1 meter, activate.*

A streak of shimmering black approached as Ade struggled to stand. Laster fire erupted, and Ade dodged the falling body as momentum carried it off the stage.

A shriek rang in his ears, and Nadia sprinted by and leaped off the stage.

"Nobody moves!" Ethan warned as he grabbed Ade by the arm and pulled him off the floor.

Ade winced as pain shot down his side and into his legs. He tried to raise the weapon, but the pain was too great on his left side. Then Ethan whirled around and fired on an approaching soldier. Ade's eyes darted to the soldier as he fell lifeless to the floor. Ade shifted the gun to his right hand and raised it at the audience. Then, he saw Ambassador Monroe lying off the stage in the grass. Nadia had ripped a sleeve from her dress and held it to the gaping wound in his chest. Even with the cauterization of the round, blood still soaked the cloth.

"I need a medic," Nadia shouted.

Ade glanced through the room, waiting for someone to heed her call. People in the audience ducked and cowered behind trees and bushes. Soldiers fiddled with their weapons and swore. Dignitaries cried and shrieked while others just stared.

"Snap out of it," Ethan yelled, punching him in the arm. Then

Ethan aimed his weapon at the two guards huddled at the foot of the noose platform. When his back was turned, another soldier sprang on the stage and charged Ethan. Ade swung the weapon from the crowd and fired. The round zipped by the soldier and incinerated a few leaves before shattering a glass wall behind the stage. Ethan turned as the soldier threw his weapon at him. The weapon glanced off Ethan's shoulder as he aimed the gun and fired. It was as if the soldier ran into an invisible wall. His arms flew back, and he fell to the floor.

Ade reduced his beta and set it to max. His thoughts slowed, and he looked back at the audience in search of Hollar.

"You, take off the noose and remove the restraints," Ade heard Ethan order.

Then suddenly, off to his right, a group of people dashed the broken wall. Ade aimed his weapon at the group of attendees. He paused. He couldn't see Hollar amongst them. "Stop!" He yelled. The group did not listen. Ade studied the dot on the tip of the site and aimed it at the middle of the fleeing group. "Stop, or I'll shoot," Ade repeated desperately.

"Enough!" A commanding voice echoed. "Everyone, stand down!"

"Don't," Ethan warned.

Ade turned his attention from the escaping group toward the voice. There, ten feet from him, stood Young glaring at Ethan as he pointed the gun at him. His hands raised slightly, Young ascended the steps back onto the stage. He had blood on his hands, and in the sudden quiet of the room, Ade heard Nadia crying.

"Ade, enough," Young said. "Enough blood has already been shed."

Ade looked at his brother and then glanced at Floyd as he hopped down from the stage and picked up the weapon thrown at Ethan.

"That's far enough," Ethan warned.

Young stopped and looked at Floyd as he approached.

"He's going to kill someone innocent if we continue," Young said with a nod toward Ade.

Ade dashed across the stage to join Ethan and activated the device in Floyd's hand. The weapon hummed as it activated, and the light turned green. His brow raised and jaw clenched. Floyd glanced at the gun and looked at Ade. Then he aimed it at Young and stood beside Ade.

"Agreed," Floyd grunted. "Ethan, watch the room." Keeping a keen eye on Young, Floyd leaned into Ade. "What's da fug is going on," Floyd whispered.

"All network devices are disabled," Ade said. "Well, all but ours."

Floyd's eyes shifted from left to right as he pieced together the puzzle. His eyes widened, and he glanced at Ade. Then his brow lowered over his eyes, and he nodded.

"We're leavin'," Floyd shouted at the audience. "Stay on the ground, and nobody else gets hurt."

"Where's Hollar," Ethan demanded.

"You're not taking him," Young stated. "You can leave, but you're not taking the president."

Floyd took a moment and gave Ethan a quick look before turning back to Young. "Fine. On da ground then."

Young looked back at the room. "You heard him. Everyone on the floor. This will be over soon. Then he shook his head slightly as he looked back at Floyd. "You've got more lives than a damn cat," Young said.

"Just get on da floor, Chad. I'll let ya take off yer fancy coat first," Floyd said.

"Did you know the boy had it all along?" Young asked, dropping to his knees.

Floyd paused and glanced at Ade. Then he shook his head and looked back at Young. "To be honest. I still don't know what da fug is goin' on."

Young licked his teeth under his lips and nodded. Then he placed his hands behind his head. "Looks like he chose a side," Young motioned toward Ade. "If I see either of you again, I will kill you. It's just how it is."

Floyd nodded. "Till Valhalla. Maybe then we're friends."

"In another life, perhaps," Young responded.

Floyd carefully stepped back, and his eyes scanned the room for threats. Then he grabbed Ade's arm with his free hand and backed toward the shattered wall.

"You'll pay for this," Nadia hissed from the floor.

Ade looked down, and her seething emerald eyes bore into him. In a split second, any doubt as to her intention became clear. *Young isn't the only one.*

Floyd tugged on Ade's shirt and pulled him away. Ade gave her one final look and followed Floyd through the broken pane into the hall. Ann followed closely behind, and Ethan hurried after them.

"What now?" Floyd grunted.

"The elevator at the end of the hall," Ade said.

"Why is there no backup? Dey musta saw it on da tube," Floyd said, glancing down the empty hall behind them.

"I killed all communication out of the room."

"But da people who escaped had to go for help," Floyd surmised.

They backed down the hall, watching the people in the atrium slowly rising to see their departure.

"The entire floor is locked down — all doors. They have no way to leave or call for help," Ade said plainly.

Floyd shot Ade a quizzical look and focused back on the people in the atrium. Then he nodded and gave Ade a sideways glance. "Still, I don't wanna dilly dally."

Ade peeked back at the elevator and looked at Floyd. "Floyd, do you know how to fly a cruiser?"

"Course," Floyd said, "But we can't go down to da-"

"Up," Ade interrupted. "We go up. It's on the roof."

CHAPTER 30 | 5856-W25

The elevator doors slid closed to an eerie silence. Ade tried to focus but felt disconnected from his body and deactivated his Beta. Glancing at his brother, it felt like he just awoke from a dream, but then a rush of conflicting emotions flooded in. He looked at the backs of Floyd and Ann and then dropped his gaze to the floor and wished he'd become invisible. It was a sense of relief, joy, and accomplishment mixed with guilt and fear.

It was like the time Ade won a spelling bee and celebrated by eating berries from the field across from their home. He didn't know they had just sprayed pesticide the night before. His parents were horrified when he walked into the house with blue juice dribbled down his shirt. They rushed him to the hospital as his stomach began to spasm and a fever spiked. Ade was only seven at the time, but it was the first time he feared death. They pumped his stomach and pushed fluids into his veins. Later that day, on the way home, the car was silent for a moment. Silence in the face of wrongdoing is a ticking bomb. It only took one mile into the drive home before the bomb exploded.

Then, as if on cue, Floyd turned to Ade. Ade didn't look up from the floor. He knew what was coming.

"Is it true? Em's dead?" Floyd asked.

Ade's shoulders slumped at the question. There was no way to break the news lightly or spin the facts, so he just nodded his head. He could feel Floyd looking at him, but he said nothing.

"But ya didn't do what they said?"

"No, sir. I had no idea."

There was another moment of silence, but Ade could hear Floyd's breath quicken and made the mistake of looking up at him. The sorrow and disappointment in Floyd's eyes ate at his soul. "It was

Nadia. I was just supposed to find Dad's work. I had no idea about the rest."

Floyd's jaw clenched under his rowdy red beard, and he looked at the ceiling before his glossy eyes dropped back to Ade.

"I said I'd take care of yer mum." His red eyes matched his beard, and a tear wet the dried blood on his face.

Ade looked at the man he'd grown to respect. There was nothing he could say to make it better. "I'm sorry."

Floyd's face became as red as his narrowing eyes. Then he spun and slammed his fist into the elevator wall in one explosive movement. The elevator shook as Floyd turned back and opened and closed his fist.

"How could you be so stupid?" Floyd growled, shaking his head.

Ann abruptly stepped between them and glared up at Floyd. "He was trying to save me, William. Me," she said, poking him in the chest. "It's our fault for not telling him sooner. He didn't know."

"He knew enough," Floyd bellowed in response.

"He didn't! We're to blame," Ann yelled. "What would you have done in his situation? What, Floyd?"

Floyd loomed over her. His chest rose and fell with each breath.

"It's all he ever knew," Ann continued. "Of course, he'd choose them."

Floyd looked over her at Ade, rolled his shoulders, exhaled, and nodded in agreement. Ann gently placed her hand on Floyd's chest. "We can't blame our children for our mistakes. You should know that."

Floyd looked down at her, and his expression softened. Tears began flowing down his blood-stained cheeks into his beard. He sniffed, nodded, paused, nodded again, and reached around Ann and Ade and hugged them. "I know," he mumbled. "I know."

Ade stood dumbfounded in his grasp as Floyd's grip tightened between sobs. Ade had never seen his father cry. It made him feel less of a man since he was so quick to cry, so seeing a man like Floyd cry caused his eyes to well up. He didn't understand Floyd's reaction at first, but as he felt the comfort of the embrace, Ade realized what Floyd was doing. In the briefest of movements, Floyd had decided to love rather than hate. It made sense that someone surrounded by death would live in the moment rather than dwell in the past, but for Ade, it was still hard to fathom. He had spent so much time regretting the past that his anger felt like part of him. Ade wiped away the pooling tears.

"Guys," Ethan interrupted. "We're almost to the roof."

Ade glanced up at the passing numbers. *Network, Roof Access, Devices, Disable All.*

"I got it. They're disabled," Ade said as Floyd released them from his grasp.

Floyd dried his eyes on his sleeve and nodded. He took a breath and blinked. His expression hardened as he turned to face the elevator door. "Stay behind me," Floyd commanded, raising his weapon and aiming it at the crack of the door. Huddled behind Floyd, the door chimed, and Ade peaked around Floyd's broad shoulders as the doors slid open.

There, standing on the roof, was Gunner. His eyes lit up when he saw them, but Floyd maintained his defensive position. "The fire is smokey," Floyd stated.

"It burns my eyes," Gunner grinned.

Floyd lowered his weapon, and a slight smile broke his stoic expression. "It's good to see a friendly face."

"I've secured the cruiser. The pilot is restrained in the mess kitchen. Andy said we might as well take it."

Floyd's smile widened at the mention of his son. "He would say that."

Ade's ears perked at the news of Andrew, and he stepped around Floyd and exited the elevator. "Is he here?"

Gunner pointed to the sky. "They're circling above us. Prepared to defend our escape should we need it."

Floyd nodded, and Gunner skipped backward as the group broke into a swift jog across the landing pad. Then he turned and ran beside Floyd.

"Sir, I've got twenty hours of stick experience if you want me to fly."

"No, Gunner. I'll be captaining me own escape. No offense."

"None, sir."

Ade slowed as the group picked up the pace and sprinted up the ramp onto the cruiser. A realization set in among all the other thoughts swirling in his mind. He looked out at the ocean as he walked up the ramp. And then, reaching the top, he paused to look back at the roof. The trajectory of his life had changed since departing this ship. Even if Ade wanted, there was no turning back. He was now an enemy combatant, and the Cranis Government would hunt him along with the remaining Union soldiers. There would be no placement test, shopping downtown, or relaxing at the public beach. He was now a wanted man.

"I'm not sendin' ya an invite," Floyd yelled from inside the cruiser.

Ade gripped the handle of the lastergun and then nodded. *This is my life now,* he thought. *Good or bad, this is who I am.*

Entering the cruiser, Gunner grinned as he secured his seatbelt and gave Ade a slight nod.

"Long live the Union," Gunner chirped.

Ade looked from Gunner to the cockpit as the engines fired and the heavy metal door clicked securely into place. His mother and Floyd sat shoulder to shoulder in the cockpit. Floyd's thick fingers pounded buttons, and the cruiser gently lifted from the ground. Ade looked for Ethan but did not see him.

"The skinny guy is on the turret. You should sit before he launches it," Gunner said.

Gunner looked giddy — as if anxiously awaiting a joyful event. Ade returned to his previously occupied seat and latched the belt around him.

"Creature of habit, huh?" the Gunner asked.

Ade glanced back at him and looked away.

"Hang on ta yer biscuits. We're not hanging round fer da parade," Floyd yelled.

The cruiser jolted forward, banked, and went vertical. The force of the movement pressed Ade's body into the belt. His eyes met the Gunner. "Told you," Gunner said with a smirk.

Soaring into the sky, Ade began to laugh. It was not a chuckle but a full belly laugh that carried beyond the roar of the engines thrusting them into the sky. Gunner watched Ade laugh until tears rolled down his face.

"What's so funny?"

Ade shook his head and pointed over his shoulder at the cockpit.

"What?"

"Hang onto your biscuits," Ade repeated. And he began laughing again.

It was the first time he'd laughed in months. As the cruiser leveled off and the engines hushed to a low growl, his laughter trailed off.

"I didn't think it was that funny," Gunner muttered.

Still smiling, Ade shook his head. "Maybe not."

Ade thought about his father staring back at him on that rainy night and then about the scolding he received on the way home from the hospital. He glanced over his shoulder at the large man piloting the cruiser.

The night they returned from the hospital, after Ade had his stomach pumped and Jack berated him for his stupidity, Ade sat alone in his room crying. Jack cracked the door and looked down at his son. "Ade," Jack began. "We only get mad because we love you." And then he closed the door. Ade had carried his anger and guilt for so long that he'd forgotten that sentiment. He had forgotten what it meant to be family. After his father had died, it felt like they had all forgotten, and the family died with Jack. Each in their fog of grief, they became estranged from one another until Ethan's sentencing. But, by that time, it seemed too late. It was not until this moment that they all moved together toward one common goal.

Gunner leaned forward in his seat and looked out the window. "Do you ever think about the people we're flying over? Those people are just going about their lives while we're up here."

Ade shook his head. "No. I guess I've never considered it."

"News must be breaking at this point. Can you imagine? People just going about their day. Suddenly, the ambassador has been killed, and their world is turned upside down. And here we are soaring above them — the most wanted people on both planets."

Ade took a moment to consider it. "Yeah, pretty crazy, huh?"

"Yeah," Gunner mused. "Crazy. By the end of the day, you'll be infamous. Everybody will know your name."

Ade nodded and looked out the window at the world speeding by. "Yeah," Ade said with a nod. "I guess they will."

The End

Printed in the USA
CPSIA information can be obtained
at www.ICGtesting.com
LVHW021529050124
767941LV00090B/4821